From the kitchen, safely behind the fridge, Two Bears put another burst of the silenced Crusader into one of his opponents and tried again to reach the Vindicator minigun lying so temptingly in the middle of the fire fight.

On the other side of the conflict, the air above the combatants shimmered and buzzed from whatever the two shamans were doing to each other. Then a thundering rainbow filled the room as the stained glass window shattered into a million knives, the shards swirling madly about, slicing everything and everybody into ribbons. Some of the enemy screamed as they were disassembled and the balcony torn to pieces.

"Got them!" shouted Moonfeather.

Forgoing the Vindicator, Two Bear dashed headlong from the kitchen, skirting the riddled wall and reaching the hallway door. Yanking it open, he stopped with a jerk. The blade of a Japanese short sword had flashed, and blood was spraying the floor. His blood . . .

SHADOWBOXER

SHADOWRUN

SHADOWBOXER

Nick Pollotta

A ROC BOOK

ROC
Published by the Penguin Group
Penguin Books USA Inc., 375 Hudson Street,
New York, New York 10014, U.S.A.
Penguin Books Ltd, 27 Wrights Lane,
London W8 5TZ, England
Penguin Books Australia Ltd,
Ringwood, Victoria, Australia
Penguin Books Canada Ltd, 10 Alcorn Avenue,
Toronto, Ontario, Canada M4V 3B2
Penguin Books (N.Z.) Ltd, 182-190 Wairau Road,
Auckland 10, New Zealand

Penguin Books Ltd, Registered Offices:
Harmondsworth, Middlesex, England

First published by Roc, an imprint of Dutton Signet
a division of Penguin Books USA Inc.

First Printing, May, 1997
10 9 8 7 6 5 4 3 2 1

Copyright © FASA Corporation, 1997
All rights reserved

Series Editor: Donna Ippolito
Cover: Royo

To Alexander Dumas,
the master of adventure

SHADOWBOXER: noun, antiquarian twentieth-century military slang referring to deadly combat with an unknown or highly elusive enemy. *WorldWide Word Watch*, 2058 update.

Prologue

02:50 AM Eastern Standard, 13 June 2058
Biscayne Bay, Miami, at the extreme northern territory of the Caribbean League

A trembling hand broke through the full moon, sending ripples of dancing silver across the water's oily surface. Steadily, a human hand rose from the polluted Biscayne Bay to grasp hold of a rusty iron cleat attached to the old weathered wood of the oceanside dock.

Painfully levering himself onto the splintery planks, BlackJack Terhune barely managed to roll over away from the ragged oak edge. With a groan, he peeled the scuba mask off his sweating face. Alive. He was still alive! Unlike everybody else on the hellish run. Fragging drek, it had been like walking naked into a meat grinder. Worse.

He cast the mask aside, and heard it splash back into the stinking brine. Then he began to perform a combat ritual over his military jumpsuit, hands red from the toxic chemicals in the sea. Boot knife gone, Belgium 9 derringer gone, the big Ares Predator gone—when had THAT happened?—ammo clips long emptied, night goggles burned out by that fragging Shatogunda mage, and the Narcoject pistol used to jimmy open an elevator shaft door.

Nothing remained of the equipment so carefully gathered in his years on the street. Even Laura's precious Fuchi cyberdeck had been sacrificed as a simple bludgeon over that ork guard's head. The dumb frag probably never expected any decker to be that desperate. Who would? Laura herself had seemed surprised when she did it. Wham! Chips and blood flew everywhere as the merc went down for the count. Then BlackJack and the deckless decker made it out of the hellhole to reach the safety of the waiting helo and away they soared, secure and safe.

Choking on a bitter laugh, he lay back weakly on the ancient wood of the dock, drinking in lungfuls of night air. The cold water ran rivulets off his bodysuit, the armor plating covering his vital kill zones now badly dented.

Safe. Ha. They'd been anything but freaking safe. Pure pluperfect hell, it had been. Who knew a purely local corporation like Shatogunda would have surface-to-air missile capabilities? His team's helo was blown out from under them even before they could make visual contact with their offshore boat. He and Laura had spotted the fiery dart streaking toward the helo, and jumped just in time. Big George didn't.

Underwater, they dropped everything they could and started swimming for the seawall to reach the open ocean beyond. They were only meters away, they could see it, hear the waves breaking over the coral, when the pack of chipped sharks was suddenly around them, circling closer and closer. BlackJack hadn't even known a fish-microchip interface was possible!

Neither had Laura Redbird, gauging from her blood-curdling scream as they took her down. If he could've done anything to save her, he would have, even if it meant his own life. But when four great whites each grab a limb and start playing tug-o-war, the victim's already dead. All he could do was use it as a distraction while he crawled over the ragged, razor-sharp coral of the reef and escape into Biscayne Bay, where the sharks couldn't physically follow.

Chipped sharks. What psycho would want to chip sharks! Drek, and that was only one of the many things wrong with this run. One of the thousands. The glint of searchlights off the chrome-plated jack in her temple was the last he saw of Laura. Blind rage almost made him strike back at the man-eaters, but with only bare hands as a weapon and ork and norm guards on the way in paramilitary hovercraft bristling with automatic weapons, brutal logic overcame his fury. BlackJack reluctantly used her flesh to buy him time to escape.

Used the flesh of a lover one last time. He felt dirty inside as if he'd been drinking chem slime in the sea. What he wouldn't give for a DocWagon team to come and fly him away to some warm clean hospital full of people anxious to make him stop hurting. Or a friendly shaman to sing a healing song over him. Arctic. Yeah, and if wishes were drek the sewers would be heaven. Stop ya whining, chummer. Still work to do. This run wasn't over yet. No, not quite yet. One more thing to do.

When some of his strength returned, BlackJack forced open the velcro of the bodysuit and began to peel it off. The ballistic material stuck to him in several places and had to be painfully pulled free. His body was a mass of bruises and bleeding cuts already starting to swell in spots. No chance of infection after the sea water got in, but poisoning was a fair bet. He'd already applied a slap patch to the throbbing bullet hole in his shoulder, but the polluted Atlantic had weakened the adhesive and it was starting to come away. Diluted, the metaphamines that had kept him awake and able to swim against the fragging current were finally wearing off. Only pure raw adrenaline was keeping him awake now. "And hate, let's not forget hate," he told himself bitterly.

Wearing only briefs, BlackJack struggled to his sore feet and staggered toward the small blue light that had been his goal for the past four hours as he'd followed the seawall to the south. Faintly illuminated by the tiny indigo bulb set in the wall above it was the warehouse's riveted steel door. So stained and marred from the constant acid rains this year that the ancient sign reading "Honest Bob's Boat Rentals" was almost obliterated. But the palm scanner recognized his handprint and the massive portal swung open silently. He and the others would have rendezvoused here if any of them had made it.

Stumbling as he stepped into the darkness, BlackJack pushed the huge door shut behind him and the internal lights came on automatically with blinding force. Momentarily stunned, he stood there blinking against the harsh intrusion. If there was going to be a doublecross, this was the perfect spot. A pimple-faced ganger with a two-nuyen zipgun could take him now. Not that he'd be good for much. He was so fragged to drek that even the organleggers wouldn't want him.

Tense ticks passed in dripping silence. As his vision slowly returned, he looked around the shoreline warehouse stuffed to the ceiling with marine equipment: bales of nets, bundles of oars, canvas net, sleeved props, and similar equipment. Tools designed a thousand years ago, but as viable today as ever. Equipment so basic it couldn't be improved. No matter what the techies said, ya can't improve a nail with a microchip. End of discussion.

A slim path wound through the towering jumbles of marine equipment. Exhausted, BlackJack lurched from crate to crate, trying to keep one hand on the dank plastic boxes for support. Finally he reached a huge pile of plastene bags that sat pooled in the harsh light of an EverBright in an open area of the warehouse. A momentary flicker told him that even the independent power packs of those supposedly eternal light bulbs could weaken with age.

Clumsily, BlackJack dug into the packs, tossing aside unneeded civilian clothes for dead friends until he found the medical supplies he was looking for. He awkwardly used his left hand to rig a sling for his right arm, then began to bite off strips of adhesive to tape his busted ribs. Try as they might, those hellhounds hadn't been able to use their flame breath to hurt his team through the protection song of their shaman, Iron Jimmy, and as the beasts charged closer, his Ares Predator had made short work of them. But the bodies of the dead hounds had continued on through the air by sheer inertia, slamming into them like sledgehammers. BlackJack heard Jimmy's neck snap before he went down under the onslaught.

With his chest now bound tight, the agony of breathing lessened to mere discomfort. He pawed deeper into the bag and found a fresh trauma patch, which he slapped onto his bullet wound, plus a few stim patches he applied to undamaged areas of his arms. He inhaled sharply as the organic plastic sterilized and sealed the huge hole, the taste of olives filling his mouth as the DMSO rushed healants through his body.

There was only one more thing to find now, and then he spied the small black box prominently marked with a red cross. He held it in his hand and checked to see what the Pocket Doc was set for. Damn things only held six ampoules of anything—ya had to load 'em for what you thought would go wrong. Imperfect—but they were a lot more versatile than simple medkits because the things could make their own limited medical decisions. A readout on the side displayed painkillers, stims, antibacs, antitox, and some other stuff he had trouble focusing his eyes to read.

BlackJack clumsily activated the computerized physician and held it to his side. The robotic device hummed in consultation as it ascertained his condition, then began a long series of hisses, pumping god-knows-what into his system. Finally, the Doc went quiet and he tossed the precious device away, too tired to care. It crashed in the shadows, breaking apart and spilling out its electronic guts.

Soon, a tingling wave of relief washed over him and he felt his head miraculously clear. Back on line. Looking in one of the other equipment bags for a spare gun, he found a couple of amber bottles instead. No surprise, considering how much Big George had loved his booze. No drugs or chips for him. Here's to you, George! BlackJack tried not to think about all he and the elf had been through, and that now he'd never see Big George again.

BlackJack pulled one of the bottles out, startled to see that it wasn't cheap synathol, but honest-to-frag, scotch. Something called Irish Mist, with a dated label, import seal, and everything! Not caring where the gift came from, he worked off the twist cap with his teeth, and generously poured the single malt down his throat. The chill left his stomach and he was just starting to feel almost human again when a figure stepped from the shadows. It was only partially visible beyond the circle of light, and all he could make out clearly were the shoes and a hand-held case of some sort.

"*Konnichiwa,* BlackJack," said his visitor, bowing slightly from the waist as she set down the expensive leather briefcase. "I have the rest of your payment here, as requested. A genuine certified credstick." There was a brief flash of white teeth edged with crimson lipstick in the dimness beyond. "Where is my merchandise, please?"

"F-frag you, Mr. Johnson," BlackJack coughed. He took another swig off the bottle and slumped against a barrel of engine lubricant. He'd been feeling better only moments before. Why was he now so tired again all of a sudden?

The Mr. Johnson stepped closer, her body in the light, but not her face. "What do you mean? Didn't you get the prototype?"

"Drek no."

An icy pause. "And why not?" she demanded, her voice not truly hostile, but close enough.

"Because your fragging canisters of nerve gas didn't kill the guards!" BlackJack screamed. "That's why!" He licked his lips. He tasted something foul . . . was it from the DMSO or the whiskey? Residue from the ocean?

"And?" asked the woman calmly. She was the fixer who'd

set them up on this shadowrun against Shatogunda. BlackJack
had never worked with her before, and now he knew why.

"And?" he roared, casting the bottle aside. He was having
trouble marshalling his thoughts for some reason. "*And*? Ya
muck-sucking null. *And* they had more mercs than you said
they would! They had different weapons, too, and hellhounds—not just dogs. There was even UCAS military support, for drek's sake! Plus, some unkillable ork goombah
with a slapgun showed up from nowhere and shot the living
bloody drek out of my whole fragging team!"

"Most unfortunate," acknowledged the Mr. Johnson
solemnly.

"Unfortunate, yeah," growled BlackJack, cradling his
aching ribcage. "I lost five of my people before we even
reached the main building, then the guards hit us from every
side. Tox, they were everywhere! Then some fragging
chipped sharks took down my best decker, and if the damn
tide hadn't been coming in, they'da got me too."

Making a soft consoling sound, the woman rested one
shoe on a small crate of engine parts. Her long skirt parted at
the action, exposing a lot of well-tanned, nylon-smooth thigh
and more. "Yes, I had counted on the evening tide. But only
in an emergency. I gather this was."

His mind fogging, BlackJack hawked to clear his throat,
and spit whiskey-flavored blood on the floor. "Damn straight
it was!"

A manicured hand barely managed to cover a yawn,
"Indeed. Sounds like Shatogunda security did a most thorough job."

"A thorough job?" snarled BlackJack, feeling the blood
throb in his neck. "Listen, Johnson, those Shatogunda mercs
did us up a royal treat!"

"Yes," she demurred softly. "Dunkelzahn must have
trained them well."

He felt his heart stop. "The dragon? We went up against
dragon-trained guards?" Before the Johnson could speak, the
awful truth hit him like a one-two punch. "Holy drek, this
was one of his corps then? Motherfragger! Even dead, the
dragon can still frag with you."

"Such language. Now, really . . ." the woman said.

Furious, BlackJack grabbed hold of a boarding pike lying
against a nearby plastic crate and pulled himself erect. His
limbs felt like lead weights were attached. Why was he so

sleepy? Something was wrong, but his anger somehow gave him the strength to speak.

"T-this run was a dry hump from the word go! Not only didn't we have accurate intelligence, almost everything you told us was just wrong enough that once we got started, there was nowhere to go but forward, and that direction got us promptly blown to pieces! It was almost as if we were supposed to fail!"

He bent over double with a coughing spell and for the first time, the woman known as Mr. Johnson smiled, her teeth gleaming like an animal's in the darkness.

"That's right," she said softly. "You most definitely were not supposed to succeed." She watched him carefully, smiling to herself. "Nor were you supposed to return, moron," she added, reaching behind her back.

As comprehension dawned, BlackJack balled a fist, and three carbide spikes slid out of his knuckles to gleam in the light of the EverBrights like new sin. The next instant he lunged for her slim figure, which was growing ever dimmer in his sight. A series of soft chugs stopped him, the pencil-thin flames from the silenced Heckler & Koch automatic tracking his riddled body to the floor.

"And my name actually is Johnson," said Erika Johnson as she continued to empty all eighteen of the pistol's caseless rounds into the still form. "Amusing, *neh*?" The only reply was a low, moist gargling noise almost too soft to hear.

Returning her weapon to the holster behind her back, Erika calmly went to the dock outside and found the remains of the wet suit. The mask was nowhere to be found. An inconvenience, at most. She folded the garment neatly into a square and placed the suit inside her empty attaché case. Going back inside, she stripped the wet shorts off the corpse and dressed the bloody body in a grease-stained worksuit taken from a wall locker. The pockets already contained assorted personal items, some illegal simsense chips, and a deluxe, three-ring, executive credstick with over ten thousand registered Caribbean League dollars. She smiled, thinking how on the street the tourists and merchants called them doubloons, looking for some kind of thrill of the forbidden, but this had come straight off her expense account.

She'd had carte blanche for this exercise, as befitting an executive of her high rank. Only Hakutsu Hotosama himself and that *gaijin* James Harvin were over her in the hierarchy of the Gunderson Corporation. And soon that would change too. Oh, yes, very soon.

Johnson pulled a pair of medical gloves from her belt pouch and donned them, whistling a tune as she skillfully used a surgical probe to remove all of the bullets from the dead man. She deposited the bloody lumps of metal into a small plastic container, which she sealed and placed inside her coat. Then she took a different spent round from another container and inserted it into the still warm wound. There, one left for Lone Star to find. If the incompetent fools could, that is.

Dragging the corpse over to the small machine shop in the corner of the warehouse, she carefully positioned the man under a shelf deliberately overloaded with tools. A gentle tap with a broom handle made the previously weakened support collapse, and with a mighty crash the heavy shelf smashed the runner's once-handsome features into an unrecognizable mess. Perfect. Erika stayed for a minute to look at the disfigured corpse, feeling oddly excited, but then turned and walked away, dropping the telltale broom alongside the mess.

She checked her own expensive clothes for splatters, then left the warehouse and went into the front office. There, she used a pair of tweezers to remove a macroplas business card from a glassine envelope. It bore the name of a rival warehouse firm presently at street war with this one. As if these small-timers even understood what the word meant. All business was war. These single-owner operations merely argued and squabbled like petulant children. Gingerly she placed the card in the middle of a small puddle of water directly under a leaking water cooler.

Then she moved swiftly into the hallway and opened a panel in the wall, with a simple yank tearing loose a wire to deactivate the old-style thermal fire alarm. She thanked the gods the owners had yet to spend any serious nuyen on updating the system. Chipped sensors were a lot more difficult to beat than this prehistoric piece of street drek. As she strode for the front door, Johnson pulled a cigar from the pocket of the livid security guard sitting limply in a chair behind an armor-plated desk. A swollen tongue protruded out of the dead woman's mouth, her neck dark purple where the garrote bit deep into the flesh. Her machine pistol was still tucked uselessly in its belt holster.

Puffing the imitation Havana cigar into life, Erika made a

disgusted face as she set the smoking leaves halfway into a puddle of paint thinner on the linoleum floor. A trail of the clear liquid reached across the room and under the door of a utility closet jammed full of rusty paint cans and oily rags. All lovingly stacked in a nice pyramid just for tonight.

As the glowing tip inched downward toward the fire trail, Erika patiently reviewed everything she'd done so far. Satisfied that all was well, she departed, locking the front door behind her and sliding the access card back inside through a crack in the plastic window pane.

A nondescript Chrysler Nissan Caravaner was waiting at the curb. She climbed in, and immediately the windows mirrored for privacy. That wasn't a standard feature for this make and model, but she didn't think anyone was watching. The green paint job was badly scratched, the simwood panels peeling with the typical rust spots of a car that spent a lot of time near saltwater and wasn't washed regularly. Nobody in his right mind would bother to steal the molding tires off the wretched piece of Detroit drek.

She put the multiple security systems into passive mode, then touched the ignition. The onboard computer accepted her fingerprint, and with a gentle purr the oversized 400 horsepower motor was activated. Soft halogen headlights flared on, and the powerful car effortlessly pulled smoothly away from the curb and tooled off silently into the darkness. Only its bullet-proof tires sighed on the old macadam street.

Make Your
Own Justice

1

Pain.

Agony filled her world, a swirling burning universe of searing sizzling pain beyond imagination. Millennia slowly passed with glacier speed, and the agony faded to mere throbbing in her arms and left leg. As the overload of physical sensation receded, Laura Redbird felt the world return about her as if the stygian fog surrounding her body was being gradually dissipated by a warm and gentle sun.

She was on a table . . . no, the beach? Her meat body was sprawled on the sand, the taste of sea salt in her mouth, her clothes in horrible bloody tatters and every limb beating with blood as if they were living balloons ready to pop. Her wristwatch seemed an excruciating band of thorns encircling her wrist. But each thundering heartbeat seemed less terrible than the one before. A ragged cough tore at her throat, and she rallied enough strength to turn her head and vomit brine forever. Could a human hold that much water inside her lungs, and still live? Must be. She was here and kicking. But where was here?

Memories returned like an explosion, and she suddenly jerked upright, screaming and flailing with her baby-weak arms at the great white sharks as they chewed at her helpless body. White-hot pain beyond bearing, beyond the range of the human mind to encompass, had seized her as the Biscayne waters roiled red with her blood and she was pulled from the sweet cool air and into the cold salt depths by the monsters. Then came a heart-wrenching memory of Black-Jack swimming away from her, and anger flashed at his betrayal. He left her to die!

Then her fury faded as logic told her that, no, he'd left her when she was already dead. Beyond saving. Her heart ached at the sadness on his face as he turned to swim away from her savaged corpse. And that was the word, wasn't it, chummer? Corpse. Stiff. Fish food du jour. She'd been chewed to chum. Or rather so freaking fragging near death that she now knew what hell itself was like. It stank of despair and helplessness.

Laura trembled slightly in the chemical wafting of the shoreline breeze and glanced around. She was on a remarkably clean area of white sand, on a pristine stretch of beach near the industrial sections of northern Miami—a beach otherwise covered with rotting seaweed, rusty cans, broken glass, spent shell casings, and the limp latex remains of safe sex. From the number of same, there were a lot of happy chummers tonight.

Gingerly reaching up to brush the wet hair from her face, Laura felt strength returning to her arms and then paused in wonder. She could see that her tattoos were gone. Well, most of them. The go-gang insignia from her juvie days as a gofer for the Slammers had vanished from her right bicep. And the fake yakuza designs on one entire thigh were simply not there. Now, how the drek was that possible? They'd been done by a self-taught ork artist in the Seattle sprawl, and Laura sure as drek remembered the needle full of ink going in thousands of times to permeate her skin. The yakuza stuff had been a work of art that fooled her assigned prey long enough for her to blow their nasty operation to drek. Afterward, the tats were much too lovely, and potentially useful, to be removed by lasers or acid. However, like all art, it was never fun in the forging. Where the hell were her shoes?

"Healed flesh is always cleansed," said the empty air before her in a vaguely familiar voice. As Laura recoiled, a shimmering vision of ethereal beauty swirled into being above the cresting waves hitting the shore. A male with long flowing hair and a full figure, no, a woman of ageless loveliness and indeterminate race supported by flowing mana rippling with every color of the spectrum. Not norm, or elf, or any metahuman race Laura could identify. And that made the identification all the easier.

"Savoriano," she muttered and bowed the best she could make her weak body do while sitting in the sand.

The astral vision hovering before her smiled at the attempt, and a wave of warmth took the chill from Laura's bones and the last of the pain from her tender flesh.

"I greet you, Laura Redbird," the vision said.

The decker almost fell down again trying to get to her

naked feet, but she finally managed. The two looked at each other for a few minutes. Or hours. Time was difficult to measure in the presence of the astral being. How long had it been since Laura had last seen the spirit in that top-secret lab of fragging Fuchi Industrial Electronics? Sealed and trapped behind wards while a team of dumbhoop scientists attempted yet again to fuse magic and technology by linking the spirit into a mainframe computer composed more of runes than chips and wires. Didn't work, of course. Never would. But the megacorps just wouldn't stop trying. Everybody knew magic and the Matrix didn't mix. Those brainiacs were dumber than dirt.

"I told you that someday I would repay the great debt I owe for all that you and your associates did for me that bloody night," said Savoriano, her words echoing slightly above the muted sea. Laura heaved a sigh, feeling better and better by the second. Yes, that had been the worst run of her life until tonight. And the financial repercussions of the matter were still, even years later, shaking the higher echelons of the megacorp world back in Japan. It was reason numero uno why she and BlackJack had come to Miami, here in the Caribbean League. Even the long arm of a megacorp like Fuchi sometimes found it hard to find a wedge into this association of local governments, pirates, cartels, corporations, and anyone else who happened to own land—mostly islands—in this part of the world. Everyone with the least bit of power always seemed to be struggling for power over everyone else, and the only thing they all seemed to agree on was hatred of Aztlan.

"We did what seemed right," Laura demurred, not wanting to take credit for some selfless noble action. The deed had taken only a moment and seemed a good idea at the time. The enemy of my enemy and all that good ol' drek.

"You did it alone," beamed the spirit—literally, almost blindingly so. Gulls near the shoals shrieked in response and flew away with more loud screams of annoyance. "And so I have watched for these many years to find a way, any chance to return the great releasing."

Ah, her stomach went icy even as Laura felt a flush spread over her face. "The sharks." It wasn't a question, but a statement of fact. Brought back from the dead? Reassembled like a model car? Holy drek.

"Dead is dead, beyond even my abilities," answered the

fading being. "But wounds can be healed, no matter how terrible, as long as the holy meat and the precious spark of life still remains."

"Wounds?" barked the bedraggled decker, in sudden fury. "Those fragging goldfish ate my legs!"

"Your flesh was shredded, but not removed," whispered Savoriano, the ocean vista behind her slightly visible through her form. The mana was as bright as ever, but the shape inside was dissolving. "Energy is matter, even as mana is life. You have been healed. Now I am free even of you, blessed liberator."

The light brightened, and the spirit was gone. The nimbus of magical energy hung empty in the air. Sea spray from the waves passed through the glow unhindered, wetting Laura's face.

"Farewell, my friend," whispered the winds even as the light dimmed with the coming of the dawn. Alone on her clean patch of sand, Laura Redbird opened and closed her perfect hands, watching the scarless fingers flex and move as if she really was a newborn discovering for the first time what those things were at the end of her wrists. Torn into soyburger and then healed by an act of kindness inspired by something that had happened over a decade ago. Life was too strange for words.

Waves crested over her bare feet, bringing back the chill and a metacrab the size of a salaryman's hat scuttling out of the froth to see if she was alive or dead. Blasted tide was coming in. The pale orange crustacean snapped its twin claws about in the air, its bulbous eyes supported on ridiculous bouncy stalks. It was a silly-looking thing, and fooled a lot of newbies. Its claws could cut steel, its mouth chewed concrete, and they liked to eat the damnedest odd things. And once they got hold of you, you either blew their heads off or died. They never let go. Only good point was that the crabs seemed to be especially fond of devil rats, which brought them a lot of goodwill from the locals.

Kicking at the ten-legger, which sent it scuttling off to find easier prey, Laura turned from her birthing spot and began to stride across the beach. Out here, beyond the great adamantine ferrocrete barrier that separated the luxury resorts from the public beach, the local prison didn't use prisoners to hand-clean the sand every night so that the tourists had a nice place to lay down their fat bodies and get

tan in the free sun. The only fragging thing free in this town.
The locals could fend for their own amid the corporate filth.
Off in the distance, she could see the shining towers of
downtown rising high above the rainbow neon ribbon of the
monorail that encircled Miami proper.

Reaching a battered wooden ramp that led to the boardwalk next to the elevated road, Laura started climbing.
Reaching the boardwalk, she headed southward for downtown and the nearest cab stand. First things first. She had to
get to the rendezvous point at the old warehouse and locate
BlackJack. Wouldn't he be surprised to see her!

Dawn was tinting the horizon pink as Erika Johnson drove
the Caravaner along the Miami canal toward downtown. She
maintained the speed limit religiously, despite the many
blast craters and pot holes. Just as she rounded a curve near
the desalinization plant, a barricade of overturned cars
momentarily slowed her, the hungry gang awakening to the
possibility of fresh meat.

Calmly, almost amused, Erika radically shifted gears and
wheeled into an alley. Garbage, both human and food, lined
the passageway as one of those groups frantically jumped
out of her way. A single shot hit the rear of the Caravaner and
musically ricocheted off the military armor plating hidden by
the artistically bad paint job. No further rounds came her
way, the locals merely shouting their displeasure at the
unseen driver's rank callousness.

Rejoining traffic heading to the west, she rode along with
all the other various vehicles—limos, sports coupes, rusted
wrecks looking like her own, and lots of remote-controlled
semis, some with, but most without, their lights on. This was
supposedly an industrial section of town, but from the
reports she'd seen the prime activity here was smuggling.
Several go-gangs of norms and trolls roared by on their
gleaming bikes, talismans and scalps flailing in the wind.

Streetlights lined the road, the twenty-meter posts topped
with wire-reinforced quartz lenses that offered only feeble
illumination down from the sheer distance so necessary to
keep the locals from shooting out the lights. The weak glare
was tinted gray by the inner-city smog and general miasma
of the decaying streets. The pink of the dawn was slowly
turning yellowish when all of the streetlamps winked out,
officially heralding the city's declaration that day was here.

They were wrong as usual. Or maybe just saving a few kilowatts, cheap bastards.

Standing forgotten on debris-piled corners was the occasional Lone Star callbox, the panic button showing only as dangling wires. Nobody here wanted the law; it only got in the way of making a few nuyen. And justice, like everything else in the Awakened world of returned magic, was something you made yourself or did without.

Turning onto a side street, Erika now headed south, deeper into the heart of the urban sprawl. Every window was barred or boarded. Tattooed joyboys and garish slotmachine girls called out for anybody's trade at this hour, while grim people in ballistic dusters and metahumans of assorted types in steel-studded leather coats jostled for supremacy on the littered sidewalks. Simsense parlors and the mandatory rock bars sprouted every few meters, each louder than the one before, or so it seemed to her disgust. Graffiti tried its best to hide the filth on the walls of the buildings and few stores.

The Miami sprawl embraced much of what used to be the Million Dollar Mile along the Gold Coast, going in all the way to Coral Gables. But times changed, as they always do, and now the majestic hotels were half-empty, become hives of chippers and organleggers. Ratnests for gutterkin, squatters, and gangers who preyed upon those too hopeless or too weak from hunger to fight back effectively.

The Overtown DMZ, home of the desperate and doomed. This place should be burned to the ground, Erika Johnson thought for the thousandth time. Painful memories of her own childhood in such a demilitarized zone flashed momentarily, but she forcibly shoved them back down among the rest of her scarred youth. She was out now and never going back. Except for work, of course. Here, where the law was afraid to tread, a sharp operator could make a fortune and eventually retire someplace clean. If there was someplace clean anymore. Outside of the corporate enclaves.

Westside blackness marked the middle of the next block, where a series of street lamps were out. As the Caravaner neared, the lamps burst into life, sending dozens of denizens scurrying toward less prominent locations of visibility. Rolling the Caravaner onto the broken curb, Johnson drove straight for the closed doors of a garage. The louvered portal opened before her and shut immediately after, so fast not even an elf with wired reflexes could have followed her. A few ticks later, a sleek black Mitsubishi Jaguar rolled out the other side of the garage onto the next street over. At the wheel a raven-haired woman sporting a blue silk Majeure scarf gunned her vehicle and screeched with smoking tires off for uptown proper, classic Queen blaring from the sixteen tandem speakers.

Reaching 95, Johnson was klicks away, tooling for Opa-Locka, when an explosion tinted the horizon and orange flames tongued the night sky. A glance at her digital. Exactly on schedule. Everything was going fine tonight. This had been the third attempted raid by her shadowrunner teams on the Miami complexes of the Shatogunda Corporation and was the last needed. The first infiltration had occurred via the Matrix and had sent Shatogunda troops scurrying to protect three locations: a downtown office on East Fifty-seventh Street, an underground laboratory in the swamp, and one shoreside warehouse. The second had been a magical penetration by a shaman, which sent the Shatogunda wagemages rushing to protect four radically different locations, two of them repeats from the first time. Tonight's physical sortie relied heavily on armed guards to rush and protect five points—only one of them a repeat from the other raids. Done and done. Now she knew where the main datastore for Shatogunda was located, and she could use that information in any of a hundred different ways that would all result in her acquiring a lot of nuyen. And power. Always more power.

Sirens from firefighters foolish enough, or brave enough, to challenge the sprawl, screamed in the distance when the thundering music abruptly stopped as the telecom system of the car bleeped for her attention. She stared in mild curiosity at the communications unit below her automatically paused chip-player. At this hour? Pressing a button gave her a garbled read-out of the caller's number on a small liquid crystal display. It was from the executive offices of the Gunderson Corporation. At this hour? Keying the access code, Erika activated the speaker unit.

"Johnson here," she said, lighting a cigarette with one hand while steering through the thickening traffic with the other.

"James Harvin," replied the unseen caller.

Erika stared at her descrambler, the monitor verifying that this was her boss and not a VR simulation. It was fairly rare tech, but Erika herself used just such a simulation when

working on her own side deals. When using her VR simulation with callers, she looked and sounded like a grizzled old
norm who looked and talked straight off the street.

"Sir!" she said. "What a pleasant surprise. How may I
assist you this evening?"

"What I need from you is important," he said, "And
confidential."

"Of course," Erika said. She was ambitious, but not
glitched. Gunderson Corporation owned Miami, and as far as
Erika Johnson was concerned, that meant they owned her
too. James Harvin was Gunderson's CEO.

"Good," said Harvin. "I always count on you, Erika."

She stubbed out her cigarette. It wasn't like him to beat
around the bush like this.

"Let me ask you something, Erika," he said finally.
"How much do you know about a place, or a person, called
IronHell?"

2

Only an hour after opening this morning, the mixed crowd of laughing locals at Walt's Crypt were thick as fleas on a dead gutterpunk, moving irregularly over the smooth ice of the oval rink, going round and round. Sitting comfy in his office, Adam Two Bears watched the patrons on the other side of the huge Armorlite bulletproof window struggle to stay upright, while kids over at the counter happily munched on ice cream cones dished out by his nephew and niece, and a score of oldsters just sat on benches sucking up the AC and luxuriating. It was going to be another blistering day in Miami, and that meant lots of biz.

What a gold mine this place was, Two Bears complimented himself proudly. Walt's Crypt had started as a dodge to hide his income as a fixer and from doing the occasional shadowrun here in Miami, but the damn thing took off and now was so profitable that Two Bears hadn't personally done a run for years. Last one was against the Brick Boys, a neighborhood gang who thought they could claim his place as private turf. But Two Bears wanted Walt's Crypt as strictly neutral territory, and after he did some corrective knee surgery on several of the Bricks with his fave sledgehammer, the go-gang saw the wisdom of his position and all had been arctic since. He and the bloody five-kilogram sledge were a tough combination to reason with. Or escape from. The stainless steel lady had never failed him yet as a precise negotiating tool.

"Well, chummer?" prompted the Johnson, his gruff visage filling the old telecom sitting on the corner of his macroplas desk. The screen was angled so that any callers only saw Two Bears sitting before the smooth blank wall behind him, not the rink beyond the office window. "Do you know anything about it, or not?"

"Iron hell?" repeated Adam Two Bears, scratching his

head. Self-consciously, he patted his thinning hair back into place trying to hide his growing bald spot.

The grizzled norm on the telecom screen scowled impatiently. "It's one word. IronHell."

Big smegging deal. Okay, IronHell. Kicking back in his battered easy chair, Adam Two Bears tugged on the gold stud in his earlobe as an aid to thought. Not expecting any business calls today, he was in casual attire with only a light armored vest underneath and a legal Narcoject pistol holstered at his hip. Not his best togs, but thankfully, not his worst either. Good thing he'd decided to help Louie fix the public lav tomorrow and not today. Chewing a lip, Two Bears shook his head. "No. Sorry. Don't know the guy."

"I expected as much," grumbled the norm, looking regretful.

"So, do you want me to find the chummer and haul him in?" asked Two Bears. Then he sat upright. "I don't do wetwork. Not my cuppa."

The old guy on the telecom accepted that with a Japper bow. "Termination is not necessary or required, my friend. Simply find out who, or *what* it is. And where it is. Then report to me. Any further actions will be based upon your initial report."

"Price." Two Bears didn't phrase it as a question.

"Eighty-thousand nuyen. Half now, half upon completion. Satisfactory?"

Mentally, Two Bears whistled. Not bad. "Sounds good, my man. By when?"

"Asap."

Oh, in a rush, eh? "As-soon-as-possible costs extra, Mr. Johnson."

There wasn't a flicker or a pause, as if his caller was expecting a little bargaining. It didn't matter what the cobbler looked like, Two Bears knew there were VR programs to make a man look like a woman over a telecom, turn an elf into a dwarf, or even a motherfragging dragon into a mermaid. Hard as it was to believe that anybody could be as handsome as a dwarf! And by the way this Johnson was throwing nuyen around, he figured there was probably a corp involved.

"One hundred and twenty then," said the Mr. Johnson. "But no more."

Inspecting his fingernails for a tick, Two Bears managed

to conceal his elation with a poker face honed by years of pretending his four acres and a bullet were complete drek. One hundred and twenty kay? Oh, momma!

"Accepted," he said. "Scheduled reports?"

"Call when you have something." Or don't report at all, was the implied message. And that was chill with Two Bears. Nothing he hated worse than offering a customer a fistful of nothing.

"How can I get in touch?" he asked.

A number scrolled along the bottom of the telecom screen. "Got that logged?"

That particular circuit was out of order on the old telecom, had been for months, so Two Bears just nodded yes while constantly repeating the number to himself.

"Goodbye then," said Johnson. "I expect to hear from you soon."

Looking stoic, Two Bears nodded and bowed formally, and as soon as the screen was clear, he hurriedly jotted the telecom code down in his pocket secretary. Then he leaned back in his chair, staring at the ceiling and ruminating. Hmm, IronHell. Could be anything, the name of a ship, the tag of some street samurai, the title of a bookchip, model of a European car—hell, where to start? Hey, amigo, he told himself. The best place is always to start simple.

Pressing a button on his desk, Two Bears heard his words echo over the soft jazz playing for the skaters. "Louie to the office, please. Louie to the office."

Moments later, an old dwarf poked his lumpy head through the door. His distorted features were more lumpy than even dwarfs thought attractive. With shoulders like a troll and fists large as anvils, Louie had been a former heavyweight champ until losing four matches in a row via brutal knockouts. Maybe the bouts were fixed, maybe not. Two Bears had never been able to find out one way or the other. So now Louie was retired and sometimes didn't show for work because he plain forgot where the place was. Two Bears tolerated such lapses from Blue Lou the Miami Mauler even though he wasn't a relative, because the guy was such a hard worker when he eventually got here. Besides, the kids loved to hear his tales of the ring. Most of them true.

"Somet'ing wrong, boss?" mumbled the champ. He didn't appear frightened or nervous. Just curious.

A smile. "Nah, nothing like that, Lou. Just a question."

"Sure, Mr. Two Bears. What?"

"You ever hear of something, or some guy, named IronHell?"

Rheumy eyes blinked in confusion, old synapses firing wildly to access biological data banks battered and abused. "That da southpaw from Hialeah?"

Two Bears forces a cough to hide his laugh. "Don't think it's a boxer, killer."

Grimacing from the effort, Louie's face brightened. "Oh, yeah. I scan it now. Dat's a secret pirate base 'n da Caribbean! My gramma useta tell us stories about it."

Oh, for the love of drek. The old guy was off on another magical mystery tour again. Pirates were the bane of Miami's existence, preying on both tourist and merchant craft. But what would Louie, much less his grandmother, know about them? "Great! Thanks, Louie. Go grab a soykaf and take ten."

"Tanks, boss!" he gushed and closed the door.

Pirates? Gimmeabreak. Two Bears shook his head as he wracked his brains. Where to try next? Bad Billie? Nah, the mage was out of town on family biz. Some tragedy in what was left of Chicago. And Dogface was on a run until further notice. Maybe BlackJack. The norm owed him a favor or three. He punched the runner's code into the telecom, but all he got was a recorded message that BlackJack was gone fishing and would return in a few days. So, he was on a run, too, eh? Local biz was booming.

Blast, who else then? Unfortunately, nobody came to mind. The only other thing he could think of was a long shot. But what the frag, he had to start somewhere, didn't he? He tapped in a code and the screensaver changed to a view of a sick-looking norm wearing a stiff suit, ridiculous pince nez glasses from before the Before balanced on the end of his nose, and the haggard expression worn by all city employees. It was probably issued weekly along with their measly stipend and crappy parking spots.

"Public library," sniffed the norm, forcing a polite smile. He applied a handkerchief to his nose and did a good imitation of an elephant. "How may I help you?" he continued, stuffing the nasal rag into his pocket.

The sight was disgusting, but Two Bears stayed chill. "O-hio, sir. Sorry to see you're under the weather. I'm trying to track down a mention of the name, or place, don't know which for sure. . . . IronHell?"

A quizzical expression. "From *Dante's Inferno*?"

"Dunno, chummer. You tell me."

The librarian gave a silent sigh and started typing on a keyboard off screen. "Checking, sir. Just a moment, please, sir." It took longer than a few moments, and the results were all negative. Apparently the word couldn't be found in something called Don Tay's Inferno or any other famous books involving hell.

"Metallurgy?" guessed Two Bears, taking a shot in the wild dark.

Blinking and sniffling, the librarian accepted the odious task. "Certainly, sir." After another longer wait, the clerk returned with equal negative results. Nothing in basic metallurgy, history of, modern advances in, biographies of people involved in, *Mrs. Brown's Dictionary of Industrial Scientific Slang*—contemporary and antiquarian editions.

There was such a thing? Two Bears made a mental note to get a copy of the chip. Might be handy in dealing with corps to parlay in their own lingo.

"Can I be of any further help?" sniffled the man wearily.

If you'd been of help, then I'd be gone, hoophead. "Yes, please. Would you be so kind as to transfer me to the reference department?"

A cough and a sneeze. "Certainly, sir. Just a moment please."

"Reference department, Ms. Sour speaking."

Two Bears perked up at her appearance. The image shown was anything but sour, and he leered at the tasty lady dwarf displayed on his telecom screen. A little gray at the temples meant nothing with sparkling eyes like those. Bodies got old, but never the eyes. Faintly, she reminded him of Melinda, and that thought cooled his ardor instantly.

"*Buenos días señorita,*" he said, trying to please. "I am seeking any data on the word, name, or phrase IronHell. Can you assist me, please?"

"Certainly," she replied warmly, smiling shyly in return. "One moment." She too put him on hold, but was back almost immediately.

"Sorry, sir," she reported. "I tried a global search on the library master grid, the public net, and worldwide Matrix, even used the 9.5 Hunter program, but can find no mention of the word anywhere. I do apologize."

He chewed that over for a tick. Hey, if it was easy, then the Johnson wouldn't have hired him in the first place.

"Is there anything else, sir?"

Unable to come up with another suggestion, Two Bears thanked her profusely to earn a few brownie points for when he asked her out later, then killed the telecom.

Blast. No go, not on the public net, at least. The private grids, of course, might be a totally different story. But that meant he was going to have to use his street sources, which would cut his monstrous profit margin to merely tremendous, but that was his cross to bear.

A flurry of movement on the other side of the office window caught his attention, and Two Bears swiveled about in his chair just in time to watch Louie teach a fine-wire expert that picking pockets in The Crypt was a mother-fragging bad idea. It was over and done with in ticks, and the skating continued unabated over the red spot on the ice with only minor slippage.

Back to biz. IronHell, what could it be? Might be the street name of a professional merc, or maybe even that of a Mafia or yakuza hitman. That he would never trace, unless he could by some miracle find a decker who could get past the lethal black IC protecting the datastores of either Lone Star or Atlantic Security. Between them they handled all the municipal and corporate security in the sprawl.

This was going to be a tough run. He was going to need someone laser-hot. Twist from Seattle—no, he didn't deck anymore for some reason. Maybe Shadowman, Leo the Lizard, or, no, that new kid, Sister Wizard from Orlando. For a newbie, the elf had quite a solid rep in the shadows. She also cost more than god on overtime. His profit was getting slashed like a loanshark's throat. Drek.

The decision made, Two Bears locked his desk, paused to grab a hat, sighed, rammed the hat on his head and headed for the exit. 'Kay, he'd track down Sister Wiz and see what the private grids might have to say about IronHell. Two Bears knew he couldn't use the office telecom. Too risky. Better to make the call from a mall, or on the streets. Stay mobile. Much more difficult to trace him, just in case anyone wanted to try. A distinct possibility since somebody was always after somebody's hoop in this rocking burg. Blood feuds seemed more popular than Urban Brawl. Hey, welcome to Blue City, chummer, please try not to bleed on the carpet as we steal your teeth.

Thumbs stepped off the rattletrap Miami gov bus and stood on the cracked sidewalk of SW Fourteenth Street, the sizzling sun baking down on the top of his tattooed bald head. The sounds and smells of home turf enveloped him like a soothing balm. Sixty back-breaking days in the dank hell of the Fort Lauderdale Citadel making one big one out of little ones for Resisting Arrest made an inner-city troll long for the hot open streets again. It was fragging wonderful to be back. Right where he belonged, on Slammer turf.

At the corner, a stoplight loudly changed, and a trio of bikini-clad blonde bikers frantically peddled through the honking traffic, all trying to reach the ocean alive. A remote-controlled truck rumbled by with no driver or markings. It didn't need one since trucks like these usually carried machine parts or tox chems for dumping into the swamps up north. Could be anything. Two orks, probably a married couple, were screaming at each other in some foreign language. Wafting steam carried the overly spicy aroma of soydog from a cart operated by a blind norm, her snarling hellhound keeping away fast fingers and fake credsticks at the same time. Sunlight glittered off the ancient three brass balls of a pawnshop that dealt in everything and anything that could fit through the black steel doorway. Resting against the rough louvered trunk of a palm tree, a leggy slot-machine girl in a stained white sailor suit yawned widely, trying to stay awake at the ungodly hour of noon. A snoring Japper toff—in a fragging tuxedo of all things!—was lying atop the rusted wreck of a wheelless Jackrabbit in the middle of a weed-filled lot. The drunk was getting expertly stripped by a bunch of troll kids, while amused passersby stopped to make wagers on whether he'd wake up before they finished the job. Odds were running six to two in favor.

Pausing to buy a dog with the works and wolf it down, Thumbs chuckled at the sight. They'd get no real money for the clothing, but it was good practice for them. Best schooling a young troll could get these days. This was his third stop on the way to his doss in Riverside. The first had been to recover some credsticks stashed moments before the Lone Stars nabbed him. Wonder of wonders, the sticks were still there waiting for him. Next had been to turn the stolen nuyen into untraceable Carib League dollars and there too he encountered good fortune.

Now Thumbs was prowling the main drag of Overtown, checking the scene and looking for any chummer who might want a bit of R&R with the happy pack in his vest pocket. The drug/chip combo, which tripled the simsense experience of Better Than Life chips but didn't burn out your brain like 2XS, was a real find—too good to sell since Thumbs was flash at the moment. And the original elf owner wasn't in any condition to complain. The nullhead organleggers had sliced and bagged all the good vitals from the corporate pixie, but not gone through his pockets. Incredibly stupid. Staggeringly dumb. No, this special treat was being saved purely for the family of his go-gang. But if Thumbs didn't locate some warm bodies soon, it was going to be just him and the lovely ladies in his head for the rest of the day. Not a bad proposition, at that. Thumbs had a secret taste for the group thing.

Briefly, the moving shadow of a sports car swept along the busy broiling street like a dagger-shaped cloud. Thumbs snorted in contempt. Fragging tourists getting a 45kph looksee at the amusing local inhabitants. Most of the crumbling buildings in this part of the sprawl were only shells, burnedout ruins from that fiery night in Miami three years ago. The Night of Law, the gov called it. But that wasn't what they called it on the street. Fragging cops had come out shooting with everything they had. And not too many people had dared bother a tourist ever since. Much less eat one, the way the Morlocks had.

Hey, it was just a gang initiation. Members of the Morlocks had copied the hinky bit from some stony biker gang from way up north in Philadelphia long before the Awakening of the Sixth World. Sounded arctic, so they did a mirror. Just kids playing. They didn't take a bite out of anybody important or local. But, geez, did the city gov blow a vein.

They'd sent in panzers and trucks and helos full of Lone Star, Atlantic Security, and any other troops they could recruit, with orders to shoot 'em up and burn 'em out. Ask questions later. Thousands of locals who had nothing to do with the incident died in the fire that night: norms, trolls, elves, kids, dogs, everybody. Rape and theft were apparently acceptable street dangers for tourists, but cannibalism was bad for the city's rep. Go figga.

The next day, heavily armed Slap Squads arrived to quickly spray-paint over any walls still standing in brilliant monotone colors of pink and blue. They'd also dropped a plasti-film covering over the destroyed structures so that the sprawl looked good to the tourists who still flocked to the coastal city for sun and tox-free surf.

Looked good from the air, that is. But here on the cracked sidewalks and stinking streets no such illusion was maintained. Metacrabs infested the palm trees that lined the boulevards like chewed weeds, while gang graffiti and posters from simsense parlors or local boom bands layered the monotones into a jumbled collage, the plas strips sunbleached and acid rain-washed until only sagging strips of rotting plas hung limply from the garish walls. At least the plasti-film roofs offered the starving squatters living in the ruins some meager protection from the deadly northern swamp rains.

Only a couple of the barred shops and stores along the wide boulevard had walls strong enough and intact enough to keep out the metacrabs and devil rats, who regularly fought over anything edible that didn't move, and thus these shops remained open for business, such as it was. The armored doors were propped ajar with jagged chunks of pink brain coral to entice customers to step in out of the heat. The sole exceptions were the always closed plate-steel doors of the Havana Gun Shop, and the Penguin Air Parlor, where a doubloon bought you five minutes of sweet, cold AC. And if some greedy gleeb tried to overstay, the AC was automatically cut until the other patrons threw you out. Whole or in pieces, their choice. But Thumbs liked the heat beating down on his bare chest, his ballistic vest flapping freely in the hot ocean breezes. A deep tan gave a nice contrast to his short white tusks, made a guy look healthy, and much harder to see when doing a run at night. Miami was a hot city. Always had been, always would be.

These thoughts were suddenly interrupted when cries for help from an alleyway caught Thumb's attention. Drawing the big Ares Predator from his inside holster, he checked the scan before going in. Not a tourist, or one of his Slammers. Not his concern then.

What Thumbs saw was a terrified dwarf. Dressed in

denims and loose cotton shirt, the halfer was backing away from a perfectly ordinary telecom unit, staring at the thing as if he fully expected it to spit acid at him. His hands were moving over his body in sharp slaps that Thumbs recognized as a military weapons search. Weapons against a phone?

Startled, the dwarf jerked when he saw Thumbs, but that was only standard. Thumbs was big for any member of his race. An effect he cultivated by wearing cowboy boots with fifteen-millimeter heels, and lifting weights that would crush a norm.

Ramming a hand into his pants pocket, the dwarf fumbled frantically for something, and Thumbs tensed his forearms in response, the carbide blades of his cyberware peeking a millimeter out of his forearms. The halfer couldn't have a weapon, or else he'd have pulled it by now. Hey, that was a certified credstick the dwarf had just pulled out of his jacket and he was thrusting a stout arm toward the giant troll.

"You, a hundred nuyen!" he barked in a barely controlled yell. "Shoot the telecom. Now!"

Shoot the what? The notion was ludicrous, but even loonies had credsticks so Thumbs automatically said, "Two," then after a split tick added, "fifty."

"Three!" shouted the dwarf frantically. "But DO IT NOW!"

3

Bending at his knees to adjust for angle, Thumbs brushed back his fringed vest and whipped out the Predator. The big autoloader thundered at his touch on its hair-trigger, and the telecom unit exploded in a blast of plastic, wiring, and chips. Then just to make sure, Thumbs pumped two more into the sparking equipment, finishing the destruction utterly.

Only a couple of alley residents paid any attention to the bizarre event of terminating a telecom unit with extreme prejudice, as the mercs liked to say.

"Thanks," the dwarf almost wheezed in relief. Using a cuff to wipe the sweat from under his hat with one hand, he rummaged in a pocket with the other, unearthed a credstick, and tossed it to Thumbs, who made the catch with one hand.

Thumbs winked as he slid the stick into his vest. "My pleasure," he replied, jacking the slide on the massive handgun, chambering a fresh caseless round for immediate use. It was an old habit, hard learned in grim street fighting and not one he could ever, or would ever, forget.

Without another word, the dwarf turned and began to move away as fast as he could without actually breaking into a run. But at the mouth of a garbage-strewn alley, he stopped and glanced over a shoulder. "Here's a bonus download for ya, chummer. Hot data, fresh from the horse. Beat feet."

Faintly in the distance, Thumbs heard sirens sound. Already? For shooting a stinking telecom? Feeling his scalp prickly, he nodded his own thanks, then moved into the busy street, dodging traffic with practiced ease, his mind already conjuring the bounty of chemical and fleshy pleasures now available to him. Easiest nuyen he'd ever made. What a day this was! What! A! Day!

Maneuvering through the piles of garbage and duraplas crates filling the alleyway, Adam Two Bears left the troll behind and darted between the towering norm drunks and scraggly elf chippers vibrating to the secret rhythm of the wires in their brains. All ignored him. Not one tried to stop him or ask for a handout. Gunfire followed by a running person always meant real trouble and the only way you stayed breathing on the streets was to avoid it.

Gods and demons, what had he gotten himself into? All this could happen while he was watching on a public telecom? Somebody had fragging wiped Sister Wizard while she was jacked into the fragging Matrix. And while he was fragging watching as he waited for her to jack out. With his own eyes he'd seen the IC fry first her deck and then her brain. Right there, big as life. The only good thing about it was that he'd been at a public telecom on the other side of town and not there in the doss with her.

Frag and drek! Where had she been, in whose files? Somebody who didn't like to be bothered. And it had to be somebody big. Atlantic Security? Gunderson? But the only person who could answer that question was a stiff still jacked into the smoking ruins of her Fuchi 9 with her brains dripping out of her ear. Gunderson was one of the most powerful multinationals in Miami. And being a corp like any other, they could easily have their fingers in just about anything.

Congratulations, Two Bears admonished himself sourly. One hour on the job and his best decker was toasted. A new personal record. Gotta find someplace to twig this mess and get major backup ASAP.

Stopping at the other end of the alleyway, Two Bears looked beyond the honking traffic at the telecom sitting there in plain sight. It was covered with graffiti and probably smelled like a lavatory, but the access light was bright on top, so it was still in operational condition. Help was only a call away. He could have a hundred runners here in minutes. Yet he hesitated to make a dash for the unit. Did he dare call any of his regulars? Rattlesnake, ChrisCross, Omni, Jimmy 2 Cool. Oh man . . . if they could do that to Sister so quickly, then they had to know her telecom was on and where it was connected.

Face facts, chumley, you panicked, he told himself. Maybe if god loves dwarfs, that big troll had destroyed the telecom before a trace could be done. But what if a decker someplace was able to follow the connection to the call box before Sister's brain was fried? What if who-ever-the-frag they were—this so-called IronHell—were even now tracking him down, encircling this neighborhood, ghosting his crib and known chummers? Going to any of his usual haunts could mean getting geeked big time. And anybody Two Bears knew might already be compromised by IronHell. Pros moved fast. Show up at Dogboy's doss and his knock on the door could be answered by a shotgun blast in the throat.

Forcing himself to stroll casually instead of run, Two Bears felt eyes watching him as he moved along through the tall bustling crowds. Desperately he searched for another dwarf, almost ready to call on a total stranger as long as it was one of his own kind, so great was his need. But only norms and trolls and orks filled the street. Great. Just great. Tugging on his ear, Two Bears wondered what to do, where to go?

He couldn't keep himself from looking back over his shoulder, which caught the eye of a slotmachine girl in Amerind buckskin and feathers. She called out something suggestive to him, but he never heard the words, only the tone. "Necker," he answered, to get rid of her fast. It was a trick that rarely failed. As expected, she recoiled in disgust. Few were the flesh peddlers who would hire out to somebody who liked doing the dead.

Alone on the crowded sidewalk, Two Bears watched the second-floor windows for the silenced barrels of sniper rifles and thought furiously, plans coming and going like the locals around him. Maybe he should go back and find the troll. The slag had been happy enough to do something glitched like blow out a telecom for a credstick. He didn't know the guy, but maybe he could trust him as far as he could pay him.

Keeping his back to the wall, Two Bears pulled his hat down as far as it would go and moved on quickly. No, that was too chancy. And, beside, the moment for it was past. His only hope was moving fast. After that, he'd have to see what chance threw his way. Still sauntering casually, but moving steadily as if only mildly late for an appointment somewhere, he rounded the corner and headed east on SW Seventeenth Street.

Far out at sea, a merchant ship flying the flag of Aztechnology drifted randomly in the winds and currents of the Atlantic.

Powerless, its twin rudders moving freely, the craft traveled wherever the ocean dictated. Mostly in circles. Occasionally, an ocean swell crested the foredeck and washed away another of the lifeless bodies lying in dark brown pools. Hundreds of spent shell casings first bumped into a wave prow, then noisily rained down the sticky steel stairs in the forecastle to scatter wildly on the smooth deck of the main open cargo hold, rolling about from wall to wall, encountering nothing to hinder their travels. Nothing except for a few ropes and chains and a humming Hercules lift, still idling along all by itself directly below the open armored hatch in the deck above.

In the pilot house, the navigational computer was dark, the manual wheel spinning wildly with each wave. Lying in the hatchway leading to the chart room aft of the bridge were the charred remains of the captain and her XO, their weapons baked into the black bones of their ashen hands. And hiding under the captain's desk was a dead ork cook with most of his chest missing, a score of round holes from the point-black shotgun blast riddling the antique cherrywood. His brown-stained fingers were splayed wide from the shock of his violent demise. However, hidden behind the turning corpse was a single word painted on the desk from the wide stream of blood from the two fire-charred merchant officers.

It was in Spanish ork, sea slang that was a mere meaningless squiggle to anybody not trained in the idiomatic, sub-tongues of colloquial metahuman dialects. When Aztechnology finally got a university philologist there, the scholar was able to read the crimson word as: Greetings.

Making it back to her apartment after learning what had happened to BlackJack, Laura Redbird found the lock destroyed and her doss in a shambles. The big table made from an industrial macroplas spool for holding wire was over in one corner next to the slashed ruin of the couch and the busted remains of the trideo. They had sure done a good job of trashing the place. Was it possible the word was already out that Redbird and BlackJack had both gotten geeked on a bad run? Everything of value was gone, and everything else was in pieces just in case it hid something of value. Not much remained intact, aside from doors and windows. Unless they'd somehow missed her stash.

Kneeling down on the floor next to the spool table, Laura

slid a kitchen knife along the old carpeting, following the pattern of the clean area that had been underneath the table. The canvas backing was tough, but the blade was sharp and with little effort she lifted away the patch, exposing the old hardwood flooring. Digging the knife point into the floorboards, she finally pried one up with a screech of rusty nails. With that opening established, the other boards came away much easier and soon she had a hole exposing the joints and joyces that supported the floor. Plus, an enlongated bundle of plastic and cloth wrapped with tape. Amateurs. They'd gotten some chips and clothing, but missed the good stuff.

Ripping away the protective layers, Laura brought out a credstick showing a thousand nuyen, an old Colt revolver and ammo box—better than nothing, she supposed—a medkit, and her first real deck, a Fuchi 2 with the spare fiber-op cables still attached.

First off, she checked the action of the Colt, then loaded the revolving internal steel cylinder by manually sliding in six individual .38 cartridges. Fragging thing wasn't even autoloading or caseless, no smartlink, laser sights, nothing. Just a hunk of dead metal. But the oily bullets were explosive hollowpoints capable of blowing a norm's head off or seriously getting the attention of a troll. It would do for today until she was able to boost, or if abso-fragging-lutely necessary, buy, something better.

Armed, she slid the table in front of the door and checked to make sure the windows were locked. Nobody hiding in the closets or in the empty fridge. Satisfied that she was alone for the mo, Laura connected the Fuchi and ran a quick diagnostic check. The obsolete deck hummed happily as it took entire seconds to perform this simple task, but gave a go status reading of all operational parameters achieved.

Everything took forever with this dinosaur, and the first thing she did was check her mail. Lots of notes posted there by friends and chummers who owed her on the down and dirty of the queered run last night. Most of it she knew from what she'd already picked up on the street. BlackJack was dead, shot, crushed, and burned. Ghost! Not even the yakuza kill you three times. Apparently a wetjob by their own Johnson, who'd attempted to disguise it as a counterstrike by another corp. Lone Star bought it 'cause they didn't care, but the street was wise. Zapped by your own Johnson, every runner's worst nightmare. The single flaw in the otherwise perfect wipeout was that Laura Redbird was still alive, and even though she didn't know what the Johnson looked like, she did know that the slitch worked for the Gunderson Corporation. And while faces and even voices could change, Laura highly doubted anybody would take precautions to protect herself from a decker known to be dead.

Gonna find you, *omae,* Laura vowed to the universe. And I'll geek you on the spot right in front of your guards. Black-Jack was much more than my bedpartner and fellow runner. Lovers may come and go, but we were friends. Something clean that even the sprawl couldn't steal. But you did, Johnson. And my life isn't going to start again until yours has ended, slot. End of trans.

The ancient keyboard had only some basic programs in it. She couldn't do anything fancy, but she could do one very important thing. Stored in this deck's memory was an RTG number that would grant her legal access to the main datalines of the Miami grid.

Who knew what number this was? Maybe an old lady who happened to mention it once or a local business that had used it in an ad or even the number of some poor slob who'd told her to call him in the morning. Wherever it came from didn't matter because the line opened . . .

. . . and she stood in one of the main datastreams leading into Miami. The data flowed around her like the rushing rapids of a river. After all that happened last night, now she was home. She belonged in the Matrix.

She'd once programmed her persona into this old deck, and so she appeared in the consensual reality of the Matrix as a gleaming silver falcon. The icon a decker used was of his or her own choosing, and Laura used the modified totem of her Choctaw tribe.

She knew she needed to get off such a public line; in the Matrix too much data could be as big a pain as too little. She'd never be able to navigate the data streams the way she wanted using this old deck, so she was going to have to hop out of this line and head for the private nodes. A few standard log-ons and log-offs and she was heading into the heart of Miami by an untraceable route.

So far, this was mostly kosher. Bypassing the public links, she headed straight for the private business lines, hopping from connection to connection as she had a hundred times before when playing her favorite game. Soon Laura was alone as she penetrated deeper and deeper into potentially deadly corporate territory.

In the angled distance, she spied the decahedrons of the Miami city gov, the irregular lumpy bubbles of the Gunderson Corporation's data banks, and beside them, a collection of squat stumps covered with nasty-looking barbed thorns of no known function. It looked like the Gunderson deckers had been working overtime on either some new defensive IC or system alert. Either way, she'd note it. It might be of great interest next time she stopped off at the Virtual Cabana, a node where she and some of Miami's randier shadow deckers liked to hang out.

As much as she wanted to hit Gunderson directly to try and find out who'd set them up, she reluctantly turned away from the thorn structures and continued on, flying low through a forest of transparent flowering trees and jumbled cubes all color-coded for different public uses and departments.

Now soaring high in the electron skies, Laura froze motionless in mid-air above the endless horizon of the Matrix. This area of the consenting hallucination of the world computer grid belonged to the Caribbean League Gov and vaguely resembled something by an ancient painter named Salvador Dali, a fave among deckers who'd created the initial sculptured programs.

The ground was translucent red glass filled with billions of stars—databytes—that swirled and flowed like trapped galaxies of fireflies. Rising into the sky were polyhedron skyscrapers of shining green, so large they almost blotted the horizon. They were filled with myriad tiny triangular sections that constantly opened and closed as if a million tiny mouths were accepting or disgorging visitors—databytes—and venting white steam of unknown function. The writhing sky was a vista of quicksilver, endlessly flowing into itself and reforming nano by nano, a mad mirrored plane against which she hoped her own chrome icon was not discernible.

Down on the ground, a dozen or so corporate icons of different styles and types were scrambling about near a small, insignificant geyser of gushing light that formed a fountain from an irregular crater in the dataflow. The main international RTG. From here links to nearly every country could be tapped, although this point was mainly a link to Africa, South America, Amazonia, Aztlan, and the Antarctic

Colonies. It was also what the Caribbean League used for "official government business." Which meant there was nothing of value here. The League had a one island one-vote policy for political decisions, but the rest of the time they seemed to be at each other's throats. All the various members also had their own individual nodes and their own private links to each other. Pirates had deckers too.

Laura loved this node. It was a decker's playground . . . Satellite uplinks were a blink away, and she could be anywhere in the world in nanoseconds. And the security was nearly always beatable. She loved that the best.

She was about to leave when something caught her eye. Out of the datastream another icon appeared, then another and another, five or six in all. Keeping her distance, she watched as the icons first took on the appearance of the dataprocessors at the fountain—metahumans in typical Miami neon-colored jumpsuits and sunglasses. But as they headed away from the fountain on one of the telecom lines, the icons changed into black sharks.

The sharks moved along the public telecom grid at an incredibly fast rate, and it almost seemed to Laura that the date flowing along those lines actually moved out of their way. They stopped at a public telecom unit. Or that's what it must have been before somebody fragged it up. The icons set up a new mode next to it and then changed again to public telecom decker icons. The com unit must have been only recently damaged because the node was still active, but Laura couldn't figure this one out. Public telecom nodes usually just lay there dormant until a decker used one and got fried or they closed the node. This type of activity was unique. She wondered what it meant, but she had more important things to do right now.

Laura Redbird would cruise the Matrix day and night, night and day, haunting the grid and info nets and virtual hangouts until somebody put out the word that they were hiring for a dangerous run. Any run, she didn't care, as long as it was local and the bigger the better. Eventually, she'd land a job with the Gunderson Corporation, or better yet, a run *against* the corp. Laura would use that link as the thin edge of a wedge to get closer to the killer Johnson. It would take time, but there was really no other way. Eventually, the murderer would try to find another team of shadowrunners to hose over and Laura Redbird was going to be first in line on-line.

Drek! Name. She'd have to use another name. The Johnson didn't know what her meat body looked like any more than she did the Johnson's, but the biff might know her name. She flapped her chrome wings in annoyance. It would be easy enough to change her physical appearance—some bleach for her hair and contact lenses, and she could probably pass for a deeply tanned European instead of the light-skinned Amerind that she was. Null perspiration. What she didn't want to change was her icon; all her program chips and utilities were set to recognize it. Take days to correct the software. Then again, did she need too? There were lots of bird icons on the grid, so how about changing her name to Talon or Raptor or Falcon? No, something more common, innocuous. Go slow, stay low. Let the target come to you. Hmm, what about Silver? Yeah, perfect, nice and bland. That would do fine.

Here I am, sent Silver silently to the whole world. *Please hire me, Mr. Johnson, so I can kill you!*

4

With a bandanna now wrapped around his head to hide the gang tattoo, Thumbs appeared from around the wreckage of an old radio-controlled truck—now a home for twelve, with dogs and kids included—staying low and following the dwarf. Money was honey, and if the halfer had needed muscle once, he might need it again. And the job could easily go to the next guy who happened to be on hand. Which was going to be him.

Piracy had been taking its toll on both shipping and tourism in Miami of late. The fraggers were ruthless and slippery, all the harder to catch because there were so many different groups of various sizes. Sure, Atlantic Security was on the case, but it didn't seem to be making much of a dent. That was hurting the local economy bad, the trickle-down effect slowing everybody's biz to a crawl. While Shorty there smelled like money and trouble. Thumbs' two favorite things, outside of beer and sex. Which were practically the same thing: money-trouble, beer-sex, one always got you the other. Or so it seemed.

Bending his knees to keep as low as possible, Thumbs watched as the dwarf scooted into a used clothing store. He knew the place. It was run by an old ork who'd lost both legs in a bad run and never quite managed to get enough nuyen to buy new ones. Lucky Pete was anything but. But he owed Thumbs favors, lots of 'em, and now no punksters would ever bother the cripple again after Thumbs had had some grisly fun with them. Mighty hard to ride a Scorpion or a Harley when ya can't get a good grip on the handlebars anymore.

Moving for the pink alley that led to the back door of the blue store, Thumbs froze as the dwarf came out again wearing sandals, a laser-white pair of shorts, a holiday shirt, sunglasses, and a beard almost as big as him. So big in fact that it nearly hid the Nikon & Howell portacam slung around his neck. Thumbs checked for the telltale map and there it was, sticking out of the halfer's back pocket like the dorsal fin of a shark. The official flag for I'M A FRAGGING TOURIST.

Smart move. During the day, nobody sane would ever bother him. So he was safe from molestation, unless he ran into someone who knew and didn't like him. If the locals found out he was a fake, they'd become a mob and violently tear the dwarf apart with their bare hands, then set his bloody bones on fire as a warning to any other braindeads who dared to violate the unwritten law of Overtown.

Thumbs gave a half-smile as he crossed the street to stay behind the Johnson. Little guy must be desperate to try that, and he obviously had more nuyen, a lot more, to get Lucky to cough up a disguise that fast for an alien. Just for a tick, Thumbs debated sliding into the store to get the scan from the ork. But his quarry was moving with a purpose now that he was disguised and Thumbs knew he'd lose him if he dallied.

"Take a cab, nullhead," he mentally ordered the other. Be a lot easier to track the halfer sitting down. But the dwarf scuttled along, humming pictures of everything and everybody. Which made more than a few of the local denizens scurry for cover. Last thing a SINless gleeb wanted was some alien recording the fact that he lived but did not have a System Identification Number. That could get a person killed down here.

On a littered corner, a girl troll from the Slammers raised an arm to hail him. Thumbs quickly gave her a curt hand slice and frowned, never pausing for a beat. The fem's face went neutral and she leaned back against the crumbling brick facade of the old movie theatre, now a joyboy brothel, and began cleaning her nails with a Japanese-style long knife.

Smart. Talia was shaping up real good. And not just 'cause she was reaching her teens. Big troll like him had lots of beds to warm, but drek-few chummers who knew when to keep their fragging mouths shut. If the hammer fell on this and things got dirty, Thumbs'd bring her in as cannon fodder and see if she really had the stuff. He wondered if she had a gun. If not, he could supply her. For a price, of course. Nothing was free.

Why would anybody shoot a telecom?

Moving through the thickening traffic of the wageslaves heading home, the answer hit him. To stop a possible trace. No phone link would mean no ID. Even an ace decker couldn't reconstruct what was no longer there. Then he remembered how fast the sirens had sounded. Lone Star would never race into Overtown simply for a blown phone. The police had bigger problems than that just staying alive in this town. But no, they'd been on their way. Ergo, some red-hot decker had already done a trace. If only he could check to make sure.

Another block passed before the dwarf stopped at a noodle stand, becoming third in line for service. Spying a telecom, Thumbs quickly decided to make a call to a chummer who lived practically on top of that public telecom box. Keeping an eye on the dwarf, he punched in the LTG code, and the screen cleared into the image of a sleepy troll in greasy clothes, tousled hair, and a badly broken tusk. On the wall behind him were rain-smeared sex posters and gaping crab holes. No furniture was in view.

"Yeah, who the frag is this?" the troll demanded.

"Beaver, it's me," rumbled Thumbs. "Speak fast and earn fifty."

The other's gummy eyes went wide with avarice. "For fifty I'd jump offa bridge widout lookin' ta see if dere was any woter. Whatcha need, T'umbs?" he slurred eagerly.

"Still living on Seventeenth and Cuban?"

"Sure. Ya needs a flop?"

Jail would be preferable to that cesspool. The only reason the rotting doss had no cockroaches was that the crabs used 'em as garnish for the devil rats. "Thanks, but no."

"T'en whatchawant?"

"Don't open ya curtains, but look outside and see who's checking out the busted telecom near the pawnshop."

Beaver's face contorted into unasked questions, but he merely nodded, wiping his nose on his sleeve. The tusker returned in a minute. "Man, it's a party down t'ere!"

"Lone Stars?" asked Thumbs, mentally calculating percentages.

"Der waz. But some suits in a slickmobile chased 'em way. Ya wan me ta go down and act casually like? See wa I kin see?"

Jesus, Buddah, and Zeus, no! Even on a good day, which

this was obviously not, Beaver possessed all the adroit acting ability of a busted chair. Maybe less.

"No need. It's arctic," Thumbs replied, wiping the sweat off his forehead with the back of a hand. The tiny ridges of the cyberware exits on his arm rubbed his face in a pleasantly familiar manner. So, this halfer had more than just Lone Star after him. A limo on the scene had to mean a corp was in on this too. And that meant real trouble and real money. Thumbs' price just tripled.

"Ah, Thumbs, like, when can I get my nuyen?" asked Beaver, licking the stub of his busted tusk.

Across the street, the dwarf got served his food and began walking away, slurping down the noodles barely chewed. It was good protective cover—fugitives didn't stop for lunch. His own stomach rumbled in sympathy. Thumbs had missed breakfast, and lunch didn't look like it was coming for quite awhile. "Get 'em from Lucky Pete. Tell him I said it's chill."

"Null perspiration. T'anks!"

Without saying goodbye, Thumbs disconnected and quickly moved after the departing dwarf. This could be the score of his life. Maybe he shouldn't wait to see if the dwarf had more work, but let the guy run to his bolthole and then turn him in to whoever was after him. Surely, there'd be some reward in it.

Thumbs hated the idea of dealing with a corp, even just for a minute and indirectly, but that angle could be safer and would probably pay more. When the time was right, he'd give the halfer one opportunity to hire him, and if he refused, then the corp goons would get him gift-wrapped. But either way, the guy was nuyen in the bank. Then the dwarf turned northeast, heading for General Gomez Park.

Drek! Thumbs slowed his advance, but still kept going. The idiot was heading straight out of Slammers' turf and directly into Latin Kings territory. Sworn blood enemies of Thumbs' gang, and rabid policlubbers. Racists with guns, not exactly the sort of folk he really wanted to be dealing with at the present moment. He already had Lone Star and some corp security goons after the little guy.

In a heartbeat, he made his decision. Okay, time to talk with the halfer and tell him about the bottom line. Amid a traffic jam, Thumbs briskly maneuvered his massive bulk between the slow-moving cars, roaring speedsters, and darting beach bikes, trying to reach the hurrying dwarf as his tiny form disappeared and re-appeared within the bustling crowd.

Dodging around a road crew making big potholes out of little ones, the halfer cut through General Gomez Park. Thumbs couldn't call out. It would draw unwanted attention to him as well. Come on, Shorty, slow down! Thumbs got tense, but didn't let it show. Little guy could be going anywhere. Stay arctic. Kids were playing on the concrete slabs as a makeshift jungle gym, couple of oldsters with obviously nothing to steal or take were sunning themselves on the splintery benches, and ork gangers in ballistic vests were sweating out the noon sun in the shade of the few leafy oak trees, slightly wilted but still standing valiant against the temperatures from above and dog urine from below.

Charging straight through the DMZ of the park, the dwarf was watched by a hundred eyes, but nobody stirred from the precious shade to roust a tourist. At night, he'd never have made it whole or alive to the old marble fountain. Long dry and now full of sea gulls. Noisy, smelly, and they tasted awful no matter how much ketchup you put on 'em.

Along the way, a dozen gutterkin reached out to beg, or offer a guided tour, sex, guns, chips, and other things that would have made the average visitor recoil. Here the halfer gave himself away by not blanching at the offerings. Only a local would be so hardened, and a couple of the smarter squatters backed away, probably suspecting a covert op from either Lone Star or municipal security preparing another of their infamous blanket arrests where everybody ended up in The Citadel for questioning and fragging few of them ever came out again.

Watching everywhere for the hated Latin Kings, his hand resting inside his vest on the butt of the big Ares Predator, Thumbs sighed in relief as the halfer darted across SW Nineteenth Street. In spite of his best efforts, Thumbs lost him a moment later in the milling throng crossing the streets. Moving quickly along the store fronts to try and catch up, he caught a glimpse of his prey through the gaping doorway of a pink-painted derelict building. Through it he saw the dwarf entering a glistening white building festooned with coconuts and flamingos, which stood alongside a row of less fashionable structures on the next street over. The Sunshine Bowlarama. Not a simsense parlor, but actual physical bowling. Balls and pins. Very retro. Just for juves and nostalgia freaks, of course.

Cutting through the doorway, Thumbs decided to slow down for a precious minute, so as not to trod on the dwarf's toes. But before he could follow Shorty inside, the halfer came out again, zipping up his shorts as he headed directly next door. An unmarked building sporting all the usual effluvia of a cheap bar, but no sign.

The Casa Cabana. No wonder the guy hit the lav before going in. Thumbs felt the urge to do the same thing. It was the hardsite for the Latin Kings. Was the halfer a suicide? Drek. Maybe the dwarf was a nutter after all. Thumbs knew little about magic, so he didn't know if a cloak spell disguising a norm as a dwarf could be that perfect in every detail. But why the frag would the halfer want to try to get into the LK's den? To see how quick they could geek him? No, Thumbs must have been wrong about this guy. The halfer had to be tripping in the twilight. A skydiver. Software corrupted. Loft for rent. Better living through chemistry.

Thumbs shrugged. Had to be. Minutes passed and when no explosions erupted from the establishment to mark the abrupt demise of the halfer, new possibilities began to occur to him. Crossing through the ruined building for a better looksee, Thumbs suddenly ran into a shambling figure swaddled in rags, who charged from behind a pile of rotting mattresses wielding a spear made from a broom handle tipped with a busted beer bottle. The razor-sharp glass lanced for his vulnerable throat, but Thumbs easily sidestepped the clumsy charge. As the would-be killer went by, Thumbs thumped him once on the head with a fist bigger than an airline pillow, and his attacker collapsed at his boots with a shuddering moan.

Ignoring the corpse, Thumbs moved to a better vantage point to watch the Casa Cabana. Maybe, just maybe, the dwarf wasn't simply an omelet brain, but novasmart with cojones of beryllium steel. Who'd ever look for a dwarf on the run in the HQ of a policlub? Jesus, Buddah, and Zeus, it was fragging brilliant. Smoking! Einstein on overtime! And if the guy was really that desperate, then Thumbs' price just tripled again.

The whispering sigh of uncoiling rope pricked his ears, and Thumbs turned around just in time to see half a dozen forms in street combat gear descending from the ceiling. A steady flashing came from one of them, and the dusty dirt around him puffed little geysers. Then something humming past and hit him in the chest, his vest slapping against his right side with triphammer force. Thumbs dropped to one knee, unable to breathe for a moment. *Madre mia!* A silenced rapid-fire. This close to their HQ, had to be perimeter guards for the Latin Kings. Frag! Nobody let squatters live in their lookout, so he'd naturally assumed that the presence of a gutterpunk meant it was a clear zone. Fragging gleeb had only been a diversion!

Instantly, the Predator was in his hand and it thunderously boomed twice, the muzzle flash illuminating the dim interior of the burned-out building to near daylight levels for half a tick. Each time a figure flew off the ropes, an explosion of red blood from the unarmored throats marking a lethal hit.

Chatter guns don't mean drek if ya can't hit the target, Thumbs thought smugly, forcing himself to breathe as he moved painfully with every discharge so they couldn't track his location. Spend time on the gun range, or forever in the dirt, as his daddy used to say. Nuff said.

The remaining four reached the ground, and were in a circle firing wildly, high and low. Crouching behind a chunk of busted concrete, Thumbs hastily buttoned up his ballistic vest and heard flechettes ricochet twice off his impromptu barrier. Bad. This was bad. Three visible exits, but he was nowhere near any of them. No back-up, no grenades, not much ammo, and it was their home turf. Reinforcements could be on the way already. Pulling the long monofilament-edged knife from his boot, he hacked off a chunk of concrete and threw it across the open expanse of the dilapidated structure. It hit with a loud clunk-clatter-crash, and two of his attackers turned to fire that way, the others expertly concentrating on the exact opposite direction, neatly cutting off his bid for the open doorway.

The wall aft of Thumbs and his concrete shield got hammered hard with dozens of rounds, and twice more his vest slapped him on the back, but now it was closed tight so the impacts were only an annoyance. Would have been closed before too, but it was just so freaking hot today! Ballistic cloth was thicker than end-of-the-year miso soup, and a troll's gotta breathe. Well, not according to the Kings he don't, that is.

Maintaining their circle formation, the policlubbers were spreading out, firing irregularly to conserve ammo. Nobody called out for surrender or quarter. Thumbs knew he was a metahuman in racist territory. If they got him, his pointed ears would be nailed to their Wall of Honor. Horns carved into pistol grips, tusks sold to tourists, and the rest of him would go to feed their dogs and gators as a special treat, trying to cultivate in the beasts a taste for metahuman flesh. As if the freaking things needed any additional encouragement.

Cutting off two more chunks of concrete, Thumbs sheathed the blade and then threw one of the chunks to his left and waited, standing erect. As the policlubbers fired in the same response pattern, he pulled back a powerful arm and threw the second chunk with all the strength he possessed. It hit one of the guards squarely in the face, and the man's head snapped back so hard Thumbs could hear his spine audibly break. As the body dropped and the others turned for a moment to see their comrade mysteriously fall, Thumbs shifted position to a stinking pile of assorted junk where the dead gutterpunk had been hiding. Okay, three down, three to go. Without a doubt, he'd had fun before, and this wasn't it.

Firing twice more, then again, and again, Thumbs saw one guard crumple and another have her knee blown off before they all started firing in his direction. In counterpoint, the wounded fem started screaming curses in every language she knew.

Hastily, Thumbs was reloading, pocketing the spent clip, when something hissed and crackled around the hot barrel of his Ares and the gun was brutally yanked from his grip. His eyes searched the darkness as he shifted position and the air hissed again. Stun baton? Drek! Reinforcements must have arrived! Drawing his knife, Thumbs shoved his back to the dirty wall, frantically searching for a way to escape, but saw only darkness and enemies completely surrounding him. No other choice then. Arctic. He touched the third molar on the right side of his mouth with his tongue and felt his body vibrate with power. The reflex trigger would accelerate his reactions to triple-speed.

"Rock and roll!" he screamed, charging headlong at the guards at thrice norm speed, his cyberblades swinging like a hundred scythes.

5

Checking the safety of his Fichetti needler, perfect for flatlining people but lousy on telecoms, Adam Two Bears pushed open the double doors to the bar and boldly walked on in.

Icy air wafted over him, and he fought back a shiver only partially caused by the low temperatures. All talk stopped the moment he entered, and a dozen faces went grim as death, hands darting below table tops and into jackets. Two Bears knew the only reason he was still sucking air was the city map in his pocket, a reminder of the Miami gov's fire-bombing of anybody who harmed tourists. Even still, he was on thin ice here. Cross the line, drek, come close to the line and they'd be mopping his brains off the floor.

The place was decorated in early schlock, with all the usual fishing nets, plastic crabs, and cork things you saw in most of the bars in town. Bloody tourists expected the whole drekking city to be nautical. Walking slowly to the bar, hands well away from his sides, Two Bears hoisted himself up onto the norm-size stool and gave a smile to the bartender, who did not return it, but continued to polish a clean glass and looked ready to spit in his face.

"Fat Jake here?" Two Bears asked, placing both hands flat on the counter.

"Who wants to know, runt?" demanded the barkeep, curling a lip in disgust.

So much for being nice. "The man who saved him from a Morlock axe, that's who, butt-wipe."

The bartender's eyes went wide, and he smashed the glass on the floor. "You ain't no man, crit!" screamed the norm, brandishing a fist the color of boiled chicken. "You're a stinking metafreak!"

Two Bears did nothing. He just sat there and waited. Crit. That was new. Short for critter, he supposed. So now they were calling metahumans animals. Made sense for them. Animals had packs and cubs, not families and children. Made his kind easier for them to kill and still sleep at night. I didn't kill a man today, dear, just a nasty walking animal. Smelly thing had the audacity to wear clothes.

"Your opinion," Two Bears said low and soft. "But if you don't get Jake out here pronto, it's your pecker in the blender."

Tense moments passed with the bartender just breathing hard, and the other patrons scraping their boots and shifting chairs all around him. Moving into better positions so they wouldn't be hit in the crossfire? Two Bears knew this had been a wild gamble. Pure dice. But nobody would ever look for him in here, and he needed resources fast. He could get them if Fat Jake still remembered old debt and hadn't let the fear or hate boil away what honor he used to have.

Long ago, a million years it seemed like nowadays, they had run together. Side by side, they'd ganged against the Morlocks, the very go-gang who'd cannibalized the fragging tourist and got half of Overtown toasted like marshmallows in their sleep a few years back. Including Melinda. Sweet gentle Mel had died in the city's brutal retaliation—the so-called Night of Law. That same night the various rival gangs put aside their differences and swore a blood oath of peace until they caught and killed every stinking Morlock sublife joybag and did them up a treat proper. There were special chummers for this job—frizoids and glitches who lived in the sewers and swamps, too twisted in the brain for any use except letting them have a hated foe to play with. That's where the Morlocks went one by one, never to return. Street justice. Hard and permanent. Trans end.

Setting a trap to take down the last few members of the gang had gotten Fat Jake, who was skinny as a laser and hence the name, on their ghoulish dining table. The Morlocks' turn for revenge. Two Bears had taken a knife in the belly busting the rival ganger free from their funtable, and Jake lost an ear but kept his life. Together they slaughtered the rest of the go-gang, saving the mage boss for last, a motherfragging insect shaman. The screaming freak unleashed some flying things like hornet-bats or something, but couldn't survive the big batch of fire-death from the packages of C10 plastique they brought along. It was a rocking party. Would have made a hell of a trid-of-the-week.

The spellcaster died in a chemical fireball better than any he could conjure and, unconscious, Two Bears and Jake both got saved from the burning wreckage by the city firefighters, of all things. Then they did a year in the Citadel for destroying public property and possession of restricted materials. Lone Star knew what had gone down, but refused to sanction any independent action that made them look bad. Welcome to Miami, chummer.

It would have been so much simpler to juke the gangers' hole to the ground. Slab the Morlocks and Jake at once. Easy as shooting crabs off a tree. But your word was your bond on the streets. The only thing a chummer could not buy was his own rep. So Two Bears saved the man who'd gotten his one true love. Melinda. He tried not to wonder if she'd have stayed with him when the change hit him later and he became a dwarf. Did she stay with Jake because she loved him more, or because Adam Two Bears was different now? Two Bears would never know. Sometimes, the truth was better not known. There was great comfort in lies.

Reaching below the counter, the suddenly smiling bartender started to pull something large and metallic into view when a voice stopped him.

"Hoi, Two," rumbled a human standing in the doorway that led to the back storeroom. Light poured in from behind him and it wasn't until the norm closed the portal that Two Bears could clearly see who it was.

The years had not been kind to Jake. Although still skinny and dark as a stick, Fat Jake was wearing a sleeveless tee that showed a network of thin scars trailing up both arms. His left ear, half hidden behind graying hair, shone with flawless health. Plastic ear, and wires. Chipped or skillwires, Two Bears had no idea. But in his youth, the other man had scorned both as crutches for the weak and stupid. Guess Jake was showing his age at last. Then again, he'd been a full adult when Two Bears was a snotty juve who didn't know the difference between bullets and bullshit. How old was the norm now, fifty? More? No matter. It would be best not to mention the physical changes. Never insult the hand before it feeds you.

"O-hio, Jake," returned Two Bears deliberately using the casual Japper greeting between friends. A little reminding couldn't hurt here.

"You know this . . . thing?" snarled the bartender, returning whatever it was to back under the counter. The rest of the patrons did the same with their own ironmongery. Slowly and reluctantly.

So this is what a skeet feels like, thought Two Bears.

"Yah, the runt's mine," said the gray-haired norm. The two old friends cum enemies looked at each other, and the norm cracked a half-smile. "You got that data I sent you to steal, crit?"

Inside, Two Bears went stiff, but refused to allow his fury to show. This was a game the dwarf didn't want to play, but he'd started it without warning, and what could he do? Challenge the norm here among his chummers? All bets would be off, and Jake would have to geek him on the spot to save face. Eat a little pride, live another day. It was drek sandwich time. But he made a mental note of the humiliation for the future.

"Yes, sir," Two Bears replied humbly, giving a short bow. "Of course, sir. I have it right here, sir."

Jake waved a hand and turned without waiting for a response. "My office, meta. Now."

"Ya sure it's housebroken chief?" taunted a leathergirl at a table full of steins.

"Why should it be?" he retorted. "You ain't."

The bar patrons roared in laughter, and the snipes flew thick as the heavy door cycled shut, cutting off all sound.

Inside the office of the Casa Cabana, Two Bears straightened his bent shoulders and glared at his host. "Having fun?"

Leaning back in the chair behind the duraplas desk, Jake levered his boots on top of the scarred surface, his boot heels dovetailing into worn grooves there. Clearly, a daily position.

"Absolutely," he snorted. " 'Bout time you learned proper respect for true humans."

Demons of chaos, give him the strength not to strangle this man before they could even talk.

"Not telling my people you're not a real tourist should even us out, eh?" added Jake coldly.

Check and balance. So it begins. "If that's what you think, done and done," said Two Bears, crossing his arms. "I'll take my problem elsewhere.

"After a bit to eat," he added sotto voce. "Any good places around ear?"

Fat Jake reacted to the words with a jolt, his hand

automatically going to the right side of his head. "Point duly taken," he rumbled, low and menacingly. "Download me."

"I'm doing a lobster and need backup. Now. As in fifteen minutes ago."

"In hot water, eh? That explains the beard and map. Must be big trouble for such a risky ploy. On the run, or on the lam?" he demanded suspiciously.

Two Bears arched an eyebrow. "What do you think?"

Jake relaxed. "Okay then. So the local SWAT isn't in hot pursuit, you're just hiding from them. What's the glitch? Need a piece? I've got a couple of nice Mag fives, and an 88V in the backroom. Heavier stuff too, if need be, but those will cost you."

Hooking a chair from behind, Two Bears pulled in close and sat. "Got a weapon and know how to get more. I need people."

"So whatcha want?"

"All three."

"Muscle, mana, and machine?"

Gods, yes. What Two Bears actually wanted was a small army, but three pros was all he could afford until he squeezed more juice from his Johnson. The old man hadn't been straight with him about the deal and that was going to cost him a stack.

But god, how he hated this! Should be making his own calls, contacting his regulars, solid chummers he'd normally trust to the marble slab. But after Sister got brainfried, he didn't know who to trust, or where to turn. If only he knew what corporate file she'd been raiding, that would help, but he was totally in the dark. Not since he was a kid running solo through the streets of Overtown had he ever felt so alone and vulnerable.

"You got the nuyen to feed them, kemo sabe?" asked Jake.

The old Amerind term of friendship invoking days long past hurt worse than any insult. Goddamn the norm. Calling in a debt of honor wasn't supposed to be a lesson in humility. "I got codes for the decker to get it for me."

"Fresh from a cold one?" chuckled the man.

A brisk head nod. "Haven't robbed a corpse in six. The codes are my own. But I don't dare go near my accounts. They might be waiting for me. Gotta access 'em from outside."

"You're that hot?" gasped Fat Jake.

Two Bears shrugged.

The human lowered his boots and leaned on the desktop. "What the hell'd you steal, Two? Or who'd you cack? Some maf chief or a yak boss?"

Removing his hat, Two Bears inspected the brim and said nothing.

No boasts, no denials, no lies, or evasions. Fat Jake's expression melted like ice on the beach, then got nasty. "Anything goes down, I burn you," he warned hastily. "Got to protect my place."

"I scan. You can always get more customers, but those plastic crabs must cost a fortune."

"Stuff it, halfer," retorted the norm. "This reeks of tox and you fragging know it. Why come to me? You're a fixer now. Ain't you got own fragging regulars?"

Two Bears shook his head. "No can do. They might be compromised. Find me new talent. No virgins. No groups. Make it all loners. Better chance they aren't morkhans that way."

"Traitors?"

"Or gov ops. I'm paying top nuyen and a slice of the pie, so I want first string."

"A slice off the top? It's that hard?"

"Straight as a laser."

A variety of expressions came and went on the norm's face, none of them happy, so Two Bears quickly added. "I got insurance."

That snapped Jake around. "Yeah, who?"

"Ask him when he sends in the drones with all guns firing."

"Drek," snorted the norm. "But it's a good lie. Let me see who's looking for work." Reaching under the desk, Jake retrieved a datacable, slid the end into his temple, and started his fingers dancing over the deck built into the desk top.

Two Bears felt oddly disturbed by the event. Fat Jake a decker, that was also new. What else had changed with the man? Gods, what a different place the world suddenly seemed.

After a few minutes, Jake removed the cable from his forehead and laid it down between them. Two Bears read the act as a formal line of disembarkation.

"Done," said Jake, coiling the cable. "I got what you asked for, and I set the meet for the old place at Palm and Cove. Second-floor ballroom. You remember?"

"Natch." It was where they used to get drunk, get high, and make plans to take over the city gov. Youthful dreams of avarice.

Satisfied, Two Bears stood, and after a moment, offered his stout hand to the other. Jake stared at the hand as if it was infested with crabs, then rose and took it. The two released their respective grips almost immediately.

"Now we're even, Two," said Jake, stepping to the wall and palming open a door. The alley showed outside. In a flash of memory, Two Bears recalled the secret door. It was an escape route from the old days, clearly still in operational condition. Probably just in case the old days came back with a vengeance.

Staring down at the dwarf, Jake went on, "Now we're even. If I pass you on the streets, I'll ignore you. But if we meet on a run and you're on the other side, finito."

Two Bears scowled. "Crosshairs, we're even. No debt, no sweat."

"Done and done."

Two Bears moved past the taller man, then paused in the doorway. "With one exception."

"What?" demanded Jake gruffly. "Some fave club? A bix bop? I'll never go to The Crypt, so you can forget that."

"Ah, too bad, my boys would love to meetcha," Two Bears returned, then softened his tones. "But no, Jake, I was referring to Melinda's grave. I put flowers there occasionally and—"

A roar cut him off. "So it's you!" bellowed Jake, spittle spraying from his mouth. Razorspurs sprang out of his hands and Fat Jake reached for Two Bears' throat. Two Bears ducked low and backstepped into the alleyway, giving himself combat room. What the frag was going on here?

"Get this straight, mutie," growled the human through clenched teeth, his thin chest heaving. "In twenty-four hours our deal is done, and your hoop is mine. How does it feel to be a dead man, freak?"

Staying out of reach, Two Bears was startled by the reaction. "But Jake, I . . ."

"And if I ever catch you near her site I'll geek you on the spot and then go do your whole fragging family!"

Stunned, Two Bears just stood there, staring at the raving norm.

"OUT! GET THE FRAG OUT! AND NEVER GO NEAR HER AGAIN, YA STINKING ANIMAL!"

Moved more by the sheer power of emotions in the norm's words, Two Bears stumbled further into the alley, the slamming door cutting off any further conversation. Standing alone on the sunny concrete, he wondered why Jake was so hyped on him paying his respects to a gone friend. She'd chosen Jake, not him. Was he that selfish he couldn't even share her in death?

Quickly Two Bears moved off, dropping the map into one dumpster, the beard into another, trading his camera to a squatter for a soiled duster comprised of more patches than fabric, changing his appearance as much as possible as he headed for the rendezvous point. As looped as Jake sounded, he might go back on the deal at any time because of this. Everything was luck and speed from this point on.

Dropping into his chair, Jake fought to control his shaking. The son of a slitch! Muck-eating gleeb! Running stiff fingers through his thinning hair, he ground his teeth in impotence, then took a glass paperweight from his desk and threw it at the wall. Tears welled in his eyes, and he dropped his head into his arms, sobbing uncontrollably.

The big plan had always been to build up enough to live on and then take off for one of the Independent Keys. Largo, perhaps. Good coastal defense, lots of trees, non-aggression treaty with the other Keys and part of the Caribbean League itself. Sounded like heaven. And if he'd had to kill to get there, what better place to do some penance than paradise? But with Mel gone, it all became meaningless. His life became meaningless.

Fat Jake never told Two Bears, never told anybody, but Melinda had made her choice the afternoon of her death. She was going to go back to Adam, even though he was changed and their kids would probably be dwarfs. Their kids! The two of them, living together, laughing, loving, in bed. Together. Melinda with a crit! A scream boiled into his throat and Jacob Anderson clamped his jaw shut, biting back the noise, but the awful visions still filled his brain like a hellish hurricane. Two Bears had won, wasn't that enough? But no. She was dead and buried, and still he fought Jake for her attention. Denying him even the solace of the lie. Would this ever end? Ever?

Reality threatened to shatter and break apart into pieces. Fervently, the weeping man wished he could go out the door and kill the filthy thing that had stolen the heart of his woman. But even to an animal, his word was his bond. Unbreakable, sacrasanct. For today, the runt was untouchable. Protected.

The tears slowed as a bitter smile broke through and his face took on a feral expression. Safe for today. That was all he'd guaranteed. One day. Twenty-four hours at the most. However, tomorrow was another matter. Oh, tomorrow. . . .

After that, he would leave this stinking town forever.

6

On patrol in the royal gardens, Oswaldo Fontecchio found the knotted rope dangling down the west side of the Minister's Pavilion and immediately touched the commlink on his collar, sounding a yellow alert. It might be only the media again, or one of the prime minister's twenty-two children playing another prank on the house guards.

The bushes parted and two other of the Imperial Hand came into view, Hiko and Seami. Wearing matching blue suits of exquisite tailoring, both samurai stood more than two meters tall with a calm grace only obtainable with years of rigorous martial arts training. Their ward, Minister Manjiro Nakahama, director of power and light for the royal city of Tokyo itself, was protected by a serious contingent of guards, human and machine. But no metahumans or altered lifeforms were involved, as the Nipponese considered any variance from the human standard utterly repulsive and abhorrent. And there was no richer or more powerful nation than Japan in the Awakened world of the twenty-first century.

Incredibly, Fontecchio was a member of the elite Imperial Hand. One of the fiver personally assigned to the Minister. For such a staggering honor to be bestowed on a barbarian, a half-Japanese, half-Italian *gaijin* from the UCAS, was almost beyond belief, and was solely a tribute to his unchipped abilities. Political clout and nuyen meant less than nothing when considering security personnel for such an exalted person.

"Yuki and Kaye are in the palace directing a sweep," said Hiko smoothly. "Perimeter reports no unauthorized vehicles, bikes, or carts." Even to the emotionally controlled main islanders, Hiko was considered unflappable. Solid stone. Ice 4. He was the son of a son of a son of a gov bodyguard. A family responsibility Fontecchio knew the samurai did not take lightly. His own daughter of two was already in training.

"*Hai,*" Fontecchio said, responding to Yuki's transmission. The Hand were linked together by head coms twenty-four hours a day. Privacy was not a privilege they enjoyed.

"We found nothing," she said.

"Join up here," he said gruffly, then quickly added, "please."

"*Hai.*"

Fontecchio turned toward Seami Motokiyo. A distant grandchild of the legendary poet, the burly man's chromed eyes were scanning the forest around them, searching for anything untoward. In private, he also wrote poetry; in public he taught najuitsu classes. A true warrior.

"Brother, I want a Matrix status stat."

Seami gave a short nod and his head kept going, falling to the ground at his feet as his neck stub gushed red blood into the air. From out of the bushes behind the falling corpse appeared a half-dozen figures dressed in solid black, their diakote katanas shining in the filtered light of the private garden.

"Ninjas," said Hito as if ordering miso soup, his cyberware extending from both arms. He dove forward in a shoulder roll, the twin monofilament blades removing the legs of two of the intruders. Falling, the dying assassins vivisected the bodyguard with the blinding speed of chipped reflexes. Only his unorthodox attack had allowed the warrior to get so close, so fast, before death.

Watching his friend die as his intestines spilled onto the manicured grass, Fontecchio coolly and calmly extended both hands as if to embrace the ninjas. Instantly from the belt holster at his waist a ferruled cable snaked upward, a massive pistol attached to the end of the metallic support. The Colt Manhunter slapped into his right palm, automatically firing, and then slammed into his left, firing and returning to the right to fire again. Three of the invisible warriors fell back, their throats crimson geysers.

The last ninja, the one prominently in the front, shimmered with distortion like a jumbled class nine holograph and was gone. A common trick. A childish ruse for the unwary.

"Jade palace, go hard," commanded Fontecchio, reloading his weapon with explosive-tipped flechettes. Chipped ninjas,

every bodyguard's worst nightmare. "Full coverage on the
lake, *wakarimas*?"

Silence.

"Palace, report!"

Static, faint words of questioning, then screams.

"Yuki!"

Nothing.

Instantly, Fontecchio was sprinting for all he was worth
through the delicate trees. The palace was compromised, two
of the Hand dead already, maybe more. This was no rebel
strike but a full assassination attempt by one of the Old
Houses, or worse. A bush moved against the evening breeze
and Fontecchio fired. Leaves exploded in the strident blast,
along with blood and a spray of gray brains spiderwebbed
with silver wires. Loping alongside the forest trail, Fontecchio pulled out a small device and flicked at it with his
thumb. The signaling device would summon the military
within minutes, letting them know this was not an exercise
or practice. In all probability, he might get killed himself
with the arrival of the overly excited troopers. But that was a
part of the job. *Hai*? he asked himself. *Hai*, he answered
solemnly.

Red ribbons attached to tree limbs and bushes, the
streamers fluttering happily about. Fontecchio burst from the
foliage and jerked to a halt on the perfect white sand of
the sculptured shoreline, staring anxiously at the house.

A tiny wooden structure sat alone on a grassy island in the
middle of a small lake of such sophisticated design none
could tell if it was artificial or natural. Nor were such
boorish distinctions important regarding the ancient tea
house. It was a most private spot where the Minister Nakahama, infamous for his familial temper, could ritually go to
seek forgiveness of whichever wife he had slighted this
week. It was a thousand-year-old ceremony, very solemn and
sacred. None but rogues would dare to disturb.

Before stepping onto the flagstone path that led to the tiny
lacquered bridge, Fontecchio gestured and fired a round at
the stones. Steelloy spears ten meters tall lanced from the
soil, then razors snapped out along their shafts and began to
spin in a tight interlocking pattern. A drifting leaf was
sucked into the vortex of the machinery and disintegrated.
Drek! Tea house defenses were on full. There were wards to
hold off impetuous family members, but nothing to stay a

determined assassin. It was not believed that such could penetrate this far into the grounds. Impossible. Unthinkable!

Staring at the paper windows, Fontecchio seriously debated firing a round in to warn the minister, but without knowing where his ward was, he might kill the man. And the walls were so thin as to offer scant protection from his weapon. Drek, frag and fragging drek! he raged silently. What had he washed with this morning? Couldn't remember. Damn, no other choice. And without further hesitation, he dove into the lake.

Fire ants crackled over his body from the electricity coursing through the clear water. It was painful, but not debilitating. Twice carp of unnatural size and tremendous jaws approached him hungrily, but backed off as they detected the lingering traces of the royal family soap on his skin. Mines of various types buried under the lake bottom allowed him passage once they ascertained his ID from the coded signals of the circuits implanted under his skin.

Reaching the shore, Fontecchio shrugged off his coat, the ballistic cloth heavily soaked with water and thus drastically slowing his responses. But as he stepped onto the grass, he was fiercely driven to his knees by an invisible barrier. Mana or technology, he had never been told. Holstering his weapon, he stayed perfectly still until his identity was confirmed and the barrier parted, allowing entrance.

A hand gesture and the Manhunter was back in his palm, rigid at the end of its support cable. Fontecchio took two steps, gave a savate kick, and the tea house door flew open. Sitting with crossed legs on opposite sides of a miniature coal brazier, the ceramic tea pot whistling softly under a perfect low boil, Minister Nakahama and the First Wife, Murasaki, were holding extremely small cups, frozen motionless in the process of turning them the necessary three times before taking three sips with a three-second pause between each.

Frowning, the Minister silently demanded an immediate explanation while Murasaki moved away from the bodyguard as she always did when one of the Hand burst in on them unexpectedly. This gave both the illusion of privacy to her husband and a modicum of combat room for the guards.

"Monkey and the tiger," said Fontecchio stepping close, giving the code for an assassination attempt in progress.

The Minister laid his cup aside and stood, waiting for

more information when pain exploded in Fontecchio's back and he was brutally hurled forward to the floor.

Hurtled forward . . . forward . . . forward . . . the body, the blood, the screams, the hospital, the grave. That tiny cold grave.

Drenched in sweat, Oswaldo Fontecchio awoke in the darkness gasping for breath, both hands outstretched in an automatic defensive reaction. But the Manhunter did not slap into his open palm. In the dim light from the wall washstand of the coffin motel, he saw the VPR2 lying nearby on the fold-out table. Memories returned as his dream-state induced by too much saki slowly wore off. Rivulets of sweat running down his face, Fontecchio cradled his head trying to shut out the memories of his day of shame. How could he have been so stupid? He'd removed his wet coat because it slowed him down. Fool.

Reaching under his damp tee, he fingered the puckered scar below his right arm where the heavy-caliber slug had exited his body. If the slug from the assassin's rifle had not slammed into his collarbone, it would have struck the prime minister. As it was coated with a bio-toxin specifically tailored for his chemistry, he would have been dead in seconds.

Instead, it hit Fontecchio's internal bones, shattering them like glass, and ricocheted off, piercing his latissimus dorsi muscles to strike the Lady Murasakiti in the right temple, exiting through her pons. No toxin was necessary. Before she slumped to the floor, there was no life remaining in the tiny frame, her brains were literally splashed on the lacquered wall behind her.

Fontecchio nearly died himself as the medtechs battled the poison in his system. But as the toxchem was not designed for him, the effects were diminished enough to offer survival. But at a cost. Needing a scapegoat, his superiors naturally blamed him, the sole survivor of the Hand, for dereliction of duty, but the Emperor himself stayed the execution and banished Fontecchio forever. Death would have been kinder.

Incredibly, waiting for him at the airport gate as he shuffled toward the General Dynamics SV250 suborbital transport was a little girl all in white, her hair pulled back into a painfully tight bun. It was Tusiato, the daughter of Hiko-*san*. The child silently offered Fontecchio a red lacquered box and turned her back on him. He was speechless at the supreme insult.

Weakly, he boarded the stratoliner with the tourists and business executives bound for NorthAm. In the privacy of his seat, Fontecchio thumbed open the cyberlock on the armored box. Inside was his VPR2 and favorite Manhunter lying on a bed of white velvet. A deathday gift for a man who was no longer alive to his friends. And they had sent a child to deliver it. Fontecchio's resolve cracked under the awful impact of the gift, and he wept for the first time since the death of his parents.

Arriving penniless and friendless in North America, it had taken Fontecchio years to save half of the return fare, even with hoarding his funds by living in dumps like this.

Reaching for the bottle of synth-saki, he gave a start as the telecom beeped. Who could possibly know he was here in Miami? His last wetwork job had brought him here only hours ago. Fontecchio glanced at the dirty wall clock. Lie, he arrived yesterday. The N'York yakuza fixer who pimped for him would have word of his presence on the Matrix by now. Could be biz.

Taking a swig from the bottle, he only got a tiny sip of the horrid, lukewarm liquid. Bah, nothing tasted worse than warm saki. However, out of booze meant he should get back to work. A single night of drunken forgetfulness was all he allowed himself after a job. To do more was always tempting, something he often fought against, but it might threaten his reactions and risk getting killed out here among the barbarians where none would sing at his grave, or burn flowers at a shinto shrine for his spirit. Alone, he would be truly alone forever, if killed here. And that thought was even more intolerable than his disgrace.

Swinging his legs off the tiny bed, Fontecchio pushed it into the coffin wall, and wrapping a threadbare robe bearing the Imperial crest of Japan about himself, sat down heavily before the tiny com unit and hit the Accept key. It took two tries. The screen cleared to the picture of a gray-haired norm almost as skinny as a skeleton. A decker.

"Delphia here," Fontecchio said, slipping an herbal cigarette into his mouth from the pack in his robe pocket. "And you are?"

"Mr. Johnson. I have heard of you from Dr. Salvatore and Raincloud. You come most highly referred."

With a pocketflash, Fontecchio lit the cigarette. The pungent cloying fumes set fire to his lungs, but the misty cloud of the fledgling hangover quickly fled under the harsh administrations of the burning herbs. "What is the job and how much?"

"I've got work for you with a dwarf named Two Bears," the norm stated, his hands very white on the old macroplas desk before him. Then he quickly ran down what he knew and what it would pay.

"Interested?" the fixer asked.

Thoughtfully, Fontecchio stared at the telecom. How had he fallen so low? A spark flared for a nano inside him, but he quickly ground it out like the cigarette butt. He lit a fresh stick and pulled the smoke deep into his aching lungs, letting the white smoke out in a stream at the rust-stained ceiling panels.

"Hai," he said, and then added, "where and when?"

7

Sitting at a table inside a wide tent on the tenth floor of an ancient condoplex at Palm and Cove, Two Bears and Thumbs field-stripped dirty weapons, spraying lubricant where needed and slipping on nylon bushings wherever possible so that lubing would never be needed again. The sourceless lights in the cool tent clearly illuminated the spacious table piled with guns, ammo clips, some nice knives, several grenades, and a couple of credsticks coated with sticky blood.

"Latin Kings didn't take very good care of their iron," observed Two Bears, working the bolt on a Ceska. "Dumb slots."

"It's why I'm alive and those guards aren't," smirked Thumbs, contemptuously peering down the barrel of a Beretta. "A dirty weapon will always jam at exactly the wrong moment. Law of the street number fourteen."

"That's hard data," agreed Two Bears, slamming a freshly loaded clip into the machine pistol and laying it aside. "So nice of the Kings to donate these fine weapons to the run."

With a whisper, the four long monofilament blades slid out of Thumbs' left forearm. "They didn't do it willingly."

"So I guessed," harrumped Two Bears.

A shrug. "I sliced as few of the guns as I could. But I gotta admit, some of those gleebs refused to let go no matter how much I killed 'em."

"And we got their credsticks too!"

"Those? They're fakes to scam tourists," said Thumbs. "Nice work, but useless."

"Pity." Two Bears started to disassemble a Light Fire 70. "Fat Jake sure isn't going to be happy about this."

"Think he'll queer the deal?" asked Thumbs, a worried note creeping into his gravelly voice. He'd connected up with Two Bears after mopping the floor with the Latin

Kings' lookout team across the street from the Casa Cabana. Then he'd hung around the area until the halfer reappeared and he could approach him. The little guy hadn't needed much persuading. He said his name was Adam Two Bears and that he was putting together a team to help him find out the identity of someone or something called IronHell.

"Nyah. He doesn't know we're working together, so why should he?" said Two Bears, placing slides and chips carefully in order on a clean cloth. "But just in case, be ready to geek any others who arrive until I decide they're friendlies."

"You're the boss."

"Yeah, right." Two Bears squinted at the big troll so absorbed in his work. "You know, I damn near had a coronary when you appeared in the alley behind the Casa carrying a pile of guns."

"You did look pale," said Thumbs, busy stripping a pistol. "Aw, crud, bad spring. Gotta toss it." He did so, adding to the small pile in the macroplas box in the corner of the tent. "But I figured you'd pay to find out about the corp limo. And if I can get nuyen for toasting some downtown yammerheads, that's granite. Merry Xmas."

"Data is gold. Say, why'd you take these?" Two Bears asked, nudging a stack of loaded clips. "Nice, but we don't have any iron to fit them."

"Hey, less toys in the hands of the unfit. Besides, I know some folks we can sell them to for a few extra nuyen." Thumbs gave a wink.

"Flash move, *omae*." Two Bears was impressed. "You ever miss a chance to make a profit?"

"Gimme a doubloon and I'll tell ya."

Chuckling at the touristy reference to nuyen, Two Bears wiped the silicon off his hands with a napkin and bit into a steaming golden burrito lying on a sheet of waxed paper. "This is good," he said, munching happily. "Father John's?"

Thumbs dry-fired a pistol next to his ear, listening to the works. "A little tight. Gotta reset the ejector. Where's the tools?"

"Here. Father John's?"

"Course. Is there any other burrito stand in town fit for a chummer to eat at?"

"Not unless you got a taste for devil rat." Two Bears wolfed down the rest, then cleaned the grease off his hands, and then started checking the next weapon, a lovely Crusader with silencer. "This one's for me."

"Done and done. Check the trigger action. It felt sloppy when I pried it out of the guy's grip."

"Yeah, it is loose. Good call. Hex wrench?"

"Here. Damn, we're out of bushing. Pass the silicon spray."

The can was relayed again. "Once the fragging decker gets here we'll do a search on the limo that showed up after you blew up the telecom. Maybe it's from IronHell."

"Gonna be tough."

" 'Cause of the way IronHell zapped Sister Wizard so fast?" Two Bears shook his head. "That's got to be some serious IC protecting whatever file she got to."

"Nyah, it's going to be tough because I didn't get a registration."

Two Bears grunted, both hands busy gently adjusting the tension on the bolt spring. "Drek. Any special markings?"

"What?" asked Thumbs, assembling the mechanical works of a pistol without looking at it. "You mean something like a nice big neon sign saying, 'This is a covert operations limousine. Please do not notice the men with guns.'? Sorry, but no."

Two Bears plunged a wirebrush down the barrel of the Crusader, and carbon deposits sprinkled down like black snow. "Too bad," he sighed. "Woulda been nice."

"Lock. Morons are easy to outwit." Thumbs reached for another gun, but the pile was gone, so he took one of the unbent knifes from the fight and started stropping the military blade on a whetstone from his vest. "By the way, chief," he said. "What's with this tent inside a building? The roof leak that bad?"

"Low-level stealth tech. The fabric masks our heat signature to hide our numbers," answered Two Bears, stuffing clips for the Crusader into his pockets. He slung the chattergun over one shoulder, and it hung to his knees. "Norms," he muttered. He removed the weapon and adjusted the strap length. "Plus it effectively muffles conversation against masers bounced off the windows."

"Yeah, I noticed they're painted. Does that help?"

"Some, but not much," he admitted. "This was an old meeting spot for the local gangs, neutral territory available for anybody's use." A rueful grin. "But that didn't mean the chummers wouldn't snoop on one another every now and then."

Testing the edge of the knife on one of his spare thumbs, Thumbs looked around again. "Tox, I've slept in worse dosses. And this is toff compared to my little visit to the Citadel."

"Yar, but no protective wards," said Two Bears, the Crusader now hanging at his waist. "Without magical defense, we're sitting naked in a glass house."

"A chill thrill, most anti-arctic."

Sweeping the tools into a plastic box, Two Bears latched the lid shut and laid the box on the floor. "Agreed. We need a decker, fast, and after that, the best damn mage we can find."

"But none of your usual support," mused Thumbs, working the metal with a steady rhythm. "You sure 'bout that?"

"Definite." Two Bears picked up a container of soykaf, snapped open the cap, and took a sip. "Gak, this is awful! Tastes like the solvent."

Sheathing the blade in his boot, Thumbs kept a straight face. "That is the solvent. What you been soaking the guns in?"

Just then, the elevator at the end of the room gave a musical ding and the doors parted. Both men sat upright with loaded weapons in hands as they watched through the opening. A woman emerged and hesitated a moment before approaching the tent. She wore a jumpsuit with matching vest, and carried a tan shoulder bag large enough to hide a medium-sized space shuttle. Her hair was jet black, and her skin was nicely tanned.

"She looks like a tourist," said Two Bears incredulously, screwing the silencer tighter on the Crusader.

"Yeah, but that bag's big enough to carry a deck or even a machine gun." Thumbs eased the safety off the Predator and put it out of sight below the table.

"Small gun in the waist holster."

"Right side. Check. And no highlights in the hair."

"A dye job. She might be the mage. Or have a bomb."

"You think?"

"Dunno. But if the hammer drops, go for a head-shot so she can't cast a spell. Just in case."

"Will that work?" asked Thumbs. He knew little or nothing about magic.

"Dunno. But at least it's a plan."

The woman stopped outside the tent and paused once more, maybe wondering if she was in the right place. Inside, Two Bears and Thumbs calmly waited to see what she would do next.

A tent inside a doss? thought Laura Redbird. Then she berated herself. *Silver, the name is Silver now, chica! And don't forget it.* Or else she'd say it out loud and blow her cover.

Nervously, she shifted the strap of her shoulder bag to a more comfortable position. Calling in some favors and borrowing a few hundred nuyen from an elf shyster whom she occasionally cleared of municipal tax problems, Laura . . . Silver had been able to parlay her old obsolete deck into a hot Fuchi 8. Not a Fairlight by any means, or even a Fuchi 9, but then, she wasn't one of Babbet's Bastards, the rogue gang of wildhoop deckers who cut more IC everyday than a professional figure skater. An eight would do fine.

"Hoi, Two Bears?" she called out.

There was an awkward minute of silence.

"Come in," said a soft voice.

"Slowly," added a deeper gruffer one.

She entered without stooping. The inside of the large tent was spacious and well lit, with clusters of Everbrights hanging from the central pole. A poker table was off to one side, with an elderly dwarf and a fragging huge troll covered with tattoos sitting side by side. She didn't know either one—strangers, thank the gods. There were some food wrappers on the table, the air pungent with the distinct smell of gun lubricants, metacrab burritos, and cheap soykaf. A pile of busted weapons filled a macroplas box in a corner. Housecleaning?

"Good afternoon," she said, staying where they could both see her. The opening ceremonies of a first meet were always critical. She was dressed in tourist casual, her Amerind hair dyed solid black, trying to appear Latino. It was a classic mirror ploy. If a person naturally had, say, black hair, and she dyed it black, then any trained observer would spot the lack of natural highlights and deduce that black was not your natural color, but a dye job, which perfectly hid the fact that black was the original color. A double reverse, or in street parlance, a mirror. The trick often worked against the truly paranoid, or fools. Which gave it a wide range of success in Miami. However, Silver was nervous with the disguise, and a good, dependable handgun would have gone far to making her feel better, but it had boosted all of her creds to obtain the used deck in her bag. Besides, she had the Colt .38, though the cold weight of the crude mechanical wheelgun wasn't very comforting on her hip.

"Sit," commanded the dwarf, laying his hands openly on the table. The big troll did not, however, and she tagged him as a street samurai. Chromed? Possibly. And those marks on his arms looked just like BlackJack's. The street sam was, of course, a razorboy. Dangerous.

"Roger sent you?" the troll probed without any preamble.

Silver paused in the act of taking a seat. "No. Fat Jake called me. Sorry. Do I have the wrong address?"

The dwarf smiled and waved her back down. "That's the correct name. Just checking."

"Null perspiration. Kings," she said, and waited.

The dwarf blinked in surprise.

What the frag was this? Silver thought. They didn't seem to know the answering password to confirm their identity. Adrenaline flooded her stomach like ice water and her hand edged closer to the Colt. Was this a trap? Had the killer Johnson found her instead of the other way around? Gods, no . . . no, wait, consider the principals. A policlubber and some metas. Drekfire, Jake was playing a game with them! A frigging game, the bastard. Arranging a meet and not telling the Johnson what the countersign was. Fuming at the idiocy, Silver kept her face neutral as she waited for the dwarf to answer correctly, or start blasting.

The dwarf took a breath and let it out slowly. "Morlock," he stated calmly.

Yes! Smiling in relief, she nodded and sat. "I'm Silver. Heard you're looking for a decker."

"Two Bears," he grumbled.

"And I'm Thumbs," said the troll, jerking one toward his chest.

"Hoi. Love your tat," Silver said, brushing a loose strand of black hair away from the chromed jack in her temple.

"Me gang tat," Thumbs responded, running a hand over his bald pate. "Da Slammers."

"Ah, the legendary Slammers. Toughest trolls in town."

"Dat's right." He puffed up with pride. "Youse knows us, eh?"

Silver smiled nicely. "Never heard of you."

The two locked gazes for a tick. Thumbs laid his Predator openly on the littered table and turned to the dwarf. "She'll do fine, Chief."

Ah, a minor shifting of diction there. This guy played possum and attacked from behind. Good. Silver liked that. Especially in somebody she might be running with. The smart stayed alive longer.

"Sussed," said Two Bears.

"So," she said, making herself comfortable. "What's the run?"

"Data hunt and retrieval. Forty kay."

Blast. The going rate for a standard run. Probably nothing special or the kind of run that would lead her to her prey. Still, nuyen was nuyen.

"Accepted," she said flatly. "What's first on the list to do?"

Two Bears picked through several credsticks on the table, as though only one were any good. "You gotta access my account at the CitiBank Central and drain it."

"Your own account?"

"Yes."

She pursed her lips. "You got the access codes?"

"Of course."

"Cake," Silver replied, pulling the Fuchi deck from her bulky shoulder bag. Thumbs got up and moved some food wrappers, grenades, and guns to expose a jackport in the wall near the table. She sat down on the floor, took out her deck and set it on her lap, then jacked in. She typed in a few commands, and after a tick the indicator lights showed green. Lines were hot and tight, no interference, no static. Arctic.

"Codes, please," she said, slim fingers poised over the keyboard.

Clearing his throat, Two Bears leaned close and whispered the two sequences. Closing her eyes, Silver tapped wildly on the Fuchi. "Stick," she said a moment later. Two Bears slid across his credstick. She took it and slotted it into her deck. Soon a light changed color, and then she pulled it out again. "Done. What's next?"

He stared at the stick and then her. "That fast?"

Silver gave him a cool smile of professionalism. "You

gave me the primary codes," she said. "I simply rerouted, did a backdoor, accessed under an assumed, did a dump and seize. Aced the line and left. Easy. You've got double your account."

"That's not what I asked for," Two Bears barked angrily. "Fragging hell! I don't need the freaking city bank hot on my hoop along with everything else!"

"They can't trace the funds. I did the entry from a public telecom in the Citadel." She gave a brief grin. "I visited a relative there once and memorized the LTG code. Then I used the main access code for your account, but not the personal one. When you've got the prime and the password, the rest is easy. But rather than withdraw the funds, which is always traced, I simply stole the nuyen outright. Cleaned you out for exactly that amount."

"Brilliant," chortled Thumbs, impressed. "Since the nuyen was stolen, the bank will reimburse him for the loss. May not even tell him there was a security breach, to maintain the illusion they're secure. So you got the same amount as before in your account." Blue eyes flashing amusement, he smiled at her. "Nice scam."

"Thanx."

Two Bears pocketed the stick, saying nothing.

"So," prompted Silver, pleased that the troll at least appreciated the art of her maneuvering. "Are we expecting anybody else, or is this the team?"

"Three? Hardly. I'm also waiting for a gunsel and a mage," said Two Bears, checking the wall clock. "It's 17:15 est. We got some twenty hours until my grace period runs out. By then we gotta be deep gone from here and with no traces. Savvy?"

"Savvy."

Reclining in his wooden chair, Two Bears reached for his soykaf, then pushed the container aside. "Here's the down. I was hired this morning by some Johnson to discover who or what the frag something called IronHell is. I went to the public datanets first and got squat. Then I hired a chummer of mine, Sister Wizard, to browse the Matrix, see what she might find in the less public databanks."

"Know her," said Silver. "She's very very slick."

"Was," corrected Two Bears sternly. "Now she's very, very geeked. Don't know where she went for the scan on IronHell, but she got brainfried faster than jackspit."

"You think it was IronHell geeked her?" repeated Thumbs.

Eloquently, Two Bears raised his palms to the ceiling.

"IronHell," murmured Silver, chewing her lip. "IronHell, IronHell. Where have I heard that name before?"

They both turned toward her.

"You know something?" asked Thumbs curiously. The canvas walls of the tent wavered in the gentle filtered currents of the building's enviro-system.

"Yeah," she whispered thoughtfully. "I do believe I do."

8

"So, spill it?" demanded Two Bears of the decker. "What do you know about IronHell?"

Silver pulled the datacord from her deck, her forehead wrinkling in thought. "Something . . ." she demurred. "I have a . . . ahem, a cousin, who works on the docks as a night guard. He lets me, uh, visit, the warehouses every month or so. Souvenir-hunting. You know."

Understanding nods from both males.

"Do the same thing myself in the trucking trade. Those remote-controlled semis often have stuff fall out the back," said Thumbs, grinning widely.

A roguish smile. "Cousins are always useful."

"Got a few myself at airport Customs," put in Two Bears. "But this one on the dock told you what?"

Silver ran her fingertips over the deck, struggling to remember exactly. "He only mentioned it once, and pretended he hadn't afterward, which is what made me remember it. I think IronHell is sailor slang for something to do with . . . pirates? Yes, pirates."

"Pirates?" echoed Two Bears, clenching the edge of the table. "That's what Louie said!" The last was spoken half to himself.

"Louie who?" asked Thumbs.

Two Bears shook his head, angry at himself for not listening to the champ. "Old chummer soft in the noggin who works for me. But I guess he still might have a few synapses connected. Who'da thought?"

"Don't wanna tango with no pirates," stated Thumbs flatly, crossing his herculean arms across his bare chest. "Those motherfraggers don't care what they do or who they scrag to get what they want. When they're done with you, the only person could love you is an organlegger. Atlantic

Security, the local corps—there ain't nobody been able to get to them. You can stuff that into your stick."

"And the megacorps don't care," sneered Two Bears, " 'cause the pirates are too fragging smart to try looting those ships!"

"You got that right, *omae*. Some megacorp versus the pirates of the Caribbean." Thumbs exposed both tusks. "Now, there's a fight I would truly love to see."

"From a great distance. Like deep space."

"Def," said Thumbs with a slight laugh. "But I wouldn't know which side to root for."

"Okay, so it's something to do with pirates," said Two Bears. "Jesus, Buddah, and Zeus, what does that tell us? A pirate *what,* and *where*?" He turned to Silver. "A ship, chief buccaneer, their supply depot, main base, arch-enemy?"

"Sorry," she said. "Honestly, don't recall. But it's something to do with pirates."

"Can we ask this Louie guy?" inquired Thumbs. He smacked a huge fist into an equally huge palm. "Maybe we encourage his memory a bit?"

"*Ichi,* he's a chummer," said Two Bears angrily. Then relented, "Besides, he's so near the edge, he forgets where he lives sometimes. A simple kick in the hoop might scramble his internal software forever. And if they traced my call to Sister Wizard, they might know who I am and be watching my place."

"Telecom?" squeaked Silver, staring at them. "And all this happened this morning?"

"Yes," said Two Bears slowly. Thumbs just stared at her.

"You did catch somebody's attention," she said. "I was in the matrix myself then and saw some deckers from someplace rush to a public telecom node."

"Frag!"

Two Bears rubbed a hand over his face and asked, "Who was it? Lone Star?"

"No, I never saw anything like them before," said Silver.

"True. Anybody who could fry Sister like that had to be some corp bastards. Probably Atlantic Security—they write their own programs and their deckers are real burners. Top flash."

"Yeah," drawled Silver. "Nova hot and their codes even hotter."

"Atlantic also imports major bangbangs from the Confederated American States," added Thumbs, eyeing the pile of guns they'd just finished cleaning.

"So, what do you scan? Think it was AtSec, or even Gunderson itself that hit Sister?" asked Two Bears.

"Null program," said Silver. "Gunderson does own Atlantic Security, but I don't think the good Sister was enough of a zerobrain to try a Matrix run on the mainframes of TGC without major protection. That's not something you do off the fragging cuff or on a freaking whim. I'd want three, four deckers to back me up, and one drekload of whitehot programs to even try."

"Yeah, guess you're right about that." Thumbs opened a cold container of some takeout soykaf they'd brought with them and gulped it down. "Maybe it's one of the megacorps trying to put Gunderson in their place cause they're getting big ideas?"

"All multinationals wanna be megacorps. What's new about that?"

Thumbs crumpled the container and tossed it across the tent into a macroplas box serving as a dumpster. "So maybe Gunderson found a way to do it."

"Battle the big boys?" Two Bears snorted sardonically. "Earth to Thumbs, try again, please."

"If this IronHell thing does have to do with pirates," insisted Thumbs, rubbing his chin with the sound of sandpaper, "then who would know more than Atlantic Security? That's what they do, hunt pirates." Atlantic Security had contracts with many of Miami's private corps and local sectors, but their ships also patrolled the seas around the sprawl.

"Or is the big secret that they really are the pirates?" asked Silver quietly.

"And are working both sides of the fence?" finished Thumbs for her. "IronHell being their codename for the covert op? Slot me like a surfer, lady, but I do not like the way you think."

Two Bears sucked air in through his teeth. "God's blood, but if that's what's really going on. . . ." His thoughts were interrupted by the elevator sounding a ding and the doors sliding open wide. Nobody was visible inside the cage.

"Get hard," snapped Two Bears, pulling the chattergun in front of him and working the selector from single to full auto.

Thumbs closed his ballistic vest, then lifted the Predator into view, snicking off the safety.

Colt in hand, Silver studied the elevator. Tilted off-angle, the corner security mirror showed only the tiled ceiling. Then a tall norm stepped into view from the area behind the door normally shown on the mirror. Dark hair, dark eyes, sideburns, and moustache. He was wearing a tropical synth-cotton suit, loose and easy-fitting. A large dull black gun was tucked into a crossdraw holster on his left hip. The metal was totally non-reflective, the window light seeming to fall into the ebony finish and vanish. Something ceramic hung around his neck on a thin woven band but was hidden under his soft linen shirt.

Slowly and steadily, the norm approached the tent as if he was dead sure that everybody knew who the frag he was and stayed awake at night worrying about it. Without so much as a pause, he entered the tent and stood unblinking in the strong light of the EverBrights. He ignored the collection of death-dealers lying openly on the table, but instead looked at each of the three people sitting there, moving his neck stiffly with a slight mechanical jerk like some robotic drone locating their positions to the exact millimeter.

"Good afternoon, I am looking for Adam Two Bears," he said. "Are either of you gentlemen he?"

Two Bears grunted yes.

"Fat Jake said you were looking for a professional mechanic," said the norm softly, his voice strangely accented and with the scholarly tones of some professor or high-level corporate suit.

"Depends," returned Two Bears gruffly, the deadly barrel of the Crusader pointing straight at the man's gut. "Morlocks."

"Kings."

Forcing himself to relax, Two Bears lowered his weapon, and the others did likewise in stages. "Okay, you're kosher," he acknowledged and kicked out a chair. "Take a load off. Let's talk."

"Call me Delphia," the norm said, taking the chair and turning it around to straddle the seat backward. "What's the scan?"

"Datasteal."

"The pay?"

Two Bears pulled out his credstick. "Forty thousand. If you're any good with a gat."

"I am," responded Delphia. "Very good."

"Oh, yeah?" said Thumbs, laying the Predator on the table.

Delphia shrugged.

"Captain Cool, eh? You that good?" asked Two Bears gruffly. "Or am I yakking with a used chip-dealer here?"

"Perhaps a small demonstration," said Delphia, sounding bored. Standing smoothly, he reached a hand toward Two Bears as if offering to shake. His arm was fully extended, the sleeve pulled back to show the bare skin of his wrist, when he bent a finger. Instantly, Two Bears saw nothing with his right eye as a click sounded. Shaking his vision clear, the dwarf pulled back, realizing he was looking down the ebony barrel of a Cold Manhunter and that the click had been the hammerless auto triggering an empty chamber.

"Holy drek," whispered Two Bears. "N-nobody's that fast! T'ain't possible even for chipped reflexes!"

"Bah, it's a trick," said Thumbs hotly. "A holograph, or something. Nice try, gleeb. But I got chummers who love yakking about iron more than bopping with the bettys. And if something like that was out there, they'd have been short-stroking themselves into a frenzy. A gat that draws itself? Bulldrek."

Removing an ammo clip from his pocket, Delphia loaded the Manhunter. "If you say so," he said, working the slide and putting the loaded pistol into the holster on his hip. As his hand came away, everybody saw that there was a slim ferruled cable of burnished metal connecting the butt of the black weapon to a powerpack on his right hip.

"This guy is for real, chummers," said Silver weakly. "I know, because I've seen one like that before."

"Have you?" asked Delphia turning about to look at her as if noticing Silver for the first time.

"*Hai,*" she grunted.

There was a pause. "Indeed," he said softly.

"It's a VPR2, right? I've heard about it—all shadowtalk, so I thought it was only smoke for the gunbunnies and boom-freaks. Wet dreams for wannabes. Some story about banned research. Secret weapons for megacorp exec bodyguards and gov assassins."

"I am no assassin," Delphia replied in a low tone, his face a mask.

"And I believe you," Silver said. "But something like that doesn't just drop out of the sky or magically appear from the Land of Oz."

The dark-haired man's demeanor did not flinch or crack, but Silver saw his eyes react and knew she'd hit home with that shot. So the rumors on the grid had been correct, Oswaldo Fontecchio hadn't been executed for his failure to protect an Imperial Minister of Japan. And now he was a street samurai in Miami? Muscle for hire? Excellent.

"Ya mean that thing is for real?" asked Thumbs, pointing.

Silver nodded emphatically. "Oh, yes."

"Where can I get one?" demanded Thumbs urgently. "How much and where? Name the price."

"They're only ten nuyen, eight if you buy them in a bunch. Got mine in a pawn shop on West Fourteenth," said Delphia woodenly. "But it burned down ten minutes ago. Sorry."

Thumbs sat back in his chair with an annoyed expression, then he broke into a smile. "I asked for that, didn't I?"

"Yes, you did," said Delphia.

"Truce?"

"I am the essence of peace, sir."

"Truce?" pushed Thumbs.

A minute passed. "Truce," agreed Delphia.

"Two Bears, you wanted an edge on this run, and here he is," Silver said eagerly. "This guy's for real. Worth twenty streetcorner bangers."

"Well, real or not, I don't like show-offs," snapped Two Bears. "They got a nasty tendency to get fancy, and thus sloppy, in a brawl. And this hump is already tough enough."

"Then do not retain my services," said Delphia without emotion, removing some lint from his cuff. "However, I can assure you that once engaged, I am the epitome of diligence."

"No more games then?"

"Sir, I am always serious."

"Well . . ." hesitated Two Bears. "Okay, done and done. You're hired."

"With the understanding," added Silver quickly, "that you're part of this team, one of us, with all that implies and infers."

Silence from the dapper norm in the chair.

"Agreed?"

Without comment, Delphia stood as if to leave. Then formally retook his chair, sitting in it properly this time. "I am yours to the death," he said quietly.

"That's fine," said Two Bears, passing over his credstick for a transfer. "Cause the very first thing we're going to do is kill me."

9

The afternoon sun was low in the sky, but still blazing like a fireball from hell, and everybody on the open streets was moving as little as possible. Night couldn't come soon enough. Sporadically, an enclosed vehicle would hum by, radiating even more waste heat and fumes from the internal cooling system, making the passengers nice and comfy but adding the waste heat to the streets, turning the usual summer simmer into a momentary broil.

Wesley was sweaty in his macroplas crate when he saw them go by, walking fast and sure as if they owned the world. Every so often, one would stop and let the others go by, and then do it again. Just like on the trideo. Rotation surveillance, or some kinda fancy drek like that. It was a military thing. Rigidly casual, the six took positions across the street from the Biscayne Bar. One of the bigger guys, an ork, was standing in direct sunlight and not sweating a drop. As if he was poured from solid rock. Or had an internal cooling system. Was that possible? Wesley guessed so. Heck, anything was possible these days. Just ask Rich the slith. There was one chummer who'd never mouth off to a lady shaman again.

Could this be a raid? Nyah. Here? This dump? What were they gonna liberate, the cobwebs? Yet this weren't the neighborhood watch checking for solos cutting in on their gambling. No smell of the street on 'em either. Not a rival gang. Something big was going down right here and he had the best seat in the house. Pulling his sweat-stiff rags tighter around him, Wesley hunched lower in his box.

Someday, he would run the shadows and the whole world would know and fear him. He even had a name picked out: Attila. Some brass warlord from dusty times. But it had a sound, a feel. Attila. Yeah, solid. Abso-fragging-lutely solid as steel.

The gunshots from inside the doss did not come as much surprise when they started, and they didn't last very long. But then the screams began. Not the angry shouts of battle, or the sharp yelp of a wound, no, these were the long, drawn-out howls of someone getting their living guts ripped out. A few of the folks on the street glanced toward the old apartment building, but that was all. Such things happened in Overtown. As long as it wasn't happening to them, life went on.

The blood-curdling noise rose and fell in horrible waves, fast becoming the inarticulate squealing of mindless agony. Whimpering himself in sympathy, Wesley closed his eyes tight and stuffed fingers into his ears, fervently praying to anybody listening to please-please let the poor sodding chummer flatline. Nobody deserved to get scragged like that, no matter what they did.

The sun was finally starting to dip behind the skyrises of downtown Miami, the sparkling colored vista spread out below her windows like a miniature dynarama at World Park. Sheathed in only the sheerest gossamer silk, Erika Johnson stood before the Armorlite windows sipping a perfect iced gin and tonic, the limes fresh and cut with a silver blade. Ordinary steel ruined the flavor. How many bartenders had she fired over this obvious and important point? Too many. How ironic that she could find competent help on the street to do a run, but for inside her penthouse? *Ichi.*

Softly, the oak-paneled wall telecom hummed for her attention, and Erika sauntered over, loosening the ribbon at her throat a bit. If this was her current bedpartner, she wanted to look a little slottish for the man. He might bring a friend along tonight, and if she was going to be the toy of a couple of nastyboys, then she should seem properly gutter. Just a touch, of course. Nobody actually wanted to play in the street, only to pretend they were.

Then the second circuit beeped and Johnson went cold. The private line. She knotted her robe shut, then put the first call on hold while setting her drink on a shelf full of BTL simsense chips. Hitting the VR mode and scrambler, Erika took a chair and wondered if the dwarf had something to report already. This was good work. Unless it was trouble.

However, the pixels on the telecom screen did not show the Overtown halfer she'd hired, but an extremely handsome norm in a hand-tailored suit. Dull yellow that was almost white, with a raw silk tie, and what looked like a Gibraltor VPR2 holstered on his belt. Impossible. Nobody outside of Japan had those. And a *gaijin*? It was beyond impossible into the fantastic. He also appeared to be calling from within a tent. Who the frag was this?

"It's your nuyen," she drawled. A bad habit of hers to begin to talk in the manner of the VR simulation that her caller would see—a scruffy old norm, unshaven and with lots of scars. Let the machine do the work, damn it, she scolded herself. That's what it's for.

"Two Bears is dead," said the man bluntly. "Killed by an assassin from a local policlub. I'm his partner and in charge of the job now."

Now, that was interesting. If true. "Do partners have names?" Erika inquired politely, knowing her alter-ego said something along the lines of: "Slot me, chummer. Sowaz's yor mudder call ya?"

"Delphia." The man's space-black eyes showed no emotion, but he seemed to be intently studying the background of the image she was sending him. If he was looking for a way to ID her location, he'd need precog to do it. The VR doss shown was totally false, a composite from hundreds of the more interesting layouts offered by decades of *Architectural Digest* chip. No way a gutter samurai could know those. She sat up straight in her chair and stopped herself just in time from tugging on her earlobe thoughtfully. Her other self would have copied the action and Erika didn't want this Delphia person to know her telltales. Possibilities were opening here, most of them unpleasant. Did he somehow know this was a VR telecom?

On the screen, Delphia removed a bloody credstick from his inner jacket pocket. Erika nearly recoiled from the ghastly object. Taken off a dead man, obviously. Somebody cut to ribbons. Or was he scamming her?

Stolidly, the shadowrunner told her about Sister Wizard and the instantaneous arrival of both Lone Star and the corp limo.

Pursing her lips, Erika leaned back in her chair and thought about this update. It could only be Atlantic Security. That had to be where the decker had gone hunting. This whole run was starting to sound like a bad idea that should be punted. But that wasn't up to her. She worked for James

Harvin, and he was the one who'd given her the order to hire runners to find IronHell. But if AtSec was somehow involved in this, why would Harvin need to hire runners? Gunderson owned fragging Atlantic Security. Anything they knew Harvin would know. Did he have some other hidden agenda?

"I am, of course, sorry to hear of his demise," she stated blandly. "Has this change affected the status of the assignment?"

Delphia barked a laugh and jammed the stick into his telecom. Erika's beeped to show the transfer of nearly all the nuyen back to her. "It was supposed to be a dataswipe, not a hardprobe." She knew that was street slang for a war. "Deal's off. I quit. Here's your down. Haveaniceday." And he actually reached to cut the connection!

"NO!"

On the screen, Delphia stopped with his hand off keys, and she cursed herself. Never, ever, show the staff you needed them. Frag and drek! Could she get another team fast enough? No, time was against her. So be it.

"This is very unexpected," she forced herself to say smoothly. "Perhaps it is time to renegotiate." The telecom did its best to translate that into street lingo.

"The run's gone sour. Not to my taste any more," Delphia returned, but didn't try to kill the connection.

Ah, Erika smiled to herself in understanding. "Perhaps I should sweeten the deal so it's more to the taste of your delicate palate?"

"Your nuyen, chummer," Delphia said again as he lifted the bloody credstick into view. She got the hint. No two-bit drek. "Talk to me."

Going round to her desk, Johnson was forced to admit she liked the man's style. Subtle as a velvet sledgehammer. Briefly, she wondered what he would be like in bed. Forcing those irrelevant notions from her mind, she pulled a credstick from her cherrywood desk and slotted it into her console. "Double the original price and a survivors' fee of . . . an additional twenty kay apiece."

His face expressionless as a dead crab's, Delphia waited for two heartbeats before saying, "Triple."

Erika paused. Bluff or a deal-breaker? She waited a full clock minute before answering, "Agreed." Letting him know no more was coming. The ceiling had been hit.

But then he added, "Plus, we need some immaterial assistance."

A mage? "Shouldn't you supply such special support yourselves?"

Delphia reached away from the screen, then brought a cup of soykaf into view and took a sip. "The word's already out that Two Bears got cacked," said Delphia, after taking a sip. "And now . . ." He spread his hands in explanation.

Erika understood completely. The streets were exactly like a board-room meeting. If the word had already spread that the run had gone bad almost from the start, they were going to have frag's own time trying to hire anyone smart enough to do the team any good. The similarities of their worlds were often amazing. "Perhaps I can help you there."

"Got a singer on tap, sir?" There was only a momentary shifting of vocal tenor at the last word, and Erika wondered if this was his way of saying he knew it wasn't a norm male he was addressing.

With this rationalization, her heart beat faster, the decision made. "Yes," she told the screen, scratching herself on the jawline as an unshaven male would. What details she missed, the VR program of the com would cover. "Likes Cat. You savvy?"

"Not a virgin?" asked the screen.

A short laugh, and Erika's VR image stroked a non-existent moustache. She thought of how Delphia's would feel on her skin. "Oh, no, she's done many . . . errands . . . for me and my associates before." Associates, let him chew on that word.

"Mage got a name?" the picture of Delphia asked gruffly. "Or do we just call her cat?"

What a caustic man. Erika Johnson was liking him more and more. And the powerful width of his shoulders offered pleasures of a more personal nature. She mimed lighting a cigar for the benefit of the others watching. The light for her double-date winked off. Too bad, so sad. But this was biz.

The arrangements for obtaining the shaman had been so slick, that Silver exploded into pleased laughter as the telecom screen faded to black. She yanked the datajack from her temple.

"The Johnson agreed to pay triple!" Two Bears cried out,

also beaming with pleasure. "Triple! With a fragging bonus! We're riding the gravy train with biscuit wheels!"

"Yes, the pay is quite satisfactory at this point," said Delphia, stepping out of the canvas tent. He turned toward the dwarf, who was sitting in a corner by himself safely away from the telecom pickup. "You were correct, my friend. The Johnson probably responded more favorably to a suit than to, say, Thumbs' more highly functional urban clothing."

"Suits like suits," agreed Two Bears with a knowing smile. "The only thing that bothers me is how easily he agreed to pay more. I think there's something important he's not telling us, which could mean we run into major complications down the line. Plus, when the nuyen flows like that, it's got corp written all over it."

Delphia nodded agreement, stroking his moustache thoughtfully. "The Johnson will surely check the Matrix to confirm the death of Two Bears, but Silver assures us the upload to the city morgue files will be accepted as a legitimate coroner's report. That should remove any possible retribution from the policlubbers, making the job much easier and vastly increasing our remuneration."

"And don't forget the bonus!" crowed Thumbs.

Two Bears checked his watch. "Sundown in less than an hour. Rocking. Let's blow this dump, snatch the singer, and bust open IronHell."

"How?" asked Thumbs succinctly.

"I got an idea," responded Two Bears. Removing the ammo clip from the Crusader, he checked the load and slammed the clip back in. "I know a gal who might be able to help us."

And what a lovely gal, she was, thought Two Bears, remembering her beautiful eyes. He'd only seen her once, but now they'd meet again. And so much sooner than he'd thought.

10

The screaming had stopped over an hour ago, and Wesley finally let his curiosity get the better of him and he started creeping up the stairs of the old apartment house. A zillion years ago it had been some rich toff's summer home. Nobody remembered who he was, or cared. The place had a solid roof, and that was enough.

The side door was too old to close properly, and Wesley eased inside with no sweat. It was on the steps that he halted, frozen in his tracks as he watched the tiny rivulet of red blood drip-drip-drip down the bare wood, coming straight for him from the top landing three full floors away.

The powerful motor of the big black Toyota Elite was working quietly and efficiently, venting its toxic exhaust fumes into the twilight air, just as a hundred thousand other vehicles were doing this evening in beautiful downtown Miami. It was what made the sunsets so amazingly colorful, and pigeons drop from the sky like broken water balloons.

Delphia was at the wheel, handling the vehicle like he was rigged into the controls. Riding in the front passenger seat, Two Bears shifted the Crusader in his lap and wondered where the gunsel had gotten the posh vehicle on such short notice. There were no rental tags. No tags at all, actually. And as with so many things about the mysterious gunsel, Delphia didn't want to say. Jacked it, likely. Or was it his? Who knew?

Two Bears considered the Sphinx garrulous compared to the fancy-dressing norm. He wasn't inclined to ask for details, as it wasn't his prerogative. And it didn't really matter. The power plant under the hood was solid, the windows tinted, the AC icy, and the tank full. A stocked bar would have been nice, but Two Bears hadn't expected miracles. As long as Lone Star SWAT teams didn't come skydiving down to get it back, he couldn't care less who the car's owner was X hours ago.

"Coral and Brickel," said Delphia, slowing the Elite to a stop at a corner.

"Redhead at two o'clock," said Thumbs from the back.

"I see her." Silver threw open the back door on the driver's side.

In climbed a slim norm, her hair a riot of blazing red with lots of highlights. She wore skin-tight denim cutoffs and tied-off T, exposing a lot of valuable assets and looking more like a bouncy beachbundle than a hotdrek shaman.

As she closed and locked the door behind her, Two Bears changed his opinion. The norm had an elaborate tiger-stripe tat running up one arm and across her back. Very costly work. She also wore bracelets, rings, and necklaces. Fetishes? he wondered. Cosmetics made her eyes slant like an Oriental, or a cat. Her nails were very long, sharply pointed and every color in the spectrum, with a few more besides. In strange contrast was the bandolier cross her chest.

Pulling away from the curb and merging with the uptown traffic, Delphia looked a question at Two Bears, who shrugged in response. What was there to say? All mages were crazy. It went with the job. Who knew how it twisted their minds trying to access and wield the magical energies as only they could?

Glancing about the interior of the Elite, the shaman gasped as she saw Two Bears. "You!"

He returned her attention. "Yeah? Me, what?"

"I heard you were dead!"

"The rumors of my demise have been greatly exaggerated," Two Bears quoted.

"Apparently," the shaman growled deep in her throat.

"How did you recognize him in that disguise?" asked Silver. "He's bald and that stomach padding adds years to him."

"I see all," purred the shaman, making a mysterious gesture in the air. "My name is Moonfeather and I sing for Cat."

Introductions were accomplished with a minimum of fuss.

"Upload me," Moonfeather said, kicking off her sandals and curling her dainty feet up underneath her.

"First things first," said Delphia, looking at her through the rearview mirror. "Scan the car, please."

"My pleasure." Moonfeather smiled warmly, the tip of her pink tongue running lightly over dark red lips.

"No armor?" snapped Silver, staring. The mage was obviously wearing nothing under her tee. "That's not smart."

"Got my spells," said Moonfeather, smiling like the cat who'd swallowed the canary. "And my Beretta." Closing her eyes for a few ticks, she hummed softly to herself, then opened them wide. "The car is clear."

Delphia glanced at her in the mirror again, but said nothing.

"Now, let's get down to biz," said Thumbs. "We need ya to change the dwarf into an ork."

"Are cameras or scanners involved?"

"Shouldn't be," grumbled Two Bears. "Not in Dorsey Park, where we're going. The whole turf shoulda been zapped to the ground years ago, but then the cockroaches wouldn't have anyplace to go for a honeymoon."

"Make him an African, or a Swede," said Delphia. He swerved around a slow-moving truck and found himself staring at the aft end of a Lone Star cruiser. The steel hotel in the back seat was empty and the two norms in the front were vigorously polishing their riot guns, obviously in the mood for a little Overtown head-bashing. Increasing the tint in the windows, Delphia slowed by tiny increments until the natural flow of traffic separated them from the street patrol.

"Just make him different," said Silver, both hands tight on the strap of her shoulder bag.

"We're going to pay a little call on an ork," said Thumbs, the SMG bouncing as the Elite hit a pothole. "If he's not feeling too talkative, the sight of another ork face might loosen him up some."

"Good enough." Closing her eyes, Moonfeather rested her hands on her knees, palms up, fingers forming circles. She began to hum softly as she placed one hand around a single bead of amber she wore on a knotted leather cord around her neck.

Inhaling sharply, she smiled in satisfaction and removed the necklace. Reaching forward over the divider, she placed it around the dwarf's neck, rubbing a soft breast against Delphia's shoulder in the process.

Two Bears fingered it curiously.

"Done," she said with a smirk, retaking her seat.

The dwarf looked in the rearview mirror, and saw no

change in his appearance. But when he turned about so the others could see him, they gasped and recoiled.

"It worked?" he asked.

"Of course it worked," said Moonfeather, resting a shapely arm on top of the front seat, a single finger touching the back of Delphia's muscular neck. "Tell him what you see."

Thumbs grimaced. "The most motherfragging ugly ork in the world is what I see!"

"That's hard data," ventured Silver. "You're black as coal with the hideous orange hair of a junkpunker on a week-long bebop bender." She bent closer. "Your face is a hodge-podge of acid scars, there's a mottled eye, some missing yellow teeth, a lot of very badly done prison tats, your left ear has been chewed to the gristle, and you've got acne." Silver looked down. "Both hands are discolored from some kind of skin disease, maybe cured, maybe not, every nail is broken, with dirt permanently embedded in the quick."

"You twisting my willie?" demanded Two Bears suspiciously.

"Good job," said Delphia, taking his eyes off the road to give the dwarf a quick glance. "He's almost ugly enough to be a Lone Star cop."

"An insect shaman's joyboy," corrected Thumbs with a tusky grin. "Devil rats would run from you, *omae*." Roaring with laughter, Thumbs whacked the shaman on the back, making her whole bracelets jingle. "Out-fragging-standing!"

"Sir, never travel to Kingston like that," commented Delphia dryly, shifting about in his seat. "The zombies would worship you as a god."

"Or a male centerfold," added Silver, pulling the deck from her bag.

"Ha!"

"Should last till you want me to stop it," said Moonfeather, not joining the jocularity. "Then I can do it again, but this will be tiring to keep up for long periods."

"Shouldn't need it for more than a couple of hours, max," drawled Two Bears in a gravelly tone.

"Talk lower," instructed Thumbs. "And curse more."

"Frag you, pud-licker."

Thumbs grinned. "Good. How 'bout Psycho Pete?"

"Huh? Oh, a name. Gimme something more macho," the dwarf said.

"Cannon?" tried Silver.

"Nitro?"

"Mackie?"

"Do I look fragging Scottish?" asked Two Bears demanded.

Thumbs said no. "But we can say a Mack truck hit you, and you won. Well, sort of."

Everybody burst out laughing.

"You are magnificently hideous," agreed Delphia, brushing at the back of his neck. "Nobody will be able to recognize you."

"Hell, they may not even talk to you in Dorsey!"

"Good. Mackie it is, then."

"So, we're going to Dorsey Park," said Moonfeather, glancing out the window. The Elite was passing under the elevated neon people-mover that circled downtown Miami. Chilled fountains and colored sand augmented the usual forest of healthy, crab-free palm trees. "I don't know that part of town much."

"Yar, Dorsey Park," said Two Bears, experimentally making faces at himself in the mirror. Still him. "Near the boneyard."

"Recon?"

Delphia set the Elite on auto, and the Manhunter slapped into his palm with blinding speed and he began attaching an acoustical silencer to the big-bore muzzle with trained ease. "Data extraction," he corrected, concentrating on his work for a tick as the vehicle maintained course and speed.

"Ah, my second fave pastime," Moonfeather purred, flexing her fingers, the rainbow nails glistening. "How nice."

"Oh, yeah. Here. This is for you," said Thumbs, reaching inside his fringed vest and retrieving a gat. He passed it to Silver.

"I already have a Colt," she said, hefting the sleek ergonomic pistol he'd handed her. "It's so light!"

"But no reliable backup piece. That"—he gestured—"is a Seco LD 120 loaded with armor-piercing rounds and tracers. It'll put holes in a wendigo and set the damn thing on fire. That two-bit Colt wheelgun of yours wouldn't stop a sick devil rat."

"Thanks." Silver ejected the clip, inspecting the caseless ammo neatly stacked inside. "Hope you don't mind."

Thumbs waved that aside. "Course not. The only folks you

should trust are your enemies, because you know what they want."

"Too true," she agreed.

"That's Bushido," said Delphia.

"Oh, yeah? Around here they call it the law of the street."

Silver dry-fired the Seco a few times, then rammed in the clip. "Good gun. Excellent balance. If you'd sell it to me, I'd like to buy it from you after the run." Removing the Colt from her belt holster, she stuffed it into her shoulder bag under the Fuchi and tucked the Seco into the empty holster. It was a bit snug, but did fit.

"Keep it," said Thumbs. "A gift from the Latin Kings."

Silver adjusted her jacket over the weapon. "Arctic. Any more goodies?"

"Care for a grenade?" he asked, offering her one.

"Def." Silver took dull metallic sphere and hefted it. "Always nice to have some boom in your pocket. What is it? Anti-personnel, concussion, flare, thermite?"

"Ah . . ." Thumbs seemed embarrassed. "Don't know, actually. Didn't have a tag when I stole it."

Silver looked at the grenade as if it was going to explode in her hand. "Are you jerking my strings?"

"No tag?" repeated Delphia from the front. "Well, what color is it? Most armaments are color-coded."

"Green," said Two Bears, looking over his shoulder at it, "with stripes."

Delphia adjusted the mirror to see for himself. "Green stripes? There are no striped grenades."

Moonfeather snickered.

"An unlabled willy peter. This fragging thing could do anything!" Silver gingerly added it to the weapons in her shoulder bag. "I'll save it for a special occasion. Such as when I'm already geeked and want to take the other sonof-aslitch with me."

"Hey, better than nothing," rumbled Thumbs.

"Agreed. But not by much."

"Dorsey Park," said Delphia, slowing through the traffic and pulling the Elite up to the curb. The vehicle nearly dislodged a dozing ork slotmachine girl with frizzled green hair from her precarious perch on a busted parking meter. The lounging locals stared at the slickmobile invading their turf, but didn't approach it. Just the opposite. Many of them started to saunter away, casual but quick.

Two Bears didn't blame them. A tinted limo meant one of two things, corps or shadowrunners, neither of which were desirable to be near when the drek hit the operating turbine.

Thumbs pulled his vest shut tight and stared bullets at a leatherboy lustfully checking out their wheels. The punkster smiled shakily and ambled away, hands stuffed deep into his pockets, whistling innocently.

"Perimeter clear," Thumbs announced. "What was the ork's name again?"

Two Bears answered. "Gordon, Scott Gordon. Research librarian for the city gov. Now retired." He'd called the lovely little dwarf clerk from the library. She hadn't been able to help him at first, but this time she'd located just the scan.

"And this slag wrote some book on pirate action in the Atlantic?"

Two Bears nodded.

"Stone. Just the chummer we need to flap gums with."

"Exactamundo."

"Not much farther now," Thumbs said. "One block up, over one block. Twenty-one seventy-four northwest Eighteenth Street, fifth floor."

"Didn't think anything around here was that high."

"Loft doss."

"Ah." This far away, there was no way this Gordon guy could have seen their car arrive. If he actually knew anything about IronHell, however, he might be just a little bit jumpy about strangers with guns.

"My search earlier showed that this dump is too old to have security cameras, or sensors, or anything," said Silver. "I'm surprised it's got running water."

"Neighboring buildings?" asked Delphia, sliding on dark glasses.

For night? Two Bears considered that odd, until he got a peek from the side and saw that they were IE boosted. Image enhancers. To the gunsel there would be no shadows. Where did he get stuff like that? How did he get stuff like that? Who was this norm?

"No regular security patrols and no known wired buildings," said Silver, reporting on her earlier recon of the neighborhood via the Matrix.

"Escape routes?" asked Thumbs.

Dusk was falling, and with the coming darkness the civilians were hurrying for home and the predators were coming out. Go-gangs on their hyped-wheels, razorboys in their leather and chromes, the full assortment of Miami gutterkin. But this was a residential hood. No flash bars, topless jis arenas, simsense parlors, or anything of real interest. The muscle would head for better hunting grounds. Soon the area would be clear.

Silver half-shut her eyes, trying to remember the layout from the city plans. "Front door, back door. Windows too small, coal chute welded shut. Fire escape solid rust. Take a week to make it work."

"Roof is out then. Any pools nearby for us to jump into?"

"No," she frowned. "And you're being paranoid. This is a fifty-five-year-old ork. We'll be lucky if he's not senile."

"Yeah, but if he's feeble he might have purchased insurance from the local gangbangers," Thumbs said. "He yells help and we could find ourselves hoop deep in flying lead."

"I agree with Thumbs. It is the wise man who prepares for disaster," said Delphia, adjusting his tie in the rearview mirror.

"Going cruising for quim later?" asked Moonfeather softly.

"Civilians are always shocked when a well-dressed person slaps a gun across their face," he answered, combing his hair into place. "It mentally throws off their center of balance. A basic interrogation technique. If the ork is not friendly, or buyable, then rougher means will be necessary."

"You bother me, chummer," admitted Two Bears. "You really on our side?"

Behind his shades, Delphia smiled. "Of course."

Yeah, sure. "Ready?" asked Two Bears, hand on the doorlatch.

"Hold!" snapped Moonfeather staring out the window into the passing crowd. An elderly elf in tattered leathers and embroidered duster stopped to stare at their vehicle. Behind the one-way windows, Moonfeather seemed to go into a trance, then gestured at the oldster. Oddly, he repeated the gesture exactly, then shuffled on.

"A guard?" demanded Silver, working the bolt on the Seco.

"No. Just a Dog shaman," she said, rubbing a bracelet. "We don't get along very well, and he caught my . . . call it my scent. But I told him this was nothing to do with him or his and we parted in peace."

"Arctic. Let's hoof."

The four doors opened, disgorging the team, all except Silver, who slid back into the driver's seat and took the keys from Two Bears. "Keep cruising around the block and be ready to rock if we shout 911," he told her.

She nodded. "Scan."

"Stay toothy, people." Two Bears tucked his canvas bundle tight under an arm. "We're here for info, not combat."

"Captain Friendly, that's me," grinned Thumbs, stretching mightily.

"Confirmed," said Delphia, looking over the street in that weird mechanical way of his.

Bored, Moonfeather yawned. "Yeah, yeah, sure, right. Then why you got so many zappers, short stuff?"

"We got one dead already," said Two Bears. "I'm not planning on acquiring any more. Let's go."

The group spread out to cross the street, headed for the apartment doss near the graveyard. Two Bears privately hoped it wasn't a prophetic location.

11

Dusk enveloped the streets in ever-darkening purple, and the summer mosquitoes arrived in buzzing droves. Staying loose, and swatting constantly, except for Moonfeather, the group traversed the short distance to the building, a gray stone monolith with the aesthetic appeal of hair clog. The steps were covered with gang graffiti and spit. They tried to avoid both. As they entered the front door, the runners found the foyer lit by a single EverBright in a wire cage, the post-boxes merely holes in the cracked plaster walls.

There were no names on the crevices; each tenant obviously knew which hole was his or hers. The inner door was sprung, barely hanging from one hinge. The lobby was floored with faded Spanish tiles from long before the Awakening. There was a battered baby carriage against one wall, a bullet-marked elevator before them, dark stairs on either side. A cracked dish of metacrab poison lay untouched near the sweat-stained newel. The elevator was busted, of course, so they proceeded up the stairs. The building smelled of cabbage, urine, and garlic.

"Reminds me of Brooklyn," said Moonfeather in disgust. "Before the big quake."

"That where you're from?" asked Thumbs, watching slits of light click off under every doorjamb as they passed by.

"No," was all she offered.

A second flight of stairs led to many more, and finally the ramshackle door to the attic apartment. The hallway was cramped, barely a meter wide, no more than an afterthought of the builder. Taking positions on either side of the portal, Two Bears tried knocking on the door. The only answer was echoes. He nudged Moonfeather.

"Mr. Gordon?" she called out sweetly, affecting a Southern belle accent thick as honeysuckle. "Scott Gordon?

I'm from the city benevolent association? I have a cred voucher for you!"

Nothing.

After a tick, Two Bears motioned Delphia forward to disable the maglock with a gadget from his pocket. In a doss like this he was sure it wouldn't set off any alarms. The lock gave with a soft click, then Two Bears banged the old door open wide with a gentle kick.

Immediately, guns came out in everybody's hands. Predator at the ready in his right hand, Thumbs made a fist with the left, and four blades extended from his left arm to the full nineteen centimeters. They could see that the doss was huge, occupying what should have been another floor above it. Place was large enough to land a helo here without hindrance. They followed a dim hallway through a string of closed doors, which led to a stained glass window of a lighthouse sweeping the sea at night. Illuminated by the street lamps, it was beautiful. Above the hallway, a balcony edged a second tier with curtained windows on either side of a second corridor. Pure rotting posh. In its heyday, this must have been some deluxe doss for toffs like visiting royalty and other drekheads. Nowadays, it was a flop.

And it was completely trashed, cushions slit open, telecom smashed apart, carpeting hacked to pieces to expose the old four-n-groove floorboards from another era. Bits of trash and busted glass were everywhere like party confetti, the walls were lined with empty shelves, the ripped remains of books stacked in chest-high piles. Actual paper and leather books. Actual bound volumes you could hold and read.

Several of the bookcases had been ripped from the wall, the paneling itself removed to show the studs and cats on the interior support system. Only one wall had escaped such an ignoble fate. Gordon was nailed to the smoke-stained paneling, arms outstretched and legs together. Crucified. Wrists and throat were sliced to the bone, his blood pooling underneath the corpse and trailing away in a slim stream dribbling out under the kitchen door. White things in the dark pool seemed to be his missing fingers, and other bodily parts.

Silently, the four approached the dead man, skirting the piles of his possessions and furniture. Nobody made any attempt to see if he could be resuscitated. Only a DocWagon fanatic would have thought of that.

"Motherfragger," whispered Thumbs, making the sign of

the cross in deference. "I've aced my share, but never like this! Are the Morlocks back?"

"No way," stated Two Bears, studying the ork. "And this wasn't done for robbery or revenge. Everything here is junk."

"Then he had something he shouldn't have," reasoned Moonfeather, her own Beretta out. "Maybe a chip he found."

"But they didn't get it," said Delphia, silenced Manhunter in his right hand.

Moonfeather looked at him. "And how the drek do you know that?"

Two Bears motioned at the piles of destruction. "His blood is sprayed on top. They trashed the place, then cut him to bits. No reason for that unless they didn't find it."

"Find what?" she demanded nervously.

Two Bears undid his canvas bundle, then loudly worked the bolt on his Crusader. "Let's see if we can find out."

In response, the door slammed shut behind them with a strident retort, and a fusillade of rounds suddenly blasted the curtains. Pottery exploded on both sides of Thumbs, and he grunted loudly as the bullets hit his vest but did not penetrate.

"Trap!" barked Two Bears, returning fire with his chattergun, the hail of fire raking the living room and hallway.

"Jules Verne!" shouted Delphia, heading for the center of the room. He threw himself down on the floor, furious to see the others separate and go for cover behind tables and columns. Blasted civilians . . . no, it was his fault. They didn't know his coded battle phrases. If, and when, they got out alive, he'd teach them a few critical commands. But for now, it was yell the instructions out loud for the enemy to hear. Not his fave thing to do.

Thunderous gunfire raged non-stop for a solid minute as both sides sought for the advantage in the first few critical ticks. Ricochets zinged everywhere and more busted stuff got smashed further. Moving and firing constantly, never giving the attackers a stationary target, Delphia heard his Zeist glasses whine as the IE circuits adjusted to the lack of light. Suddenly, he saw the doss clear as day, although in black and white. The dozen or so ambushers were norms in denim and leather, mohawk do's and go-gang tats. Typical street samurai. Except that they were hammering with Mossberg CMDT rapid-fires, the glowing red dots of the integrated laser sights bouncing all over the place. Not the usual sort of bangbang for a punkster.

Delphia savagely twisted the silencer off the Manhunter, and snapped off a fast series of shots at the overhead rafters thick with black shadows. There sounded a crack of old wood, and down hurtled a tremendous ceiling fan, its rotating blades slicing and smashing two of the opposition.

That'll teach them to gang up, he thought bitterly. Just too bad there weren't any more fans.

Thumbs was secure in a corner behind the barricade of a table, his SMG and Predator maintaining a steady response to the CMDTs. Ducking under the lasers, Two Bears was crawling through the bloody muck on the floor, heading for the kitchen to set up crossfire. Pointing with his left hand, Delphia slapped the Manhunter into his palm, fired, then swung over to his right and fired. It was a deliberate, showy move to shock the opposition.

But the punks showed no surprise at his abilities. None at all. Drek! Delphia thought. They weren't expecting *some*body to show—they fragging expected us personally! Street gang, his hoop, these were corporate security goons. These zonies had been waiting for them to show. And that was extremely bad. Delphia wanted to warn the others, but how? How?

Suddenly the bull roar of a Vindicator came from the hallway as a woman in armor and a bobbing ponytail stepped into view from out of a closet. Furniture and junk simply disintegrated under the monstrous assault of her minigun, caseless rounds hosing about like a stream of water. Books jumped, shelves splintered, mirrors shattered, plaster came off the walls. It was a fusillade, a drekstorm from hell! Then she stopped firing and yelped in horror as her body lifted helplessly into the air.

It was Thumbs, Delphia, and Two Bears pumping rounds into her torso, seeking vulnerable joints until blood showed. She dropped the Vindicator and went limp. The others slowed their barrage at this slaughter, clearly unsure of how to proceed. Had they accidentally killed the leader? wondered Delphia, slamming in a fresh clip. That would be most satisfactory.

Then the first dead man's head exploded for no discernible reason. Delphia noted the odd event with interest. What was that about?

Gotcha, thought Moonfeather as she pointed a finger at another norm whose weapon burst violently as if something was blocking the barrel solid. But his ballistic gloves saved his hands, and he pulled out a LightFire 70 pistol to continue banging away.

Annoyed, Moonfeather started to gather her mana for a really major spell when a fist of ice clutched her heart, cutting off her air. She stopped stone cold. There on the second level stood a man dressed oddly even for the sprawl: tight trousers, an open long coat, mink or some animal skin fedora hat, dreadlocks sticking out from underneath like hairy octopus tentacles, gold earrings, a big gold tooth. He was gesturing with a thick elaborately carved cane, dripping with beads and feathers and bones. A juju staff. His hairless chest was painted white and then covered with red symbols and runes. A small leather pouch on a twine necklace dangled about his neck. He was a hougan, and that was a voodoo soul bag.

"He is bad," thought Moonfeather. "Voodoo is bad."

She raised both hands to deflect a swirling wave of something from the hougan. In a perfect circle, everything around her roiled from the impacts of invisible bees, knives, needles, whatever form of mana darts he was throwing at her. Didn't matter. Screaming a short song for Cat, she raked her nails through the empty air, and the enemy mage stumbled back with deep bloody furrows slicing open his handsome face and chest. Shocked but defiant he still stood there. Drek!

The hougan recovered, his eyes going solid black as the pupils totally expanded. He was scanning her aura, looking for weaknesses. With a cry, he shoved his staff forward and a fireball rumbled down from the balcony toward her, filling the doss with blinding light. Moonfeather hissed at the thing and gestured. The fireball burst apart over his own people, two of them screaming as they hit the floor, rolling about to extinguish the flames covering their bodies before their handguns cooked off.

The balcony under Dredlocks began to sag, then leveled itself with a groan. Moonfeather slapped a stim patch to her thigh, going fuzzy as to what was happening here, but then the stims hit and she jerked back to reality, spitting and radiating fury. She sacrificed the power held in a ring and a bracelet, and the doss got icy cold, the dripping blood frozen solid, and then the air got even colder. Age lines creasing on his slashed face, his breath fogging, the hougan screamed unpronounceable words at his stick and a broken chair hurled across the doss like an upholstered meteor. Every muscle painfully weak, Moonfeather forced herself to duck underneath the deadly bludgeon, just barely keeping her head intact.

She triggered her Beretta non-stop, but only two rounds hit the hougan on the armored coat as he shoved himself loose from the fallen balcony. The impact seemed to refresh him, and just as he began to laugh at her pitiful attack, the wooden railing in front of him detonated. The blast nearly knocked the staff from his grip and covered his bare chest with bloody splinters. Immediately, the hougan fell to the floor.

Feeling terribly nauseous, Moonfeather knew she could no longer fight. She grabbed a crystal hanging around her neck and spoke a few words. The invisibility spell locked into her oldest and most cherished fetish activated and she could breathe. She could only wait now.

His neck bloody from a graze from across his throat, Thumbs aimed his big chattering SMG at anything moving. Firing to the right, Delphia caught a motion off to the other side and jerked out his left arm. The VPR2 shifted the Manhunter to the other hand in a nano. It boomed once, and a norm in combat armor was blown off her boots to crash over a table and hit the floor upside-down.

Dropping the spent clip, Delphia dove over a smashed table to land behind a ripped couch, and slapped in another clip, wishing he'd taken a grenade from the Elite. This was a Scarlet Ribbon, a three-on-three formation with the corpse a diversion. The door the key in, and no way out. To even try was death. It was a beautiful trap, and they were in serious drek. He chided himself angrily, but the dwarf wanted a soft penetration first. Smiles and flowers. Howdy, neighbor! So much for fragging subtlety.

Another dead man's head exploded, brains and blood spraying everywhere in a grisly rain.

Wiping gray matter off his face, Thumbs dropped his exhausted SMG and charged at a pile of debris, slashing through the stuff with his forearm blades. Whoever was on the other side screamed and stumbled into view minus an arm at the shoulder. Grabbing the man's dropped Mossberg, Thumbs started firing again as a new punkster arose behind him swinging a laser axe. He strained to swing the CMDT around to meet the sizzling blade when the leatherboy jerked back, a hole in his head gushing blood.

From the kitchen, safely behind the fridge, Two Bears put

another burst of the silenced Crusader into the ganger and tried again for the Vindicator minigun lying so tempting in the middle of the bloody carnage. Then he also spied a deck lying amid the papers and body parts. An antique Fuchi 2. It had been stepped on, or shot, and was busted wide, but decks meant data, so he tucked the relic under an arm and moved on, firing controlled bursts as he went.

The air above the combatants shimmered and buzzed from whatever the two shamans were doing to each other. Then a thundering rainbow filled the doss as the stained glass window shattered into a million knives, the shards swirling madly about, slicing everything and everybody into ribbons. Some punksters screamed as they were disassembled and the balcony torn to pieces amid spraying blood.

"Got him!" shouted Moonfeather.

Jerking a look, Thumbs gave a bellow of victory over the burping of his CMDT while heading for the exit.

"NO!" screamed Delphia, when a pile of trash erupted and he found himself face to face with a razorboy who'd been digging a tunnel through to him. Sons of slitches were buried like land mines in the wreckage. The guy was in patent leathers, garishly painted, dripping with chrome, but he wore it like a costume, not reg clothes. Razor spurs jutted from both hands like cactus thorns, and he was packing a netgun. Not a kill, but a capture-them-alive weapon. Both moved to aim and fired. Delphia won. But as the man doubled over, a woman behind him fired a burst from her Mossberg and Delphia was hit in the arm, stomach, thigh from the stream of high-velocity lead. He went down firing in return.

Off amid the reeking destruction, another deader's head exploded.

Forgoing the Vindicator, Two Bears dashed headlong from the kitchen, skirting the riddled wall and reaching the hallway door. Yanking it open, he stopped with a jerk, the elegantly wrapped handle of a wakazashi, the formal Japanese short sword, sticking out of his belly. Blood was pumping everywhere. His blood.

The Crusader dropped from the dwarf's hands as the troll in the hallway shoved the blade upward, gutting him like a fish. With a shuddering sigh, Two Bears keeled over to the filthy floor. Katana and wakazashi in both hands, the troll samurai administered the death stroke and moved into the doss with chipped speed.

Blowing off the face of his newest attacker, Delphia was staggering for the door when a blurry image moved into the peripheral field of his sunglasses. He fired blindly without turning. The blur stopped, and dropped.

"Now!" screamed Moonfeather, her body seeming to appear out of nothing. At the same time a shimmering barrier of crackling electricity formed a curved wall between them and the remaining attackers. Stumbling outside as best they could, the three had just cleared the doorway when the hallway was filled with light and the building shook as if drop-kicked by a god.

"Green means high-explosive," Thumbs said with a grin, not a scratch on him.

"*Hai,* I noticed," wheezed Delphia, holding his bleeding leg. He'd been hit with a mixed clip of rounds, the tracer splattered on his hip not setting his clothes on fire because he'd paid extra for protection against that. The next was a dumdum that had hit his gut like an express train. Ballistic cloth stopped full penetration, but that kinetic force had to go somewhere. And the fragging third and fourth had been an AP round that went through his suit and him too. Couldn't get a slap patch on until he dropped his pants, and this was not the place for that.

"I gotcha, *omae,*" said Thumbs, sliding a massive arm around the smaller norm. "We're gone."

"What about—" questioned the now visible Moonfeather, starting toward the still form of the dwarf sprawled on the floor. There was something in his hands. A deck. She raced to snatch it.

"Leave him, he's dead," gasped Delphia, fumbling to reload his gun with one hand, just in case more were outside waiting for them. His fingers refused to obey and he dropped a full clip as they stumbled down the stairs. Nobody bothered to pick it up.

And nobody attempted to hinder their departure. The lobby was as empty as before, and when they reached the street, the Elite was at the curb, Silver at the wheel, Seco in hand. Both doors sprung open as they approached, and the runners stumbled in like drunken tourists lunging for the last taxi in Overtown.

"Duck!" shouted Silver as she tossed something globular and striped green over the roof with her left hand. Bullets pinged off the light armor of the Elite, one side window cracking from the deflection of a heavier round. She peeled away ticks before a deafening blast shoved the vehicle off at an angle and the front of the Dorsey Park dossplex disappeared in smoke and flame.

Sirens were sounding in the distance as Silver wheeled wildly into traffic, dodging bikers, pedestrians, and other cars in a pinball game of slam and rebound. Horns filled the night-time darkness with a cacophony of noise.

Delphia lay pale and bloody on the back seat. Moonfeather slit off his pants and placed trauma patches on every wound. Awkwardly, Thumbs fumbled to operate a PocketDoc, a device he'd never used before. Silver kept the headlights off to reduce targetability, and the battered black Toyota Elite disappeared into the northbound traffic of the Miami sprawl.

The sounds of fighting in the doss long over, Wesley pushed open the back door to the upper-floor apartment cautiously as if expecting resistance. The rusty hinges creaked horribly, and when the door finally reached a half meter wide, he froze at the awful sight of the carnage displayed. But even as Wesley started to retch, his dirty hands moved expertly over the broken bodies, taking weapons, credsticks, optical chips, and everything else he could stuff into his patched pants. The smell of feces and blood was thick enough to taste, but he ignored the stench. He'd encountered worse, much worse, on the streets. Just never this fresh. Some of the bodies were still warm. That was the bad part. The suggestion of life where there was none.

Loaded down to where he was barely able to waddle, Wesley slipped quietly out the back door, closing it behind him and locking it with a key taken off the wall. An extra knife, solid and made of good steel, was slid under the jamb as a shim to hinder the pursuit he knew would be coming.

Minutes later, a squad of combat troops dressed in Lone Star uniforms came bursting in through the front door, weapons out and ready for anything but what they found: naked dead, smashed furniture, numerous small fires, and a crucified ork. By the time the officers finished searching the two floors of the huge doss and decided to break down the back door, all they found was a trail of bloody bare footprints on the stairs going up to the first floor and then out again into the alley. They lost the tracks in the prickly weeds of a vacant lot. When more Lone Stare reinforcements and a DocWagon team arrived, everything and everybody of any importance was long gone.

12

Pink neon blinked constantly outside the bedroom window. On, off, on, off. Primitive Morse for look-at-me. The one table in the sparse room was covered with wire and bits of equipment from a dozen different decks, radios, and even selected parts from the telecom. If old Walter Gibson and Rube Goldberg had a kid, this would have been their first creation. A 3D Jackson Pollock.

Swung around to point at the wall, the trideo was showing the wallpaper the classic 'Vampire Hunter D!', the noise of it masking their soft conversations from any possible eavesdroppers beyond the thin foamboard dividers.

"Is it working?" asked Thumbs hopefully.

"Ssssh," said Silver, eyes closed, fiber-optic cable connecting her to the Fuchi 8 and then the sparking ruin of the Fuchi 2 recovered by Moonfeather from Two Bears' hands. Seated uncomfortably in a cheap macroplas chair, Silver was jacked into the mess.

"Why did Two Bears risk his life to grab this?" she mumbled, not taking her attention off the cobbled-together Frankenstein. "Files corrupted, recovery programs scrambled, databytes flickering about in here as random as snowflakes in a storm! Gods, this is totally trashed. A complete waste . . . whoa, what was that?"

Silver became perfectly still, except for her fingers tapping variously on the keyboards of both Fuchi decks. "I'm going in!"

Dressed in only boxers and T-shirt, Delphia was shaving in the washstand with the complimentary free soap and a cheap razor. His wounds were still sore as hell, but for a man who'd been shot a half a dozen times only hours ago, he was doing fine. All the way here, Moonfeather sang a healing song over him, and as they pulled the Elite into the parking lot of the north Miami Domino Motel he stumbled out with the others on his own feet. Starving, but alive. Gods, was he hungry!

The Domino was a classic by-the-hour. And even though it wasn't Saturday night, or a holiday, four people of assorted races and different sexes renting one room for the whole night did raise the clerk's interest. The stickful of creds lowered them, though, allaying his suspicions, and they got the rent-a-doss. It was cheap, but relatively clean.

Rinsing the razor off under the tepid tapwater, Delphia wondered what the magic done on him was going to cost. He already had a sneaking suspicion what pound of flesh the Cat shaman wanted from him.

"What do we do about Two Bears?" asked Thumbs, watching Silver work.

"Word on the grid is that he died yesterday," said Moonfeather. "Now it's true." She was sitting on the bed, her bracelets, rings, and necklaces spread out before her. Occasionally, she would sing to them, or just hum to herself. Nothing seemed to be happening, but she looked pleased.

"The services are tomorrow," added Delphia, drying his face.

"Buried so soon? How come?"

"Some religious thing. He's got to go under within twenty-four hours."

"I liked him," said Thumbs for no apparent reason.

Pulling on fresh clothes he'd taken from the trunk of the Elite, Delphia shrugged. "He was a Johnson. He fragged up. Now he's wormfood. Happens to everybody eventually."

"What do we do if there's any usable data on the chips in that relic?" asked Moonfeather. "Call the Johnson and collect the fee?"

"We have the number," confirmed Thumbs, reaching into a plastifoam box and pulling an icy beer into view. He popped the top with a callused thumb and took a draft. "So who makes the call?"

"Me," said Delphia in his no-nonsense tone, buttoning a shirt. "I'm the one who talked to the J. Anybody else chats him up and we could blow the deal."

"And all those lovely nuyen," added Moonfeather.

"Hey," said Silver softly, getting their attention as she jacked out. "I'm starting to download." She spoke in a whisper as if afraid a loud noise might terminate the tremulous connections. Everybody crowded around her, but not near enough to jostle an elbow.

She spoke ever so softly, "Found something. My Fuchi 8 can download a thousand times faster than this old thing could when it was brand new." Fingers tapping, keyboards clicking. "Yeah, there we are, sweetie. This is a lot easier than running the Matrix. Don't need anywhere near the concentration to twig the job. But if I pull on the data too hard, the jury-rigged system will crash, scrambling all those zeros and ones and there'll be nothing left but a half-melted paperweight people paid blood to get."

They others stood and watched the cracked lights on the old Fuchi change color and patterns, moving to the technological tune of the decker, who played the keyboards like an ambidextrous pianist. After a few ticks, a thin stream of smoke curled up from the Fuchi 2 and it went dark.

"Dead," announced Silver. "The recovery program burned her out. Just couldn't take it. Poor dear." Removing the fiber-optic cable from her temple, she looked at the technological rat's nest lying before her with a puzzled expression. In the background, Vampire Hunter D confronted the dark shogun and revealed who he really was. A fight between the titans immediately ensued.

"Beer?" asked Thumbs politely.

"Any kaf?"

"Nope."

"Beer'll do. Thanx."

"Well?" asked Delphia, straightening his cuffs. "Anything?"

"Yes and no," Silver said, rubbing the cold can along the side of her face. "There was a record of the original transaction about the book chip. Not the contract with the publisher, but the private contract between Gordon and the author."

"Say again?" asked Thumbs, thrusting out his tusks.

Silver still held the beer to her throat. "Gordon didn't write the fragging book. It was a lie. He was the ghost author. A front for the real writer."

"Why hide that you wrote a book?" inquired Moonfeather making a face.

Thumbs crushed an empty beer can. "Why write the book is the real question?"

"Because he had too much to say, and wasn't allowed to talk," rationalized Delphia, adjusting his suspenders. "Somebody who knew great secrets and could not speak of them." He started to walk and talk. "It's a common problem among the upper echelons of any gov or business. Bursting with forbidden knowledge, somebody hired a nobody to front for his public confession. He got to talk, and stay safe at the same time."

"And Gordon got some nuyen and a hot rep for basically doing nothing," observed Moonfeather. "Sounds like a win/win to me."

Leaning forward, elbows on knees, Thumbs snorted rudely. "Yeah, except for that getting crucified part at the end, a sweet deal."

On the trideo, lightning crashed as the mutants escaped, and norms attacked vampires while the great castle began to fall apart amid the civil war of blood relatives.

"Was there a name?" asked Delphia bluntly.

Silver sipped the beer. "Yeah, some chummer named James Harvin."

Moonfeather gawked. "*The* James Harvin?"

"There might be another," Delphia growled. "But I have only heard of one in town."

Thumbs halted in the process of opening a beer with a tusk. "Harvin," he said.

"James J. demigod-this-town-is-mine-frag-you Harvin. The CEO of Gunderson Corporation. The guy who ordered the Night of Law. *That* James Harvin secretly wrote a book about pirates?"

"Apparently so," said Silver, starting to pull wires and turn off switches.

"Whafor?"

"Maybe he likes pirates."

"Maybe he is a pirate. Or used to be, anyway."

Thumbs drained his beer and opened another quickly.

"How are we going to arrange a meet with a top drawer like him?" asked Moonfeather, polishing a large catseye gem on her T-top.

Swallowing a mouthful, Thumbs laughed bitterly. "God needs an appointment to see Harvin. Us? Null program."

"Silver, think you can get into their system and dig some data?" Moonfeather breathed on the stone and polished some more. "What Harvin knows, I'll wager his mainframes do also."

"Yeah, buried under so much IC it'd sink the Titanic II. Pillage the frames of TGC?" She shook her head. "No way."

"So what about Atlantic Security? Use it as a back door," offered Delphia, taking a seat. "One owns the other. They must have a sweetheart deal to exchange data."

"Zero sum there. AtSec also writes the IC guarding most of the major corps and multinationals in the Carib League," said Silver, patting her deck as if it was a pet. "Nobody's getting past their black ice without at least one executive access code or using the master terminal in Harvin's private office."

Accepting a beer, Delphia vetoed that. "The system's probably triple-sealed too. That's standard. Unless it's Harvin accessing the mainframe, it'll blow and bring a drek-load of guards with shotguns and chipped hellhounds and tox knows what else. Blessed Yomi, just getting into his office would take a miracle!"

Silver shivered.

"Yeah? Well, I can get us the access codes," said Thumbs, setting aside his beer. "Maybe a couple of the codes. Fresh, hot, and tight."

For a tick, nobody could speak. Vampire Hunter D finished rolling the credits and Mobilesuit Gundham began immediately, the intro music fast and jazzy, with lots of bass and brass.

Something banged on the wall from the other side. "Turn down the fragging cartoons!" shouted a muffled voice. "It's three in the bloody hack, ya gleebs!"

Reaching for the bedside table, Silver turned on the radio too.

"Argh!" screamed their neighbor, and then his trideo started blaring the jazzy fight music from Xabungle. "Ha! Take that!"

"You're telling us you can get us into Harvin's files?" smirked Moonfeather contemptuously.

The floor creaked under his awesome weight as Thumbs crossed the room to look out the curtained window at the blink-blink of the electric motel sign. He stood, haloed in pink neon, his horns curving above his smooth bald head.

"Yeah, that's what I'm telling you," he said. "Ever started a riot?"

13

With two ork guards behind them, two in front and one on point, the corporate executive and her escort came down the inclined ramp of the underground parking lot. She wore a slingaround spidersilk dress in the latest mode, the fabric mimicking flowing water as it rippled with every step. Her ankle-strap highs perfectly matched her long scarf, and complemented her elaborately coiffed hair. He was less noticeable, as befitting his lower status, in a simple black on black tuxedo, slicked-back blonde hair, a slight stagger in his walk from too much good champagne and too little food.

The ork bodyguards were in somber ballistic suits, their shirts lumpy from the armor plating attached to their skin underneath. They were wired to each other via headcoms, and wore silenced machine pistols slung over their shoulders, backup smartlink handguns on their hips, and flash grenades on their belts. It was an average night out, nothing special. Their suit had gone out on the town, and now they were escorting her and her paramour back to the penthouse for sweaty vanilla. No big jewels involved, no corporate data, no unknown or dangerous turf, no high-crime neighborhood. Cake. A yawner.

The guards proceeded toward the Mitsubishi Nightsky limousine in standard two-on-two formation, the point man drawing any potential fire in the lead. Following them was the couple. The man was smiling and laughing, probably in anticipation of whatever fleshy delights awaited them at the apartment. She was more serious, frowning slightly as she studied the limo with its tinted windows.

The driver had not come to the front door of the restaurant when she beeped. Most unacceptable. He had done this once before, passed out from sampling the liquor in the wet bar. It brought him a reduction in rank and pay, which should have been sufficient punishment for the indiscretion. Well, the old norm had seen his last drop of her liquor supply. She would fire him here and now, and he could walk back by himself through Overtown. It would serve him right if the gangs killed him.

They stood in the shadows, silent, waiting. Silver had accessed every restaurant reservation in greater Miami and this was the couple they'd chosen. A Gunderson exec and her playmate. Delphia whispered to Moonfeather and she released the spell held in check for the past hour.

Instantly, everybody but them was entwined in a mana web, their reactions slowed tremendously. With an audible slap, the Narcoject pistol was in Delphia's hand and he snapped off six fast shots. Then two more. Slowly, as if trapped in invisible molasses, the unconscious couple and the bodyguards slumped to the floor of the underground parking lot, tiny darts protruding from their vulnerable necks.

Kicking the guards aside, Delphia and Moonfeather lifted the woman bodily to the limo and hauled her inside, where they stripped off her clothes as quickly as possible. The chauffer was already taken care of, out like a light and dumped into the trunk of the limo. There were two more hours of darkness before the dawn, and they were exactly on schedule. Delphia and Moonfeather climbed into the limo and drove to their next stop.

Leaning against the pounding wall of the Fiesta Grande nightclub, Thumbs watched as the street began to fill with the denizens of the night—predators and victims, the lost, the lonely, the jinked, chipheads, dopers, fools, and gutterkin. He had one arm around Silver, and she snuggled against his big form as though she was his biff. This was Slammer territory, with gangers standing on every corner, in every doorway, sitting on every stoop, and nobody dared give Thumbs and Silver a second look.

A soft trilling in his vest almost made Thumbs reach reflexively for his Predator. Slightly embarrassed by the overreaction, he pulled out the pocket telecom instead and activated it. The screen lit with a jerky picture of a view through a car windshield.

"Thirty seconds," said a familiar voice and the connection was terminated.

"Thirty and counting," relayed Thumbs, tucking the device away.

Within moments, the stolen limo pulled up in front of an

abandoned building. Moonfeather got out from behind the wheel, some women's clothing in her arms. Delphia awkwardly climbed out the passenger side, favoring his side. He then pulled a nude female norm out by her ankles, and slung her over one shoulder.

Nobody on the street paid any attention even as Moonfeather started dropping items of torn clothing behind them, leaving a trail from the limo into the abandoned building. It was a fire-gutted wreck, but with a solid roof. More important, its sewer system led to a manhole just steps away from the building.

They made their way into the gutted shell, its once-polished terrazzo floor now carpeted with trash. Moments later Thumbs and Silver followed them in. Thumbs took up position by the window, watching the street, waiting for what was soon to come. Silver found a semi-clean spot in a corner and sat down with her deck and jacked in. Delphia and Moonfeather took the stairs down to the basement, Delphia still carrying the inert body of the corp suit.

Within minutes, they were back, stinking of the dank muck of the sewer where they'd stashed the body. Silver was just jacking out as they reappeared.

"It's confirmed," she said. "When their base command lost contact with the suit's bodyguards, it triggered an alert. Atlantic Security's been tracking the limo by air, and they've got a helo is its way here now. ETA five minutes."

Delphia gestured and a gun slapped into his palm. Not the Narcoject this time, the Manhunter, no silencer. "Then let's do it."

Stepping outside, Thumbs placed two fingers in his mouth, whistled long, short, short, long. Instantly the whole street erupted in gunfire and explosions while everywhere were the running, howling members of the Slammers looking for fights, looking for fun, looking for trouble, rocking and rolling the street as only they knew how to do.

Zooming over the Miami skyline, the Atlantic Security pilot of the massive Hughes Sky Stallion saw the street riot long before he was in firing range. Pinpoints of gunfire strobed the shadows as countless handguns, and some automatics, blasted away constantly at everyone and everything. Windows were smashing, store alarms screaming, and a thick billowing cloud of acrid smoke from burning car tires hid much of the street and the action.

"Free drug night?" asked one of the troopers aboard, lowering the blast shield of his helmet over his face. "Moon sure ain't full."

"Drek knows," responded the sergeant. The badge on his amored breastplate read "Tanner." "But we got a confirmed on a Gunderson exec, Sharon Palmer. She's down there somewhere."

The helo bounced from a thermal caused by the streets still releasing their heat of the day, and more than a few rounds zinged off its armored hull. The gunner sitting next to the pilot responded by sending a flurry of soft gel rounds from the twin belly cannons, dispersing the crowd faster than drek down a loo. Nobody wanted to get intimate with gelatin rounds coming in at over Mach 1. At this distance, they stung like a Cuban fire bee. Any closer and they'd hit like a rain of sledgehammers, busting bones and shattering skulls if the wrong part of your anatomy got in the way.

"Great, some suit slitch goes slumming and starts a street war," snorted a bored trooper.

Another said, "Probably fighting over her bones."

"Bio-med says she's alive," said the pilot, "but the locator signal is erratic."

"Jammed?" asked Sergeant Tanner, instantly alert.

"Can't say. Maybe only scrambled from strong magnetic fields, big speakers from the thumpclub down there, or shielded by dense metal."

"Touchdown in five," called out the pilot over the PA without any preamble. "Four, three, two, one!"

A stinging hurricane swept the street as the Sky Stallion landed in the middle of the intersection near where the Mitsubishi was parked. On contact, the team of nine AtSec troopers and their commander charged out and assumed a half-circle defense pattern. Rounds came their way, but they withheld fire until target acquisition was achieved. Kill the customer and they got a week's suspension with no pay.

The limo's doors were wide open, nobody inside. But the troopers quickly saw pieces of a torn dress, and then more scraps of clothing leading into a burned-out building.

Even as they were deciding their next move, one of the troopers took a painful shot to the head. He staggered from the impact of the slug, his combat helmet dented but still intact.

The rest assumed a more aggressive posture, a double circle, and hosed the nearby windows with small-caliber fire to discourage any further incidents. It worked for a minute or two.

"Tanner to base, we have a level two fight in progress," reported the Sergeant over his headcom. "Client Sharon Palmer not on site. Found torn female clothing leading into a burned-out hive. I suspect level four personal assault in process. We will advance and advise, requesting backup, stat."

Static crackled inside his head, then came a response.

"Roger, Tanner, this is base. Confirm. Gunderson has authorized additional emergency expenditure. Additional teams en route. ETA fifteen."

"Where the frag they coming from, Bermuda?" muttered a corporal, kicking open the door to the ruin, his laser-beam spotter flashing over the smashed remains of what looked like it had once been an illegal operating room. "Gotta move fast or blow our recovery bonus."

"Move with a purpose, people!" Tanner subvocalized into his throat mike, his words booming over the speakers of his helmet. "Go-go-go!"

With the hatches locked tight, the pilot and gunner of the Sky Stallion sat side by side in their tandem cockpit, vid-scanners sweeping the street. Directly underneath the helo, a manhole cover carefully slid open and Thumbs crawled out, followed by Delphia, Moonfeather, and Silver. Crouching low near the armored belly of the assault helo, Silver gestured to the others.

Moonfeather waved one of her cat trinkets as she began to sing softly. A few ticks later, the gunner and pilot in the helo gently slumped over, asleep. Delphia immediately stood up alongside the hatch and used a pencil-thin device to unlock the port door. But the inner mechanical bolt had also been thrown and it refused to budge. Thumbs grabbed the handle, and bracing a boot against the hull, gave a heave that burst the door free, throwing him to the ground and leaving the door dangling.

Thumbs was back on his feet in a tick. Sluggishly, the pilot stirred. As his eyes opened, he was looking down the big barrel of an ebony Manhunter.

"Don't," said Delphia softly. But the groggy trooper clawed for his holstered Colt anyway. Without hesitation,

Delphia blew the man's face off, the blood exploding all over the cockpit and windshield. Thumbs by now was back on his feet and had pulled the bodies of the dead man and the still-unconscious gunner out of the cockpit. He threw them aside with his powerful arms as though they were crumpled MacHugh's wrappers.

Silver then climbed onto the slippery seat and jacked into the control console. This was the risky part. Thumbs had told them the story of a badly wounded Atlantic Security officer stumbling into a helo, which then flew off by itself back to their fortress station. Not that AtSec really cared about the troops, they just wanted their very expensive helo back. But a story like that told the runners there was an autopilot onboard. Somewhere.

Wiping the windshield clean with a hand, Delphia smeared blood over the pinhead vidcam in the console to mask their identities. Thumbs meanwhile was rigging the hatch door into place using a seatbelt to hold it.

"Better than nothing," he stated. "It'll keep some of the smoke out. Hozitgoin?"

Delphia shrugged as he glanced over at Silver. She was frowning over the controls.

Pursing her lips, she tapped a key, and the aftmotors roared into powerful life, the rotors above them revving to flight speed. In a hurricane wash, the gunship lifted clumsily into the air and angled away between two condoplexes, steadily climbing for altitude.

Thumbs grinned at Delphia, but the other man had never taken his eyes off Silver.

"Base command to Helo Eighty-six," crackled the control console speaker. "What's wrong? Why are you leaving the drop zone on auto?"

Grabbing the dead pilot's headset, Thumbs gargled something about lasers and nerve gas while Delphia fired a round into the console radio link. It exploded with a spray of sparks.

"Lasers and what?" took over the ceiling speaker. "Repeat, Number Eight-six, what is your problem? Main transponder down. Reserve radio-activated. Awaiting authorization code."

Moonfeather mouthed an obscenity, Thumbs smacked a palm into his forehead, Delphia was pointing his gun at anything resembling a radio, but not firing. It was all up to Silver now.

14

The trail of clothing led the Atlantic Security rescue team down through a grating in the rubble-filled remains of the basement and into the city sewer. The walls were slime-covered brick and moldy ferrocrete, the stink thick enough to chew.

"Sir!" called out a trooper, standing near the edge of the open trough sewer. The light of his flash was centered on a credstick bobbing in the stinking city waters.

"They didn't take her stick?" asked a trooper. "Drek. She's dead, chief."

"Maybe," groused Tanner, playing his flash around the stygian tunnel. "But I'm not gonna report that unless we're fragging positive."

A rusty iron ladder was set into the wall not far from their position. On a hunch, Tanner went over to check it out. When he spotted moist drek on the rungs leading up to the street, he turned back to his men, waving his arms for them to follow.

"*Motherfragger*! It's a scam!" he screamed. "Back to the helo!"

Slinging their weapons, the troopers began to scramble hastily up the ladder, their boots clanging on the corroded metal rungs.

"Lose that helo and we're stranded until backup arrives," cursed a corporal. "Move it, people. Move it!"

"O'Malley, it's a trick!" Sergeant Tanner transmitted over his headcom to the helo, still climbing frantically. "Go hard, *omae*! Report, Palmer's down. We've been tricked. Go hard and shoot everything in sight! Hose the hood, geek 'em all you want, but do not go skywise until we return. Do you copy?"

Static.

"O'Malley, do you copy?"

More static.

"Helo Number Eighty-six, report!"

Nothing, not even a carrier wave.

"Base, this is Tanner. Main radio is down. Helo Eighty-six may have been compromised!" Still no response. "Fragging manhole must be blocking the signal!"

A voice in the dark said, "Or else the helo's already gone."

"Shut up!"

The point trooper strained to shove aside the manhole cover, and in orderly formation the rescue team clambered onto the macadam. A snoring rigger and a faceless pilot lay on the ground where the help should have been waiting for them with its big guns and armor.

"Fuck!" exploded Tanner. "Goddamn it to hell!" The brawl had evaporated, the streets now strangely quiet. Smoke from the fires wafted over them as fireflies imitated the starry sky above. Then dozens of Miami cocktails began to plummet down from every rooftop, the homemade bombs bursting into pools of liquid fire as they crashed on the hard street.

As he fired his Mossberg CMDT into the sky, Sergeant Tanner's helmet sensors went crazy, indicating his people were being hit with black powder, cordite, thermite, rubbing alcohol, soap flakes, bathroom cleaners, bleach, ammonia, lye, gasoline, ol' Uncle Sizzle—kitchen-brewed red fuming nitric acid—fragging drek, anything explosive that could fit into a plastic bottle!

An inferno rapidly built on the street.

"But we're not Lone Star!" cried a trooper over the chatter of his SMG.

"They don't give a frag! Bug out!" ordered Tanner, slamming in a fresh clip. "First squad give us cover. Go-go-go!"

Coughing and hacking, six troopers cut loose with everything they had, while the others retreated back into the sewer. The rest soon followed, fighting to be first in. Whooping and howling, the locals moved in for the kill, throwing their crude bombs directly into the open hole. More than one fell back, torn to pieces by weapons fire, but the others crowded in close to get their chance.

"Night of Law! Night of Law!" became the mob's wild chant. Inside the Fiesta Grande, the slaprock thundered on as the club's patrons danced and drank and chipped their way

into oblivion, blissfully unaware that anything more interesting was happening in the sprawl tonight.

Twenty stories above the streets of Overtown, the Sky
Stallion hovered in position as the voice of base command
again demanded identification and codes immediately.

Delphia mouthed words: Can they hear us? Jacked into the
Stallion's control console, Silver shook her head no.

"Good," he said aloud. "What are our options?"

"I don't know. I can't find the fragging code," Silver
snapped, her face a mask of concentration. "I can try to override the autopilot, but they're trying to activate the anti-
intruder systems."

"Stop them," Delphia commanded coolly.

Her fingers tapped at the keys of her deck as if with a will
of their own. "I'm trying, frag it! I can't fly this thing, do
that, and try to use the satellite uplink to access their node in
order to jack into their system all at once. Nobody can!"

Rising up, Delphia stuck his head into the aft compartment. "They're going to haul us in soon if we don't do something," he said grimly. "We'll jump when we reach the
canal."

Thumbs started divesting himself of his heavier items,
while Moonfeather began to search frantically under the
seats.

"What're you doing?" asked Thumbs, frowning.

"Can't swim," she replied on her hands and knees, head in
a storage locker. "Where are the parachutes?"

"Helos don't carry 'em," he told her.

Moonfeather jerked out. "You fragging me?"

"No."

"Drek!"

Removing his ballistic cloth coat, Delphia folded it neatly
and placed it on an empty seat. "What's our altitude?"
he asked, looking out the port window. "It looks like a long
way down." Removing his sunglasses, he turned to Silver.
"Are you done yet? Can you find out if there's a maximum
height from which you can jump and still survive? Undamaged, that is."

Silver said nothing, staring at her motionless hands.
Memories of her chummers in BlackJack's team getting
geeked came vividly to mind, and she gasped aloud at the
recalled pain of the shark attack. *No, never again.*

"Silver?" he prompted, as the console beeped steadily.

"Could it be that simple?" she wondered out loud. "That easy? Do it backwards?"

"Yes!" snapped Delphia, shaking her shoulder. "Whatever it is, try now."

Slow and sure, Silver pulled an optical chip from the pocket of her blood-smeared jacket. Slotting the chip into her deck, she tapped in commands. Instantly, the satellite link opened up. She could see the fountain, her favorite spot in the Miami grid, and then the resistance cleared. She was flying down the datastream. No IC, no system alerts, nothing. She had the golden codes, and they blew her straight into the Atlantic Security mainframe.

Yes! She ripped the operational codes from the mainframe, and then stole everything she could stuff into the banks of the hot Fuchi in her lap.

Sending the codes back through the radio, with a mumbled message about snipers and radio interference, she watched as the intruder alert went clear and the autopilot kicked in.

"We're clear!" she called over the internal PA a second later as the Sky Stallion started moving again to gain altitude.

"Roger Helo Eighty-six," said the ceiling speaker. "You are on independent recall. Troops are en route to your street team. See you in ten."

In the aft compartment, the wind whipping his clothes, Thumbs gratefully closed the side door. "Thank Ghu."

"How?" asked Delphia, slumping heavily in the pilot seat.

Wearily, she beamed at him. "It was dicey for a bit, but I let them control the helo and I went for the satlink."

"But how?" he insisted. "What was that chip? Some special can opener program?"

"A ten-year-old data chip, nothing more."

"Say what?" gushed Thumbs, filling the doorway. "Oh, I get it!"

"Gordon," said Moonfeather from behind him. "You used his old chip."

"*Hai*," replied Silver unjacking the deck. "Gordon had an access code to talk privately with Harvin about the book. It got him through the Matrix for secret yaks with the big cheese. Damn code also worked via a satellite uplink and it was cleared for Atlantic Security. It let me past their IC to talk to them directly. After that"—she snapped her fingers—"done deal."

"Indubitably a superb demonstration of non-Euclidian logic conquering corporate jacdictation," breathed Delphia, with a lopsided grin. "Utterly outstanding."

"Crab poop, why can't you ever speak English?" demanded Thumbs, sliding his sunglasses back on.

Flying over downtown Miami, the massive helo skimmed low over the jumbled rooftops, running lights out, motors on hush, a whispering ghost masking the stars one by one.

"I'll land us on the next rooftop and send this bucket back to AtSec headquarters on George," Silver said. "Look for a likely spot. No power lines or antennas."

Stuffing loose items into a bulging dufflebag, Moonfeather stared at the other woman. "George?"

"Aviator slang for the autopilot," Silver replied gaily, crossing her arms as the gunship neatly pirouetted in the sky before beginning its angled descent.

"Great Ghost, I love beating the bastards!"

Every light in his penthouse office was on, removing any chance of a stray shadow. His tie was removed, jacket gone, shoes off, and James J. Harvin had wrapped a silk kimono about him. An untouched gold tray of food sat on the low table between twin couches nearby. Also untouched on his empty desk was a decanter of chilled wine spotted with dewy moisture.

Harvin sat facing the windows, looking at his reflection in the triple Armorlite barrier. A squarish head, gray hair cut in a buzz, tiny ruby earrings, large hands, no age spots yet, but he knew they would come. Maybe it was time to violate his body and get chipped—skillwires could make him an instant violin maestro. Replacement muscles would give him the strength of a troll weightlifter. He could be strong, fast again.

But that would just be the meat, his soul was tired. Did he even have a soul anymore? He had taken so many parts from others, their organs beating and living inside his chest. They'd taken him apart and put him together with the lifestuff of other people. Was he still Jim Harvin anymore? The face resembled him, but that too could change in less than a day. His illness was in recession. He'd fought the mutagenic cancer and won. Or so they said. So why did he feel as if he was still dying?

He poured himself a glass of wine and took a sip, rolling

the vintage about on his tongue, breathing in through his nose to savor the bouquet as his father had taught him decades ago. How to relish good wine, cut the throats of the competition, and avoid friends. *Muchas gracias, padre.*

So many dark thoughts for such a lovely night.

Faintly, on the other side of the windows, Harvin could see the twinkling lights of Miami. Resorts, hotels, casinos, schools, brothels, air defense centers, his. So much of it was either owned or run by his Gunderson Corporation, which really was the same thing. What other Caribbean League gov could touch him? He ruled Miami. The telecom beeped musically, calling for his attention.

"On," he said, without turning. "Code fourteen," answered a VOX, the artificial voice flat and flavorless. He swiveled his chair about. "Accepted. Do not monitor, record, or trace. Unrestricted access granted on my command."

"Acknowledge," spoke the mechanical words. Harvin had been expecting this call ever since receiving the report about the Atlantic Security rescue team less than an hour go. Those street samurai Erika Johnson had hired were supposed to be second-stringers, at best. And yet they still stayed one step ahead of the game. He smiled.

The indicators on the telecom lit, but the screen remained featureless. "Report," came another voice, though the screen displayed no visual.

"They're close. Very close," said Harvin. "They've acquired the datafiles on IronHell."

"When?"

"Less than an hour ago."

"The real files?"

"No. The basic files only. No detailed data."

"How?"

"Used a private passcode to gain access to the Atlantic Security system, and then on to their central data processor. They got the pirate files."

"Whose code?" the faceless voice asked from the telecom.

"Mine."

A minute passed. "The ork?"

"Yes," said Harvin.

"Kill him."

"Gordon is already dead."

"But not soon enough, it appears."

"No." Harvin shook his head sadly, thinking of Scott Gordon. "Not soon enough."

"I warned you that trying to write about this could jeopardize our whole operation."

"Yet you have published several articles on undersea living in the scientific journals," Harvin returned quietly.

"Which have not incommoded us."

"Yet. Even you find it hard to resist telling someone after you've solved a most difficult problem, eh?"

A few silent ticks passed. "Granted. But that is irrelevant right now. Was the ork terminated by in-house staff?"

"No." Harvin breathed deeply, faintly tasting the wine again. "My friend was killed by unknowns. Crucified. When we find whoever did it, they'll go straight to the medical labs—dead or alive."

"How did they get away with this?"

"They had very good help."

"IronHell?"

"It is likely, or else . . ." An awkward pause. "Or else the elves have developed an interest in our business beyond the wall." The last words were not stressed, nor spoken loudly, and Harvin wondered if the other heard the meaning he intended.

"Understood. That would be most unfortunate," stated the voice without emotion. "This changes everything. Stop the investigation immediately. Pay the runners off with a bonus."

"Impossible. They're incommunicado. Until they report in, I have no way to contact them."

"None?"

"None."

"And they have a chance at success?"

"Expect them at your door any day now."

"Most unfortunate. In the chaos of this situation, they may discover what is actually happening."

"Yes."

"Terminate them. Immediately."

Pouring more wine, Harvin softly laughed. "You have such difficulty with the world kill, don't you, dear sister?"

"*Hai,* I suppose so."

"And what about the other matter—the trouble we've been having with our system? Is it heat again?"

"The matter is being attended to."

"So, no success from your side either, eh?" Harvin said to the black screen. "Good. Failure loves company. Only success stands alone."

"That is one interpretation of the facts."

"Have you found the needed personnel yet?"

"Yes. And he's on his way."

"The first good news of the day. Do your best."

"Acknowledged, dear brother. Out."

"Off," he said, toying with the full glass. As the connection broke, Harvin watched to see the brief image of a blue triangle bisected by an irregular red line fade in and then out. Confirmation of an untraced transmission. Then that too was gone, and he was alone again at the top of the world.

▼

Into the Abyss

15

Stumbling out of the fresher, Thumbs braced himself against the rusty wall and breathed in through his nose, out his mouth, a few times. They'd been out to sea three weeks aboard this rustbucket and he still couldn't stop yarfing out his guts every time they hit a wave. The sea, the sky, the deck, and his wobbly self were all gently rocking back and forth, to and fro, with the overhead light fixtures swaying sickeningly in squeaky counterpoint. But he was feeling much better after giving the fish of the Atlantic Ocean a hearty meal.

"Try this," said Silver, tapping him on the shoulder.

Thumbs look down and accepted the steaming mug.

"I asked Moonfeather to make it double strength this dose," she said. "Maybe that'll do the trick."

Thumbs nodded and swallowed the herbal brew. Remarkably, in a few ticks his stomach stopped doing the cha-cha-cha. "Better," he said around a tongue like shag carpet. He repeated the word, "Better."

"Another?" she asked.

Thumbs gave her an expression of total agreement and started to stumble off. Taking hold of a hairy arm larger than her leg, Silver turned him about. "Engine room is down there, galley this way. We're on deck five, not two."

"What the frag are we doing out here?" Thumbs demanded, trying to ignore his throbbing horns. "I'm a street troll, not fragging Popeye the sailor guy. El trains and alleys are my turf."

"Hey, chummer, this was your idea, remember." She was holding open a heavy hatch in the causeway for him.

Yeah, yeah, he'd have to take the fall for this brilliant

twig. The files Silver had uploaded from Atlantic Security showed that they were definitely hunting pirates for the Gunderson Corp. The files had also offered up lots of rumors about fields of sunken ships and secret cities inside mountains. But you could take all the hard data, carve it in granite, stuff it up your nose, and never be aware that anything was there.

With one notable exception. They'd learned the meaning of the word IronHell. According to the AtSec files it was a special code word for the headquarters of one of the bigger pirate groups preying on ships in this part of the Atlantic. The location was apparently well-hidden even by shadow standards. Atlantic Security had no idea where or who they were. Half the time IronHell seemed to refer to the organization and the other half to its secret base of operations. Whoopdie-fragging-do. Thumbs was not impressed.

However, unlike Queen O'Malley and her ilk in the waters around California Free State or the Black Mariha gang operating in the coastal waters of the Mediterranean, these Caribbean brigands were well-organized, heavily armed, and none had ever been taken alive. Not one. Ever. Delphia considered that a significant fact. Silver thought it was unnatural. Moonfeather said it was a lie to cover AtSec incompetence. Thumbs' personal opinion was that the slags had simply never been captured by a meanhoop Slammer with access to handcuffs and a cheese grater.

Apparently, there was a nifty little bomb surgically implanted inside their brains. Not just inside the skin and bone of the head—lots of folks had com units, decoders, and all sorts of drek stuff in there. No, this device was deep inside the living brain. If the pirate was captured alive by enemy forces, even unconscious, his head would explode, making interrogation what you might call difficult. Neither deckers nor mages had been able to circumvent the security device. X-rays and CAT scans set the thing off instantly.

Once the wearer was dead, he or she always went boom. It was obviously the IronHell pirates who'd tried to ambush the team in Dorsey Park. Whoever built those headbombs knew what they were doing. Thumbs didn't think even Aztechnology and Fuchi could have done better.

From other data in the files, they learned that Atlantic Security had investigated every isle and cove from Bermuda to the equator. But IronHell remained elusive. The pirates ruthlessly sank search parties almost as soon as the vessels left dock, proving they had plenty of chummers on the inside feeding them info. Cargo ships were sometimes hit, sometimes not. But they seemed to specialize in hitting military craft, sending them straight to Davy. Rumor had them working with new experimental equipment, nova-hot stuff that had never seen the light of day. Sailors called it the return of Atlantis, but then again, Thumbs knew sailors spent too much time in the sun and not enough time on land.

Outside the old hull, he could hear the wind and waves getting rough again, but Thumbs felt his stomach accept the condition without qualm. Thank Ghu. And half their job was done. They knew what IronHell was. Delphia had called the Johnson and left him a telecom message. Now all that remained was finding something the Gunderson Corporation, Atlantic Security, Lone Star, and every independent shipping line operating in this ocean couldn't locate. Where the frag IronHell was.

The team had decided they needed to go straight to the source if they were ever going to find the truth. They began to hang out at the dockside hiring halls, and had landed work as security. This was their third trip in as many weeks, but they hadn't seen a whisker of anything vaguely pirate. The *Esmeralda*'s cargo had seemed plenty hot enough, but maybe they'd get luckier on their next trip.

Silver found the others sitting in a corner of the galley picking at their food. Delphia was in the usual natty suit with tie and soft brim hat, while Moonfeather was in a cut-off jumpsuit that hugged every curve tightly.

Sullen sailors, mostly grizzled norms and tattooed orks, sat at other, more distant tables, talking in low voices about what sailors always have since time immemorial: how much they hated their jobs, and then, once they got to shore how soon they could get back out to sea again.

"You'd think El Segundo Lines would feed their security personnel better than this swill," said Delphia, removing the napkin from his shirt collar and placing it over the food on his plate like a death shroud. "Bah. Swill is a compliment."

"I'm sure they do," said Moonfeather, gnawing on a strip of baco-flav soyjerky. "But don't forget, Handsome, we're lowly mercs. Neither corp nor captain give two dreks about us till the hammer falls. The crew thinks ballast is more important than us."

"The laborer is worthy of his pay," said Delphia, wiping his hands and moustache clean on a pocket handkerchief.

"Bulldrek. Why do you think there's only the four of us for a ship this size? The only reason we're here is to help keep the insurance premiums low, that's all." She stopped her attempts to consume the undamaged strip of soymeat in her grip. "Maybe I'll sew some of this into the lining of my duster as armor."

Delphia gave a dry laugh. "Good idea. Ought to stop a nine-millimeter easy, but I don't think anything short of a missile could breach the pancakes."

"Broke a tooth on a waffle."

"*Hai,* the pay is pitiful, and the food wretched." Delphia shoved the plate of fish stew aside. "Three miserable weeks at sea and no sign of pirates. The *Esmeralda*'s haul should have attracted their attention by now." He glanced out a nearby porthole. The weather had been growing steadily worse ever since the freighter had departed the coastal waters of Africa and begun steaming for Rio de Janiero, then back home.

Home? he thought, taking a sip of his kaf. And since when had Miami become home to him?

"Who knows what they're looking for these days," Moonfeather said, studying his face. "Nuyen for your thoughts."

Delphia shook his head. "Almost tastes like the real thing. Incredible."

"Should. It is."

He paused, the deliciously fragrant brown liquid moving back and forth from the motion of the ship. "Beg pardon?"

"It's from the private stock I brought on board." Moonfeather gestured behind her. "I bribe what they laughingly call the cook on this floating grease lump with a cup a day to make it special just for you and I."

Turning about, Moonfeather stared across the room and shook a wrist, her bracelets jingling softly. In the galley, the fat ork in a stained apron and ridiculous hat stopped smearing soylard on a sizzling grill already thick with it to look up abruptly and smile innocently toward her. "I also threatened to turn him into a toad if he crossed me."

Delphia took another sip, watching her closely. "None for Silver or Thumbs?"

"Frag 'em," she purred leaning closer, nearly popping out of the tiger-stripe leotard under her jumpsuit, her cascade of curly red hair framing a lustful grin.

"And how can a simple sprawl shaman afford real coffee?" he inquired softly. Enjoying the view.

Her smile vanished. "Stole it."

"O-hio," greeted Silver, sliding into place between them. "Figured out how to cut the soup yet?"

Moving as if made of glass, Thumbs eased himself down into the fourth chair, making the cheap steel creak ominously. "This place never have a troll on board before?" he griped. "Hey, shaman. Thanks for the herbal stuff. It helped a lot."

"Null perspiration," said Moonfeather, flipping curls off one shoulder. "Catch a bullet for me in a brawl and we're even."

"Ha! I'd rather bed a rabid swamp gator."

"Granite."

A tick. Two ticks. "Catch a bullet where?"

"Anyway, we were just talking about the . . . " Silver tapped her head meaningfully. "You know, and we're wondering if there's any way to know who's got one before it goes off?"

Thumbs nudged Moonfeather. "Can't you look astrally inside their heads to see if they got one?"

"Possibly. The problem is if they're only adding and not replacing."

"How about some kind of truth spell?" probed Delphia.

She snorted. "If we take one alive and I can mind proble him, sure. But that won't make the bomb not go off or disarm it or even give us any info. The power of the spell might just make his head pop, and personally I don't want to be that close when one does."

His stomach rumbling, Thumbs looked at Silver. "So much for secretly hypnotizing a pirate to get him to spill the chips." Then he looked over at Delphia's covered plate and pointed. "You gonna eat that?"

"The fish stew?" Delphia recoiled askance. "No. Please. Help yourself. Enjoy."

"Thanx." Thumbs removed the napkin with a flourish and starting making serious inroads into the greasy concoction.

"I see your appetite is back," said Silver dryly.

"Yar," he mumbled, mouth full of seaweed and bones. "Starved."

"It's part metacrab."

"Hey, axe da cook," slurped Thumbs. "I dunno wats in it."

The ship pitched and a heavy wave crashed over a porthole, throwing the window open and water streaming in to flood the deck. Cursing and grumbling, sailors rushed to force the porthole closed. As the salt water rushed to the walls and down the causeway stairs, the deck inadvertently became clean in several areas.

"It's painted blue," said Moonfeather in wonder.

Then an alarm sounded down the corridor, to be repeated all over the ship in echoing repetition. "Red alert," warbled the decrepit PA system. "Storm at force five levels. Repeat. Force five levels. All hands to battle stations."

Scrambling in every direction, the crew tossed aside beers and card games to grab weapons from wooden wall lockers and rush up the causeway for the higher decks.

"Time to earn your ride, lubbers," said First Officer O'Shanassey, a grizzled woman with missing teeth and no direct knowledge of soap. She thrust a large canvas bag at them.

Thumbs dropped his spoon and spread the salt-stiff canvas wide. "Jesus, Buddha, and Zeus!" he swallowed. "It's fulla grenades!"

"Are we to slay the storm for you, madam?" asked Delphia emotionlessly, sipping his coffee.

"We didn't hire ya for ballast," O'Shanassey snorted. "Well, maybe the troll."

"Stuff it, breeder," he rumbled dangerously, pineapple in hand.

"Scare me later, stud," said the norm, working a tobacco wad. "We got real probs. Sonar's going crazy. Big storms like these occasionally drive them from the depths into the higher regions. And then all fragging hell breaks loose. We gotta be prepared, just in case."

"In case of what?" asked Silver pointedly.

"Pirates?" asked Moonfeather excitedly, twisting an onyx ring about her index finger.

"Ha! We should be so lucky," said O'Shanassey, flinching from another crashing wave. "Don'tcha know what a storm can bring up in these shallows?"

"Shallows?" scoffed Delphia. "The ocean is over a thousand meters deep out here. More in some areas."

Silver lifted a grenade from the bag, inspecting it. "Gods, UCAS military, high-explosive, anti-personnel."

"Worth a fortune on the streets," confirmed O'Shanassey. "So don't lose one overboard. Or it's ya hoop."

A bellow sounded outside, overwhelming the fury of the squall. The noise seemed to summon thunder, and the storm increased in power to near deafening proportions.

"What the motherfragging heck was that?" asked Thumbs, cyberblades poking out from his forearm as he raced over to the nearest porthole.

"Don't go near the ports," warned O'Shanassey, taking a step after him. "They can see yaz outline and likes to bite da glass."

"Who?" asked Delphia, tensing his hand as he rose. Smooth and silent, the Manhunter was back in its accustomed spot.

Another roar, louder than before, and accompanied by the sound of machine-gun fire and dull explosions from the aft and starboard.

"Snakes," replied the sailor, making the sign of the cross as fresh sweat stained her dirty uniform. "Big'uns."

16

Ignoring the howling storm and noisy commotion outside his plush cabin, Attila relaxed in the softly vibrating leather chair, allowing the mechanical massage to augment the one he was receiving in the flesh. He was naked save for an untied silk dressing gown, which dangled loosely off his wiry frame. Attila was sipping champagne from a crystal goblet and smoking a fine Havana cigar, the picture of contentment. Kneeling between his open thighs was a young Angola girl, bound with the chains of her slave auction. Her long black hair visually, but not audibly, hid the fact that she too was engaged in an act very similar to smoking.

A frantic knock came at the cabin door, and then the portal slammed open, a frightened engineer from below decks too fragging busy to be either shocked, or titillated, by the carnal scene.

"Sea serpents attacking the ship!" he cried, tossing a chattergun and a belt of mixed ammo on the carpeted deck. "All passengers to the foredeck to help defend the Emmy!"

The slave slowed her ministrations. But Attila only chuckled and refilled his glass. "Nothing to do with us, little flower," he sighed, drawing the smoke of the pungent cigar deep into his lungs and then letting it out slowly. "I paid for a first class cabin, and that means they fight for me. Not vice versa." He lowered the goblet, offering her a sip of cool wine, then pushed her head back to its earlier position. "Continue." Meekly, the girl did as commanded, her chains rattling as she shifted to a more comfortable position.

Ah, life was good. The credsticks he'd stolen from the deaders at the old ork's doss had carried a small fortune in them. A fortune! As expected, the Overtown stickshyster offered him only a tenth of the nuyen shown. So Wesley displayed a few of the handguns he'd also acquired while a trusted gutterchum waddled in hoisting the Vindicator mini-cannon. Suddenly, the price was raised to half.

After paying off his *omae*, Wesley bought toff rags and split for Africa. Leaving town was a necessary move, and Africa was the most faraway place he knew. In Casablanca, he officially became Attila Abelovzsky, a Hungarian arms dealer, and managed to auction off the rest of the weapons, including the Vindicator, to some paramilitary suits in the Congo really hungry for top-string bangbangs. Oddly, the data chips he'd found around the apartment brought an even greater price from an Arab sheik than all the guns combined. Weird.

Now Attila was rolling in wealth, a fragging mil in the Cayman Island banks, eighty-five kay on his personal stick, and a confirmed chip dealer. He knew a good thing when he found it. Smuggling guns was crudcreds compared to boosting industrial chips. Some serious nuyen spread about on the streets of Addis Ababa gave him names to contact in Angola. A deal was quickly cut with some slaves, surprisingly easy too, and here he was sailing to Brazil in style, the little lovely at his feet carrying his next million surgically implanted inside her collapsed left lung. After the stolen Chinese chips were extracted in Rio, he'd sell her to the local snuff jockeys, then see what Seattle had to offer in way of fun and biz. That was the place to be these days. Yar, life was almost too fragging wonderful to believe. And he was supposed to worry about some snake? Ha!

Howls, screams, and explosions sounded constantly above the growing noise of the storm. Who was attacking, and more importantly, who was winning, was completely unknown. Privately, the female servicing the boy fumed in rage over the cowardice of the idiot. If the situation was so bad topside that they were recruiting the fragging passengers, then their own lives might depend on one extra gun in the fight! Of all the buyers at the auction, why did she have the bad luck to be bought by this motherless gleeb?

Not soon enough would they be off this bucket and then she'd be able to cut this fool's throat, establishing herself in society as a woman of means with a mountain of nuyen from the hot chips tucked inside her. A fine dinner, a good wine, a massage, a lot of the kinky sex he liked so much and afterward the exhausted boy would fall asleep without setting the

security system on her collar and never awaken again. It was
how she'd gotten out of jail, and what better way to escape
the death sentence and the magistrates than to be smuggled
off the island using somebody else's nuyen and connections?

However, her slave masquerade must continue until they
were once more ashore. With a girlish giggle, Ruby the
Razor pretended lusty enthusiasm, consoling herself by
imagining what she would do to the naked flesh of her
master when she was free. Oh, yes, what she and her lovely,
lovely straight razor would do.

Stopping at their cabin only long enough to grab their personal weapons, Silver and the others charged up the main
causeway to the forecastle and burst into the bridge room of
the lurching cargo ship. In dripping poncho and hat, Captain
Villiers was lashed to the wheel, shouting details of their
location and situation into a standard black crashbox, his
shoes anchored to the deck with stout steel clips. Silver recognized it as the deadman pose. With a shock, she realized
he didn't expect to succeed. Or even survive.

Industrial wipers struggled uselessly to clear the rain off
the Armorlite windows of the bridge. The storm raged
unabated outside, lightning flashing as waves crashed over
the ship, covering the deck with foamy brine. And writhing
about in the maelstrom was a dark shape barely visible
through the heavy downpour, a sinuous length of muscles
and scales thicker than a tree. Howling in fury, the beast
coiled about madly, crushing crew members, passengers, and
splintering a lifeboat as if it was made of balsa wood, not
duraplas. The gunfire never stopped for a moment.

"Rock and roll," breathed Thumbs, sucking a tusk while
checking the clip in the Mossberg CMDT, which he'd
adopted ever since the shoot-out at Scott Gordon's doss.
"Seen worse."

"Been to Chicago lately?"

"Yar."

Something crashed into the bridge, rattling the whole
structure and damaging a window, causing a spray of sparks
to erupt from a console as the cold ocean water gushed in
through the thin cracks. With a cry, Lieutenant O'Shanassey
rushed over to the main control board just as a petty officer
grabbed a mike from the console.

"Main guns, firefirefire!" shouted the bosun, and from

above them a barrage of fiery darts lanced out past the colossus coiled around the bow of the struggling ship.

"Get away from there!" cursed O'Shanassey, cuffing the man aside. "It's aim, lock, fire, you fragging gleeb!" She pointed furiously at the control board. "Look! Half our missiles gone and no hits!" Snapping open the flap on her belt holster, the lieutenant pulled a handgun into view and laid a finger on the trigger. At the slight pressure, a moving red spot appeared on the bosun's face from the laser clipped under the big barrel. "Outside!"

His face went white, eyes darting to the howling thing on the foredeck. For a tick the storm parted, exposing the creature's tremendous head, diamond-shaped eyes, yellowed fangs, and the bloody legs of somebody jutting from its hellish mouth. "But, sir, I—"

The safety clicked off. "Outside or die here!"

Whimpering, the bosun forced open the side door and rushed out into the melee, the driving rain hiding him completely from view in a heartbeat. The metal door slammed shut behind him, and continued to bang until Moonfeather dogged it shut.

Streams of burning tracers dotted the darkness, highlighting the ocean beast as the phosphorus smashed against its scale hide and failed to penetrate.

"We're armed against pirates," shouted Villiers over the storm. "The Emmy doesn't stand a chance against that!"

A shrieking ork sailor stumbled past the wheelhouse, something black attached to his back. Another of the crew spun about fast and hosed the dying ork with tracers and bullets, tearing him and the black lump to bloody pieces.

"What the frag are those?" demanded Silver, checking the clip on her Seco.

"Leeches!" shouted Captain Villiers.

"They live on the snakes in the depths! Or on sharks! Anything with blood. Up here, us!"

Delphia frowned deeply. Manhunter in hand. "Apparently a meta-version of *macrobdella valdriana*. But the size! Never seen one larger than a meter before. These are giants!"

Moonfeather gestured at the open hatchway. Her hands glowed with power, and one of the enormous leeches crawling through the opening suddenly burst into flames, then was instantly washed away by a frothing wave. "At least they're killable," she said. "Unlike big daddy out there."

Moonfeather yanked some magnesium rounds from the bandolier across her chest and began ramming shells into the pump-action Remington. She hefted the weapon onto a shoulder, but then did nothing more. She simply stood and watched the fierce struggle amid the violent storm, her eyes like slits.

"This ain't no time to get mystical!" yelled Thumbs. "Go throw a lightning bolt or a death spell or a mana dart the size of a telephone pole, but geek that crit!"

Moonfeather seemed not to hear, but remained standing there, one red fingernail pressed against her full lips, deep in thought or reverie.

"Frag this!" With blinding speed, Thumbs opened a storage locker and retrieved a length of thick rope. "Tie me!" he shouted, tossing the loose end to Delphia.

Delphia wound the rope around the middle of the big troll and knotted the end tightly. Then Thumbs lurched out the hatchway, struggling through the raging bombardment of water to reach the railing and tie a second rope about a stanchion to anchor himself. His boots constantly threatened to slip underfoot, and his clothes were soaked in mere ticks.

"Moonfeather?" said Silver. No response. Even when a horde of leeches started for the bound troll at the starboard gunwale.

"Delphia, cover fire!" Silver screamed, her Seco firing away. Assuming a combat stance, Delphia unlimbered his Japanese-made SCK 100 submachine gun and cut loose with short, controlled bursts.

The noise seemed to rouse Moonfeather suddenly. She ripped open the bag of grenades and rushed over to the port hatch. Speaking to each grenade first, she began tossing them fast as she could, underhand, overhand, and sideways. The spheres and pineapples flew toward the monstrous serpent, the blasts illuminating the night but barely damaging the creature.

"Aim!" shouted Lieutenant O'Shanassey into a mike above the howling of the storm. "Lock!" But the final command never came as a leech smashed through the weakened windshield and landed full on her face. O'Shanassey fell back into the bridge, clawing wildly at her head.

From his position at the wheel, Captain Villiers drew a

Colt and blew the First Officer's brains out. In mindless
feeding frenzy, the leech didn't stop sucking the juices of the
decapitated corpse until Villiers fired again, and again, punc-
turing its slick, rubbery skin. Black ichor poured out thickly
as the dying thing continued feeding, human red tinting the
ebony blood in pumping swirls.

"Captain on the com," announced an unshaven Lieutenant,
saluting smartly as the commander of the pirate submarine
Manta stepped through the aft hatchway of the submarine.
The rumpled crew at their posts merely grunted at the
announcement and continued working, the rainbow of lights
from the controls giving the cramped room of the military
killing machine an almost holiday feel.

"Carry on," growled Captain, moving past the effete
nancyboy in annoyance. Bloody hoopkisser. His First was a
deserter from the UCAS Navy, and still followed regulations
meaningless to a pirate boat. Who cared about such drek? As
long as the crew instantly obeyed his every command, Captain didn't give a frag if they washed or stood straight. Damn
idjit. At least the gleeb had stopped shaving every day. It
was a waste of good hot water.

When Captain first joined the IronHell pirate group, he
found it disturbing that most of the crew were called by their
jobs when on board: gunner, engineer, cook, rigger, etcetera.

"Have we found them yet, Number One?" he asked, taking
his chair—not original equipment, which he considered
foolish of the old submariners. Why should the commander
stand?

But the vessel was very old, an *Acoola* Class Red Star
from before the Awakening. The original crew had disappeared from within the locked sub during a mana storm in
the dreaded Triangle some twenty years ago. It had only
recently been found intact by a Gunderson oil survey probe
his Bermuda contacts had followed out to sea. After locating
the sub, his contacts had notified him and he'd notified Iron-
Hell of the vessel's location, as usual. Nuyen changed hands
as it always did in such scavenger activities, enough nuyen
to make those contacts his for life.

Within a month, the wreck was upgraded and renamed
Manta. Her liquid crystal display on the rusty conning tower
converted from the innocuous serial number of a bogus

oceanographic institute to a blazing skull-n-crossbones at the flip of a switch. Startled the drek out of people.

Eventually, his prize was given a choice assignment—hit a merchant class ship for the contraband it held and try out the newest piece of IronHell tech, some sort of laser gun. If all went well, he might be able to split from IronHell and form his own band. Maybe even own a piece of the Caribbean. But the Captain was no fool. He knew dreams never came cheap.

"Aye, aye, sir. Radar contact is confirmed." Lieutenant passed over a handcomp with a datachip already in the slot. "Here's the manifest and purser's list."

Captain pressed the search pad, then skimmed the info it presented, interested only in passengers. They already knew this was a rich ship, a ripe plum. A cornucopia of Italian machine parts made from valuable ceramic composites. On top of that were the Asian chips: simsense prototypes, military Hunter/Killers, biochips, and more. Not to mention the secret stuff being smuggled in from the labs of Angola. Oh, yes. This fruit cart would never reach home port.

No passengers worth ransom or good-looking enough for the white slave market, however. Merely the standard crew of malcontents and some gutter mercs. Nothing to worry about. No mages on board. Good. The last thing you want on a sub is a mage. Can't control those mana freaks.

"We're taking everything on this one, so kill as you please!" Captain shouted to the crew. They muttered assent. Aye, and after they were done stripping the ship clean, he'd send her straight to Davy with a torpedo in her belly. Always a fine sight. His masters would be very pleased. Put the fear of IronHell back into the corp's belly. Damn suits were getting uppity again. "Storm status?"

"Wave height increasing," announced Tactical. "Winds up another twenty kph."

The squall was getting worse. "All stop," Captain ordered, reversing his cap. "Gimme periscope depth. Stabilizers on full."

"Aye, sir. We are."

At fifteen meters depth, their periscope was above the ocean's surface, but the endlessly crashing waves hid their target in a choppy maelstrom. "Up five meters," said Captain, forearms resting on the side supports of the 'scope. Someday, he'd get jacked and see the outside inside his head through their pinhead cam on the hull. But he'd yet to find a chummer he trusted enough to stand guard over him while he was unconscious and under the laser.

"Aye, sir," said Lieutenant, scratching his stubble. "Helm, up five, zero bubble."

Rigger nodded, fully jacked into the sub's brain so man was boat and boat was man. His hands also hovered over the main control panel as he watched the dials before him intently. "Confirm. Five at zero!"

As the periscope focus adjusted automatically for the distance, the captain of the *Manta* punched for night vision. Lights were flashing over the craft. What the hell was going on? "Ah, drek!" he said finally. "They're fighting a snake!"

Murmurs came from the bridge crew.

"Sea serpent," corrected Captain grimly. This was not part of their plan. But the sea was always full of surprises. "Big fragging mother. Forty, fifty meters long."

"Leeches?" asked Lieutenant grimacing.

"Tons of 'em."

"An old snake then. Bloody hell."

"Aye." Standard procedure was to wait for the target ship to come out of a squall and then attack while the crew was still weak and disorganized from battling the elements. But a sea serpent!

"Prepare torpedoes," ordered Captain briskly. "No, belay that! Prep the Firelance."

The Weapons officer awoke from his dozing. "Sir?"

"You heard me, Wep. The big laser. Now move! Let's give this baby a test run. That's why we got it!" There were rules at sea, even for pirates. And one of the most important was, everybody killed snakes. Just for different reasons, that's all.

17

Standing in the open doorway of the bridge on the forecastle, Delphia squinted against the sheets of rain. He lowered the SCK and reached into his jacket for his Zeist glasses. He put them on, the frames giving a low hum, the lenses swirling with colors, and suddenly his machine gun was back in action, chattering away into the raging darkness.

Just steps away, Thumbs touched the third molar in his mouth with his tongue and his reflexes kicked into overdrive. He always liked using his reflex trigger, it gave him such a rush. He slashed his monofilament blades at the sea serpent with chipped speed, a blur in the rain. The rest of the crew was battling the leeches crawling over the deck of the *Esmeralda* like roaches on a wet kitchen floor. Green-black waves rose above the radio mast to crash on the decks harder than piledrivers, smashing the last few lifeboats and washing off everything and everybody not holding on for dear freaking life.

Silver meanwhile had found her spare cable and had jacked directly into the automated weapons control panel of the ship. She was no rigger, but she figured it was now or never. It wasn't a rigged vessel, thank the gods, and it only took her a nano to seize control of the weapons systems. The Emmy seemed to have only one defensive battery, class four, honeycomb formation, Rockwell and Boeing manufacturer. Carried 10 four-meter-long missiles. Loaded with old-style Amsterdams, almost a decade out of date, all-purpose missiles: surface-to-air, ship-to-ship, and ship-to-land.

Drek! Only three remaining, and all set for detonation upon impact, not penetration! Useless against the adamantine scales of the fragging snake. Frantically, Silver raced through the menu, changing the codes to alter the timing sequence on the big 15-kilogram warheads. She hoped to drek the others could keep those leeches off her while her consciousness was here doing this. With its doors open and lights full on, the elevated forecastle and balcony seemed to be a lure for the filthy things. Bloodsucking monster leeches. She shivered.

Grenades used up, Moonfeather was shooting at any leeches that tried to gain entry into the bridge. But easily half her rounds twanged off the steelloy deck, and one big leech got so close it almost bit her with a fanged proboscis even as the thing horribly exploded.

"Thanks!" she called over her shoulder.

"Not a problem," shouted Delphia from the other side of the bridge. "Can't you see through the storm?"

"Hell, no!"

Four more fast shots. "Then I'll give cover! You do something else!"

"And make it big!" Villiers added.

Nodding, Moonfeather holstered her weapon and moved over to the center of the room. She sat down crosslegged and pulled a leather fetish from her belt. Holding it like a sword, she took a deep breath and went very very still.

Moonfeather was standing on a vast desert, its shifting dunes reaching to the shimmering horizon.

Her combat gear was gone. She was dressed in a flowing garment made of purest white silk and leather sandals. The sand under them was rippled like waves on a lake, and Moonfeather noticed her feet were in shadow, at the very tip of a pointed triangle of darkness. Turning around slowly, she flinched. The afternoon sun was blazing directly behind a huge structure of some sort.

Impossibly, the sun rose into the sky as if on celestial tracks. The shadow receded toward the structure, pulling her along with it as if she was attached to it. As the sun reached azimuth, she crested a low hill and saw a tremendous stone pyramid rise majestically before her. It was enormous, bigger than anything she had ever seen, towering three, four hundred meters tall. Dominating the entire desert, the featureless expanse of the geometric shape seemed brand new, not crumbling and ancient like those of Egypt or Mexico.

Reverently advancing in the shifting sands, Moonfeather spotted a small opening on ground level. It was a metal doorway, the detailed stone skindle and jambs edged with elaborate hieroglyphics and cartouches. On either side of the entrance, supporting the massive lintel with inhumanly muscular arms were twin statues. Apparently carved from hard mountain granite, not soft sandstone, the statues were of norms with the heads of cats, their angled eyes glittering the same color as the door itself. Some sort of amber gems? No, polished bronze, or gold. Golden doors?

In the distance, Moonfeather heard soft voices singing sweet songs of praise, and the silvery tinkle of bells. A soft wind blew the sands away from before her, exposing a walk of polished jade leading directly to the mighty door.

Approaching, she noticed the statues moving slightly, tracking her every step. Their granite hands were claws, and ebony swords hung sheathed on their belts, but Moonfeather felt no fear. Theirs was the kindly gaze of an amused friend or perhaps an elder sister.

Distance fooled her sense of perspective. As she stood before the massive door it stretched above her like a golden cliff. No hinges or lock were in view. Moonfeather walked closer, and as she moved between the guardians, the door slid silently aside, going into the pyramid. Beyond was the sandstone side of the structure and a normal-sized passageway, a minuscule mousehole compared to the gigantic door.

Tricks and illusions. Moonfeather knew she was being played with. Every time she visited her totem, the landscape was different; a hollowed-out tree larger than any megacorp skyscratcher—its branches stretching out to cover the world, bejeweled cities of paper and silk, steaming savannahs, always different, yet always the same. Tricks and illusions, games and tests.

As she stepped into the passageway, soft fur brushed her cheek and the door closed with a whisper of the air pushed out of its gargantuan way. It was much cooler in here, even though the corridor was lined with dozens of smokeless torches. The steady light illuminated a long narrow passageway whose walls, ceiling, and floor were completely covered with painted scenes of solemn ceremonies attended by endless hordes of worshippers lovingly offering tribute to whatever was down the passageway.

The far end was open, the golden doors spread wide, inviting entrance. Walking at a steady pace, Moonfeather could almost taste the mana in here, it was so thick. She felt invigorated, almost giddy and fought the feelings down. Another test. Remember, dignity, always fragging dignity!

Beyond the doors was a single massive chamber larger than any sports arena, the vaunted ceiling stretching out of sight. The floor was covered with thick rugs and piled with plump cushions. The interior walls were mirrors, reflecting everything. Prominent in the exact center—and somehow she knew it was the precise and exact center—was a tiered rise of jade, framed by statues of brawny humans holding aloft a golden bower edged with sparkling jewels. Sprawled almost bonelessly on a silken divan in near obscene comfort was a large tan cougar. Although the creature purred in pleasure, the black tip of its tail was a metronome of impatience. Only the overly large eyes watching her minutely showed startlingly human expression. It was Cat.

"Little one, I do not like to be kept waiting," throated Cat, giving a long slow blink of welcome.

"I did not know I was expected," said Moonfeather honestly.

"My followers should think ahead of the now." Cat hunched her shoulders as if preparing to pounce, then relaxed and tilted her head. "However, you are forgiven. When you struck that hougan and left My mark upon him, that was very good. His kind had no fear of me, now they do. I am pleased."

"Thank you, I—"

"You wish a favor?" Emerald eyes narrowed and widened. "You have not asked of me for many years. Yet you always boast of my songs, tell of my power, and wear my marks. Even when it endangers your life. Your request is granted."

Moonfeather was stunned. So easy? Words filled her thoughts, but she forced herself quiet. Here was the game. Don't ask for two things when offered one. Don't ask for what cannot be given. Magic had limits.

"Beloved mother, sister of the night, please touch me . . ." She shook her head and began again. "Show me a song to summon an ocean spirit to banish the storm."

Cat purred louder and gave a smile. With a sigh, Moonfeather knew she'd asked correctly. As the storm departed, so would the serpent. Teaching her could have taken hours or days, depending on how attentive she was. Showing her was much faster, and time had nearly run out. Cat only gave what was asked. It was part of the game. Without rules to secretly break there was no point to life itself.

Leaping from the divan, the great feline padded close to

Moonfeather and rubbed her stiff whiskers against the palm of her hand. Moonfeather stopped herself from stroking the head or scratching the ears as she had not been invited to touch the Old Mother.

Another purr, deeper, almost a rumble.

"You may touch," said Cat, circling the woman.

Moonfeather tenderly stroked the velvety fur, feeling a sensual pleasure at the contact. After a few moments, she stopped, although she ached to touch her totem more. Rising to stand on her hind legs, Cat rested both massive paws on Moonfeather's shoulders, their eyes centimeters apart. Moonfeather tried her best to show no fear, but she felt her reverence tinged with impatience. Deadly black claws slid out from the soft pads and Moonfeather felt her skin pricked by the needle-sharp points, but said nothing. There was nothing to say, this was Cat. Implacable as the wind. You did not argue or cajole, but accepted whatever was offered. Pain or pleasure. Life or death.

"Ah, wisdom at last. You are no longer a kit," throated Cat, releasing the woman. Reverently, Moonfeather blinked once slowly and purred under the praise.

Sitting on her haunches, long tail wrapped around her on the floor, Cat licked her paws with a rough tongue, and the claws retracted.

"A song of summoning, little sister? Very well, listen and learn." Cat began to croon, a low melody of tranquillity. It steadily grew in complexity and power, and Moonfeather followed as best she could, trying to remember the song for herself. From outside the pyramid, she could hear the silvery bells ring louder and louder, until the noise shook the structure like primordial thunder.

With a deafening boom, sheet lightning crashed among the thunderheads in the boiling sky. In the open doorway of the bridge, Delphia stopped firing at the leeches when a missile whooshed by close overhead. Backing away, one arm held before his face, he cursed as the leviathan snake twisted out of the way at the last moment and the missile disappeared into the churning sea.

"Close! Try again!" he shouted at Silver, as the ship plowed through a turbulent swell. The craft was tossed upward, then paused in midair for a breathless moment, before crashing back down into the yawning trough. Delphia grabbed a stanchion near the doorway with both hands, losing the SCK 100 as it happened again. On the bow, the fat ork cook screamed and was gone.

A red light flashed on the bridge control board. "Gods almighty, it's over! We're done for, matey!" shouted the captain, his dark face contorting with effort as he fought the stubborn wheel.

The Manhunter slapped into his wet hand as Delphia turned to look at him. "What are you talking about, man!"

"The stabilizers are gone! We're helpless at the mercy of the storm!"

Delphia's jaw dropped. "We're helpless?"

Her body motionless as a statue, Silver's fingers raced over the old controls of the bridge console as if she was playing a silent piano.

Tightening its grip about the ship as another wave battered the little craft, the snake went motionless and a snarling Thumbs attacked with a vengeance. But the deck underfoot was slick with the rain, and once more he nearly lost his balance and went into the roiling sea, only the nylon rope keeping him secured.

Lightning illuminated the world as Thumbs charged and rammed his blades through the scales and deep into the soft flesh underneath. The noise of the storm was eclipsed by the scream from the serpent as Thumbs twisted his arm about and yanked, pulling out a plug of flesh larger than a soybeef roast. The whole ship shook as the beast trembled from the wound. Another fiery dart lanced by, but the serpent batted it with its neck, and the missile hit the hoist near the cargo hatch. The detonation blew a dozen sailors to fiery pieces.

Blood gushing from the hole in its torso, the sea serpent swung its gigantic head toward Thumbs, jaw wide, rows of fangs exposed, its open gullet filling his universe.

"Scrag you, worm!" screamed Thumbs, rearing back his arm for another slash when a scintillating rod of destruction sliced through the deafening storm. A burning rainbow rod of blinding intensity that vaporized the tips of his blades and struck the beast just behind the flared fins on its thick neck. Deck metal crunched, as the snake screamed in shock and pain, a fountain of pale blood gushing from the gaping wound.

Thumbs staggered in shock, staring at the slagged tips of

the cyberware jutting less then five millimeters from his forearm. His blades were gone above the wrist, his skin red and blistered from the passing of the deadly beam.

"My blades!" he screamed in shock and rage. "My fragging blades!" He switched off his reflexes with a quick flick of his tongue.

Its scales rattling, the snake's squeal of anguish climbed higher and higher. The leeches swarmed over its thrashing form, trying to stanch the pumping wound with their own bodies. The energy beam struck again, but only vaporized leeches as countless more coated the serpent as a living shield.

Firing his Mossberg, a trembling Thumbs fell against the chain railing. Delphia holstered his own weapon and was just grabbing a bloody Crusader chattergun from a corpse when Moonfeather pushed him aside and walked boldly out into the storm. As if on cue, the winds died sharply and the waves ceased crashing so violently across the bow of the battered ship.

As the rain noticeably slowed, twice more shimmering stilettos of energy stabbed at the beast, killing only leeches. Stumbling over the bodies and wreckage, Moonfeather charged insanely at the snake. Bounding onto the twisted ruins of the cargo crane, she took a deep breath and jumped.

She hit the snake's body hard, gasping at the impact. Frantically grabbing the sharp scales with her bare hands, she forced herself to concentrate. Out of her hands came a bolt of electricity that she focused directly into the pulsating hole. Instantly, the reptilian flesh turned yellow and large blisters full of virulent white puss began to form. The sea beast doubled over in agony, jaw agape, its eyes fully dilated in unbearable pain.

"What the . . . she's insane!" screamed Captain Villiers.

"We all are!" shouted Delphia, the muzzle of his appropriated weapon searching for an opportunity to shoot.

At the console, Silver smiled.

Releasing the scales, Moonfeather dropped to the littered deck and rolled away from the writhing snake, seeking protective cover underneath a smashed storage locker. The moment she was clear, the last Amsterdam rocketed from the ship's battery, slamming directly into the open mouth of the heaving beast. A strident fireball removed its head com-

pletely, hot gobbets of flesh and shrapnel peppering the sur-
viving crew members in a gloriously grisly spray. The whole
tremendous length of the serpent shuddered so hard it
seemed as if the ship had run aground.

Once more the laser stabbed through the quieting storm,
slicing the serpent off at the prow. In limp pieces, the
metabeast slid off the *Esmeralda* into the choppy sea, the
leeches now wildly burrowing into the dying body of their
former host.

Struggling to his feet, Thumbs smiled wearily. "Just like
on the streets," he said. "Get stupid, get dead. Nice to know
some things never change."

"A-men," said Moonfeather weakly. Thumbs shuffled
over to the wreckage as the thinning gray clouds overhead
gloriously parted and sweet sunlight bathed the battleground.

"Alert," said the voice of Silver over the PA, and the
searing ray appeared again, dimmer in the spreading areas of
sunlight. At the console, Silver recoiled as if physically
struck. Shaking uncontrollably, she started to sway and Delphia rushed over to catch the woman before she fell.

"You okay?" he asked, setting her in the navigator's chair.
Silver's trembling hand reached for her temple, and Delphia
gently eased the cable out. As it came free, she stopped
shaking and went limp.

"Whoever that weapon belongs to must have thought we
still had some missiles."

Captain Villiers strode onto the promenade and raised
Zeist trinoculars to his face, sweeping the ocean.

"Cap'n, waddaya see?" called out a troll bosun, bloody
and battered, a broken axe in hand.

"Black shape in the water at a klick!" Villiers adjusted the
focus. "A raft, no, it's a sub! Got a lot of radio antennas . . ."
He lowered the trinoculars. "Antennas, my hoop, those are
gun batteries!"

"An escort?" asked a hopeful sailor, holding a busted arm
close to his chest.

"Aztlan?" asked another from the bloody crowd.

"Fragging drek, no," said Villiers, stuffing the trinoculars
into their holster on the promenade. "Those're pirates, and
they're coming our way!"

The beam stabbed in from the distance again, neatly
taking off the *Esmeralda*'s radio array and radar.

"That, my friends, is definitely a laser," stated Delphia.

Silver was in shock. "But that's impossible in such a large-scale weapon."

"I guess someone made one possible and decided to bestow it on a gang of pirates."

"Red alert!" boomed an ensign, touching his throat as the PA system repeated his words throughout the ship. "All hands prepare to repel boarders!" Resembling badly risen zombies, the crew shuffled out to different locations, kicking dead leeches overboard and picking up dropped weapons.

"Laser guns," said Silver, still shaken. "What the frag next, two-headed moon men?"

18

Near total darkness and a drekload of acoustical padding completely surrounded the bodies of Silver, Thumbs, Delphia, and Moonfeather. They were stuffed into a packing crate along with weapons, air canisters, food, medkits, halogen gas tanks, a hydraulic jack, and other assorted equipment. And it was jammed into this crate that they planned to get themselves aboard the pirate ship. Cargo was, after all, what the pirates were after.

"Why did the pirates save the Emmy from the snake?" whispered Silver, stuffed between Thumbs and the side of the crate. "Because they wanted the ship intact?"

"Probably," muttered Thumbs, endlessly rubbing his right forearm.

"But they've got a submarine. Why not just recover the cargo from the sea bottom?" asked Moonfeather softly. "Or is the pressure too great?"

"Squash you flatter than a pancake," Delphia said.

"I don't like hiding," grumbled Silver petulantly.

"You'd enjoy getting sold into white slavery even less," said Moonfeather. "It's better to geek yourself than be taken alive for the leatherlovers."

"So we kill with impunity," said Delphia calmly. "Lone Star may be corrupt and bastards, but they're essentially police officers. Pirates, on the other hand, are fair game."

"Natch."

"Thumbs, is that your foot in my hip or a rifle stock?" grunted Moonfeather, shifting about.

Fingers the size of dinner sausages checked. "Air tank. I'll gladly trade ya for the nice ammo box up my ass."

"Boxes have sharp corners. I'll stay with the smooth round tank, thank you."

A mountainous leather shrug. "Hey, never hurts to ask."

"Ssssh!" hissed Silver, placing an ear to the soft material lining the inside of the crate. "Listen. Can you hear?"

An assortment of muffled sounds followed.

"No gunfire or explosions," offered Thumbs.

"Hai," agreed Delphia. "With us gone, the rest of the crew has probably surrendered. I hear that's what most of them do when boarded by pirates."

"Feel kinda bad about not fighting," rumbled on Thumbs, scratching his chin on his knees. The whole team had gone to get Delphia and Silver immediately after Moonfeather finished off the sea serpent, and they'd headed directly for the hold. The whole point of signing on with the cargo ships was so that sooner or later they'd run into some pirates, and they'd held this plan in readiness.

Moonfeather breathed. "Our contract says we fight until reasonably unable to save the cargo, the ship, or the crew. The crew coming last."

He gave a low snarl. "Naturally. Typical corp drek. Even if El Segundo Lines was only a local company. Eh, gunsel?"

Delphia disagreed. "No, it is a logical clause. Nobody but a fool would agree to fight to the death over something they don't care about."

"Talk on the Matrix says most pirates will leave the crew alive if they don't fight too hard," said Silver. "If you ruthlessly kill every crew, the next group would fight to their freaking deaths against you. Leave 'em alive—"

An interruption from outside, a heavy thump and an odd ratcheting noise. "Maybe even slip them some nuyen. And the next time, nobody fights—"

"Quiet," Delphia hissed. The noises were louder now.

Though the sounds were muffled by the thick walls of their packing crate, the four could almost hear conversations. Something, or somebody banged on the side of their crate, followed by an odd mechanical noise, which stopped, then came again. Moonfeather questioningly tapped Delphia on the shoulder and he shrugged. A rumbling crash sounded from overhead along with the clatter of heavy chains.

"It's working!" whispered Silver in barely controlled excitement, "Welcome to the pirate express, when you positively, absolutely, have to get on their ship overnight."

Delphia gingerly rechecked the clip in his Manhunter. Moonfeather closed her eyes and crossed her arms.

The clatter stopped for a moment. Abruptly the crate

moved, halted, moved again. Then it rotated about in a circle and there came the muffled noises of creaking ropes and winches chugging. Bouncing like child's piñata, they went up, up, up, and paused. For a while they swung back and forth.

Silver ran a fingertip along the hair-thin edge of their escape hatch. Not a glimmer of outside light showed around the trap door in the side of the crate. The seal was perfect. Shouts came, more chains, and they began to descend. More ropes and chains. Next a steady rumbling noise, then silence.

"Are we in the submarine?" asked Thumbs as softly as he could.

"Moonfeather?" asked Delphia, shaking her.

Roused from her nap, Moonfeather yawned. "What? Are we there?"

"Please go and see."

Mumbling an affirmative, she took a deep breath and went very still.

Moonfeather stepped out of her meat body and floated amid the equipment inside the jam-packed crate. Invisible to ordinary vision, she drifted past the material boundaries of the container and emerged into a much larger area.

The floor was perforated like a grill, the walls sloped in curves, and the ceiling was an array of panels held in place by plastic togs. All of the crates from the *Esmeralda* marked as military chips and machine parts on the manifest were here, but none of the barrels of crude oil. Several boxes had been levered open, the plastifoam strewn about as the pirates took inventory of the booty. Only the runners' crate was untouched.

Amused, Moonfeather ran an astral digit along the huge fluorescent label: "Experimental chips. Danger. Halogen gas refrigerant packing. Do not open for inspection unless in Class Four sterile laboratory conditions." She knew experimental chips would be worth a fortune on the black market, especially to the Mafia, tongs, or yakuza, who were always desperate to get their hands on state-of-the-art booty.

"And the dumb gleebs bought it," Moonfeather smirked in satisfaction.

Curses and laughter in the outside corridor caught her attention, and she moved through the bulkheads to see a good-looking adolescent male in a flimsy robe being hauled along in chains, the nude woman chained to him meekly following. So they did take slaves.

Then she spied a familiar box full of cans on a shelf. Jamaican Mountain Blue fine ground, her coffee! All of it! The utter and complete bastards. The pirates would pay for that transgression. She drifted about a bit, looked here and there, making a few mental notes. When satisfied, she returned to the crate and stepped back in, slipping into her meat body as if donning some comfortable old clothes.

Moonfeather opened her eyes. "Guards everywhere doing inventory," she announced. "They took some prisoners and stole my fragging coffee."

Delphia slid on his sunglasses and looked at her directly in the dark. "All of it? Good. Something for us to drink in celebration after we're done."

"Coffee?" said Thumbs. "I love real coffee. Haven't had any since I was a kid. Where'd it come from?"

Moonfeather smiled at him. "Surprise!"

"Ouch!" said Silver, testing her blackjack by swatting it onto her hand.

"Ouch?" asked Thumbs in concern.

"Ah . . . splinter," replied Silver.

"In a macroplas crate?"

"Tell me about the exits," said Delphia.

Moonfeather pulled a small pocket secretary from a bag at her waist. She unfolded the palm-sized flatscreen and started doodling on the luminescent display. "Main door . . . sorry, main hatchway is over here. Side, port, no, starboard, aw, drek. The right-side door is here by the hoist controls. Small personal storage lockers over here. Equipment and hoists etcetera, over here. They have the crates and macroplas containers laid out in nice neat rows, lashed down tight. Very tidy for wavejockeys who eat their own young."

"Arms?"

"Every guard has a holstered pistol and a cybergun."

"All of them?"

"Yes."

"Motherfragger. Everybody be careful if one of them tries to raise his hands in surrender. Any vidcams?"

"Two. Opposite corners."

"Excellent. Silver?"

Reaching above her head, Silver found a small valve, eased off the lock, and gave the handle a quarter turn.

The cargo-hold hatchway, a half-meter thickness of layered metals and duraplas, undogged with an oily series of clangs, and swung open ponderously upon counter-weighted hinges. Billowing clouds of blue-gray mist filled the cargo hold, masking everything.

"Bloody hell," cursed the First Mate bitterly. "Must be the halogen gas coolant. That experimental box musta sprung a leak!"

"Aye, First," agreed Cargo Guard, chewing a bit of seasoned soybeef like a plug of tobacco. "Ta captain will be furious less we plug it. Prototype chips could be our biggest haul ever!"

"Don't I know it, squint," she growled. "If it goes wrong, you'll take the fall."

The Chief Guard said nothing, but gestured to the younger crewman standing aft the big door. The newbie nodded at his section chief. "Should we go topside and vent this stuff, sir?"

"No need," answered First Mate. "Come on, bring a number nine patch kit and some duct tape. That'll fix bugger all." Hands outstretched to feel her way, she shuffled into the cool swirling clouds, carefully placing one foot ahead of the other. "Halogen won't kill you, 'less ya breathe a lot of it for a long time. We'll be done in tick."

She disappeared from view into the mist, and as the others found the requested items, they carefully joined her.

"Whaddaya mean, fifteen?" demanded Captain suspiciously.

"We keep sending people down into the hold, but they don't come out," repeated Chief Cargo Guard. "We even used SCUBA and they still don't come back."

"An' it took you this long to tell me?" Captain roared, spittle flying from his bearded mouth.

Chief Guard did not flinch or wipe his face. "Did our best to fix it without bothering you, sir."

"First concurred with the plan, sir," added Spanner, the pockets of his greasy coveralls bulging with tools and chip-readers.

Captain growled at the news.

"Maybe it's poison gas," suggested Sonar. Massive

headphones covered his ears and a cord ran from his console to the datajack in his temple.

Everybody shivered. Poison gas was the oldest death for submariners, and the most feared. Bust a wall at the big depths and the pressure killed you before you even knew it. Slam! You're paté. Fast and painless. They all knew the horror stories from World War Two back in the pre-Awakened days. Those old boats used nickel-lead batteries for power when they were under, and didn't have reserve air to feed their massive diesel motors. If the hull got a leak and sea water hit the plates, it formed chlorine gas and whole crews died in screaming agony, skin bleached white as ghosts.

"Shut up, Sonar," snapped Captain, and the man flinched. "Second, close all internal hatches!"

"Aye, sir!"

Captain assumed his chair near the map table. "We're going to vent that hold now! Emergency stop!"

"Emergency stop, sir," repeated Navigator formally. The great submersible slowed to a gentle halt. Not a dish rattled in the galley, not a stylus rolled off a console.

"Zero bubble, level ascent, blow all tanks, surface crash, now!"

"Aye-aye, Skipper. Express to the roof!"

Feeling oddly like an elevator, the floor rose underneath the crew, driving them ever upward. Then lights began turning red all over the status board.

"Internal hatches unlocked and opening, sir!" called out Chief of the Boat.

Captain glared at the man. "Impossible, COB! Override and close them!"

Hands racing over the controls, COB said, "Can't, sir. Something's stopping me."

"A short from the gas?" asked Sonar, just as a thick, billowing cloud of blue-gray smoke poured into the bridge, completely hiding the hatchway.

"Close that fragging hatch!" bellowed Captain furiously.

"Aye, sir," snapped Gunner, and taking a deep breath, she charged into the thick swirling mist. A spray of her blood came back first, then the woman stumbled out, both hands clutching her neck. Her throat was gone, red blood pumping out from a huge ghastly wound.

"What the fragging hell?"

"It's a mutiny!"

"Red alert!" boomed Captain, drawing his pistol. "Security, intruder defense goes on . . . now. Code Romeo-niner-alpha!"

Silence from the intercom. Dead silence.

"No response from security, engine room, the galley," said Communications. "Slot me, skip, the whole boat is off line!"

Then, from out of the cloud, a knife came swooping through the air to slam between the eyes of Sonar. He went limp in his chair. There followed a series of soft chugs, and now the rest of the bridge crew also began to spurt blood and drop in their tracks. In mere seconds, Captain was alone on the bridge.

Galvanized into action, he raced for the map table, firing blindly into the cloud. Ricochets zinged everywhere. Clawing at the table, he ripped off a macroplas cover, exposing a small control array. He jabbed a finger toward the sensor plate, but his hand was stopped in midair by the massive grip of a troll in a fringed vest.

"Surprise," said Thumbs, lifting the norm into the air as if he was a child. "We win."

His wrist crushed, Captain let the pistol fall from his hand. Twisting about furiously, he finally just fired his cybergun. The small-caliber round went through the ceiling panels and did not ricochet. Thumbs grinned in victory, and the pirate kicked him in the chest with no appreciable effect.

Enraged, Captain loudly hissed like a bad impression of steam radiator, and twin steel fangs long as pencils jutted from his upper gums, tiny drops of a clear fluid glistening on the needle tips. Horrified, Thumbs released one hand and used it to fast-punch the pirate as hard as he could. Captain flew across the bridge to smack into the bulkhead and then drop to the deck limp as a ragdoll.

As Delphia, Silver, and Moonfeather emerged from the smoky mist, somebody leapt out from under a console and charged, swinging a monofilament knife in a practice arc. The blade whizzed centimeters from Silver's face. She whipped out her shock baton and Delphia leveled his silenced Manhunter, but Thumbs stepped between his fellow runners and the charging pirate. Ducking low, he kicked the man in the groin with the flat, not the point, of his boot. As the pirate tumbled, gasping and pale, Thumbs thumped him once gently on the head. Groaning, the norm sank, then tried to rise again, his palm outstretched. Thumbs kicked the pirate in the face with his boot and the norm collapsed twitching on the grisly deck.

"Why'd you leave him alive?" asked Delphia, checking the rest of the bridge crew. Down the corridor came the grisly sound of exploding heads.

"IronHell told me to," Thumbs said, really, really loud, pointing at his own head, and then the pirates.

Nodding in understanding, Delphia asked a silent question and Thumbs pointed at the crumpled norm. "IronHell needs him alive," he said theatrically.

Moonfeather turned the man over to see. "Yes, the rigger is okay," she said. Removing a necklace, Moonfeather laid it on the man and stood up. "He can't hurt us now, nor can the bomb."

"Smart move leaving him alive," whispered Delphia, moving away from the rigger anyway. Thumbs gave him a wink and a nod.

Under the consoles and behind the map table, the heads of the slain crew started to regularly explode.

"Jesus, Buddah, and Zeus, am I glad this thing has a grilled floor," said Thumbs, slipping a little. "This is disgusting!"

"And that's fourteen here," announced Silver, toeing the fallen captain with her gore-streaked shoe. "According to the manifest, that's the lot of the . . . mutineers against IronHell. The ship is ours."

"Boat," corrected Delphia, coolly removing the silencer from his Manhunter. "They call it a boat."

"Anybody know why?" asked Moonfeather.

"Unknown," said Silver, taking a seat at the Security console and jacking into the submarine's operating system. She tested the keyboard with some taps. "But the first submersible ever built was a converted rowboat. So perhaps it stuck."

Lifting a bit of bone from a dead pirate, Moonfeather pocketed the grisly item and shrugged. "Yeah, maybe."

A tendril of wafting mist obscuring his features, Delphia asked, "Silver, can you vent this smoke out of here, please."

"Null perspiration." After a few ticks, a soft whirring noise permeated the bridge and the cloud noticeably thinned, taking a lot of the stink of the dead crew with it. Cool, fresh sea breezes wafted about. Then there came an unexpected banging and clanging sound. A steady rhythmic noise like a rain of hard hail.

"More exploding heads?" asked Thumbs, glancing about unsure.

Sonar went bang, followed by COB, and then Captain.

"That's an exploding pirate. The other noise is from outside," said Moonfeather, glancing upward and wiping off a wet cheek.

"Activate the monitors," said Delphia, looking around, Manhunter back in hand. "Screens, windows, whatever the frag they're called. Activate the view screens!"

Pursing her lips, Silver nodded, her fingers moving awkwardly over the unfamiliar console. "Drek, this is a mess. Odd design, very old and reworked by some tech on drugs." Daintily, she pressed a sticky red button. "I have no idea what I'm seeing. You all seem to forget I'm a decker, not a fraggin' rigger!"

"Can you do it?" asked Thumbs, towering over her.

Every screen surrounding the bridge flickered into life, clearing into a panoramic view of the ocean around them. "There are only so many commands," Silver said slowly. "This one has View Screens On."

The choppy Atlantic Ocean was shown on four different screens, the dying squall moving away in an easterly direction. North was clear, as was the south and west. Some birds in the far distance, but that was it.

"No sign of the *Esmeralda*," Silver reported. "Low-level radar shows clear."

"It's been a couple of hours, and from what we know, the pirates rarely stick around after looting," Delphia said, studying the horizons. "And the storm is way the way over there. So what's that weird noise?"

"Fish?" suggested Thumbs.

"Jets!" said Moonfeather, pointing a hand at the western screen.

High in the corner of the view screen, almost off-camera, were three tiny shapes hovering in the air, motionless black birds with swept-back wings as if struggling against a powerful wind. The water below them was turbulent, nearly roiling. Lights sparkled from their noses. The rattling on the hull of the submarine continue nonstop.

"Eagles!" identified Thumbs. "Aztlan patrol!"

"Thank Yomi, no missiles yet," said Delphia, nervously holstering his gun and drawing it again. Slap-slap. "Those jump-jets can trash this can in a tick."

"They must think we're pirates!" growled Moonfeather.

Thumbs rapped a hull with a knuckle. "Lady, we ARE pirates!"

"Drek!" Delphia moved to a control console, staring helplessly at the array of buttons, switches, dials, levers, knobs, jackports, meters, telltales, and indicators. "This is a technophile's wetdream. How can anybody run this thing? *Eta gaijin* motherfragging pirate hoopheads ... Silver, get us out of here!"

Thumbs went over to the weapons console, touching this and moving that, proceeding with extreme care and achieving nothing.

"Outrace a military jump-jet?" scoffed Moonfeather.

Delphia motioned. "Straight down will do. A hundred meters and nothing they've got can touch us. Water is almost as good as dirt for stopping bullets."

"That would be artic if I could, but I'm sorry to tell you I can't," announced Silver over her shoulder. "The rigger setup is too tight, too specific. I can't override it. Only that guy can get us out of here!"

Sprawled by the map table, the rigger lay limply on the filthy deck, bubbling with every ragged breath.

"Moonfeather, heal him!" ordered Delphia, pointing at the pirate with his Manhunter for no sane reason.

"Gimme room," she said, kneeling alongside the man. "Cat! His jaw is busted into pieces. Even when that dumbhoop troll tries to take 'em alive, he still hits like a freaking express train."

"Thanks," said Thumbs, flipping a switch. A whole row of lights came on, and as he touched one, they went out again.

"Can you do it?" Delphia demanded.

Moonfeather laid a glowing hand on his face and the bubbling slowed, but didn't stop. "Yes, given time."

"Done." Delphia spun about on his toes in martial arts stance. "Silver!"

"Yeah?"

"Send them our surrender. Full and unconditional."

19

In the cockpit of the wing position Eagle, a young officer touched his ear, then his throat. "Spike to Hot Dog. Sir, I'm receiving a surrender request."

"Did not copy." Hot Dog adjusted the gain on his helmet radio while staring at the pirate sub in the middle of a freaky cloud bank. As protective covering, it was laughable. "Come again? They're asking to surrender?"

"What cojones!" sneered Sky Dancer, glaring through the tiny cockpit windows of the third jump-jet. "Let's toast these muchachos and glide, Capitán."

Touching the joystick, Spike put a burst of his nose guns into the waterline. The anti-personnel rounds did no appreciable damage. "Correction, Sky Dancer. They are surrendering to us."

"Hot bulldrek. Hot bulldrek on toast."

"Maybe we've hurt the ship with the Victories?"

Watching the stream of their 10mm rounds take paint off the submarine's conning tower, Hot Dog was not swayed. "Boat," he corrected. "And I don't know, compañero. I've seen 'em sink from machine gun fire, the old ones anyway. The pressure and temperature of the deep sea make their armor brittle as glass over the decades. Some of them are only held together by mana, not rivets. But surrender?"

"We sure they're pirates?"

"Got a skull and crossbones on the conning tower. What else could they be, Free Masons?"

A barked laugh. "Point taken. Sí, tell 'em to send the captain and rigger out in sixty or else we launch the Hellfires."

"Sir? We going to waste Hellfires on a sub?"

Another burst. "Don't be tonto. Of course not. We'll use Stingrays. But you always threaten with your big stick."

"Understood, wing commander. I'll relay the message."

* * *

Silver spoke without moving, "They're giving us sixty seconds or else."

"Not enough," said Moonfeather, her hands shimmering over the supine pirate. "He's not conscious yet."

"I'll give 'em or else," snarled Thumbs. The controls were unfamiliar to him, but the basic operation seemed similar to any defense console. And thankfully, the switches and buttons were clearly marked. Made sense because it would be all too easy to flip the wrong switch in the heat of battle and get the crew geeked instead of the enemy. So everything was clearly labeled to try and keep friendly-fire accidents to a min. Cross hairs formed on the screen, and an indicator showed that the accumulators were fully powered. "Main gun is ready!"

"Great," said Delphia, sliding into the captain's chair. "What is it?"

"Let's find out," said Thumbs, and he pressed the stud.

A shimmering, multicolored beam of coherent light lanced out from off-screen and missed the foremost hovering jump-jet by the thickness of a coat of paint. The heat flash of the beam's passage through the atmosphere caused severe turbulence, and the fighter wavered, wobbling to recover its balance. Thumbs fired again, and the Eagle silently formed a fireball of truly impressive proportions. "Got one. I got one," said Thumbs.

"Hey! The other two are backing off," announced Silver, watching the radar screen.

"Getting combat room," corrected Delphia grimly. "They'll be back in half a tick."

"So I'll zap 'em again," smirked Thumbs. He beamed in pleasure at the console. "Here I am with my hands on the trigger of an Ares Firelance, and my mother said I'd never amount to anything."

A low moan came from the sprawled rigger, his face no longer an imprint of the troll's boot. "Kill the lights," snapped Moonfeather, stepping away from the norm. "He's coming around."

Struggling back to consciousness, Rigger saw that the bridge was black, only the emergency chemical lights dimly showing vague forms here and there. The air smelled fresh, with only faint lingering traces of that weird mist and death.

"Wazhappened?" asked Rigger. "Cap?"

"We're under attack by Aztlan jump-jets," said a muffled voice in the darkness. "Get us the frag out of here or we're all meat for Davy!"

"Firelance?" he asked as somebody really big helped him to the navicom.

"It's damaged," said the gruff voice. Sluggishly, Rigger grabbed hold of the control surface at the main board and started boosting systems.

"Dive, damn ya. Dive!"

Rigger slumped into the seat and grabbed the controls. The pattern of lights radically changed to indicate rigger control, but that was all.

"Well?" barked the figure in the captain's chair.

"You're not the captain," said Rigger coldly.

A tense tick passed, then the lights snapped on. Rigger saw a troll and three norms: two women, one guy. All of them had weapons not pointing in his direction.

"No I'm not," the norm in the suit admitted. "We're a snatch team. Your captain was going rogue, so we geeked your crew and took the sub for ourselves."

"Would have done you too," the troll chimed in from behind the map table. "But our own rigger got cracked in the takeover."

"Bloody smeg," Rigger said. "So you swabs're in complete control?"

"Yes," said a woman's voice over the ceiling speakers.

Rigger flinched. "A decker, eh?"

The black-haired woman sitting at the navicom paused to wave a hand briefly. "So, okay, who's outside?"

"Aztlan Eagle with a major hard-on for this ship," said the redhead in the tiger-stripe leotard.

"Boat," Rigger said, his face hard and determined. "And how the frag do I know any of this is the pure quill?"

"We're from IronHell," said the guy in the skipper's chair.

He gave a sneer. "Good enough. I'm Rigger."

"I'm Delphia."

"Thumbs."

"Moonfeather."

"Silver," said the decker, then as the radar screen began to beep more incessantly, "they're coming back!"

"Dive, motherfragger!" shouted Delphia. "Now!"

"Aye, aye. Down we go!" Klaxons sounded over the vessel, announcing a crash dive. Swirling water flowed past the multiple screens of the *Manta* and daylight was replaced by the greenish hue of the upper levels of the ocean. What sounded like hard rain or hail peppered the conning tower.

"Brace for evasive maneuvers," announced Rigger. The perforated deck tilted as the submarine angled off in the sea, moving to port, slowing and then accelerating to starboard. The sea went dark, then became grass-green, emerald, jade, brown, and finally black as the vessel plunged deeper.

"One hundred meters," croaked Silver, a silhouette from the rainbow lights of the control board. Instantly, a sizzling hiss sounded from the built-in speakers of the sonar console, followed by a deep thrum.

"Missile," said Silver, as a dull boom shook the sub.

The hissing came again, closer. Then further away.

Manhunter in hand, Delphia walked from one wall of controls to the other in a few steps. "They seem to be firing blindly."

"Thank the gods for small favors," noted Thumbs wryly, powering down the Firelance.

"D-directions?" asked Rigger, slurring the word a bit. He found it necessary to squint and keep moving further away from, then closer to, the board.

"You okay?" asked Thumbs.

"On l-line and cooking."

Delphia grunted. "Head for home, but go deep."

"Aye, aye, sir."

A barrage of pings sounded from the sonar board. "Incoming!"

"Odd, doesn't sound like a missile," Rigger said, tilting his head.

"Some sort of canister, or barrel," said Silver.

Thumbs rumbled, "Depth charges?"

"Could be."

Ever darkening, the rectangular views of the sea ringed the bridge. Beautiful, endless. On the aft monitor were two sinking canisters, discernible by the trail of air bubbles each left to the surface.

"Where the frag are the aft torpedoes?" demanded Thumbs, a hint of anxiety tinging his voice.

"The *Manta* doesn't have any."

"No rear torps?" sputtered Thumbs. "But that's stupid!"

"I agree," stated Rigger, commanding the engines to maximum speed. The shaft bearings on the main rod were starting to overheat, but that was just too damn bad. Whatever those canister were, they had trouble with a capital T written all over 'em.

"However, it does not alter the reality that we don't have any."

"Drek!"

In precise mirror movements of each other, the two canisters reached the 300-meter depth and both burst apart in globular explosions. Darting out of the force bubbles came two sleek needles riding fiery exhaust cones.

"Underwater missiles?" squeaked Thumbs. "B-b-b-but that's impossible! Can't be done!"

"Go tell them that," snapped Moonfeather, both hands clenching the arms of her appropriated chair.

"Bull. No missile exhaust will work underwater."

"Yes, it can," said Delphia softly. "Because there it is."

The aft screens showed the things as black dots surrounded by a halo of savage fire.

"Range, two thousand meters," announced Silver. "Blast! Radio waves won't travel underwater. I can't even try to seize control of them."

"Gertrude," said Rigger in explanation, redlining the engines to emergency status.

"What? Huh?"

"Later. Bilge, look at 'em travel! Never seen anything move like that underwater."

"Rigger, top speed of the sub, please," said Delphia calmly.

"Nothing faster in the sea," boasted Rigger proudly, puffing his chest. "Sixty-five klicks per hour!"

Moonfeather snorted in contempt. "My Suzuki scooter is faster!"

"But it doesn't weigh five kilotons," said Thumbs.

Delphia ignored them. "Speed of the Azzie missiles?"

"Two hundred klicks," Rigger said, astonished. He boosted the ship's computer to double check the figures coming from the defense CDP. But the integers were solid.

"Two hundred," he repeated, looking sick. "They're too damn fast for the old *Manta*! We're dead meat on a stick. Davy, here we come!"

"Can we lighten the load for more speed?" asked Thumbs, swiveling his chair.

"Throw stuff in their path, make them explode prematurely?"

"Not without opening the main cargo hatches, which would effectively slow our speed to zero for a couple of minutes," answered Silver. "A tactic not highly recommended for continued existence."

Thumbs sighed. "Been nice knowing ya, Silver."

Thrusting out a hand, Silver flashed a smile at the troll. "Been nice running with you, chummer."

"I'll save you a seat in hell, amiga."

Oblivious to them, Moonfeather had by now spread her arms wide and begun to sing. The words were inarticulate, merely soft crooning noises, and then she began to slap her hands as a backbeat, bracelets tinkling. The music was rough, but as if in response, the sub lurched forward and half the instrument boards flashed bright red.

"What the frag is she doing?" demanded Rigger. Then he added, "Whatever it is, don't let her stop!"

"Speed, one hundred forty knots!" shouted Silver. "No, one forty-five, no, one forty-eight. Way to go, Cat!"

Delphia stroked his moustache as if it could help increase their velocity. "Engine status," he demanded. "Can they take the awful pressure?"

"Turbines have dropped to nineten thousand rpms."

"Dropped?"

"How is this possible?" asked Thumbs, intently watching the missiles. "They're still coming, but a frag of a lot slower."

"External pressure on the side of our hull is nineteen tons per square centimeter," read off Rigger, speaking carefully. Goddamn, his jaw really hurt.

"Pressure on the front of the hull is fifteen psi," finished Silver. "That's air pressure."

"She summoned a water elemental to move the ocean out of our way," said Delphia, smiling at the crooning shaman, who seemed to be in another world just then. "Would only have to do it for a meter or so, maybe less."

"A traveling pocket of air that we endlessly charge into," smirked Thumbs. "Mega arctic. Ice IV."

Silver added, "More important, it's working."

"Yes and no," said Rigger, feeling a wave of weakness wash over him. Nerves or reaction from his beating, it made no difference now. "Moon lady bought us time, but that's it. Ya see, if those things are Interceptors, they'll have fantastic speed but only for very short ranges. Distance sacrificed for max velocity."

"Great!"

He went on. "However, if those are HKs, hunter/killers, they may be holding back to try to force us to show them where our home base is, then they cut loose with their full speed and pierce our hull like it was cheap origami."

"Which?" demanded Delphia, clenched fists in his lap. "How will we know?"

Concentrating on his console, Rigger shrugged. "When we die, or live."

"Any armor on the sub?" asked Thumbs, rubbing his forearm.

"Sure. Forty millimeters of the best around. Outer armor is forty millimeters flexible impact alloy, cushioning wall half-meter of power cells, inner hull fifteen millimeters beryllium steelloy composition."

A tusky grin. "Hey, sounds good to me!"

"Are you saying that we can survive a direct hit?" asked Delphia.

Coaxing the engines back to maximum, Rigger actually laughed. "Survive a hit? Zero reality. Don't you swabs know anything about subs?"

"Know enough to seize this one," snarled Thumbs.

"No offense meant. However, even normal torps could toast a boat this size if they hit. Motherfragging nasty things, some sort of gelatin, epoxy, thermite combo."

"Underwater napalm?"

"Dunno. But it clings to anything hit like it was alive and peaks at 2k Kelvin."

"That's the temp of the sun!" said Thumbs.

A shrug. "If you say so. I'm no techie, just a rigger."

"Must be a thermitic reaction," declared Silver, eyelids closed, chemical formulas scrolling on the screens of the console. "Salt water would actually feed the chemical reaction, not slow it down."

"Accepted," snapped Delphia, watching the missiles creep ever closer and closer. "So what can stop it if they hit?"

"Nothing in science or magic can do that," stated Silver. "Thermite is a one hundred abso-fragging-lutely unstoppable chemical reaction."

"Nothing? So if those thing hit . . ."

"We die. End of trans."

20

High above Miami, Emile Ceccion dropped his silver spoon with a clatter and started to choke on his clear soup. Managing somehow to swallow the boullion, he gasped for air like a fish out of water. *Merde!* Breathe, he couldn't breathe! The air before him swam and filled with the image of other elves dying for lack of air. They lay sprawled like winter leaves on the ruined streets of the sprawl. Many held wands or fetishes, and all had a strip of red cloth tied about their left arm. A symbol? A badge? Then even as he watched they crumbled into dust.

Mon dieu! Heart pounding, Emile called out to his familiar under the table. Grand yipped in response, startling Emile so violently that he jerked forward in his chair, nearly tumbling out onto the plush carpeted floor of the penthouse.

With ragged breaths, he gratefully drew in lungful after lungful of cool sweet air, the environmental systems of the Gunderson Corporation tower having done their job of removing every trace of pollution from the ambient air of Miami. Soon, his vision cleared of the horrid nightmare, and Emile stumbled from the dining room table to the gleaming white lavatory and splashed mineral water on his face and neck. The back of his mind still echoed with the vision of his people dead and dying. Shattering like broken glass. How many had there been? Four, six?

Emile closed his eyes for a moment as Grand leapt from the floor onto his shoulder, and nuzzled his master's cheek. His sight swept through the fourteen rooms of his spacious penthouse and out beyond the steelalloy-plated walls and bullet-proof Armorlite windows. All was well, his home safe. His watcher spirits kept their vigil against physical or magical threats.

What was this horror that dogged his thoughts? Was it some vision, a dire warning . . . oh, what nonsense. It was just a stupid daydream. His mind had been wandering. On the other hand, this might be what came of drinking red wine with fowl. His mother would have beaten him for such a gross practice. Propriety with food was as important as wearing the proper clothing.

Opening the medicine cabinet with calmer hands, Emile found a prescription bottle and took several draughts. He had work to do in six hours and needed to be well rested. He kept his toff doss and vaunted position in the corporate world because he was very good at the work he did: corporate defense, industrial espionage, debugging, wards, and so on, services vital to any major corporation. Gunderson was a mid-sized multi-conglomerate, specializing in transportation, inventory systems, and external security. TGC was solid in its slot and secure in the business of helping other corporations do their business. Maybe that was why they weren't as ruthless as most. At least, not to the best of his knowledge.

Feeling much better, Emile walked calmly back to his dinner, even though it was midafternoon. Like many mages, he was not on a set schedule, except during a business emergency. How different was this place than his home in Paris. Warm and sunny, with its kilometers of beaches and the smell of the sea. He loved the ocean in all of its myriad moods. Stormy, calm, seductive, playful, it was like visiting a favorite lover, ever new, ever familiar.

The memory of salt water brought a nano flash of panic, but the draughts were taking effect and soon Emile was preternaturally calm and continued on with his dinner. The steak Dion was delicious, the Waldorf salad superb. During the dessert, which he shared with Grand, he was suddenly struck with the exact number of dead and dying elves in his momentary flight of imagination. Twelve. There were twelve of them. Odd, eh? A mystic number.

Ducking in through the open hatchway, Delphia burst back onto the bridge of the *Manta*, hastily buttoning his fly. "What happened? What's the situation?"

Thumbs did not turn from studying the main view screen of the weapons console. Everything was peaceful and quiet in the sea around them. "It was awful. The missiles hit and we blew to pieces."

"Then sharks ate us," laughed Moonfeather at the security station.

Plugged into the navicom, Silver shook her head slightly at the callous banter.

"Those were interceptor missiles," Rigger explained. "They ran out of power and simply dropped away. We're safe."

"No sign of pursuit. Or trouble?"

"Clean as a politician's conscience."

Delphia took his place in the captain's chair. "Excellent."

"By the way, where did you dash off too in such a . . . oh, never mind." Thumbs spotted the bit of T-shirt sticking out of the norm's hastily sealed trousers. "Barn door."

Delphia was confused for a tick, then smiled in embarrassment and took care of the matter. "Sorry, but the call of nature does not await convenience."

"For thirty minutes?" admonished Thumbs, tying a bandanna over his gang tats in pirate fashion. "Fall in afterward?"

"In spite of all the study on seacraft we've been doing while riding the waves these last weeks, I was completely unprepared for the bathroom . . . I mean, the head." Delphia gestured vaguely. "It was like trying to relieve yourself in a nuclear reactor! I had to read the instruction panel twice just to get the lid up!"

The submarine slowed around them as Rigger removed his hands from the console. "But you did flush correctly?" he asked urgently. "And properly seal off valves nineteen through thirty-five in reverse order, then open the main negative flow pipes?"

"Most assuredly," Delphia assured him coolly. "And I dogged the hatch and checked the sensors before repressurizing."

"Good."

"Are they all like this?" Delphia asked.

"Sure. And we call them heads."

"Hmm. Most annoying."

"Agreed."

Thumbs arched an eyebrow. "Are you two making this drek up?"

Rigger spun about in his chair to face him directly. "Ah . . ."

"Thumbs," the troll told him.

"Right. Thumbs, there's no machine more complex on a submersible than the head. Or more deadly."

"Deadly?" laughed Silver, attaching the Fuchi 8 to the navicom console. "A killer toilet?"

"Oh, dis I gotta hear," said Thumbs curiously.

Rigger scowled irritably. "Look, lubbers, you can't have a chem toilet on board. Thirty people using one head for a month? The storage tank would have to be bigger than the cargo hold, and the stink—" He waved the air as if dismissing a remembered odor. "You don't want to know about the smell. Suffice it to say, flush toilets are the only way to go. And with external pressures sometimes exceeding fifteen tons per square meter, the water could explode out of the pipes like a Juggernaut, cutting the boat in half. To get the job done, and not risk sinking the boat, the operator needs to carefully access secondary seals, pressurize the bowl, trim the safeties, and on and on." To their confused expressions, he added, "A lot of submarines were lost due to improper use of primitive bathrooms in the preAwakened world."

Standing, Delphia nudged a corpse with his shoe. "As fascinating as all this is, let's get this meat below before we start smelling like a slaughterhouse in summer."

In short order, the dead were hauled to the bilge and slid unceremoniously into the ballast tanks. Rigger told them algae would dispose of the bodies within a day or two. Standard procedure. After tromping back to the bridge, they all reassumed their earlier positions.

"Can this thing cruise for awhile without your guidance?" asked Delphia, reclaiming his chair.

Removing his hands, Rigger rotated his chair. "Simple. It will go straight until it hits something or runs out of fuel in nine more months."

"*Hai.* We need to talk biz for a tick."

"Download me," said Rigger.

"Bottom line, we've got the sub, but can't operate it with our own rigger gone. Also we don't know as much about subs as you."

"So, in short, you can't kill me," Rigger said. The next instant shining steel was under his chin, the beating of the blood in his veins forcing flesh against the razor-sharp blade with painful sharpness. A ruby-red drop formed on the edge and trickled down Rigger's neck, disappearing into his shirt.

"Wrong," said Thumbs removing the knife. "You're meat anytime the Big D says so. You scan?"

Touching his neck, Rigger's hand came away smeared with red. "I scan."

"Good."

Unperturbed, Delphia went on, "Of course, you can ram us into an underwater mesa when we're asleep. So, how about signing on with our crew as First Hat."

"I thought that was First Mate," muttered Moonfeather.

"When it's official, he's First Mate, pro tem it's First Hat."

Rigger chewed his lip and scratched his head. "XO sounds good to me. Would have taken me a decade to get that far under the old Captain."

"A real bastard, eh?"

"Yar."

Instantly, the Manhunter was in Delphia's hand. Rigger gasped in shock. "I am too," Delphia told him, holstering the gun. "We're on a special run. Not the usual thing. The haul will be big." He looked at the others and after a tick they nodded yes. "I offer you an equal share. A full fifth of the haul."

"XO and a fifth of the booty?" Rigger ran a finger behind his ear. He displayed the dry digit to the others. "Fair enough, Skip. What're we after?"

"Silver?"

Having prepared for this ploy back on the *Esmeralda,* Silver shoved an optical chip into a slot on the control board, and the main screen displayed a map of the world. "Almost fifty years ago, just before the return of magic, the Jappers built a supersubmarine called the *Emperor Yamato.* It carried every bit of advanced technology of the day. And was supposed to be unstoppable, the ultimate war machine."

A long, low whistle from the rigger. "I heard of it. Thought it was a fable. Like Atlantis or the Flying Dutchman."

"Oh, no, it was very real." She paused. "It also sunk one day."

"Why?"

She shrugged. "Nobody knows. But we've got a rough location." Silver changed chips for one showing the floor of the ocean. "Lost military tech. You tell us how much that's worth. On the market, or off."

"Done and done. I'm in," Rigger said, smiling.

Satisfied, Delphia stood and walked over to the pirate. "Good." He stood alongside the man and read the name tag on his shirt pocket. "Is Rigger your real handle?"

"Huh? No, 'course not. That's my position and job."

"Change it. We use street names."

"Never heard of a pirate doing that."

"New captain, new rules. You copy?"

"Tone and bars, Cap."

Delphia nodded in satisfaction. "Now show me what this tin can is capable of."

Silent, Chief Captain stood before the window, marshalling his thoughts. Dressed in casual clothes chosen for comfort, not appearances, he was trim and well muscled, with the physique of a trained athlete rather than a stevedore or laborer. His hands were badly scarred, but well manicured, which would have told a lot to any trained observer, which the small norm holding the chipboard in the middle of the executive office was.

Beyond the thick Armorlite windows was a vista, an expanse of wrecked ships, vessels of all kinds, surface ships and all manner of submarines. Barnacles and coral added colorful touches to the mass of gray paint and rusty hulls, as huge schools of brilliant fish darted among the sea-going ruins.

Turning from the observation window, Chief Captain clasped his clean hands behind his back. "And what exactly the fragging hell do you mean we lost a sub, you brain-dead, hoopkissing gleeb?" he screamed in fury.

Executive Yeoman noisily cleared his throat. "Well, sir, I . . . that is . . . we . . ."

"Well?" roared Chief Captain, slamming a fist against his desk, splintering the valuable antique wood. "Was it sunk? Stolen by privateers? Destroyed in a storm? Torn to bits by magic?"

"Boat Number Sixty-five got caught in a storm, killed a snake, looted a cargo ship, then simply went off the air," reported Yeoman quickly. "There are unsubstantiated reports from our people in Atlantic Security of an attack by a wing of Aztlan Eagles."

"And one of our subs didn't get off a single volley?" Chief

Captain scoffed. "Not likely, unless the whole crew was already visiting Davy."

"Our thoughts exactly in Tactical, sir."

"Hmm. Might be rogues. Unless Old Dome is trying something again. Honorless zombies. Which sub, by the way?"

The name was already highlighted on his chipboard. "The *Manta*, sir. Formerly the *Gahanna Girl*."

"Julius Romy, eh? Might be a mutiny then. No love lost between him and his crew. It was the man's greatest flaw. A commander has to be hard to inspire discipline, but not so hard his men lose their fear of death."

"Truly a narrow line to walk, sir," agreed Yeoman.

"Shuddup," snapped Chief Captain. "Clear my schedule for the rest of the day. I want a full meeting of the entire council within the hour. And that includes Port Captain and Attack Fleet Captain. Understood?"

"Aye, sir." A pause, followed by a diplomatic cough. "And if perhaps Attack Fleet Captain is, ahem, busy, sir? Indisposed, as it were?"

"Then call the brothel guards, put the drunkard in chains, and haul his hoop into the council chambers. Along with his First Mate. Maybe we should make her the damn captain. What's her name again?"

"Her real name, Chief Captain?"

"Yar."

Executive Yeoman quickly checked the board's flatscreen readout. "I.R. Helen, sir."

Chief Captain snorted. "Damn funny her ending up down here with a moniker like that."

Taking a seat, he pulled a portacomp closer to him on the desk and began to scroll through some supply reports. "Iron-Hell takes care of its own," he said softly, as if repeating a daily oath.

"The *Manta* is ours, and we'll get her back. Even if I have to send out my whole damn fleet to do it!"

21

In a tuxedo and evening cape, Emile Ceccion walked into the main lobby of the Miami Opera House flanked by a pair of trolls in severe hand-tailored Armanté suits of the deepest blue. They stood quietly, relaxed and at ease, while front-door security personnel ran sensors over their employer. The handscanners beeped twice. The guards noted the positions and nature of the devices, then waved the Gunderson mage onward. The trolls received only the most passing inspection and, although the scanners beeped constantly, they were passed into the opera house without comment.

The bodyguards took their employer's cloak and deposited it along with their own elegant ballistic overcoats in the cloak room. The next couple were scanned and forced to check their automatic weapons with Security.

Beyond the entrance, a milling throng of Miami's elite was sipping champagne while talking music and money. The ladies were mostly in formal ball gowns or slash dress displaying everything and hiding nothing. The few exceptions were slim, smiling women whose eyes tracked everybody, talked little, and wore beautiful, but loose garments that gave them great freedom of movement. The gentlemen were locked in the mandatory tuxedos and white ties, only the most minute differences in the fabric and cut indicating which was an inexpensive rental and which a high-ticket import from England, hand-tailored by the acknowledged masters of the tuxedo.

Sculptured ice in the form of the Gunderson corporate logo, the interlocked TCG, cooled a tiered fountain of champagne that poured into a marble basin alive with genetically altered Japanese carp. Smiling servers dressed in pristine white moved ghostlike through the crowd, continuously offering glasses of wine or cold hors d'oeuvres. Set high in alcoves above the patrons were clusters of vidcams whose telephoto lenses swept the assembled faces in programmed curves, scanning for known troublemakers.

From beyond a line of closed doors came the sound of the summer Philharmonic orchestra tuning its instruments. Strolling among the rising young executives, vice presidents, department heads, old money, spouses, escorts, bodyguards, millionaires, and gawking tourists, Emile breathed in the excitement of the evening as if the air itself was rife with mana. He accepted a program book from a liveried norm child standing behind velvet ropes, then beamed in delight as he read.

"Ah, Señor Puccini's *Manon Lescaut!*" he murmured to himself. "Not his greatest, but a favorite of the more discerning connoisseurs of classic opera."

"Sir?" asked one of the trolls, unbuttoning his suit jacket. His hand was always in motion, scratching his stomach, adjusting his tie, straightening the flower in his lapel. Several of the patrons who noticed the activity also recognized it as an ancient samurai trick of constant activity to mask the readiness to draw a weapon instantly. Many moved discreetly away from him.

The other troll simply kept both hands in his lumpy pockets, foregoing subtlety for better response time.

Accepting a glass of chilled champagne, Emile smiled at the towering metahuman, "Nothing, Bertram. I'm just pleased at what's on the program this evening."

"Yes, sir," said the troll impassively, while the other guard tilted his head, apparently listening over his headcom.

"Monsieur Ceccion," he said, not totally successfully with the French pronunciation, "your presence is immediately requested at the Tower, please."

"Indeed?" Emile took a sip from a glass he'd just been served. "On my night off? Who is it?"

Emile, of course, would never have a com unit installed inside his cranium. Any mage worth his salt knew that magic and cyberware were a disastrous mix. Besides, magic offered him abilities that technology could only dream of. While on assignments, he did, however, carry a particularly nasty Fichetti 1mm needler—one with a specially designed oversized clip, a safety installed backward to befuddle anybody trying to use it against him, and a hairtrigger sporting a featherweight half-kilogram pull.

"It's Mr. Harvin," whispered the troll guard urgently, motioning for the exit.

Listening to the orchestra run a few arpeggios, Emile shrugged with Gallic unconcern.

"He says he wants to see you right now."

The CEO of Gunderson wanted to see him? Emile handed his glass away and headed for the exit. He didn't hear it shatter on the floor, so somebody must have taken it from his hand. But he wasn't really paying attention.

The indicator blinked "99" and the elevator doors opened wide with no noise to announce their parting. Emile briskly walked out, leaving his escorts standing on either side of the waiting elevator. It was his own private transport around the Tower for the duration of his stay here.

Crossing the manicured jungle of the foyer, he nodded in friendly passing to the cleaning staff, the guards, and smiled politely to the blonde receptionist. A pretty little norm, tan and bouncy. Emile had scanned her astrally once on a sheer whim and was stunned to discover that she was heavily chromed, with muscles replaced, forearm guns, various cyberblades, and other things that he could not identify. Since then, he always thought of her as Lady Cerberus when he went by.

Passing between some foliage that he knew was artfully tracking his approach, he reached a frosted glass wall extending meters in every direction. The heavy doors swung open with a soft sigh of powerful hydraulics. He was obviously expected.

Emile proceeded through and into the office, where he stood waiting for the doors to close behind him. The huge room was tastefully decorated in a somewhat antique style. Leather couches formed little conversation niches, while two walls of solid windows showed Miami sprawled around the towering home of Gunderson Corporation. Lester Parrish originals hung in illuminated frames on the other two walls, and the desk was a massive slab of cherrywood bigger than a Toyota Elite. An enormous telecom shared a wall with a woodburning fireplace made of tan bricks, the andirons and screen obviously of purest gold.

Over by the bar pouring himself a cognac from a dusty bottle was a powerful, squat man with a military-style flat top crewcut. James J. Harvin.

"Good evening, Mr. Harvin," said Emile with a bow.

"Emile," said Harvin.

Emile walked closer, but kept a polite distance. "Always a pleasure. How may I assist you this evening, Monsieur?"

Harvin swirled the cognac in his glass, inspecting the color. The purest smoky caramel. "We are finding it necessary to reassign you, Emile."

"Indeed? Has there been a problem with my work? I knew that my failure to completely cure your ailment has caused you much distress . . ."

Harvin dismissed that with a grunt. "Nothing like that, Emile. Your performance is exemplary, the best we've ever seen. No, we need your help in rectifying a special problem of great importance to Gunderson."

"An extra-corporate matter?" asked Emile.

Harvin stoppered the 400-year old bottle of cognac. "No, nothing like that Seafront matter. This is an internal problem, but very delicate and extremely dangerous."

Amused, Emile gave a polite little snort and waved a hand at the city twinkling below them. Everything was dangerous in Miami.

James Harvin moved to his desk and sat down behind it. "As per your contract, we will pay you for the additional risks."

Twelve of them. The thought came violently into his mind, and Emile nearly spoke the words aloud. He had difficulty breathing, and a cold clamminess unlike anything he'd ever experienced seemed to permeate his bones.

"Emile?" asked Harvin in concern, a hand reaching for a control panel on the desktop.

"I . . . am fine," Emile said, taking a chair without asking permission. "Merely a headache. Perhaps too much of the good life, no? Hard work may be just the prescription needed. Something different to clear the cobwebs, eh?"

Harvin studied the fluid in his glass once more as if searching for answers, then set it aside untasted. "Yes, Emile, but time is of the essence. You'll leave in the morning, and you will likely be away from Miami for quite awhile."

"May I ask how long, Monsieur?"

"Indeterminate."

Emile gave a small bow. "Whatever is required, Monsieur Harvin. I shall be glad to offer any assistance or service required." As Harvin began to explain to Emile where he was going and why, the mage could not completely shake the sensation that had seized his very soul moments before. It had the taste of death.

On board the *Manta,* it was close to midnight when Silver finished with her work and jacked out of the CDP of the military submarine. She coiled the datacord and tucked it into a pocket of her blouse, then accessed the console-to-console function of her board and started sending messages.

At the map table, Delphia gave a start as words began to scroll across the picture of the Atlantic Ocean. Thumbs at the weapons console did likewise, as did Moonfeather sitting cozily in the captain's chair watching the tiny monitor built into the arm. Rigger at the navicom continued piloting the vessel unaware of the private conversations occurring around him.

I HAVE FINISHED ACCESSING THE ONBOARD FILES, sent Silver in straight test. THERE IS NO MENTION ANYWHERE OF IRONHELL. NOR OF ANY PLACE MARKED A PRIME LOCATION TO RETURN TO IN CASE OF TROUBLE OR FOR SUPPLIES.

At their posts, the other three runners frowned.

SO I LOOKED FOR SOMETHING NOT LISTED IN THE FILES, she continued. AND THERE IT WAS. OR RATHER THERE IT WASN'T. SEVERAL LOCATIONS MARKED AS DEAD ZONES. AREAS NOT TO BE ENTERED UNDER ANY CIRCUMSTANCES.

WYH? mistyped Thumbs.

UNKNOWN.

SO LET'S GO AND SEE, typed Moonfeather slowly.

AGREED, sent Delphia. ANY LOCATION SEEM MORE FORBIDDEN THAN ANOTHER?

NEGATIVE, Silver replied. IT'S A CRAP SHOOT. THEY COULD BE A LOT OF THINGS. SUPPLY RENDEZVOUS POINTS, SECRET REFUELING STATIONS, AMMO DUMPS. OR ANY ONE OF THEM COULD BE THE IRONHELL HQ.

WHAT ABOUT THEIR SHAPES? sent Thumbs, hunting and pecking the keys with one finger. ANY OF THEM PERFECT CIRCLES OR SQUARES OR SUCH?

QUERY? asked Moonfeather.

AN IRREGULAR SHAPE WOULD INDICATE A NATURAL LOCATION SUCH AS A VOLCANO OR

MESA, sent Delphia. BUT A PERFECT SHAPE WOULD DENOTE AN ARBITRARY DESIGNATION.

CHECKING, Silver returned. YES, HERE'S ONE PERFECT CIRCLE, NEAR THE BERMUDA TRENCH.

GOOD, typed Delphia. PLEASE GIVE ME A POINT EXACTLY THROUGH THE MIDDLE OF THE AREA FROM OUR CURRENT LOCATION.

MOMENT. A moment passed. ON BOARD MAP REFERENCE 19.5-4A.

LET'S SEE IF WE CAN GET A RESPONSE FROM OUR PIRATE. "Rigger, we're going to map reference 19.5-4A. Please set a straight course there. No deviations."

"You sure about that?" asked Rigger. Both of his augmented hands were on the steering wheel, while the manual controls on his console constantly moved into different positions without his touching them. "That'll take us awfully close to the war zone."

THE WHAT? typed Thumbs.

Moonfeather sent, WAR ZONE? WHOSE WAR AND WITH WHOM?

BEATS ME, answered Silver. BUT I'LL LOOK FOR ANY ADDITIONAL REFERENCES.

Blanking his screen, Delphia shrugged. "We'll have to chance it. It's a prime location for the *Yamato*."

"As you say, Skip," Rigger responded. "Grid reference 19.5-4A it is, sir."

"Oh, chosen a name yet?"

"Yes." The man gave an embarrassed grin. "Boomer."

"Ah." Delphia went back to scouring the map as he spoke. "As in lowering the boom?"

Rigger hid his annoyance. Didn't these slags know anything? A boomer was slang for a missile ship. What the *Manta* used to be before IronHell tore out her guts and made her a raider instead of a deadly attack sub. From race horse to plow horse with one snip. But all that could change once more when this Delphia cobber was dead, and the boat was Rigger's to command. And he certainly knew better than to believe they were actually searching for the long lost *Emperor Yamato*.

"Exactly, Skip." Boomer grinned. "Exactly."

22

Silent and invisible in the dark waters, the *Manta* hovered over the stygian plain like a black dirigible in endless night. Her running lights were extinguished, the liquid crystal display on the conning tower blanked, the housed propellor beating soft and slow, active sensors off, passive sensors boosted to maximum.

Two thousand meters away, hovering at the same depth, was a small orange submersible about the size of a semi-trailer. It carried the insignia of Gunderson Corporation. Its every light was ablaze, its two mechanical arms extended as if offering an embrace. Fluorescent cables dangled from its open belly, extending all the way down to the ocean floor some three hundred meters below the craft. The ends of the rope were tied off to illuminate mooring assemblies anchored in the rock-hard sand of the seabed. Waddling away from the lines were tiny yellow dots bobbing along in comical slow motion, like bad animation or astronauts walking on the moon.

On the quiet bridge of the *Manta*, Silver adjusted the magnification on the main screen and the view zoomed in closer. The figures were encased in bulky suits of armor resembling yellow spacesuits with smooth louvered sleeves and balloon joints. The armored figures were hauling what appeared to be centuries-old wooden chests into the wreck of a two-masted surface ship lying on its side in the silt, the hull of the sailing ship half hidden by a copse of seaweed. Only tattered streamers remained of the huge canvas masts, and gaping holes dotted its side. But the gilded name of the vessel was still faintly discernible on its aft, below the captain's quarters and along its bow under the mermaid figurehead. That noble wooden protector was still intact among the waters that had long ago claimed her craft and crew.

"The *Santa Cordova*," murmured Delphia. "Spanish. Looks like she got sunk by cannon fire. See those impact holes?"

"You know ships?" asked Boomer in surprise.

"I know explosives," Delphia replied.

"Swell," said Thumbs, sucking a tusk. "Next question, what the frag are they doing?"

Boomer laughed. "They're putting chests of gold into the wreck, what else?"

"Into?" Moonfeather sat upright and studied the screen set above the map table.

It was Delphia who answered. "Dinkers! They're corporate dinkers."

"Sussed," smiled Boomer, adjusting the trim of the boat against the currents.

"Dinkers? Oh, fake antiques," said Silver, baring her teeth. "I get it. Whenever they find a sunken ship hundreds of years old with nothing of value in its hold, they quickly manufacture gold coins and lost treasures, then hide the stuff inside."

Moonfeather grinned as understanding dawned. "Then they 'return' with a vidcrew and record 'discovering' the treasure?" She laughed. "Spirits, that is clever. The base metal is only worth, say, four hundred nuyen a pound on the Tokyo exchange. But as antiques, the coins are a hundred times more valuable!"

"Typical megacorp drek," grumbled Thumbs, rubbing his forearm. "Cheating everybody and making a profit from it."

"What are those things, power armor of some kind?" asked Silver, zooming in on one of the waddling lumps.

Boomer punched a button on his console and a side screen displayed a beginner's tutorial on the equipment. "Jym suits," he told them. "Don't know what the name means. Whatever it originally stood for is long forgotten. They're built to withstand the pressure at the bottom of the ocean."

"Why don't the corp gleebs just send down a sub?" Delphia asked.

"There's not a sub in the world that could go down there," said Boomer. "The pressure would crush us flat as a sand dollar. See?" He pointed at a wall monitor of odd design, a simple dial with a free-swinging needle to indicate external pressure. It was hovering just above a red patch.

"And we're hundreds of meters higher," gulped Thumbs, studying the dial. "I thought that thing was something for the engines. Manifold pressure or some drek like that. Or temperature."

"Engine gauges are over there. And deeper than half a

klick the whole fragging ocean is at zero Celsius. Although no ice forms 'cause of the pressure. No, that gauge shows our external hull pressure. We're currently at five hundred meters, with a static weight of seven hundred kilograms per square centimeter."

Seven keys per centimeter? The runners looked at each other. It was as if they suddenly felt the awful staggering weight of the entire cold ocean pressing in on them from every side.

"Pressure goes up fast down here," said Thumbs, adjusting the strap of the Mossberg hanging across his chest.

"Roughly seven kilos psi every ten meters." Boomer glanced at the quivering indicator needle. "Another hundred meters down and we'll start hearing creaks and groans. Another hundred after that, welded seams split, rivets pop out like caseless rounds, and then it's pancake time."

"Whoa," said Moonfeather, crossing her arms over the bandolier of ammunition she wore. "You mean those divers can go places this sub can't?"

"Absolutely."

She wrinkled her nose. "Bulldrek."

Boomer shrugged. "Something to do with surface area versus displacement. I'm no scientist. Under normal circumstances, the *Manta* here can only descend to a maximum depth of six hundred meters. Jym suits can naturally reach four."

"Thousand?"

"Yar. And that's the bottom. Well, aside from the deeps, like the Trench—don't think that has a bottom."

Delphia worried his moustache. "Most impressive," he said. "Do we have any of those Jym suits?"

"Sure, aft in Storage A, near the conning tower. Got a dozen patched together from spare parts stolen off ships or found in the wreckage of corp fights. Not SOTA by a long shot." Boomer grinned craftily. "On the other hand, they were free."

"Interesting," murmured Delphia. "Purely for exploration and rescue, or do they have any military applications?"

A bitter laugh. "Captain, there ain't nothing on this bucket that doesn't have a military use except the toothpaste."

"Why?" asked Moonfeather pointedly. "What's there to fight about down here? Fishing rights?"

"Got an hour?" snorted Boomer, looking at her reflection in the dark green glass of the deactivated radar screen. "Drek, ocean has more untapped natural resources than all the dry land put together. Oil, coal, diamonds, steel, drugs,

medicine . . . Weird pressure makes alloys tougher and
cheaper than diakote, and there's enough fragging food to
feed the whole freaking world twice over. And more lost
goodies than you can shake a cutlass at. What's down here?
Everything, little biscuit, absolutely everything."

Moonfeather scowled at the epithet, but refrained from
commenting.

"I wonder why there aren't any underwater cities then,"
rumbled Thumbs thoughtfully.

Boomer returned to his board and said nothing.

"Oh, there are," said Silver unexpectedly. She unjacked
and swiveled her chair about. Her Seco lay on the console
behind her. "I've talked online with deckers from dometowns off Seattle and Jersey. Just little places, couple hundred chummers and no more than thirty meters down at the
max. Mostly they do farming and fishing. Tap some oil.

"No, wait," she added, touching her cheek. "There's a big
domecity off the CalFree Zone. Kalamari Incorporated. It's a
hundred or more meters deep and has fifteen thousand folks,
plus. They do genetic research, I think. And fishing, of
course."

"Japan's are much bigger," Delphia said with a note of
pride. "They have at least one farming arcology in the
shallow seas off the main island, with a bubbletown permanently housing its population. I've seen reports from the
Imperial Navy debating the wisdom of such, as the place is
impossible to defend properly. Even with diakote coverings,
a single salvo of armor-piercing torpedoes will destroy the
protective bubble and a billion-nuyen installation is gone."

"Well, we're not going to find any of those down here,"
said Silver, swiveling back to her screens. "If an armored
sub can only reach six hundred, no dometown could possibly
survive the pressure."

"True enough. I've never seen one," said Boomer, not
facing them directly.

Conversation slowed as each person became absorbed in
his or her own thoughts. Then a ventilation fan clicked on
with a whir, making everybody jump.

"Let's go, there's nothing here," said Delphia, hoisting the
Crusader onto one shoulder. "Silver, was this the . . ." He
left the sentence hanging and she shook her head no.
"Boomer, continue on original course and heading."

"Aye, aye," said Boomer, returning his augmented hands

to the control surfaces. The perforated deck below them took on a gentle cant as the *Manta* angled off in a new direction, building speed as the orange submersible dwindled on the aft and port screens.

A hundred klicks away, and six hundred meters straight upward, a rubber life raft bobbed in the low swells of the open sea. The sun was hot overhead and the surface water devoid of any sign of land or other ships to the empty horizon three klicks away in every direction.

There were two occupants, young norms. Both were shoeless and only partially clothed in loose garments, and already flushed red with the beginning of serious sunburns.

"Whaddaya mean, no?" raged Attila at the slave, sitting bolt upright in the dingy. His dirty silk robe was knotted about his waist.

Ruby tugged down her oversized T-shirt and glared at him defiantly. "You may have gotten us off that ship, but I grabbed the water and food and it's mine! Mine, do you hear me? Mine! You can't have any."

"No, you're mine!" he shouted, brandishing a fat barrel flare pistol. "I bought you, and I own you!"

"Own this, jackanape," she said making a gesture.

"You slitch!" screamed Attila as he leveled the flare gun, which she promptly kicked out of his hand. The gun discharged from the impact, sending a sizzling round high into the brilliant daylight sky, where the exploding charge was virtually invisible. The empty gun hit the water way out of reach, and sank instantly.

With a scream of rage, Attila dove forward, going for her throat with both hands. Ruby whipped out her homemade plastic shiv and stabbed for his stomach. He dodged, she missed, and the two collided, cursing and wrestling, food containers splashing into the sea as they fought over possession of the razor-sharp knife in their inflatable rubber raft. Nearby, a shark fin cut the water and began to circle the bouncing dingy. But the two cursing combatants were much too busy to notice the presence of the third killer. Not yet anyway.

Far below the surface of the sea, lunchtime came and went on the *Manta,* with the runners taking turns getting chow, somebody always watching Boomer. During the break, Thumbs readied his Mossberg and checked the brig of the boat to see if there were any guests. But the iron box with its leg irons and wall-mounted neck clamps was empty of guests, alive or dead.

On his way back to the bridge, however, Thumbs did note that all the escape pods were missing. Unless, of course, the ship ... the boat, frag it, simply didn't carry any. Who knew? If cleanliness was any indication, the pirates had been rather lax about maintenance. Then again, logically, even if they survived a wreck or something and got rescued at sea, they might still have their heads explode, so why bother?

It was late afternoon when the *Manta* crested a mountainous ridge and the forward vidcams showed a wild flurry of movement on the plateau below.

"Life, at this depth," breathed Silver, astonished. Her hands moved over her console, activating the disk memory and replaying what they had just seen in slo-mo. As the submarine crested the ridge, there came into view a valley below them with a horde of merrows fighting a huge kraken. As the lights of the *Manta* illuminated the fight, the creatures all darted away.

"Sea is full of it," commented Delphia, polishing his sunglasses with a pocket handkerchief. Both went into a pocket. "But I didn't think either merrow or kraken could go this deep. Guess I was wrong."

"How much further to the center of the target zone?" asked Thumbs, reclining in his chair.

"Just over those mountains," said Silver, hunched forward over the console. Her hands never stopped tapping keys, turning dials, or adjusting the controls. "Range eighty klicks."

Filling the dark bow screen were the faint outlines of an undersea mountain range. The jagged granite peaks registered taller than the Andes.

"High or low, Skip?" asked Boomer, retarding their speed.

"Umm?" asked Delphia. "Oh, ah, keep us low. Can you maneuver through that central pass over there? Between those two jagged peaks?"

"Def. Plenty of room."

As the submarine started forward again, Moonfeather shuddered violently from head to foot. Deathly pale, she gasped out as if in pain, nearly falling from her chair.

"Mother goddess, stop," she pleaded in a strained whisper, as if mortally wounded. "P-please, s-stop the b-b-boat!"

23

Smoothly, the megakiloton *Manta* glided to a complete halt.

"W-what did we just go past?" Moonfeather stammered, hugging herself as if freezing cold.

"Umm? Nothing," reported Silver. She checked her board. "Bare stone below us. Just an empty plain. We're not even close to the foothills of the mountain range yet."

"Empty, my hoop," chattered Moonfeather, going to the aft starboard screen. Only blackness showed. "Go back."

"Why?" asked Thumbs, puzzled.

"Just do it!"

"Skip?" asked Boomer, looking over his shoulder.

Drumming his fingers on the arm rest, Delphia was studying Moonfeather. She was staring at the aft screen intently. Her whole body said she was looking for something she knew was there. "You heard her," he said at last. "Reverse course."

A shrug. "Aye, aye." Slowly, the submarine eased into motion and started the long slow process of backtracking to its earlier position.

"Stop!" cried Moonfeather after a few minutes. Boomer did so. With trembling fingers, she reached out to touch the screen. "There. Can you feel it? Cat, it's big. Huge!"

"What?" asked Delphia, checking the monitors in the arm of his chair. "Thermal is clear, no metal registering, no movement, no magnetism."

"There's nothing there," affirmed Thumbs at weapons. His view screen was black, the sensor panel underneath showing a vector graphic of the area below them. In glowing green outlines was a cartoon seabed, rippled sand dunes, a few copses of hundred-meter-tall kelp, a couple of rocks, some brain coral, and not much more.

"Sonar is clear," added Silver, touching her ear. "Not even any fish in our immediate vicinity."

"No fish?" said Delphia, shaking his head. "That's not right."

She gestured. "See for yourself! There's nothing out there!"

"Something invisible?" demanded Delphia, slipping on his sunglasses. He frowned. "Damn, nothing."

"A magical shield," she confirmed. "Biggest I've ever seen. Ever heard of! Must have taken some hotdrekking mages to create it!"

Twelve.

"Who said that?" barked Moonfeather, whipping around.

"Said what?" demanded Thumbs.

"You okay?" asked Delphia in concern, lowering his glasses.

"Nothing. Forget it. Just nerves, I guess," she said after a tick, and went back to studying the black screen. But she began to hum softly, a wordless song none of them had ever heard.

"This could be the *Yamato*," Boomer said eagerly. "Maybe somebody else found her first and left her protected by magic."

"Get us closer and lower," said Delphia, loosening his necktie. "Z minus one hundred. But go slow. I want elbow room."

"Gotcha, Skip."

Moving in a long slow curve, the submarine adjusted the angle of its hydroplanes to descend to a lower level. Time passed in silence, everybody straining to see whatever was out there on the ring of screens. The *Manta* was coasting at dead slow over the empty vista, every sensor on the trips, sonar beeping steadily when the monitors suddenly winked out and the lights died. Silence engulfed the bridge as the sonar, sensors, ventilation fan, everything stopped working at the same time.

"Trouble," came Silver's voice. "We got trouble."

"Aye, roger that," said Boomer, the clicks of dead buttons being pushed painfully loud in the darkness. "We're dead in the water. Motors off line. We got nothing."

"Starting to drift," said Thumbs, voice tight.

"How can you tell?" asked Delphia.

"I can see just fine. There's plenty of heat in here," he said. "Power's off, but the compass and bubble float are still working. We're . . . five, no, six degrees off plumb and getting worse."

"Caught in a cross current," Boomer reported emotionlessly.

"I can't see drek," Moonfeather complained.

"Chemical lights," said Delphia.

"Nada," said Boomer, releasing the non-functioning controls. "Haven't replaced the ones used up earlier when you sprang your surprise."

"Great. We blow a fuse?"

Swiveling his chair, Boomer turned to face Delphia. "Hey, you tell me. I got thrown off-system when the mains died."

There came a low hum from the captain's chair. "Ah, that's better," said Delphia. "Everything looks okay." There came the sounds of him walking surely across the bridge, his steps going around the periscope.

The deck was canting seriously by now, the angle of degree steadily increasing. Somewhere aft in the boat, something crashed and a loose hatch swung open to slam into the bulkhead with a thunderous boom.

"We're gonna be floating sideways real soon," said Thumbs nervously. "Hey, there's no seat belts!"

"What? Oh, of course not," admonished Boomer. "If we hit something hard enough to throw you out of your seat, the boat's busted to drek and you're already dead."

"Silver, was the current going in the direction of the mountains or the plains?" asked Delphia from the darkness beside her.

She turned toward the sound of his voice. "Sorry. I honestly don't remember."

"Just in case we're heading for the mountains, did anybody think to check the escape pods?" asked Delphia. "Are they in good shape? Do they have air and battery power?"

"They're gone," rumbled Thumbs. "We ain't got one on board."

"All of 'em?" gasped Boomer. "But that means we're trapped!"

"Yar. Unless you wanna walk home."

"So we just sit here?" Moonfeather hissed. "Boomer, do something! You're the expert. It's why we kept your hoop intact, chummer."

"Yeah, I remember," he muttered. His chair squeaked once, and was silent.

Then a spark flashed in the darkness, and a heartbeat later

a hundred lights winked over the boards as they rebooted. The overhead bulbs flickered and strobed back on with full power as the floor gently vibrated from the engines kicking on.

Caught halfway across the bridge, Boomer scowled and returned to his chair. "We're on line," he announced, jacked back into the controls. "Fusion plant at full power. I'm taking us away from that freaky plain."

As the submarine leveled off, Delphia made no direct response as he reclaimed his seat and removed his sunglasses.

"Was that a magical attack?" asked Thumbs, rubbing his forearm nervously.

Exhaling, Moonfeather ran fingers through her hair, brushing it away from her face. "No, that was some sort of technological interference."

"Technological interference?" Silver seemed shocked, and repeated the word. "Technological, eh? Can you do an astral projection to check it out?"

Going back to the map table, Moonfeather barked a laugh. "Against juju like that? Frag you and the horse ya rode in on. Lots more easy ways to get my butt kicked."

"Then how about sending a water elemental to check it over?" asked Delphia. "Or an ally spirit. Don't you have any spirits?"

Moonfeather shook her head and pointed a finger at the view of the empty plains. "I don't want anything to do with that thing!" She shivered again, in spite of the fact that the bridge was a balmy twenty-two degrees Celsius.

"Want some hot soykaf?" offered Thumbs, rising from his chair.

She gave a chattering nod. "Cat, yes. But I'll get it. Thanks."

"Hey, Boomer," said Silver, eyes glued to her screens. "Any chance we're in an especially cold area of the ocean?"

He looked at her quizzically, then checked his board. "Yeah, we are. Smack in the middle of a polar stream. An undersea river that comes straight from the North Pole. Howdyaknow?"

"Technology," she murmured, keying in commands. "Deep underwater, icy-cold area, took us out in a nano. Everything but the batteries. Magically protected by a shield of invisibility. Can't be anything but that . . . What else could it be? Nothing. So there's the answer."

"A coldframe?" said Delphia, incredulous. "Down here, in the middle of nowhere?"

"What better location?" she responded.

"Possible," he mused, stroking his chin. "Unlikely, but possible."

"They're almost always war computers," Silver reminded him. "And combat always generates a lot of heat."

"Nyah, can't be a cold frame," said Thumbs. "Of this size?"

"What size?" asked Delphia. "Damn thing's invisible!"

"Yeah, but the shield seems to cover the whole rocky plain . . . oh, I guess that's just to help hide its location. It wouldn't be no larger than a refrigerator, right? Just a big cube."

Silver studied him carefully. "You know about this stuff?"

"Got a cousin who's a drekhot decker, loves to talk about uniques and specials as if they're bedpartners."

"How many cousins you got?"

"I dunno, fifty, sixty, the usual."

"Lucky you," said Boomer. "What's a coldframe?"

Delphia nodded at Silver, who answered. "It's a computer built to operate on modified electronics. Superconductor wires and circuits that allow electrons to move without hindrance. Only gravity itself slowing them down, and that's barely appreciable."

"And this stuff is faster than maser relays?" Boomer asked. "Drek. Fiber-optics operate at light speed!"

"Don't you believe it, cobber," Silver told him. "Best cables in the world—even Fuchi lab bench stuff—only goes at about ninety percent LS. Cables are never a hundred percent clear, even under perfect conditions, which means distortion and reduced speed. But still a quantum leap faster than the best electronics." She glanced at the plain below. "Till now."

"Why's it called a cold frame?"

"The original superconductor wires wouldn't operate unless chilled to hundreds of degrees below zero. Pretty fragging useless for inner city work. But decker talk says that just before the Awakening some big brains got it up to room temperature. Down here, in this arctic subzero cold water, there'd be no variations of temperature to affect processing. No regular deliveries of liquid nitrogen for competitors to hijack, etcetera, etcetera. A coldframe is delicate and expensive, but will go a million times faster than anything in existence." Silver stroked her deck and closed her eyes. "Ghost, what it must be like to jack into that mother!"

Delphia exchanged glances with Silver. "Maybe."

Keeping his head low, Thumbs stood and advanced to the map table. Pressing buttons, he scrolled and advanced undersea charts across the flat screen. Some of them were hand-drawn from hundreds of years ago, some brand new and bearing the marks of Atlantic Security. None of them showed anything but water in their present location.

"No record of something here that was moved. And this thing musta cost a fragging gazillion nuyen to build," said Thumbs, accelerating the scroll function, maps flashing by at flickering speed. "Had to be somebody strictly major league."

Serenely, the sub continued to circle the suboceanic plain.

"Maybe it's some other pirates," Moonfeather said from the hatchway, a steaming mug cupped to her chest.

Throwing back his head, Boomer laughed heartily. "Sweet Davy, no! Freaking IronHell don't have that kind of nuyen, and neither do any of the others."

"Silver, can we jam this phenomenon—whatever it is they're doing?" Delphia asked.

She pursed her lips in thought. "Maybe. We still had battery power during the blackout. I checked as soon as I could jack in again. But there wasn't enough power to run anything important. It was the fusion reactor that scrammed on us. And I have no idea how they did that little trick."

"So we move on?" asked Boomer, sounding disappointed.

"Leave? Frag, no," whispered Silver, caressing the chrome jack in her temple. "If it's technology, then it has to have a control system. All I have to do is find an access port or locate the fiber-optic cable connecting the coldframe to whatever system it's operating."

"And then?"

"And then I'll go jack into that mother and find out."

"No. Too dangerous," said Delphia. "Any other ideas?"

Fiddling with the controls, Thumbs spoke from the map table. "Perhaps we should damage the machine. Stir up a little mess. See who comes out to repair it."

"And talk to them," said Boomer, grinning. "We got a special room down in the hold, strap-down chair, electrodes, all sorts of toys."

"Silver, can coral live at this depth and temperature?" asked Thumbs, turning off the table and going to a port screen.

It still showed the large clump of pinkish brain coral, all alone in the vasty rocky expanse and receding in the distance.

"No way," she replied. "It's too cold, too deep. They like warm shallows. But storms do break off chunks and send whole reefs off into depths like these."

Thumbs tapped the screen. "Completely undamaged?"

"No," said Delphia excitedly. "And it's the right size too. You twigged it, *omae*. Silver, sweep that coral with the sonar. Let's see if we get a picture of irregular branches or a compact cube."

"Done and done." Her hands moved over the console, and the sonar screen sounded with a single powerful ping. It returned almost instantly. "Cube!" she replied. "We found it!"

"It's beyond the depth the sub can go," Delphia noted. "We'll have to use the Jym suits to get closer. Where are they?"

Boomer was studying the signal image of the cube. "Down aft of the conning, near the portside machine shop."

Suddenly, the sonar was beeping wildly, the pings coming faster and closer together with every tick.

"Holy Davy, red freaking alert!" screamed Boomer, staring horrified at the navicom screen.

"Incoming!" shouted Silver, grabbing hold of her console. "Brace yourselves!" The entire vessel shook as if it had just rammed the world, throwing everybody out of their seats.

"Report!" snapped Delphia, hauling himself upright.

"Did we get hit by a torpedo?" asked Thumbs from the deck.

"No, drek for brains," said Moonfeather. "We're still here, ain't we?"

The *Manta* shook again, more violently, whole sections of the control boards going dark as klaxons sounded.

"Both of those were hits," reported Silver, standing at her console. "We've got a double breech in the engine room. Fusion reactor dying, engines dead." She tapped the controls with a finger. "Something odd here. The internal temperature is down a hundred degrees. How the frag can that be?"

"Down? High explosives should make our internal temp go up, not down," snorted Thumbs.

"It's a Snowball. We're being hit by bloody Snowballs!" shouted Boomer, slapping the panels as if playing the drums. "Reactor to max! Life support to max. Sealing off the . . ." He rattled the controls. They sounded loose and lifeless. "Frag it, they're all dead again!"

Another tremor.

"Hit again!" cried Silver. "Hull breach sectors nine, ten, and eleven. Bilge temperature is at minus four degrees!"

"Boomer, what the frag is happening!" demanded Delphia standing, Crusader cradled in one arm.

"Snowballs! Armor-piercing torps loaded with liquid nitrogen. Kills the crew, saves the ship. A fav tactic of AtSec. Why the frag did you pinpoint it with the sonar, ya stupid slitch? Drek! There's flooding along the main corridor and the cargo hold," Boomer ranted, checking everything on his board. The boat shuddered again. "Propeller is gone, aft section damaged and taking on water. Auto-seals have closed the internal bulkheads, pumps gone." He swiveled about. "We're sinking like a rock."

"Depth at five hundred meters," reported Silver, stuffing the Fuchi into her bag, fiber-optic cables dangling like tails. "Five hundred fifty meters, six hundred, six-fifty . . . a hundred till crush depth!"

"Abandon ship," said Delphia, shouldering the chattergun.

"How?" asked Thumbs, slinging the Mossberg over his neck. "Escape pods are gone."

"Head for the Jym suits!"

As everybody dashed for the hatchway, another tremor shook the submarine, nearly knocking Thumbs over as he frantically typed commands into his console with his over-sized fingers. "There," he grinned, stepping away. "Whoever boards this baby will never know we were here."

"With nobody on the bridge and the bilge filled with corpses?" asked Boomer, moving around him to get to the hatchway and almost slipping in Moonfeather's spilled coffee.

"No prob. I got it covered," said Thumbs grimly, ducking low to make his own sprint through the hatchway. Another shake and the ring of monitors winked out behind them. The *Manta* was blind.

"Covered how?" shouted Delphia, clambering down a metal staircase far ahead of the troll.

Moonfeather was right behind him, followed by Silver gripping her bulky bag, and trying not to bump into anything. Boomer traversed the stairs by grabbing the rails, lifting his boots off the deck and sliding down in practiced ease.

Thumbs simply jumped to the next level, landing in a crouch. "I set the Firelance to fire, full power in ninety seconds."

"Underwater?" screamed Boomer aghast, his breath fogging.

"It'll be a sight to see."

"Yar. From a distance. Let's book."

Creaks and groans sounded from all over the vessel. Struts snapped free from ceiling joyces to lethally swing across corridors like scythes. Hatches popped open randomly, and the lights flickered as the fusion reactor fought to stay on line against the encroaching cold.

Following the others, Thumbs banged his head on a norm-sized hatchway. Blood trickled down his cheek, but he kept going. "I sure hope you had a troll in the crew!" he said, shaking the blood off his face.

"No," Boomer answered, punting down a corridor. "But we once had a really fat ork, and his suit is still here."

"Close enough!"

The *Manta* was starting to list severely as mists crept along the decks, icy crystals forming on bare metal by the time the team reaching the airlocks. A deadly chill was in the atmosphere and getting worse by the tick. Delphia wrapped a pocket handkerchief around the latch, then hauled open the hatchway. Everybody tumbled in, then Boomer slammed it shut. He grabbed gloves from a locker and put them on to spin the locking wheel to seal the portal tight.

The lights were dim in the pressure chamber, the filaments of the bulbs easily visible as the power to them was so low. Lockers lined the bow wall, with dressing benches bolted to the deck before them. Hung on the opposite side were the Jym suits. They lined the bulkhead like overstarched tuxedos, flat black instead of orange like the ones the Gundersons had been wearing. Resembling military power armor, the suits were in two pieces, top and bottom, the waists open. However, the arm and legs were fastened to the bulkhead with chains and one mother of a padlock. Delphia gestured, the Manhunter spoke, and the lock exploded into pieces.

Thumbs dogged his waist seals tight, then punched the

emergency start button clearly marked on his sleeve control panel. The Jym suit came alive with power, lights, and air. Frost was creeping along the bulkheads at an incredible pace, and the thickening mists made it difficult to see as he searched for the keypad to open the huge hinged hatch in the deck.

"Where's the switch?" he shouted, his voice muffled by the thick metal and plastic of his helmet.

"Here," said Boomer clearly from the twin speakers inside each of the helmets. He pressed the keys on the icy pad. Nothing happened. He tried again, and again, with the same result. "The safeties have shorted out!"

"Then we improvise," said Silver, and she flipped the safety latches off with a metal kick. Instantly, the pressure hatch slammed back, indenting the perforated metal floor, the hinges cracking apart. A solid column of water thundered into the room, impacting against the ceiling and punching through the deck above them.

Fascinated by the sight, Moonfeather reached out a gauntlet, and Delphia pulled her arm back. "Don't. The pressure will shear off your hand. Wait for the water to come to us."

Bitter cold began to creep through the bulkheads, ice forming around their suits as the thundering sea water rose to knee depth, waist, chest, and they were finally under. One by one, the runners stepped into the gaping hole and dropped through.

Truly resembling shadows, the ebony Jym suits plummeted through the cold sea, the running lights of the *Manta* wildly splaying about as the hull buckled and writhed like a huge beast dying in anguish. Then a perfect sphere of fire brighter than the sun replaced the submarine. The deafening shock wave brutally shoved the falling Jym suits into the killing depths below as hot shrapnel hissed by in a deadly rain and darkness swallowed them whole.

24

"Here they come again!" cried a sonar operator.

Filling the forward display with gentle majesty were the waving forests of the undersea farms, organized hexacres of crops colored in brilliant hues growing in wild abundance under the powerful lamps of the undersea arcology. And traveling straight in from the west came several pirate submarines, their advance heralded by a fusillade of torpedoes, arcing and spiraling toward the shimmering bubblecity in an ever-expanding cone formation.

"Anti-torpedoes launch, activate countermeasures. Deckers proceed with jamming and whiplash!" ordered the duty officer, using both hands to operate his console. Seated next to him in the command dais was the XO officer. She was slumped in her seat, comely features charred from the electrical explosion of her console. It was caused by a freak overload when an enemy torpedo hit a power relay junction Beyond The Wall.

In fast precision, the amber cross hairs on the screen surrounded each of the enlongated submarines, and the anti-torpedoes streaked away. The tiny needles lanced through the ocean to slam deep into a pirate boat, and then the vessel vanished, engulfed in a globular fireball that expanded, contracted, and was gone.

Outside the mesa, alarms sounded on the streets of the city as the shock wave hit and thousands of tiny cracks appeared over the section of the dome facing the blast. Slowly, the fissures started to close, but water sprayed in through the hairline fissures, knifing through buildings, carving off chunks, and cutting passenger vehicles in half.

In the Command Center, the side screens displayed a hundred bubbling trails crisscrossing in wild patterns as the pirates released anti-anti-torpedoes to counter the city's defense. Made of ceramics and powered by compressed air, the deadhead projectiles were invisible to magnetic sensors, so The Cube master-computer formed vector graphics of the incoming projectiles based on sonar readings; glowing green lines to show the silhouette of an enemy incoming where the passive sensors indicated they should be located. The accuracy of the plotting and graphics was highly doubtful.

Two rumbling explosives blossomed on the horizon and the computer screens as a pair of torpedoes were destroyed. Then the easterly screen went speckled as dozens of pirates in green camouflaged Jym suits were released and disappeared into the farmland of the city. The duty officer cursed. "The pirates never used troops before!"

"Launch salvo of anti-sub limpet mines," the commander snapped. "Needlers, fire at will. Prepare to trigger outlying depth charges."

A chorus of acknowledgments greeted the orders, when an entire panel of controls went dark and an alarm began to howl.

"Another hit," called out the female operator at the damage control console. "Missile strike in Section Ten, breach in Quadrant Four of Old Dome. Explosive decompression in Quadrant Three and Two!"

"Sonar is down," called out the operator at engineering. "Fusion reactor number two is down. Shunting emergency power to back up sonar and the Wall."

With the resurgence of power, the althropic dome over the city closed the hissing cracks faster, but the streets were already flooded in some sectors, with traffic snarling in the outer divisions.

Almost undetectable against the mass of the arcology, a swarm of microscopic dots launched from a battery hidden in the surrounding mountains. Under independent control, the sleek drones curved away at full thrust, a trail of bubbles streaming behind them like a jet's contrail in the atmosphere. Rapidly accelerating at ten . . . fifteen . . . thirty-five knots, the finned bombs dodged around the lamp posts in the farm field to zoom in on the Jym suits amid the greenery. Balls of fire erupted in the cropland, grisly bits of armor and clouds of red blood forming a dense cloud. Needlers, plain steelloy rods with barbed tips stuttered out of nests through pressurized ports, the thousands of quills riddling the Jym suits by the score and detonating incoming torpedoes everywhere.

Then a lone torpedo pierced the defensive barrage and struck the bubblecity dead center on the west side. Fifty tones of diakote and marcoplas glass vaporized instantly, leaving a hole the size of a fist clear through. A stream of water shot out of the puncture, lancing across the city.

One tick later, explosive decompression hit, the dome rupturing from the shock and spiderwebbing cracks for hundreds of meters in every direction. Unstoppable, the ocean poured in through the ever-widening rupture. Clawing at anything, men and women screamed, their bodies banging helplessly against walls as the deluge poured into the city, smashing everything.

Alarms sounded everywhere, from The Cube to Old Dome, and banks of monitors were flashing red in the Command Center.

"Breach in Sector Ninety-four!" cried a technician, frantically throwing switches and levers. "No . . . Sectors Eighty through One-twenty! And on levels eight, seven, and six!"

"Launch everything!" screamed the duty officer, brandishing his fist at the computer screen. Overhead the lights flickered and died. "Motherfragger! They got the fusion plant!"

The sea outside the wounded dome was filled with spheres of fire as drones and torpedoes battled for supremacy. A flash, and a pirate submarine was gone. Another, then a third! Then the roof of the city violently shook as tremendous bombs dropped from out of the dark sea overhead to pound the dome in unrestricted fury. Cracks spread to every quadrant, knives of water roaring in through splintering cracks. A geyser of boiling water shot across the center axis of the city, toppling buildings into the central granite mesa. A thousand death screams were drowned in the titanic roar of the sea unleashed.

A bomb larger than the rest combined hit the top of Old Dome. The five meters of resilient dome material held for no longer than a heartbeat against the blinding fury of the hellish onslaught. The upper city burst apart like a cheap lightbulb, the inhabitants jellied from the stark implosion. The steelloy girders of buildings were driven into the reinforced granite of the central mesa like tent pegs, splitting the rocky edifice to pieces.

The fuel tanks of liquid hydrogen for the fusion generators detonated, sending out a death cloud of shrapnel toward the damaged city below. Overloaded, circuit breakers exploded into molten metal, power relays slagged solid and the superconductor cables heated to the point that they ignited their own fireproof casing. Soon, billowing clouds of poison gas were added to the chaos. Busbars hissed into nonexistence, then the mighty fusion reactors exploded and melted. Gigawatts of stored power were released, and blue lightning crackled over the wounded arcology, setting fires everywhere that were promptly extinguished by the flooding from above and both sides.

More torpedoes arced in through the weakening defenses and struck the dome, embedding in the transparent material, then detonated in unison, the titanic force vectors separating the crack with a screech of tortured glass unheard by any living soul. The physical shock wave rippled along the streets and granite of the central mesa, shaking off chunks of cliff. The main dome split asunder, the remaining atmosphere woofed out as the sea rushed in, carrying with it a million tons of debris and failing bodies. Bridges, buildings, streets collapsed, crushed flat under an avalanche of falling concrete. A hundred unoccupied escape pods launched. Even underwater a chemical fire raged unchecked in Industrial, and the bubbletown went dark.

The pirates fired salvo after salvo of torpedoes into the ruins as bombs dropped from overhead to complete the utter destruction of the trillion-nuyen arcology and its many inhabitants.

The tridscreen went dark and the theatre lights gradually came on to rosy levels. The rows of seats were completely empty except for two patrons, a man and a woman. Both were norms, both elderly, and neither seemed the least bit pleased.

"Pitiful," stated the skinny male slumped in his seat. "Absolutely pitiful."

"Agreed," replied the distinguished woman, sitting alongside. She was lovely but severe in a restrictive dress of formal function. "And that was our best combat simulation so far."

"I can see why you hired me, Ms. Harvin."

"My Miami contacts recommended you highly. Lights, please!"

Instantly, the theatre was illuminated. Turning about in her chair, Barbara Harvin studied the old norm siting near her. Pole-thin, with gray hair and a chromed datajack in his temple, the decker wasn't physically impressive. On the other hand, she could hire all the street muscle ever needed, and it wouldn't do the job. Shawn Wilson could.

"So you agree with my assessment?"

The decker nodded. "Totally. Your people seem to lack the necessary . . . um, non-linear thinking mandatory to defend this type of installation."

"Pirates attack in a straightforward manner, why not? All the advantages are theirs. They're small and mobile, we're large and stationary."

"A single torpedo and the dome is gone."

"Oh, more than just one. Our althropic"—she stumbled over the word—"glass shell is the most resilient material known."

"Radio waves can't travel through salt water," he observed. "How do you communicate with your subs and control the torpedoes?"

"An acoustical phone called a Gertrude. It's limited only by the thickness of the water, compounded by the distance needed and the power of the sonic transmitter."

Wilson rubbed the chrome jack on his forehead. "Like shouting at a car in the wind?"

"Exactly."

He chewed that over. "Bad for your subs. The pirates can hear every command."

"We have a solution for that," she said, but that was all.

Wilson gave a wry smile. "Only one way to shout in public and not have the world understand what you're talking about. Codes."

She nodded. "Changed daily."

"What about cutting off the problem at the source?" Shawn Wilson lit a cigarette. "The dead can't hurt you."

"If we knew the location of the pirate base, it would have been over long ago," said Harvin.

Wilson sent a puff of smoke toward the ceiling as a perfect ring. "You must have already tried capturing one and torturing the location of their main base out of him. What was the name of this gang again? IronHell?"

"Yes, that has also been tried and also failed. The pirates have cerebral bombs surgically planted inside their skulls set to explode if anything happens to them. We believe that the upper echelon do not, but so far it's been impossible to confirm this, much less find and capture one of their leaders."

"Drugs? Hypnosis? Magic?"

"All tried and failed," Harvin said. "Mr. Wilson, if these are the best suggestions you can offer, then perhaps it was a waste of time bringing you here."

"What about infiltration?"

"We already have a very special team working on that particular angle."

"Any progress?"

"Oh, most assuredly. Our contact is incommunicado at the moment, but we expect good news at any time. They are most resourceful." A pause. "Of course we'll never be able to use them again after this."

"Ah, they know too much," Wilson did not state it as a question.

Barbara Harvin stared at him. "Quite the contrary. They know absolutely nothing about what's really going on."

Thoughtfully, Wilson ground out his smoke in an ashtray, and lit another. "How much time have we got?"

"For the moment, all the time you need."

He raised his eyebrows in surprise. "How is that possible?"

"Gunderson currently has an . . . agreement with IronHell. In exchange for leaving the city alone, we provide them with all the food and medical supplies they can carry in ten ships every month. Other times they want money, and sometimes they want ships."

"Expensive."

"Extremely expensive. It cuts our profit margin to the bone. It is, however, necessary for the present."

"Any reason this place is so attractive to them?"

"None to our knowledge. Aside from the obvious fact that they know it's here and can successfully extort supplies and nuyen and ships from us. Only the deep-water location of this city is unique. People have been successfully building underwater cities since the 1970s."

He stared at her.

"Incredible, but true." Harvin took a cigarette case from a pocket of her suit, removed a slim cigarette and puffed it into life. "The difference is that until now the dometowns have always been located in shallow waters. Old Japan and America both tried deep-water cities and failed. So did Brazil, Australia, France, and Russia."

Harvin gestured expansively. "The ruins are still out there somewhere. Secret cities of the dead. A fortune for anybody who ever finds one, figures out why they failed, and brings back the data."

"Interesting."

"However, until confirmed, the reason those primitive arcologies are believed to have failed is thermal inversion. There are rivers of water running through the ocean, some hot, some cold. They shift about and move freely, so there can be a dynamic difference of twenty degrees in ocean water within a mere ten meters. For a dometown a thousand meters tall, the differences can be incredible, and deadly. Mini-fissures are created by the temperature differences. These lead to a general weakening, then cracks and explosive decompression and total dome failure. Millions, and in some cases, billions lost in an eyeblink."

"Then how is it that yours is still standing?"

She inhaled deeply, letting the smoke trickle out her nose. "That information is on a need-to-know basis only."

He took a deep drag on the cigarette, the tip glowing red as a laser sight. "I may need to know," Wilson informed her.

"Demonstrate that, and I shall personally brief you."

Another puff and the cigarette was ground out on the expensive carpet underfoot. "Fair enough."

Harvin rose and started for the exit, trailed by her entourage of guards and aides. "There is a tremendous profit to be made down here from pressure-welding unique alloys, superconductor chips, and the near limitless supply of food for the surface."

"Which you will happily sell to the starving of the world."

"Of course. Gunderson is a business. The ocean is also a pharmaceutical cornucopia of plants with fantastic medical, and even recreational, properties."

Barbara Harvin held out a hand, and a dapper aide proffered a small wooden box. She lifted the lid and drew out a handrolled cigar with a golden band bearing the Gunderson logo. She offered it to Shawn Wilson. "This is deepweed, a prime example of the resources down here. It has much more nicotine than land tobacco, and a good dose of the chemical THC, just like fine Colombian marijuana. The world market potential for such a luxury item is staggering."

With a pocket lighter, Wilson lit the tip and inhaled, lolling the smoke on his tongue like an expert. "Draws like a good Havana," he complimented. "Very mellow."

"Yes, it is very popular in the lower districts." Harvin

watched him puff contentedly on the cigar for a moment, then turned and started along the hallway. "So you see, we desperately need the freedom to harvest the sea without hindrance or interference. The Gunderson Corporation wants those pirates dealt with once and forever."

Continuing along the plush hallway of the theatre lobby, Wilson looked at her over the cigar. "By the way, exactly how do you get staff down here?" he asked. "Not many folks would want to work in a fish tank situated in a warzone."

"Normally, we hire them in gangs through fake ads," Harvin said. "We have many thousand workers at present, but always need more. And if there is a specialist we need and cannot lure here"—she shrugged—"we simply kidnap him."

"Such as mages?"

Barbara scowled at him. "There are no shamans or mages in the city. This is important for us to maintain absolute control. Riggers and deckers we allow because of their tremendous usefulness, and because the dometown is not connected to the world computer grid. With no access to the Matrix, there is little harm a decker can do. And if they're foolish enough to try a run against our coldframe, then the problem solves itself." She smiled at this last.

"If babies are being born, you're going to have mages someday."

"When a child shows the talent, we kill him or her in an accident."

Wilson frowned. "Crude."

"But efficient. It has served us so far."

"No mistakes?"

Barbara Harvin stopped at the elevator, and an aide pressed the button for them. "Only once. And it was also corrected. Although there have been complications from the solution. However, that was before my administration, and such an event will not be allowed to occur again."

With a sigh, the elevators doors parted, and then parted again. Wilson blinked. "Just like an airlock."

"It is one," Harvin informed him. "All major doors to the executive quarters of Old Dome are. For the safety and protection of our people in case of a minor dome leak."

"What do you tell the workers when they want to go home? Pirates again?"

"Oh, no. We control all the submersibles and Jym suits.

Nobody leaves without our consent. Also, upon arrival we give them a medical injection to help their bodies cope with the terrible pressures down here. Actually, it's a powerful narcotic extracted from deepweed and genetically altered. Once administered, the worker must continue to take more of the substance daily for life. If an unauthorized person escaped to the surface, he'd be unconscious within hours, dead in a day without the antidote." She smiled. "Because, you see, they don't even know about the drug. We place it secretly in their food, beer, soymilk, candy, even the free cigars and cigarettes we regularly distribute from quote— manufacturing excess—end quote."

In abject horror, Shawn Wilson dropped the cigar from nerveless fingers. It fell to the floor and lay there smoldering at their feet, slowly dying on the plush carpeting. Nobody made a move to retrieve the item.

"Welcome to Old Dome," said Barbara Harvin, motioning him with a smile into the upholstered corporate cage.

25

Waddling through the ankle-deep silt, the five Jym suits clumsily moved along the bed of the ocean. Thankfully, their underwater armor was in good condition, batteries fully charged, air tanks at max, the DeCamp joints flexing freely, and the heaters toasty warm, although the insides did smell of old beer and sour sweat like a locker room after a game. Operating at the bottom of the sea, the runners had six hours to find some place to recharge both, or die. The suits weighed a good ton apiece and there was no way even magic could float them to the surface. Which gave them only one option.

Every shuffling step of the group puffed up little clouds of silt that settled with amazing speed. The pressure was tremendous, and they all kept a close watch on the quivering needles of the dynamic-tension gauges set with the other controls and meters along the jaw line of each helmet.

With their shoulder-mounted lights off and the sonar deactivated, the black suits were silent invaders into the briny depths. Thermographs, struggling against the polar currents, only offered them vector graphics of the world around them, sketchy green outlines devoid of color or details. It made the whole scene seem unreal. Schools of cartoon fish swam by like the radioactive ghosts of trout long past. Unbelievably, plant life was abundant in the crevices of the flat plain, waving fronds, bushy clumps that shrank inside themselves at their approach, and weird things resembling upsidedown octopi. And crabs, of course.

Silver knew that radio waves couldn't travel through salt water, not at this pressure and temperature. However, the Jym suits carried something called a Gertrude, an acoustical sea phone. The five of them could talk, and it was supposed to be impossible to tell the scrambled sonic signals from natural biological background noise. Or, at least, that was the theory. The darkness compounded with silence was intolerable, so the risk was worth it. Besides, she had other uses for her radio.

"How much further?" asked Thumbs, wheezing slightly, the faceplate of his helmet fogging.

"Decrease your oxygen," snapped Moonfeather. "You're getting too much."

"Thanks," he panted. "Thought I'd need more cause I'm big."

"No."

"Another two, three klicks," said Silver, wiggling an arm free of her sleeve. As it came out, she flexed the limb in the scant confines of her torso area and happily scratched her nose. "The explosion threw us farther away than I thought."

"If you hadn't zapped the sub, it would have sunk and we could have looted the wreckage for air tanks," grumbled Boomer.

"To what end?" asked Delphia, in the lead. "You saw that scout come to look over the blast zone, and then leave. It wasn't a rescue sub. It was a recon looking for survivors to geek."

"Yar? And how do you know that?"

"Their airlock was sealed, torpedo tubes flooded."

A pause. "Oh. Bidamned, you're right."

Easing the fiber-optic cable from her jacket pocket, Silver spoke. "External temperature, minus fifty. We're in the middle of the polar river now. Should be close."

"Gods, I wish we could use the lights!" said Moonfeather.

"Don't!" snapped Boomer. "It'll attract everything alive for klicks. And some of the larger ones will be hungry."

"Or armed."

"Gotcha. Dark it is."

Reaching an arroyo, they circled a copse of kelp stretching upward out of range of their thermographs. Fish darted in and out among the strands of kelp like birds in a tree.

"There it is!" cried Thumbs, gesturing.

Everybody hurried toward him. The clump of brain coral was sitting alone and innocent near the exposed gnarled roots of the kelp. A single squat crab peered out at them like a prisoner from his jail cell window.

Delphia moved around the illusion, hands spread wide. "Don't go near it!" he reminded them sternly. "There will be more defensives. Deadlier ones."

"Natch, kemosabe. What am I, stupid?"

"I can answer that."

"Lick my pud, mage."

"Arc-store it troll."

The group walked around the clump of brain coral at a good distance. The smooth sand seemed primordial, undisturbed for millennia.

"Anything?" asked Moonfeather anxiously, tapping her gauntlet against her forearm controls to up the heat some more, and then further still.

"Over here!" cried Boomer, standing near a crack in the seabed, kicking at the silt. His scuffing had partially exposed a thick cable buried underneath the compressed sand. It led to the brain coral and stretched off toward the north.

"Toward those black mountains," said Silver, her voice echoing slightly in the confines of her helmet. "Odd that we can see them down here," she added softly, sliding the cable into her temple jack. "Should be far out of our range." With awkward fingers, she slid the other end into the communications jack of her radio.

"Thumbs, take point," said Delphia's voice over the Gertrude. "I'll cover the rear."

"And do what?" snorted Thumbs, fists on hips. "These things don't have any external weapons."

"To trip booby traps," said Moonfeather, walking away slowly.

His black helmet nodded, and he started moving off. "Accepted. At least it's a plan."

"Can't you throw a mana bolt or summon something if we get ambushed?" asked Boomer. "Magic should work under water."

"Sure. But through the metal of the suit? No."

"Excuses, excuses," he mumbled.

The land rose and fell before them in flat rippling dunes with dull monotony, the compressed sand providing an easy walk. And the minutes became hours as their battery power and air decreased with lethal regularity. Then they reached an expanse of rolling foothills, a mud swell running between them.

"The cable goes in this end," announced Thumbs, kneeling in the hard silt.

"And comes out over here," said Delphia, unseen. "But the coating on this side of the cable is the kind they use on fiber-optics."

"Vulcanized rubber on this side," added Boomer.

"The junction box," breathed Silver. "Where the EM pulses from the coldframe are converted into maser signals. Nobody uses a combination of the two anymore, not for decades."

"Who cares whether they do or they don't?" stated Boomer urgently. "Let's find out where it goes and get there."

"Careful," warned Delphia. "The swell itself is probably armed and armored against intrusion."

"Hopefully the cable is vulnerable," offered Silver. "Supercomputer or not, it would be useless unless it could get to the data banks of the CDP, and that means terminals of some sort with access ports for inspections, repairs, and diagnostics."

"If you say so."

"Do it, girl. Go find the thing."

Bypassing the mud swell, Silver proceeded around the lump. "Ha! It's a top-hat style. The top is solid, but the bottom is open!" she said. "Maybe to vent off heat or allow the waters to cool the circuits. Whatever, the internal relays are plainly visible."

"Can you jack in?"

Silver opened the control panel of her sleeve and hesitantly started splicing plastic wires to her dead radio. She closed the lid of the service panel to help hold the fibers in place, then reached out and gently pocked the bare ends of the optic cables to the exposed ports of a transmodem. They slid in perfectly. Another triumph of Japanese standardization. She boosted power, activated a shield program, and tentatively attempted to access the data stream.

Silver's mind swirled under the explosion of data and instantaneously she was in, surrounded by a million copies of herself, reversed, backward, and inverted. A hundred datastreams silently thundered by, the lambent rivers of bytes traveling in both directions simultaneously. She reeled under the onslaught of impressions, and struggled to focus her attention on her own hands, the only non-reflective things in sight.

In here, everything was chromate, a billion endless mirrors reflecting in mirrors, in silvered pools of polished lightning. It was like the Matrix boosted on chips, a concept that made her temples throb. A neon aurora in the stainless steel sky, a coded menu shimmered above a reflective collection of nodes and relays. Oddly, the shiny ground under her was slightly dull, not as perfect as the rest of the landscape. Distorted from the minor heat of her presence? How sensitive was this thing? Tentatively, Silver tried moving further in and activating a sophisticated can opener when gray ICE suddenly hit her from every direction in a perfect globe. There was a jarring flash of brief pain.

"Drek!" cried Silver, staggering a bit. "It dumped me!"

"You okay?" asked Delphia, touching her metal shoulder with his gauntlet.

More annoyed than anything, she took a tiny sip of water from the nipple of the bottle inside her helmet. There wasn't much left. "I'll live," she sighed. "And I got inside. But it was too fast, too complex." Her gloves moved in the water trying to show them the polished visions in her mind. "It was wonderful," she whispered. "Beautiful! Ghost, I want to go back right now!"

"So do it," prompted Boomer.

She hung her head, the helmet staying motionless. "It would kill me. It's like breathing pure oxygen or running a V8 on straight nitrous oxide. Sounds great, till everything blows."

"Hey, that's arctic, kid," said Thumbs. "Were you able to get anything at all?"

Slowly, as if laying flowers on the grave of a friend, Silver disconnected the cables from the transmodem in the junction. "Yeah, I found stuff. Nothing direct, but I got a glimpse of the main menu."

"Is it . . . part of what we're after?" asked Boomer. "The *Yamato*?"

"No. It's a war computer, just like we thought."

Delphia threw up his armored arms. "Drek! A toy of some Carib League member? Or does it belong to Atlantic Security itself?"

"Don't know, but it's never been used, except in practice runs. There's no hot file, so that's a lock. And what it's protecting is about sixty klicks due north. Something really, really big."

She smiled even though she knew no one could see her

face. "Something with atmospheric and temperature perimeters suitable for life."

"Yes!" cried Thumbs, doing a slow-motion jig. "We live!"

"If we can travel sixty kilometers in . . . four and half hours," retorted Boomer sourly. "Uphill with no roads."

"Have we got a choice?" inquired Moonfeather, her voice acid sweet.

"No," said Delphia. "Sixty in four, with thirty for getting lost. Cake. Let's go."

He lurched off for the black mountains, the others close behind. As they moved away toward the foothills, an albino crab scuttled out to see if they'd left anything edible in their wake.

26

Cresting an arroyo near the top of the lowest mountain, the five gasping people in Jym suits stopped wheezing and inhaled sharply.

"Slot me!"

"Motherfragger!"

"Aí, carumba!"

"Yes! Thank the gods, yes!"

Towering undersea mountains stood proud and tall to the south, west and distant north of them, a half ring of protective granite rising klicks high into the ocean. To the east was an endless impossible nothingness, a yawning chasm in the ocean floor stretching beyond visibility. A ravine, an abyss larger than the Grand Canyon of the Ute Nation and the Marianas Trench in the Philippines combined. It was like looking over the edge of the universe and straight into hell.

Lamp pots shed brilliant white light on the thousands of hexacres of cultivated fields, with different types of submersibles tending the crops, bringing in harvests, relaying personnel in yellow Jym suits, and hauling about gigantic nets full of fish and crabs.

Dominating the center of the half valley was a double bubble: a large squat dome of transparent material with a smaller round dome set on top, a massive shaft of granite, a mesa, in the center, supporting both like a stalagmite tent pole. Inside the upper dome of clear material could be seen scaffolding and rigging similar to that used on oil fields. The large lower dome was squalid, filled with gray machines, pumps, and what looked like some kind of processing plants. On the ground level was a wall of interlocking granite slabs, thick and tall, ringing the floor of the dome, an inner wall of protection.

"Incredible," breathed Delphia. "Fantastic."

"Salvation," panted Thumbs.

"And how the frag do we get in?" demanded Moonfeather irritably. Boomer grunted a similar sentiment.

Silver pointed. "We'll use the backdoor. Follow me."

A colossal god towered above Old Dome, frowning with impatience.

Rolling up his sleeves, Shawn Wilson narrowed his eyes and stared down at his new domain. The lower level of the undersea bubblecity was mostly machines, storage and repair shops, the few housing complexes made from converted factories that had obviously been destroyed in the fighting. What fighting he didn't know yet, but anyone could see that a major battle, or maybe more than one, had been fought within the confines of the lower dome. And not that long ago, either.

The upper portion of the city was known as Old Dome, the other as Low Dome. Old Dome contained the remnants of what may have been a prototype city, though it was now in ruins.

Chewing on a stylus, Wilson walked around the colony-in-a-crater, studying the details and angles. The place was recreated with amazing exactness in the dynarama on the table. The model filled most of what was called his office here inside The Core, the granite mesa. The papier maché mountains stood at throat level, the undersea farms waving to holograph currents. Wilson gave a signal, and watched intently as pinkie-sized submarines came floating into the space behind the mountains to launch tiny torpedoes, and the city retaliated with a dozen burning lines. The slim lances of fire moving sluggishly outward like burning radio antennas rising from a car.

"Underwater lasers," said a norm in a lab smock, working a pocket computer. "Will those really work, sir?"

Standing in the great abyss, Shawn Wilson bent low to watch how the holograph workers abandoned their harvesting machines to get into the city. The procedure was slow and sloppy, endangering the whole operation. He made a mental note to see they got some practice on how to do an orderly retreat. "Yes, fire a static laser under water, and you get a backblast from the reflection that blows the weapon apart. Yes?"

"Of course," sniffed another of the labcoats.

Wilson didn't know their names yet, and had a feeling he

wouldn't bother to take the trouble. He disliked them already. Dumber than trolls, if such a thing was possible. "Granite. So, instead, start with weak beams, spotter rays like we use on weapons to show where the bullet will go, then gradually increase the power into a pulsating beam flashing through the visible spectrum a million times every tick, and you counter the reflection problem, avoid a thermal backlash, and have an underwater energy weapon."

"The range is fragged," stated another lab coat.

"Slower than drek," added a third.

"Sussed," said Wilson, hands on knees as he watched the holo torps blink out in tiny flashes one by one. "But if the pirates didn't know about such things, their tactics wouldn't include a counter move, and we could tear their fleet apart."

"An edge," he said standing upright and looking over the assemblage of the lab staff. "That's all any good tactician needs. One single advantage and the other side loses."

"What about our submarine fleet, sir?" asked a woman, hands stuffed into her pockets, chewing a pipe. "We have the subs hidden inside the Bermuda Trench. There's a mesa out there just above crush depth. When the pirates arrive, we'll flank them, hit from both sides in a classic pincer movement."

"That's good," Wilson admitted, hoisting a thigh up on the edge of the table. "Very good, in fact. But not good enough."

"If I may ask, why not, sir?"

Wilson scowled. "Because I'd bet they either know about the existence of those subs, or have a strong suspicion. And without the element of total surprise, it's lambs to the slaughter."

"I must respectfully disagree, sir," she said, shifting the pipe stem to the other side of her mouth. "To spend millions installing energy weapons of doubtful function seems wasteful and pointless."

"Tough. I'm in charge." Shawn Wilson smiled thinly. "You don't like it? Talk to Barbara Harvin." Their faces went pale and apologies poured as there came a knock on the door.

"In!" he called, taking the chewed stylus from his mouth and prodding a minuscule fireball to expose the pea-sized tractor inside. "These explode? Who designed this drek, an ork?"

"Mr. Wilson?" said an ork guard, standing there uncertainly.

"That's me," he said, not turning to look. "What is it?"

The metahuman cleared his throat. "Sir, we've just received the report of a submarine detonating near The Cube in the polar plain."

"How unusual. However, why is Reclamation telling me this?" Wilson asked tartly. "Path the sub and add it to our fleet."

"The . . . our asset was not damaged, but recon teams conducting a search for survivors on the surface located two norms in a life raft. Escapees from the pirate sub that was destroyed. They claim there was a mutiny, which is how they escaped."

Turning about, Jake paused and frowned, glaring at the guard in cold formality. "A pirate mutiny? Impossible. They're lying. The cerebral bombs prevent such actions against their leaders."

The guard lowered his voice. "We agree, sir. I have taken it upon my own personal authority, due to the unique elements of their acquisition, to cancel the usual procedures of assimilation and have Security immediately begin their interrogation."

"Good. Tell me when they learn something solid."

"Certainly, sir." As the guard departed, Shawn Wilson turned back to the dynarama table. "Lock'n load, my fellow humans, let's double the number of pirates, add our own sub, and have somebody do a suicide run at the main dome and see that happens then. Chop-chop!"

The massive airlock doors in the granite walls parted with a loud hydraulic hiss, and a small gush of water poured out onto the ferroconcrete floor. Trundling in on rusty rails, the cargo box clanked and rattled through the locks and on deep into the maze of machinery before coming to rest at a padded buffer. The double doors closed with a strident boom and then hissed again, prominent wall gauges showing pressure being reestablished on the other side.

Squealing in protest, the hinged top of the rectangular container separated with an exhale of air, exposing a pile of wiggling fish inside. Instantly, the fish stopped moving as their bodies swelled to double, triple their original size, eyeballs bursting, pale blood pouring from their open mouths and gills. Computerized locks mechanically disengaged, and the container swung over to one side, disgorging its contents in an avalanche of still bodies. Sliding across a meter of floor, the fish disappeared into a funneled chute, bands of laser lights scanning the deluge. The digital readout climbed into the thousands before the appearance of five black Jym suits. Immediately, alarms began to howl.

"Motherfragger!" howled Boomer as they careened along the metallic chute, banging and clanging off the sides as they hurtled along with the cargo of dead sea life.

"Stay loose!" cried Delphia, looking over his boots at the others close behind him.

With brutal impacts, the suits landed sprawling on a conveyor belt covered with still swelling fish. It proceeded to move off with a jerk as skeletal arms reached out from slimy gimbals to neatly align the fish, while a different set of mechanical hands a few meters away began gutting and filleting them.

Struggling to her boots, Silver saw the flashing knives converge on her and raised her arms to protect her face. The whirling blades broke by the dozen against the armor of the Jym suit, the blades careening off to ricochet among the machinery on either side of the moving belt. Proceeding past the broken shredders, the Jym suits were whisked through a thundering curtain of steaming water and came out the other side into bright lights. As their faceplates dripped clear, they saw a score or more of chairs lining the moving belt, a double line of people, norms and metas, young and old, all wearing stained jumpsuits and hairnets, the knives in their hands paused in the act of chopping off the heads and tails. Further down the line, one side was sorting the filleted bodies into different boxes. The other group was separating the heads from the tails onto conveyor belts going in different directions.

A female ork screamed as the ebony Jym suits went past her. A teenage norm followed her lead, and soon the whole area was filled with wildly running people making as much noise as possible. A battered door in a macroplas kiosk flew open, and a fat norm with a frown and a stun baton stepped out.

"Shut the frag up," he bellowed. "I was trying to sleep!" Then he lost both the frown and the baton at the sight of the Jym suits and staggered backward to hit a red button on the wall. Bells started clanging everywhere.

"Pirates!" he shouted. "Attack 'em! Kill them!" Only he was alone by now, everybody else having scrambled for safety long ago.

Jumping to the floor, Delphia snatched a vacant chair and

threw it at the clanging bell, knocking it off the wall. That bell stopped, but others continued elsewhere.

Cursing vehemently, the overweight norm fumbled a Seco into view and fired at them, the flechettes banging ineffectively off the deep-sea armor. Bending low, Thumbs grabbed a knife from the side table and flipped it at the norm. The blade hit the wall alongside his belly, going in to the handle, the plastic cracking for meters in every direction. The norm promptly fainted, sliding to the grimy floor in a heap. A stygian behemoth, Moonfeather leaped off alongside the male, and grabbed the stun baton. Advancing upon the kiosk, she removed the door from the frame and checked inside. "All clear!" she called, tossing the plastic door away.

"Over here! This way!" cried Silver, clambering off the belt, crushing a chair flat as she waddled toward a flight of metal steps leading to an upper-level catwalk.

Bounding up the steps, the metal bending under them like warm taffy, the group charged along the catwalk, the metal framework shaking horribly under their combined tonnage. Delphia yanked open a door, and cleaning supplies tumbled out. Thumbs did the next portal, and a group of people in aprons and hairnets screamed, bunching tighter together in a corner. Moonfeather grabbed the handle of the next door and it came off in her gauntlet. Silver opened the next. "Hallway!"

Piling through, they pounded past a huge machine pumping and hissing, while another complex bit of ironmongery steadily ground what looked like fish guts into a ghastly puree. Huge glass tubes rose on their right sides, filled with colorful liquids constantly churning with endless streams of gaseous bubbles. There was a riveted metal door at the end of the passage clearly marked in ork and norm Authorized Personnel Only. Both a print and a retinal scanner were on the wall alongside. It resembled a bank vault. No passage there.

Delphia stuck two fingers into his mouth and gave a shrill whistle. "Here!" he cried, stepping over the side railing and grabbing hold of a frosty metal pipe. Wrapping his armored legs about the icy length, he slid down and out of sight.

The others followed close behind. Machines and furnaces, floors and catwalks, flashed by until the conduit went through a terrazzo floor a hundred meters later. When Delphia slammed to a halt, he stepped out of the way of the person above him and raced through a zigzag maze of machinery and equipment.

27

The surface of the Atlantic ocean was choppy and rough, the swells cresting to over a meter in height, but the Atlantic Security battleship *Conquistador* was motionless in the water as if nailed into position. Resting his back against the angular armor plating of the portside gun battery, Emile Ceccion stood in a tight-fitting twilled jumpsuit of plain utilitarian gray while enjoying the shade of the triple 200mm cannons of the foredeck.

Idly breaking off pieces of hardtack and feeding the crumbs to Grand on his shoulder, Emile studiously watched the crew in their starched white uniforms finish the preparations with the bow crane of the stationary vessel. Swarms of sailors and officers were triple-checking the connection of a thick hook and massive chain to the hoop on top of a squat, flat-bottom, metal ball, its outside ferruled with bands of steelloy and bulk iron. Roughly five meters across, the bathysphere had a single entrance point, the two oval-shaped doors set on either side of the ball's dense hull facing only millimeters apart. Set along the equator were four tiny portholes whose slabs of Armorlite glass were heavily veined with reinforcing wire filaments. It seemed overly much, but Emile always preferred excess in favor of survival. The awful pressure of the lower depths was not the only known killer down there.

Grand chittered and arched his long back, as if agreeing with his master's thoughts. Emile feed him another chunk of the traditional navy bread, his long blond hair blowing in the wind. Grand accepted the treat in his tiny paws and nibbled greedily on the hard cheese-like bread with obvious delight. Emile knew his companion was an omnivore, but this seemed to be taking the definition to new heights.

"Or is that a new low?" he said aloud. Grand playfully nipped the point of his right ear. "Ouch!" said Emile, pushing him gently away. "Pax, little cub, pax. Here, take the rest."

Holding a piece of hardtack larger than his pointed head, Grand chittered in triumph and began to stuff his bulging cheeks with the greasy-gray foodstuff in unabashed glee.

Set in tandem at the very point of the bow of the ship, located between the forward missile battery, were two huge spindles rolled with cables and pressure hoses. Both lines fed to an even larger spool of cable that connected directly to the ball. From his briefing, Emile knew that these were the life-lines of his transport, designed to keep him comfortably supplied with air and power until reaching his destination: Old Dome, a bubblecity some hundreds of meters below on the bottom of the ocean. He found the concept intriguing. To be that much closer to the very heart of Mother Earth. Licking his stiff whiskers clean, Grand nuzzled his master's cheek with a rumble of contentment.

Stroking the ferret under the chin, Emile saw an ork sailor snap a salute to an officer. The norm male was using a lightpen to check off items on the flatscreen of a pocket computer that was lashed to his belt. Originally, Emile thought the bondage an odd affectation before watching a dwarf gunner trip on a loose rope, which sent the box of clay skeets for the captain's evening shoot flying out of his hands and over the railing into the sea.

Briskly, the officer pocketed the computer and started on his way, the wind tugging on his cap but not succeeding in removing it.

"Hoi! Everything ready, Lieutenant?" Emile asked loudly over the growing easterly winds. According to readouts from the Gunderson Corporation's meteorological satellite, another severe storm was brewing up northward and would be coming this way in short order. Once underwater, he would be safe from the ravages of the hurricane, but the *Conquistador* would bear the full brunt of the tempest as it stayed to lower him to the underwater city nearly two full klicks below the surface. Emile sincerely hoped the ship did not capsize while he was still linked to it. Grand hissed in agreement, his bushy tail lashing about.

"Aye, sir!" called out the officer. "The *Cousteau* is ready whenever you are, sir!"

Gathering the plastic shoulder bag and vine-covered wooden staff at his boots, Emile stolidly crossed the freshly painted deck. An ork ensign held open the outer hatch of the bathysphere for him, the inner hatch already swung out of the way. Stooping, Emile entered the metal ball.

Once inside and upright again, he was surprised to see that the interior of the *Cousteau* was pleasantly upholstered, with velvet walls, plush rugs, and a curved bank of cushioned seats from which seat belts dangled loosely. Off to the side opposite the seats was a stack of crates lashed to the hull with elastic straps. Another hatch was in the center of the floor, the lid locked with a wheel-shaped mechanism. A brief inspection of the equipment crates showed that they were secure and that his personal seals had not been disturbed.

"Any last requests, sir?" asked a lieutenant, one mirror-polished shoe resting halfway on the rim of the hatch.

"Such as?" asked Emile, tugging a strap tightly around his shoulder bag to hold it in place.

The norm shrugged. "Food, medical supplies, narcotics, weapons, bookchips, simsense chips, spare clothes . . . Mr. Harvin himself authorized carte blanche, sir. Whatever the Connie carries is yours."

"Thank you," Emile said, jabbing his staff into the flooring. The vine-covered rod of wood stayed there. "But I appear to have all that I require." Leaping off his shoulder, Grand landed on a seat and yipped.

"I stand corrected," Emile turned to face the norm. "Is there perhaps any more hardtack?"

Watching Grand with distrust, the lieutenant said, "Ah, not up here, sir. I can get more from ship stores." Outside the sky was rapidly darkening, and soft thunder sounded.

"We shall do without," Emile decided. Grand yipped again. "Silence," he said softly, and the ferret went motionless. After a tick, Grand chased his own tail until he was a small ball of fur, head and tail indistinguishable.

"As you say, sir." The lieutenant saluted. "The trip should take approximately six hours, adjusting for current drift. You do have the authorization codes?"

"Naturally," Emile said, swinging the inner door slowly shut.

"Good voyage, sir!" the lieutenant called through the closing crack, moving his foot just in time.

Emile spun the wheel to dog the hatch shut, then slid the lock in place. Taking a seat near Grand, he clicked on the straps of his safety belt, then reached up to a concealed control panel and turned on the external microphones.

"Stinking elf bastard," he heard the lieutenant say. "Hope a fragging leviathan eats him on the way down." Then much louder. "Ready at the ball!"

"Ready, sir!"

"Undog the clamps!" Metallic thumps came from four sides of the sphere. "Stabilizers on full! Release the lines! Power on! Pressure on! Drop the soap, boys!"

Emile felt the sphere lift smoothly into the air and gently swing toward the left. His aerial view of the *Conquistador* was of the deck lined with sailors standing in clusters between the banks of depth charges regularly dotting the gunwale. The middle of the vessel resembled a porcupine, its array of cannons and gun turrets pointing every which way. Personally, he found it difficult to believe that any pirate ship could survive even a brief confrontation with a technological terror such as the *Conquistador*.

The immersion into the water was flawless, and only the rocking of entering the water itself marred the descent. As the ball dipped into the ocean and the waves washed over its tiny windows, green lights flooded the bathysphere, quickly darkening to stygian blackness. The only sounds came from the soft whine of the heater, the gentle hum of the pressure/depth gauge, and the reassuring thumps of the air regenerator. With nothing to do but wait, Emile settled in his seat and closed his eyes. His regular sleep schedule had been seriously thrown akilter because of this trip, and a short nap would be most appreciated. As he drifted off to sleep, Grand hissed in warning and once more the nightmares began. But more sharp, more vivid. Almost as if they were real.

Tail abristle, Grand screamed as Emile jerked awake, his jaw working as he tried to clear his throat and breath. Air . . . there was no air! His lungs were laboring, but nothing was happening. It was as if the bathysphere had been pumped clear and he was in vacuum. No air! Gasping and choking, he fumbled with the control panel set overhead, unable to believe the dials showing that the sphere was full of good air at proper pressure and that oxygen and carbon dioxide levels were normal. The feeder lines from the surface must be clogged!

With the blood pounding in his ears, Emile couldn't hear if the regenerator was working or not, and no visible parts were moving to show its operation. Escape filled his mind. Yes, that was it! He must reach the surface! Clawing off his seat belt, he staggered to the hatch. In mindless terror he began to beat weakly on the wheel, trying to escape from the underwater coffin. Grand raced before him and stood defiant before the hatch, hissing at his master, but Emile swatted the ferret aside. All thoughts were gone except for the burning need to breath in cool sweet air one last time. A single breath, a spoonful, a sip of air . . . oh, spirits, please . . . please . . . !

Ducking under a red-hot pipe, and dodging around an array of steaming vats festooned with hissing hoses, Delphia rounded the corner of a thumping machine with numerous dials and readouts to find himself in a dead end before a massive freezer. Easing open the insulated door, he peeked inside and saw only darkness, the section of floor lit by the light behind him thick with dust and cobwebs. As he turned, the others arrived.

"Any sign of pursuit?" asked Delphia, closing, but not shutting the door.

Last in line, Moonfeather shook her head inside her helmet. "We're clear. If anybody was after us, we lost 'em on the pipe."

"Excellent." Walking into the freezer, Delphia popped the seals on his waist, and bent over to lower the top half of the Jym suit to the floor as quietly as possible. "Let's ditch these suits in here," he said.

"Sounds good." Thumbs popped his helmet and vigorously began scratching his nose. "Ah! Been wanting to do that for hours."

"Doesn't look like anybody has used this place for years," noted Moonfeather, joining them in the dim interior of the big box. "We can always reclaim the suits if we need to. These things must be worth a fortune."

"My idea exactly," said Delphia, stepping out of the lower half of the armor.

"Hey, where's Boomer?" asked Silver, glancing about.

"Drek! We must have lost him in the gutting machine," said Thumbs, checking outside the freezer. "No sign of him. Should we go back?"

"Frag that," muttered Moonfeather, stepping out of her suit and then shaking out her red hair. She checked the charge on the stun baton and stuffed it into a belt around her waist. "I don't think he knows where IronHell is, and he sure as drek doesn't know what this place is, so who needs him?"

"And if he's caught?" demanded Silver, standing alongside her suit, carefully freeing her Fuchi from its nest of wires.

"Then his head explodes," Moonfeather said.

"With reservations, I concur," said Delphia thoughtfully, unlimbering the Predator from the leg of his Jym. "He was only an asset aboard the submarine. If he was still with us, we would be forced to terminate him ourselves."

"Then it's good he's not here."

"Wherever here is," observed Silver, shouldering her bulky bag.

"That blimp breeder thought we were pirates," said Thumbs slowly. "So this place can't be IronHell."

"Indubitably," agreed Delphia. "And from the foreman's severely antagonistic response, we may infer that the inhabitants of this bubblecity are not on good terms with the seagoing palliards."

With her Remington pump-action in hand, Moonfeather draped the partially loaded bandolier of shells over her chest. "However, the local gov might know where IronHell is," she offered.

"Get me to a jack or a telecom and I'll download the whole fragging city grid," said Silver confidently, checking the clip in her Seco. "I've got programs that can strip a grid to the bare boards."

Delphia tested the VPR2 and his Manhunter. Slip-slap. "That will take time. Which would require privacy. Even if we can find something, our credsticks are probably useless down here."

"This is terra incognito," agreed Moonfeather, jingling a bracelet.

"So don't leave anything behind," said Thumbs, cradling his Mossberg in the crook of a tattooed arm. "We might need it."

"Natch."

"Done and done."

"Arctic. Let's blow."

Weapons at the ready, the four moved quietly through the deserted processing machinery, keeping a careful watch out for guards or vidcams as they headed for the first door marked Exit. It had a retinal scanner, but Silver and her Fuchi busted through that in a few ticks with a UniBlink program and they were gone.

28

Stopping behind a big vibrating reactor with lots of pipes, Boomer caught his breath and waited to see if anybody was behind him. After a few ticks, he decided it was safe and broke the seal on his helmet. Almost instantly he regretted the act. The air in the food processing plant was hideous, thick with the stink of decaying flesh and rotting guts. Davy, it was worse than a bilge full of ripe corpses!

Breathing in tiny sniffs, he forced himself to acclimatize to the stench and soon was out of the Jym suit. His clothes stuck to his skin with dried sweat, but he luxuriated in a good stretch, savoring the freedom of movement.

That stopped as a fusillade of bullets sprayed the wall above him, punching a line of holes in the metal. "Go static!" boomed a norm in a guard uniform. The guard came closer, boots and badge polished bright. "And keep 'em raised."

Slowly, Boomer lowered his arms, forcing himself to stay calm, think icy, and breathe regularly. Be calm, goddammit!

"I said raise ya hands, gleeb, or get cacked," growled the guard, the multiple barrels of his tripistol spinning in readiness.

"You will lower that gun and speak politely to me. I am a pirate rigger," said Boomer, displaying his hands, but not raising them in the surrender act. "From the submarine *Manta,* and I will speak with your sector chief immediately."

"Yeah?" sneered the guard in contempt, "Or what?"

Trying to feel in control of the situation, Boomer smiled genially. "Or else the next thing you see will be an armor-piercing torpedo the size of a school bus coming through that freaking dome outside."

Chewing air, the guard hesitated, clearly unsure of what to do next. "If this is a trick . . ." he started.

Boomer cut him off. "Get on the blower, tin star, and let me speak with your boss, now!"

Never lowering the barrels of his weapon, the guard took a handset from his belt and lifted it. "Hey, Central! Ya hear me? Well, I got me another streeter claiming to be a pirate. What's this month's code phrase?" He listened and nodded. "Gotcha. Hold on."

"Okay, gleeb," he said in low tones. "Tell me what he just said, and if ya get one word wrong, I'll blow your stinking head off."

His temples starting to throb, Boomer breathed deeply, forcing himself to be calm. I am not in danger of capture, he mentally told himself again and again. I am in charge. This man will obey me. There is no danger of capture. No danger.

"Well?" shouted the guard impatiently, thrusting the tri-barrel closer. "Tell me!"

"Many are the leaves fallen," spoke Boomer softly, "but few the trees which stand the winter."

His face going ashen, the guard released the trigger of his weapon, the triple barrels slowing to a stop. "Sorry, sir," he said, hurriedly holstering the gun. "But I had to check, ya know? Some chummers fake being pirates to try 'n avoid going beyond the wall."

"Hope you zap 'em," said Boomer, feeling the tension in his head ease.

"Yes, sir. Always have. We got a treaty, you guys and us, and Old Dome keeps its side." It obviously hurt, but the guard managed to force a friendly grin. "Anything ya need . . . sir?"

"Yar," snapped Boomer. "I want clean rags and an escort to the next food shipment to be picked up by IronHell."

"Absolutely, sir," growled the guard.

"And have a crew bring along the Jym."

"No prob. My pleasure, sir. Happy to do it." The guard checked the watch on his pinkie. "If we hurry, maybe we can get you on today's shipment. It leaves in less than an hour."

"Good."

"Don't know about your friends, though. Where are they?"

"Who?" Boomer blinked at the word. "Oh, those gleebs aren't with me. They may pretend to be pirates, but I have no idea who or what they really are. Hard data. I strongly suggest you hunt the jimps like rabid devil rats and slit 'em into chum. Especially the mage."

"M-m-mage?"

"Def. A shaman, sings for Cat. However, I will be happy to give you a full physical description, along with their names, weapons, and known abilities." Boomer could also have told the city stars how to track the Jym suits using their internal security systems, but that would reveal way too much of what IronHell knew about the dometown defenses.

Then, almost as an afterthought, he added, "That is, I'll download once I'm safely away from here and those fragging killer Snowballs out there." He gestured with a thumb.

Drawing his weapon, the guard pulled the trigger. The triple barrels rotated up to speed with a whine, and a stuttering stream of highvelocity rounds violently slammed the pirate back against the wall of the chem reactor, tearing his body into bloody chunks. After reloading, the badge waited until the decapitated head messily exploded, then grabbed his handset and hit Transmit.

"Hello, Central? I just killed the pirate. Had to. He said a forbidden word. Yeah, that one. He also said the other invaders aren't pirates, which makes it a cybernetic lock they are. We better twig those yobos double pronto."

Nervously, the guard glanced around at the catwalks above this level, the laser spot of his tribarrel searching for any movements in the shadows. "And one of them is a mage" he added softly with a shudder.

Less than an hour later, a group of workers in bright orange Gunderson Corporation Jym suits waddled out from Low Dome on their regular duty schedule. Heading for the sea-going equivalent of tractors and combines, nine of the suits carried the regulation two tanks of compressed air on their backs. But one of the group carried the unusual number of three. As the group chatted with each other over their short-range Gertrudes, one suit went casually off by itself into the tall deepweed beds. A moment later, there was a brief flurry of motion as something small and metallic streaked away over the lush farmland, moving toward the distant mountains at an incredible velocity. When the Jym suit returned, it was carrying only two tanks of air.

Nobody seemed to notice.

Unrolling a bolt of red carpet over the perforated steel flooring on the dome, the orange-uniformed crew cycled down a ladder attached to the ceiling, and one technician

climbed up quickly. Checking the validity of the magnetic
seal, he released the mechanical lock and spun the wheel on
the top hatch. The circular slab of metal swung off on a
silent pivot flange. Set within a recessed area a good meter
in height was another hatch with a similar locking wheel,
both moist with sea water. Rapping three times, then three
times more, on the second hatch, the technician undid the
second mechanical lock and spun the wheel, undogging the
smaller hatch. This one swung upward, exposing a stern-
faced Emile standing like a statue on the other side, pack on
his back, wand in hand and Grand glowering from a
shoulder. Dumbfounded, the norm was unable to speak for
awhile. Emile was not surprised at his reaction.

"Hello, sir," said the norm, swallowing hard. "Please
follow me, sir." And he quickly descended to clear the way.

Primly exiting the bathysphere, Emile climbed down to
the red carpet. Wide-eyed stares greeted his appearance, and
Grand chittered unhappily as his eyes darted about. Emile
was standing in a small undersea dome, its flat ceiling dotted
with six pressure hatches identical with the one he had just
used. The curved walls were ringed with thick portholes,
clusters of air tanks, and puncture repair kits every two
meters. The strip of carpet underfoot led to a half-circle
tunnel extending off into the distance. A group of people
were standing in the mouth of the well-lit tube; a norm male
in a standard business suit, a norm female in a severe business dress, no jewelry, and three hulking trolls in full combat
armor and sporting Mossberg SMGs with grenade launchers.
Two of the metahumans had chromed eyes, the third was
wearing darkly tinted wraparound glasses of unknown function. But Emile suspected they were of military origin.

"W-welcome to Old Dome, Monsieur Ceccion," said the
suit, giving a stiff bow from the waist. His pronunciation
wasn't bad: *Ses-shun*, he said firmly. "I am Dan Robinson,
executive vice president of Gunderson Oceanographic Indus-
tries. A pleasure, sir. A real pleasure."

Emile said nothing, concentrating on his breathing. The
noise filled his ears like gusting thunder. Yes, this place was
near the source of his feelings of suffocation and nightmares.
Very near.

As the staff began unloading the luggage and equipment
boxes, Robinson gave a forced smile. "And this is my assis-
tant, Rebecca Thomas."

"We've heard so much about you, Monsieur Ceccion," said the female, sweat trickling down her face. "I certainly hope you will enjoy your stay here."

Again Emile did not respond, but thumped the flooring with his wand as if to test its solidity. The grilled metal tanged musically and Grand hissed at the noise. The orange jumpsuits paused in the unloading, but Thomas brusquely motioned them back to work. "Ms. Harvin sends her regrets that she is not able to greet you personally," said Robinson, his artificial smile weakening. "But she asked me to communicate her regards. I trust your trip went well?"

"Survival was achieved," said Emile, feeling as if he was only linked to this plane of existence by the sheer force of his will.

The norm assumed a quizzical expression. "Come again, please?"

Ignoring the breeder, Emile walked to a porthole and looked outside. The stupendous bubblecity was visible beyond the lush hexacres of green farm land, with jagged mountains faintly discernible in the far distance. Beyond the rocky sentinels was the ultimate blackness, darker than even interstellar space where a trillion blazing stars tried to banish the eternal night. Down here, there was no light, except for the rare phosphorescence of exotic tubers from the depths and what substitute suns humanity brought along with them.

"You did not kill them here," Emile said quietly, turning away from the vista. "Not here, no."

The suits exchanged nervous looks, smiles gone completely.

Wetting his lips, Robinson hurried over. "Please, sir, accompany me to the elevators and we will discuss this in private," he whispered, stern and quick.

"No." Emile walked away from the annoyance. Long tail lashing, Grand growled unhappily as they entered the tunnel and found the slidewalk. As they stepped onto the ribbed matting, the endless belt activated at their weight and started to move slowly off, gently accelerating to a casual speed.

The tunnel all around Emile was very well illuminated by indirect lighting. Sitting on the surface of the seabed, the tunnel was forged of steelloy rings thicker than an ork, with titanium-reinforced ceramic sheets in quadruple layers. Only the visible interior was of standard macroplas, gaily painted in murals depicting the wonders and delights of the sea. Emile did not know how he was aware of these details, not yet anyway, but he sensed that the answer, and many more answers to questions unasked, lay ahead of him, deep within the bubblecity.

A manicured hand roughly jerked him around, and Emile found himself face to face with the suit again.

"What are you on, drugs? Chips?" demanded Robinson hotly. "This is outrageous behavior! Mr. Harvin himself sent you, mage, and this is how you arrive? Fried like a gutterkin?"

"Be quiet," Emile commanded, gesturing with his vine-covered wand. The length of the wood seemed to glow for a tick.

Curling a lip, Robinson moved his mouth and lips in pantomime but not a sound came out. Not a squeak. Recoiling, the norm gave a silent scream and backed away from the elf, the motion of the slidewalk carrying them quickly apart.

"Guards, stay with our guest," ordered Thomas, stepping between Emile and the Gunderson executive, holding up her briefcase as if was some kind of protective shield. "I'll take care of Mr. Robinson."

"Understood, m'am," answered the troll with sunglasses, and the armored trio briskly walked alongside the slidewalk as it whisked Emile along. He did not mind their company, as he sensed these soldiers had nothing to do with the slaughter.

Overhead, a neon script sign hanging from the ceiling proclaimed that it was two klicks till the city customs inspection. Listening and watching, Emile saw that every quarter-klick he passed a band of discoloration spanning the entire floor. He knew those to be the tops of pressure bulkheads, veined barriers of thick resilient materials that would automatically activate if the tunnel lost pressure or became punctured. For an industrial installation, purely interested in the peaceful exploitation of the natural resources of the ocean depths, the dometown certainly seemed to be armored for war.

Shifting his backpack, Emile stepped off the slidewalk at Immigration, and breezed past Customs as if their guards and fences were merely decorations. Stunned faces were everywhere and nobody made a move to stop him. Walking through a lobby, he bypassed the elevators going to Old Dome and proceeded onto a bare promenade. The Low Dome spread out before him, and Emile was forced to blink away his distorted vision. But that didn't help as it had before. He still saw the world as mixed images, a dozen facets of the shifting skyline, the moving buildings, the shifting dome overhead.

"Not here either," he said to himself and to the others not with him, but present still. Walking to the railing, he stared out at the bubblecity. It was a desolate place, a place of machines and enslavement and despair. Everybody he saw was either in a hurry or frowning. Most were both.

"Out there," Emile told his familiar, pointing with his staff. "They all died out there . . . somewhere . . . near . . . a wall?"

Grand growled in response, as if already aware of the truth.

"Come," said Emile to the trolls, moving toward the exit doors. The few people about rapidly cleared a path for them. "If Barbara Harvin wants me so bad, she will know where to find me."

29

Watching the world go by, they stood in the mouth of an alleyway.

"I want to know when the hell it will get dark," grumbled Moonfeather.

"I don't think it does," Delphia said, gesturing. "Observe the street corners. Note the configuration of the store signs."

Her eyes widened. "No lights. There's no fragging street lights, no neon. They must never turn off that blasted dome!"

"No shadows, no night," grumbled Thumbs. "A chummer could go crazy here!"

"Hey, zone this," said Moonfeather, watching the street. "Have you noticed that there's no cars, no bikes, nothing with a chemical exhaust that might pollute the air."

A squat City Guard squad car hummed by, its angular sides bristling with gunbarrels.

"Electric," Thumbs noted, hulking lower.

"And well-armed," corrected Delphia. "But I'm sure nobody else is."

Thumbs nodded. "Yeah. They might have knives or drek like that, but no projectile weapons. It's like—"

"Not *like*," said Moonfeather. "This *is* a prison and they're freaking slaves."

"Well?" asked Delphia softly as Silver rejoined them. She'd been snooping around for a way to jack into the city's grid. "Anything?"

"Yeah," reported Silver. "I found a busted telecom, wired up a port, and jacked in. Security was poor and my can openers and mimic utilities cut through easy. I don't think they've got many deckers here."

"Great. Download us."

She took a breath. "Well, for one thing, we're not going to be able to get ourselves a bolthole down here."

"Why not?" Delphia asked.

"They call this section Low Dome. It's where the workers live. Whenever a batch of newbies arrive from the surface, a doss is assigned to each one. And worse—"

"Worse?"

"Our credsticks won't work here either. The Gunderson Corporation owns this ant farm, and every stone, stick, and thing in it—everything! They flat out own it all. It's a company town. The workers get paid with a company-issue credstick."

"Ruthless," said Delphia.

"And it means we're broke," added Thumbs. "Our sticks are worthless down here."

"Zero sweat," Moonfeather said. "All we gotta do is mug some slag and snatch his stick."

Silver frowned and leaned against the rough brick wall, her arms crossed. "TGC also owns every sub, every Jym suit—drek, they own the air! Nobody ever gets back up to the surface." She paused and shivered. "Ever."

"We're trapped here?"

"Seems so."

Delphia waved that aside. "Merely an inconvenience. We have our own Jym suits, and once recharged we can leave whenever we wish."

"And go where? Walk to fragging Miami?" exploded Thumbs. "We'd run out of air long before we covered the hundreds of klicks."

"The goal I have in mind is much closer." Delphia patted Thumbs on the shoulder. "Trust me, *omae*. We can blow whenever we wish."

Silver gave a bone-cracking yawn. "I don't know about you chummers, but I say we still gotta find a place to ice for a bit. I'm dragging hoop."

"Me too," said Moonfeather.

Thumbs reached into his pocket and brought out a brightly colored cylinder. "I got a HappyPack here that'll keep us awake for a week."

"Awake and alert?" asked Moonfeather, sounding interested and suspicious.

"Well, no," admitted Thumbs. "You'll be seeing every color in the spectrum sing and dance, and watching tables fly by on fairy wings."

"Pass."

"So what do we do?"

Delphia chewed a corner of his moustache. "I have no idea," he told them honestly. "Absolutely no fragging idea."

Crossing his office in a hurried stride, Lester Dore, Chief Captain of the IronHell pirate group, rubbed his freshly shaven face, amazed at the good job. Breakfast had been stim patches instead of soyeggs with kaf, and he felt supernaturally alert. Every sense sharp as a laser. Good. He'd need that today. Belting on a holstered pistol, he sat in his chair, and adjusted the buttons on his immaculate uniform. It had been awhile since he'd called a meeting of the whole staff.

He took an antique wooden gavel from its recess and rapped on a worn wooden plate, announcing the start of the impromptu meeting. On the acoustical signal, a bank of telecoms automatically rose from the floor, each screen displaying the unsmiling face of one of his underbosses. At the bottom of each screen was a listing of their confirmed kills, income for the past year, known expenses, and the names of the surface ships and submarines the officer personally owned.

Once, meetings of the Council had been held in person. Face to face, and in the flesh. But the competition was stiffer than ever, and the corps were out after them with a vengeance. Virtual meetings seemed a lot safer.

"Hear ye, hear ye, I call this emergency meeting of the IronHell Council to order," said Dore, rapping some more.

"Chief Captain presiding. We'll pass on roll call. I can see you're all here. First item on the agenda, hell, the only item—"

"At this hour?" yawned a bald norm in a rumpled tee and boxers. In the background was a huge rumpled bed with a pair of nubile female elves sleeping on opposite sides, the middle empty. "Couldn't ya have waited till noon like a normal person?"

"Dock your skivies, Base Defense, this is fleet biz," snapped Chief Captain, leaning forward in his throne.

"Tiz?" The sleep was instantly gone from the man's face.

"Yar." Chief Captain glared at the telecoms before him, watching the faces of his commanders awake with frightening speed. "I've just received an emergency message torp from one of our mimes in Old Dome saying that the city guards have killed a pirate."

"Well, whoopdie-fragging-do," said Master Engineer,

rubbing his scarred face with a plastic face. "Send his widow a buncha roses and a death bonus and let's get back to sleep."

"Aye, what is this drek?" demanded an unshaven ork.

"We lose crew everyday," agreed an Amerind, knotting his bathrobe closed.

"Or was there something special about this?" asked a grizzled old troll, both of his tusks capped in gold, his horns diakoted to a brilliant, and armor-piercing, sheen.

"Aye, Recon, there was," confirmed Chief Captain. "Our man was kilt *after* he identified himself as a pirate and *after* it was confirmed by their security division."

Shocked faces filled the screens.

"Are ye daft!"

"They'd never do that!"

"That's a declaration of war!"

"We gots an agreement wid 'em!" raged another. "Signed in blood!"

"This is a hard-data download," said Chief Captain, speaking softly, knowing full well that would catch their attention. "End of trans. A done deed."

"Well, then . . ." A grizzled man in a flowing red beard of classic styling started, stopped, then began again. "Then I say enough is enough. Let's juke the gleebs."

"*Qua*? Zap the whole installation?" asked a beautiful black norm, one eye covered with a white patch. "Think of the nuyen we'll lose, not to mention the high-quality supplies!"

"And the ships," added a young ork, stiffly formal in a spotless uniform. "If the report is true, then they've got something special waiting for us."

"Aye, Intelligence and Escort are right," stated a grossly fat elf in a Jamaican mumu, accepting a steaming mug from off-screen. "We'll be losing a lot of tonnage and crew attacking them." She took a careful sip.

"Men and nuyen."

"Gonna kill the golden goose?"

"Aye."

"Aye!"

"No," said Chief Captain, hitting the reverb button on the arm of his throne, making his words thunder over their telecoms. "The golden goose, as Covert Ops said, has already turned and bitten us in the hoop. We know these corporate gleebs have been hiring yabos and mercs and shadowrunners to find our HQ so they can pressure us to renegotiate the deal. Threaten to expose us to Atlantic Security for smaller tribute, or none at all! Well, that's a fair dare. If we're not strong enough to protect ourselves, we should go down to Davy."

A muttered chorus of agreement.

Chief Captain slammed a fist onto the arm of the chair. "Only now they're moving openly against us. And why, I ask you, why?"

"Okay," rumbled Intelligence in a surly manner. "Tell us why."

Chief Captain stared at them for a full three ticks. "Because he said a forbidden word."

"What?"

A forbidden word?

Codes went pale as her scars. "Jesus, Buddah, and Zeus, Harvin must have some kind of military secret she's terrified we might discover."

"A new weapon," said Master Engineer, then he shouted, "they've invented a new fragging weapon!"

"Aye, makes sense," agreed Covert Ops. "But was this merely a slip? Or is it a trap to lure us in and burn our fleet?"

A thick silence.

"What's your opinion, Tactics?" asked Port Defense, looking to his left.

On Chief Captain's right, a voluptuous blonde norm cracked her knuckles thoughtfully. "I think it's a slip," she decided. "And unless we move fast, they'll be ready for us and kick our combined hoops all the way to the Straits of Magellan."

Pensive murmurs.

Scratching under a breast, Tactics continued, "I say we strike with a retaliatory fleet of, say, five ships. Just to teach 'em a lesson." A slow grimace took her features. "Unless they do have a special surprise for us, then we hit them with everything we've got. Attack from both sides and blow 'em to Davy! Then loot the ruins!"

"The whole fleet?" asked Recon.

"That takes a formal vote," decried Base Defense.

"I didn't wake ya to ogle your pretty faces," stated Chief Captain gruffly. "I second the motion for a full strike. So hit the buttons and decide. Should we ignore this affront to our authority and wait for more rebellion. Or teach them, once and for fragging all, that nobody frags with IronHell!"

Grim faces turned away from their screens to talk with aides or to check the current battle simulation to see what would be the theoretical result of a surprise attack by Iron-Hell on Old Dome using the full resources of the pirate fleet, both outside the bubblecity and within. In staggered steps, the red lights on every telecom blinked green, and the sub-monitor in the arm of Rore's chair showed the results. It was as expected.

"Okay, mateys, drop your dips and grab your chips," he said, standing up. "Cause this is Old Dome's day in the barrel. We're going to war!"

30

Stabbing out from other rooftops, four searing stilettos of shimmering light stretched across the skyline of Low Dome, converging on a big water tank set on the roof of the oil refinery. The beams pierced the macroplas effortlessly, shifting slightly in a carefully orchestrated arc. Then the top of the tank came off, the bowed plas dangling from a tow chain. Instantly, armed Guards charged out of the doorway in the roof to surround the tank, while dozens more rapelled down from other locations. Most landed around the container, and a handful landed directly inside, in a real-life strike so perfectly coordinated it could have been a computer simulation.

"Drek!" cursed a major, standing in knee-deep water. The flash clipped under the barrel of his SMG played over the vacant tank. "They're not here!" Four other troopers were stationed about him in a two on two pattern, their weapons constantly moving about, fingers on triggers as they hungrily looked for targets.

"But they were, sir," stated a trooper, freezing her shoulder lights. In the cone of illumination, a catwalk ringing the inside of the tank was visible.

"Thermograph shows residual heat signatures of four, maybe five people, within the hour," announced a Guard, his face shield down, numbers and text scrolling on the visor. He turned slowly in a circle, scanning everything, his left hand holding a Predator, his right hand operating a miniature keypad on his left forearm. "No molecular traces of plastique or powder. No booby traps."

"Thank Ghu," whispered a Guard, wiping his brow.

"But we missed them!" cursed a sergeant, splashing closer. "How the frag did they do this?"

"Maybe there's a mole in City Defense?"

"Ha! That'll be the day."

"Or one of them is a freaking mage," grumbled the major, tightening the grip on his SMG. "And they got a freaking elemental helping them."

A burst of machine gun fire from outside.

"Report!" subvocalized the major, deep in his throat.

"Nothing to report. A misfire, sir," said a familiar voice over the radio in his helmet. "Just one of the badges kinda nervous capping at thin air."

"Maybe he thought they were invisible," scoffed a trooper in the tank.

"God Two, report!" barked the major.

"Negative on invisible perps," stated a voice. "Infrared and proximity both show clear."

"I want immediate ID on the gleeb who fired!" barked the major suspiciously.

His radio crackled. "Who, me, sir? Shield 79160, Corporal Buckley."

"That's a confirm, sir," said a computerized VOX in his helmet. "Carrier sig, vocal patterns, and serial number match for Buckley, John J., Corporal."

"Acknowledged," said the major. "Buckley, you're demoted to trooper pending further actions. Random firing of auto weapons in a combat situation is strictly forbidden, general order 975."

A handful of ticks. "Aye . . . aye, sir."

"You, report." The major pointed at another trooper as he waded over to the group of soldiers clustered on the catwalk.

"Sir, it looks like they've been bouncing a radio wave off the dome," said a trooper holding a crude assembly of parts and fiber-op wiring. "Trying to access the city mainframe, bypassing the telecom circuits and jackports. The althropic plas is a perfect reflector."

"Explains why we couldn't track 'em by triangulation," said another Guard.

"Sir, could they be in contact with the U-boys?" asked a lieutenant intently, SMG held ready in both gloved hands.

Motioning the woman closer, the major raised his visor and turned off his radio. "Make friends with Buckley," he said, "because you're demoted too. Executive Order 5 states we are never to mention the Underground in front of the troops."

"But, sir, I . . ."

"Dismissed," the major said, slapping his visor down and

turning away. He subvocalized, "God One, give me general broadcast, scrambled and coded."

"Hot and tight, sir."

"All right, hoopholes, download this," the major rasped. "It's been six hours since these pirates invaded Old Dome, and they're still running around loose doing tox knows what! Until further notice all leaves are cancelled, all vacations are cancelled, personnel on sick leave will be recalled, and everybody will do double shifts until we find these motherfraggers and blow 'em to Davy!"

Triggering his SMG, the major fired a long burst into the air. "Dead! Do ya hear me! I want 'em dead, and I mean now! As in yesterday!"

Everybody resolutely chorused in military affirmatives, nobody foolish enough to mention their commanding officer's random firing of automatic weaponry in a combat situation. Rank did have its little privileges.

"Sir, shouldn't we do a perimeter search of the area?" asked a Guard, snapping a salute.

"Already taken care of, Corporal," said the major, returning the salute. "We have other teams handling that job."

A macroplas grill in the street alongside the curb was judiciously lifted by a huge hand and a bald head peeked out.

"Clear," whispered Thumbs, and he forced the grillwork aside to crawl out. After helping the rest of the team out of the hole, he kicked the grill back into place and they moved off into an alleyway, keeping low and dodging across several streets before allowing themselves to slow to a walk.

"Where the frag are we?" asked Silver. Low buildings stretched off in either direction, curving out of sight. Before and above them was the transparent dome of the city, a faint chill radiating from its surface. And only a block away was the granite wall they'd seen from the mountaintop outside.

"This must be the part they call Beyond the Wall," said Moonfeather.

"Every city's gotta have a junkyard," said Thumbs philosophically. "Might as well use it for insulation."

"We're out of that sewer, that's all I care about," said Delphia.

Coming to a corner, they paused briefly then spread out,

checking the other side to make sure it was clear of hostiles before continuing on.

"And that wasn't a sewer," corrected Silver. "It was a storm drain. And that huge machine we traversed was a pumping station. If the dome ever cracks or gets a leak, that'll return the water back outside and keep the bubblecity from flooding."

"Is that what it was?" asked Thumbs, arching one eyebrow. "We crawled through the heart of a giant pump?"

"Hey, nobody sane would follow us." Moonfeather gave a rueful laugh. "Or even believe we did it."

"I did it and I can't believe it."

"See? We're safe."

"Yar, arctic."

Half a block later, Delphia called a halt near a broken wall, the angled ruins offering excellent coverage. Everybody put their back to the wall and spread out a few steps so no single blast could geek them all in one shot.

"No rats," said Thumbs, glancing at the rubble and refuse piled high about them. "Garbage, but no rats."

"Hadn't noticed," said Delphia, checking the setting on the PocketDoc strapped to his hip. "But you're right. No bugs, no rodents, not even any crabs."

Silver nodded. "There'll be nothing down here the Gunderson Corporation didn't specifically import for its own private use."

"Except us," said Moonfeather with a grin. She was sitting crosslegged on the granite slab that was the ground here in the bubbletown. The unyielding nature of the material seemed not to bother her in the least.

"Check. And they do wish to correct that mistake, don't they?"

"Check and mate."

"So, where are we?" said Delphia, taking a seat on a chunk of ferrocrete. "Accessing the Gunderson mainframe via radio didn't work."

"Only one thing to do now," said Silver, also sitting down. Easing off her sodden shoes, she poured out the water acquired by diving down the pipe in the floor of the tank, then slid the shoes back on. "We gotta try to find some allies."

Thumbs reached into a pocket of his vest and brought out a pack of smokes soggy as forgotten breakfast cereal. "Any ideas how we do that?" he sighed, tossing them away over a shoulder.

"There have to be a few dissatisfied citizens in this place. Would you want to be trapped for life under the ocean working as a drone for some corp?" said Delphia. "Maybe we can hit some bars or brothels, and see who comes out of the woodwork."

"Not bad." Thumbs looked impressed. "Gotta say, Mr. D, you got cojones."

Delphia stared at the troll for a long hard minute. Slowly his gun hand relaxed. "Thank you," he said softly. "Thank you very much, sir."

Then he stood up. "Time to book, my friends."

"Yar, let's go find another sewer," rumbled Thumbs.

"Storm drain!" said Silver.

"Whatever."

An hour later, the group was creeping through piles of bricks and glass toward The Wall. Several of the street lamps in this area were broken, and the dim shadows generated by the ghostly luminescence of the dome itself cloaked the street. They saw that a tunnel passed through the granite barricade at this point, the truck-sized opening sealed shut with rusty doors of riveted iron. There was a sign bolted to door, its lettering long gone to ferric oxidation.

"Old," whispered Silver, hefting her Seco. "Real old."

Delphia touched his ear. "Anything?"

Thumbs shook his head no. "All clear. Can't hear a sound on this side except for us."

Bracelets jingling softly, Moonfeather stood. "Good."

"Stay on guard," said Delphia. "This place is tailor-made for a trap."

Weapons at the ready, the team looked around them for any suspicious movements. There were none.

Directly in front of the tunnel was a water-filled pit, an impressive pothole. Razor wire and the crumbling remains of a kiosk were strewn about. In contrast to these ancient guards erected against unauthorized intruders was a very modern underwater keypad on the side of the imposing iron barrier.

"Probably there for City Guards or suits who might get trapped on this side," rationalized Thumbs, unfolding the stock on his Mossberg CMDT. "Can you ramjam it, Silver?"

"Cake," she snorted. "The ThunderClub in Overtown has better locks in the ladies room."

"Thanks for sharing that."

"No prob."

As Silver unlimbered the Fuchi deck from her shoulder bag, the rest formed a protective half-circle around her. The ruins and refuse were motionless as there was no breeze to move bits of paper, no leaves to be gusted by thermals. It was like standing in a painting. All was still. Then the tiniest ripple marred the surface of the muddy pit before them. Delphia froze for only a tick before starting to angle away. "Jessie Owens," he said to them in casual tones. "Saigon bug-out."

"Who?" returned Thumbs.

"What?" said Moonfeather, not amused. "Where are you going? To drop a penny?"

"Warp speed, Mr. Sulu," Delphia said in staccato tones, moving quickly toward the dreary dossplex to their right. Suddenly, the Manhunter was in his hand.

Lowering the Mossberg, Thumbs just stared at him. "Can't you talk English, *omae*?"

Still moving, Delphia frowned and gestured at the ground.

Out of the corner of her vision, Moonfeather saw a bubbling in the muddy water. "Eh?" she said aloud. "Where the frag could mud come from in a city built on solid rock?" Then the bulbous orange helmet of a Gunderson Corporation Jym suit broke the surface, the ork face inside smiling widely.

"Dorsey Park!" screamed Moonfeather, firing her Remington at the helmet. The barrage of pellets hit the armor suit dead on, but failed to break the faceplate. The Jym suit kept on rising, joined now by several others, their massive gauntlets holding automatic weapons wrapped in plastic.

Galvanized, Silver yanked her deck free from the keypad and hit the ground in a dive roll, then came to her feet meters away. Tucking the priceless Fuchi under one arm, she started running for all she was worth, firing her Seco pistol behind her blindly. "It's a trap!"

At her cry, several rapidfires opened up from the gaping windows of the twin plexes. Caught by the crossfire, exposed in the middle of a flat ferrocrete apron, Delphia flew backward off his feet and hit the ground limp as a ragdoll, the Manhunter dropping from his twitching fingers.

31

The Remington boomed again, and Thumbs' Mossberg added its chattering fury to the battle as the Jym suits fired the bulky pistols and rifles in their cumbersome gauntlets. Silver cried out and clutched her shoulder, but then dropped to one knee and returned fire with her Seco. The small-caliber rounds bounced off the underwater armor like gumdrops.

Shouting City Guards came rushing out of doorways from every direction, and as they cleared the building, Delphia rose with the Predator in his hands, spraying hot lead death everywhere. The Guards tumbled back out of sight.

"Idiots," he muttered, snatching the Manhunter from the ground, while firing the Predator one-handed.

Moonfeather gestured with both hands, and one of the armor suits split apart in a series of ringing crashes, leaving the stunned norm inside wearing only his helmet. Her Remington shotgun spoke again, and this time killed.

As Thumbs frantically reloaded, he looked around for protective cover and saw none. The granite Wall was on one side, the Dome on the other, the pool ahead of them, apartment complexes behind. It was a perfect quadrangle set-up. They were trapped in a valley with snipers to the south, armor to the north. Dead meat. Hasta la bye-bye, amigos.

Thumbs began to run, screaming incoherently over his chattering Mossberg. He touched the third molar on the left side of his mouth with his tongue and accelerated to triple speed. Spreading his arms wide, he began to sweep down toward the others.

With a curse, Moonfeather ducked under his outstretched arm and he missed her. He did manage to scoop up Delphia and Silver as he charged the Jym suits waddling out of the water. Caught by surprise, several of them raised their weapons, but Thumbs had already reached the edge of the pit and leapt over the muddy water.

Even as he was airborne, a net spun toward them but did not connect. Landing heavy but still gripping Delphia and Silver, Thumbs stumbled for a moment. A shot cracked off the rocky ground near his boots. Then another, and Thumbs was sprinting again.

"You meta-motherfragger!" cried Moonfeather, watching the troll race off into the ruins. She threw a shield between herself and the snipers, but the net was already over her, pinning her arms to her sides. Struggling, she was hit by another net, a third, a fourth. The sticky strands of plas got tighter and tighter until she was barely able to breathe.

Slowly, cautiously, the Jym suits approached her, their big guns pointed steadily at her supine form. Unable to get a good deep breath, Moonfeather was reduced to unintelligible curses.

"We got one, sarge!" called out one of the Jym suits over the external speaker.

"Shoot him if he's armed!" commanded somebody.

"Unarmed!"

"Great! Don't geek 'im yet!"

Moonfeather hissed at them. "You gleebs won't be geeking anybody!" she stormed. "I'm not a pirate, you morons! I work for Gunderson Corporation, just like you."

City Guards in uniforms of ballistic cloth joined the Jym suits standing over her. Their faces showed disbelief.

"Yeah, prove it, biff," snarled an officer. "What's the password for this month?"

"I don't know the password for pirates, you hoop-wipe!" she raged at him. "I told you, I'm not a fragging pirate! I work for TGC—for Harvin himself—and you nullheads have just screwed up a major covert operation!"

"Yeah, yeah, sure, sure," said a Guard, shouldering his Mossberg. "Sing us another one, slitch."

"Let's stuff her into The Pit," said the officer, holstering his pistol. "We'll find out the truth later."

"I tell you I'm working for the Gunderson Corporation, you sexless gleeb!" Moonfeather spat at them, outraged.

"Nope, I don't think so," said the sergeant calmly as he lowered his pistol and shot her.

"Argh! Jesus and Buddah!" she screamed, trying to clutch

the wound in her shoulder. The pain was like a white-hot iron shoved into her flesh. She felt dizzy and sick to her stomach. "Motherless . . ."

"And that's how you subdue a mage," the City Guard told the other soldiers.

"Think again," hissed Moonfeather. She pointed at the officer, a red shimmer briefly tinting the air and then he burst into flames.

A screaming human torch, the norm beat at his burning flesh with fiery hands. When one of the Jym suits tried to grab him, he backed away, shrieking even louder. Stumbling for the muddy pit, his fiery form almost made it when he dropped to the ground smoking and crackling. The City Guards not in Jym suits covered their mouths and pinched their noses shut.

"Ghu, the smell!"

"I'm gonna yarf."

"Slot you, witch," snarled the lieutenant, drawing her gun. The Guard fired at Moonfeather, pumping in round after round until the mage's body bristled with darts. Moonfeather felt the world spin madly round and round, and then a great warm blackness swallowed her whole.

"Narcoject," the lieutenant told the others, reloading her weapon before holstering the gun. "Take 'em alive and easy. Now you and you in the Jym suits get this biff to The Pit for interrogation."

"Yes, sir!" they chorused and lifted the norm as if she weighed nothing.

"Strip her of everything that looks like a weapon . . . no, just strip her to the skin, and check inside," commanded the officer gruffly. "But don't play with her. I want her alive and sane for questioning."

"Sir, what about the sarge?" asked a Guard, swallowing hard.

The officer craned her neck to gaze at the smoking form sprawled on the ground. "Looks like his equipment is cooked. Leave it for the trash collectors." Lifting a whistle to her lips, she blew two sharp keens.

Unnoticed among a gaggle of broken and rusted-out vehicles, a wheelless wreck of a trailer truck opened its back door silently on oiled hinges. A ramp descended and technicians rolled out six sleek Hyundai OffRoader motorcycles.

The front wheels were bracketed with small-caliber machine gun ports while the fat tube of a grenade launcher protruded from the top like a unicorn horn.

"Data upload, troops," the lieutenant said, walking over to the low-slung rice-rockets. "Cars can't follow fugitives in the ruins, but these sweet roadsters can go wherever they do, and more besides." Taking the lead bike, the lieutenant climbed on and slid her sidearm into a cushioned holster under the clutch.

"Now, let's go scrag those pirates," she said, revving the electric engines to a whispery hum.

Over piles of rubble and through doorways lacking walls, Thumbs ran and ran, pushing himself to the limits of his body. He sprinted through the broken streets, gaining ground and making time. When there were obstacles, he went around, sometimes over, and occasionally underneath. Cresting a small mountain of rubble, he spied a lone figure standing in the middle of an empty lot a half a block ahead of them. Lurching off to the side, Thumbs forced himself to stop in the lee of a section of macadam tilting upward like a skateboard ramp. Releasing Delphia and Silver from his grip, he slumped to the ground, dripping with sweat, gasping for breath.

"You okay?" asked Silver, stroking his head.

Bent over double, Thumbs wheezed an affirmative while gulping air and licking dry lips. Without hesitation, Delphia pulled out a flask and offered it to the troll. Thumbs gladly accepted the tiny container and drained it in a gulp.

"S-s-s-mooth," he croaked weakly. "W-whatiz?"

"Cold coffee from the *Manta*," Delphia replied, pocketing the flask. "I also have a PocketDoc. Think you need a stim or a trank?"

His bare chest heaving, Thumbs waved the suggestion aside.

"What happened to Moonfeather?" asked Silver, turning to Delphia. "Did you see anything?"

"She's dead," he said, moving to watch the street through a sagging window frame with gun in hand. "I saw it in my sunglasses behind us. They shot her once, she fried the guy, then they shot her six or seven times more."

"Too bad." Silver yanked the clip from the Seco and

checked the load. Satisfied, she slammed it back in. "I didn't like her, but shot six times . . . !"

"Seen . . . worse . . ." gasped Thumbs, holding his sides while trying to stand erect.

"Yeah?" she asked. "How?"

"N-netgun. Modified."

"What do you mean? Electrified? Coated with poison?" Delphia sounded interested even as he peered around the side of the macadam rise, watching for pursuit. Oddly, there was none. He didn't like that.

Taking a deep breath, Thumbs held it for a minute, then let it out slowly. "Ya know what monofilament is?" He was breathing almost normally now. "Hair-thin wires stronger than a steel I-beam and sharper than a razor?"

His companions both nodded.

"A chummer in Orlando did a run against Zeller Geo-Medical and got shot with a netgun and the net was made of monofilaments. When he tried to struggle free . . . pieces of him just kept falling off . . ." He made a face. "*Madre mia,* now that was nasty. The gleeb with the netgun called it a Julieanne, for some reason."

Moving to the other side of the asphalt ridge, Delphia carefully peeked out through an irregular hole in the crumbling macadam. "You flatline him?"

"Natch. But first I shot him in the knees, stole his toy, and put four of the things on him." A wolfish grin. "I enjoyed watching him die. Frag with my friends, and you're fragging with me."

"You make your own justice on the streets," said Silver, sliding her padded bag off her shoulder.

Thumbs threw her a grin. "No bounce on that, pretty lady."

"Yama," said Delphia, holding up a hand in the universal sign of stop. "Somebody is coming this way."

"Who? Where?" asked Silver, Seco at the ready.

"An elf," said Thumbs, peeking over the ragged wall.

"Where'd he come from?"

"I passed him while we were running. I saw him down another street, searching among the rubble."

Dressed in utilitarian coveralls, the elf was standing in the middle of the courtyard, tall and thin like all of his race, the sides of his long blonde hair woven into decorative braids that hung from each temple in the latest Miami fashion. On his back was a plastic haversack, in one hand a wooden staff covered with living vines, and hunched on one of his shoulders was an albino ferret. Both of them were staring at a ragged piece of red cloth the elf held in his hand.

"Could be an outrider searching for us," suggested Silver. "Drek! He's got a staff!"

"Might be a mage," agreed Thumbs, easing the safety on his Mossberg. With a jerk, he realized what he had just done and snicked it off once more. "Think we should light him up?"

"We just lost a mage," said Delphia, tucking the Manhunter into his belt holster and swinging the Predator around in front. "If he's out here, it could mean he's either hunting us, or being hunted himself." Delphia turned off the laser spotter on his chatter gun. "Let's give him a tick before we do something irreversible. *Hai?*"

Squat and heavy, the Mossberg CMDT leveled. "Natch."

Slim and polished, the Seco did the same. "Hush," said Silver, creeping along the wall away from them. "I want to hear what he's saying."

"And to whom."

"Here is where they were killed, little one," said Emile, his senses stretched far beyond the physical limits of his meat body. The shattered visions of his dreams were clearer at this location, the anguished spirits of the long gone finally able to plead their plight to a receptive mind. "Yes, I hear you . . . all of you. Twelve shamans and mages. They gathered you together to perform a great task, a . . ." He closed his eyes and tightened his hand into a white-knuckled fist around the tatter of cloth. "A masking, yes, a cloaking of some kind to hide a large cold thing."

Grand snarled and hissed.

"Yes, then Gunderson killed you." Emile grimaced sadly. "Harsh coin, indeed, for a job well done. But they shall pay for this betrayal."

What he saw next was unexpected. At first he wasn't sure whether the raven-haired norm was real or part of the visions he'd been seeing.

"More likely killed to hide the location of the item," she said, lowering the muzzle of her Seco. "The corp zapped them to hide the location of the coldframe."

Emile stared at her, watching her aura flicker and dance in the artificial lights of the immense dome.

"Yes, it is true. But how do you know this, decker?" he demanded.

"We found it out in the deeps," said a troll, coming up to join her. The male was also armed, heavily chromed, and covered with gang tattoos, yet Emile sensed no immediate danger from him. "They probably thought it was the only way to keep the location of the supercomputer secret."

"What fools," Emile said. "Three may keep a secret only if two are dead."

"They also did it to remove any mages from this place," said a norm male, stepping from behind a crumbled section of sewer pipe. This male wore a badly rumpled suit and was also armed.

"He's alone," the man said to his companions.

Annoyed, Grand chittered in response, and Emile scratched him reassuringly under the chin. "Why would they want to do that?" he asked.

"Mages carry power in their minds. They cannot be unarmed. Twelve mages . . . you did say twelve, correct? That's a fragging army in a slave society."

"Slaves, yes, I have seen that, felt that," Emile said slowly. "I must admit, I do not like this place, or those who hold it in their power."

"I'm with you, chummer," said the troll. "If you don't like these hoopheads, then you're jake in my chip."

"How were they killed?" asked the fem. "Zapping a dozen mages is no easy task."

Emile shrugged. "I do not know. They seem to have suffocated in a white cloud of bitter cold, so cold they could not move or speak."

"Liquid nitrogen," announced the norm in the suit. "We've seen it before. The city hit 'em with a stream of liquid nitrogen. Like the Snowballs used to stop inquisitive subs. Case-hardened steel becomes brittle as glass when the stuff hits. Flesh crystallizes in a nano."

Emile looked deep into the norm. Grand bared his teeth. "I see that what you speak is true. *Mon dieu*, what a terrible way to perish. They . . . yes, they were still alive afterward, trapped inside frozen bodies until touched and then they crumbled into dust."

"No death is good," said the norm, holstering one of his weapons.

"But how do you know all this?" asked the troll nervously.

"How shall I say?" Emile paused, trying to think how to explain one of the mysteries of magic. "Under certain circumstances, places of violent death retain . . . vibrations, disturbances in the astral plane, residual emanations that can be detected by one with magical abilities."

Emile gave them the closest he could come to a smile under the circumstances. "Pray excuse my lack of manners. It has been a most trying day." He gave a bow. "I am Emile de Coultier Ceccion." There came a short hiss. "Ah, yes. And this, of course, is Grand."

"Grant?" asked the decker, smiling at the ferret. Grand purred in response. A good omen that.

"Grand, with a 'D'," corrected Emile, enunciating carefully. "His full name is West One Hundred Fifty-seventh Street And Grand Ave. It's where we found each other." A wan smile. "Grand for short."

"Gotcha."

"Both of us were formerly employees of the Gunderson Corporation."

"But no more, eh?" asked the troll, relaxing his shoulders.

Emile scowled. "Indeed, not. They must pay. The one who ordered the slaughter must suffer."

"We wish you much luck," said the suit, "but we're here on biz. Once we get what we came for, we're gone."

"Escape may prove to be impossible. Given time, they will capture us all. It is a small city."

"We have the means at our disposal," said the suit.

"A means of departure?" Emile asked eagerly.

"Yes."

"A reliable means?"

"No," said the suit stonily. "A means, yes, but it will not be easy or simple to leave."

"How honest. Excellent," beamed Emile, watching the empty streets. "Perhaps we can come to some arrangement. Assist me in my task and I shall assist you."

"And what're you going to do?" asked the decker. "Kill the entire City Guard who set the trap?"

"Oh no," he declaimed. "They were merely the weapon, not the one who pulled the trigger. I will seek out the norm who runs this city. The one who gave the orders. Barbara Harvin."

The troll gave a whistle. "A wetjob like that's gonna be a tough one. She's bound to have a lot of guards with a lot of guns. And a superslick coldframe to run her security systems."

"True," said Emile, looking at the dome above them. "But I am her only mage, a critical lack in her defenses. Plus, I believe that I can promise a distraction that will keep the City Guards very busy for quite awhile."

"Then maybe we can cut a deal," said the suit. "We're here on a data steal and the info we want is inside the coldframe."

"But it's too powerful for me," said the decker. "We need to turn it off so I can download the files from the auxiliary buffer zone. The backup data storage, you know. And the cut-off controls have to be in her office."

"Where I can deal with her personally," said Emile. "So, it appears we are fellow travelers. Both of our destinations end at the same terminus. Shall we work together?" He offered his hand and they each shook it in turn. Emile assensed that he could trust them for the moment, but decided not to let down his guard. They needed him now, but later would be another matter.

"Done and done. I'm Thumbs," said the troll, jerking one toward himself. "The decker is Silver, Captain QuickDraw over there is Delphia."

"Hello."

"Konichiwa."

"Holy drek, they found us again," spat Silver. "Incoming!"

Thumbs and Delphia spun about. Coming down the littered street running along the edge of the dome wall five motorcycles were speeding toward them, the riders hunched forward as they raced closer, silent as ghosts in a dream.

"Spread out. Get some cover," snapped Delphia. "Conserve ammo. Short burst, no hose jobs."

"Check."

"Natch."

"There is no need for such preparations," said Emile, holding his staff tight in both hands. His head was cocked slightly to one side as though listening to something only he could hear.

"What the frag are you talking about?" demanded Thumbs, slapping a fresh clip into the Mossberg. "Those are fully armed OffRoaders!"

Emile shrugged with Gallic elegance. "Are they? *Ça ne fait rien.* The distraction is about to begin."

Delphia stopped in the act of crouching behind a cracked engine block red with rust. "Distraction?"

"Have to be a fragging motherless big one to stop those gleebs," snorted Thumbs grimly, kneeling and aiming carefully.

"It is," said Emile, as the ground underneath them rocked and bucked. A thundering concussion boomed over the ruins, slamming the motorcycles to the roadway, two of them skidding off and one hitting a brick wall to whoof into flames.

"What the frag was that?" demanded Silver.

Emile merely pointed a finger upward.

As she looked, a star blossomed in the glassy sky, a rosy fireball that sent thin cracks radiating outward from the point of impact on the dome as the muffled blast slapped her in the face with a warm wind. As the blast was doused by the sea, the fissures swiftly closed. Then faint rods of light lanced out from the base of the bubblecity into the murky distance, the feeble beams steadily increasing in brilliance until shimmering with unleashed power like tortured rainbows. More explosions appeared in the sea, and sirens started a banshee shriek over the city.

"Pirates," whispered Thumbs.

Darkness crashed down as the city turned off every light. Only the pearlescent sheen of the dome offered any illumination.

"To make the place less of a target," reasoned Delphia, smiling broadly. "And giving us a perfect window of opportunity!"

"Almost perfect," countered Silver. "What if it's only a sortie, not a full attack?"

"She is correct," Emile said. "Time may be short." Down the street, the City Guards were stumbling about, trying to remount their Hyundais. "May I suggest we steal those bikes," said Emile, brandishing his wand. There was a click and blades snapped out of either end. "It will save us much time traveling to Old Dome."

"If it's still there when we arrive," said Thumbs sourly, shielding his face from the hot winds and billowing smoke of the burning motorcycle. Another explosion shook the sky, the wild cracks spreading outward, resembling white lightning against the black ocean beyond.

"*Oui, mon ami,*" agreed Emile solemnly. "If any of us are still alive by then."

32

Alarms howling, every sonar screen in the Old Dome Defense Center was covered with moving blips. People were scurrying madly for their seats before the consoles, where they began to throw switches and tap commands with practiced speed.

"More pirates in Sector Nine!" called out a gunnery from his console.

"West range torps, ready!"

"North range torps, ready!"

"City subs on the alert and moving in from the south and north!"

"Surface battleships not, repeat, not, in the umbrella position! We have no roof!"

Stoic, Shawn Wilson stood amid the chaos, watching the sonar screen and the murky view screens, the density of the water distorting the visual pickup of the telephoto vidcams. Subs of different sizes were closing in on the bubblecity in a four-on-four scissor formation. Jym suits were raining out of the ocean above them, and HK torpedoes were spiraling in. The lasers had stopped the first wave, but had not put the fear of hell into the buccaneers, as they'd hoped.

Removing the toothpick from his mouth, Wilson said, "All missiles and APTs, launch at will." The words echoed throughout the bustling room. "Repeat, launch at will! Bring down the invaders!"

Thunder and lightning filled the domed sky with the fury of warring gods as the four shadowy riders on sleek motorcycles rode steadily up the darkened spiral of stairs encircling the exterior of the granite mesa. Many stories below was the stygian expanse of Low Dome, the cityscape horribly illuminated by the flashes from outside.

Suddenly, there was a landing before them, and standing there was a lone City Guard with nightgoggles holding a

massive Barret rifle. Bouncing up and onto the landing,
Thumbs revved his engine to the max, hit the brakes,
twisting sideways. The Guard swung the big barrel of the
rifle about, trying to track him, but got slammed by the back
fender of the rice-rocket. With a cry, he dropped the rifle and
went tumbling over the chain railing and out of sight.

Braking his bike, Delphia grabbed the dropped rifle and
the Barrett and checked the cigarbox-sized magazine. "Ten
in the clip, one up the pipe," he said, working the lever-
action bolt, ejecting a tremendously large brass cartridge.
"Emile, know how to work this?"

"*Oui,* point and pull the trigger," answered Emile calmly.

"Yar, but don't forget to brace yourself," added Thumbs.
"That ain't no caseless rapid-fire with gas vents to neutralize
the recoil. This baby fires big, old fashioned bullets. It's
louder than a grenade, and kicks like a combat bike riding
the wire."

"But it hits like an express train," finished Delphia. "The
Barrett has a live range of a klick."

"Most acceptable," Emile replied, slinging the huge
ungainly rifle over a shoulder, forming a cross with his
wand. "This Colt revolver offers scant protection in any
serious firefight."

"And I seriously question the accuracy of these fender-
mounted weapons," he added, patting the Hyundai. Grand
purred agreement.

Delphia handed him an extra round, and Emile tucked it into
a breast pocket. "An emergency spare," he said. "Besides, I
dislike bouncing wildly with a live round under the hammer."

"Bouncing is done," Silver called out softly from a pool of
blackness. "The elevator is over here!" Something hit the
dome and spread in a wash of underwater flame, casting the
decker, her bike, and the elevator doors into harsh blue light
for a single heart beat.

"How long for you to subvert the locks?" asked Delphia,
climbing off his Hyundai and pushing it forward.

Silver chuckled. "The gleeb left the passcard in the slot.
Probably to give himself a fast escape route should pirates
arrive."

"Lucky us," said Thumbs happily, leaning forward on the
handlebars.

"I distrust luck," said Emile, kicking down the stand of
his bike.

With a musical ding, the double doors parted, emitting a blaze of light that bathed them in harsh visibility. The two City Guards inside cursed at the sight of them and clawed for the Mossberg SMGs over their shoulders.

A deafening roar ripped apart the night. It was followed by a finger of flame reaching out from the landing, going past the team and into the cages as the chest of the first Guard violently exploded and the other behind him slammed into the wall with most of his face gone. As the bodies dropped, a hole as big as an orange appeared in the back of the elevator.

"Yes, most satisfactory," said Emile, working the bolt on the Barrett, ejecting the spent cartridge. "I may keep this for my personal collection."

"Arctic," said Thumbs wheeling in his Hyundai, along with the others. He kicked down the stand on his bike, then appropriated the Mossbergs and ammo clips. "But from now on, warn me before you shoot that fragging bazooka, will ya?"

"Is a change of undergarments needed?" asked Delphia politely, smashing the ceiling EverBright with the barrel of his Manhunter.

"Damn near," grumbled Thumbs, stuffing clips into his pockets as the double doors closed with a hiss.

Some minutes later, the elevator doors opened onto a reception area: potted ferns in the corners, plush carpeting underfoot, indirect lighting, synthwood paneling. There was an electronic board on the wall for showing who was where, but at the moment it was turned off.

"Very nice," said Thumbs, twitching a cheek muscle. "We are definitely not in Low Dome anymore."

"And the air smells infinitely superior," stated Emile, breathing deeply. "Yes, much better." Grand looked around curiously with his sharp, bright eyes.

"Where next?" asked Delphia, checking down the side corridors, both his weapons out and ready.

"How should I know?" retorted Silver, looping her shoulder bag across her throat to keep it from sliding down her arm when she moved. "I couldn't get into the system to find a map."

"Emile?"

"Sorry, but I never did show up for my official tour of the facilities."

Delphia eased open a door, which turned out to be a supply closet filled with cleaning supplies and mops. "Great. We don't even know what building we're in!"

"Come on, I have an idea," said Thumbs. He grabbed the Hyundai and began pushing the bike down the carpeted corridor and toward the carved wooden doors at the end.

Going past a security checkpoint with a scanner but no Guards, the team came to a short flight of stairs and onto the sidewalk outside the building.

The street was dark, the street lamps not working. The noise of the battle was louder here, the dome closer and smaller, with much less room for the sounds to be absorbed in the distance.

"No sign of security cams or snipers," said Delphia, slipping on his sunglasses and checking out the windows above them. The lintel on the building they had come out of was turned off and unreadable. "Where the hell is everybody?"

Just then, several City Guard vehicles screeched around a corner and leveled out, racing for someplace else. A deafening boom sounded from above, and a concussion slammed hot air over the team.

"Whatever we're gonna do, do it fast," Thumbs shouted over the noise. "I don't know who's winning out there, but those yahoos are fragging serious!"

Silver gestured at the departing vehicles. "Follow them?"

"No," called out Emile. He took Grand off his shoulder, then tucked the ferret inside his jumpsuit and velcro'd the front halfway shut. "Follow me," he called out, revving the bike.

Rolling over the curb, the Hyundai hit the street and hummed away, taking a corner so close and so low the elf nearly lost a knee. The others took off after him, and soon caught up a couple of blocks away.

"Just like Miami, right?" asked Thumbs with a grin, riding dangerously close. However, the elf did not flinch or pull away. Delphia bracketed him on the other side.

"Correct," said Emile, giving a little nod. "The Harvins like to inhabit the tallest building in the city, smack dab in the middle, so they can look down on their little kingdom and gloat. Every hour on the hour."

Rolling down the streets, the team encountered other bikes, mostly with City Guards riding escort to semis and small limos. Sirens sounded from somewhere, a security vehicle streaked by, a car alarm wheeped constantly, and then an explosion sprayed glass from a building across the street. They wheeled the bikes onto the opposite sidewalk to avoid the shards on the ground.

Humming down the main drag of the dome, passing crowds of frightened people and darting vehicles, the four bikers received many strange looks, but nobody stopped to question them or open fire. Indeed, one truck full of Guards gave them a game thumbs-up and moved out of their way, allowing them passage.

"Did you do something?" asked Delphia suspiciously, one hand still holding his Manhunter.

"Yes," said Emile, long blonde hair whipping in the wind.

"Download us," shouted Thumbs.

"We are City Guards, wounded and bleeding," said Emile.

"Arctic. That should get us into Harvin's office."

"Oui." Emile grinned.

Watching the building come closer and closer, the team angled around a corner and came upon the monolith thrusting up into the darkness like the head of a spear. Frantically, they wheeled about into an alleyway, careening off a wall and racing right back onto the next street over.

"Keep moving!" shouted Delphia, tilting his sunglasses. "It looks clear, but they might come after us yet!"

"Just how desperate are we to get this run done and go home?" said Silver, hunched low over the handlebars. "Are we totally zoned? Brains to the wall? Are we fragging gonzo, mad dog, zoombalas?"

"Rock and roll!" howled Thumbs enthusiastically.

Running parallel, Delphia and Emile slowed their bikes.

"Perhaps we should discuss this course of action before committing irrevocably to—"

Black hair streaming in the wind, Silver leaned way back in her saddle and popped a wheelie. "Stay close!" she screamed. "We're going sonic!" Her bike engine whined with power as she twisted the rheostat handle to the max setting and shot away as if jet-propelled.

33

The runners and Emile pulled up their bikes in front of one of the emergency medical centers they'd seen scattered throughout the bubblecity. A muted gray in the dim light of the dome, the building was etched in streams of bright light escaping through the cracks of windows and doors. Along the ground, a score of armored vans sat waiting in garage bays, motors humming quietly.

"This is a medical rescue operation run by Gunderson itself," said Emile.

"Exactamundo." Silver kicked down the stand and climbed off the hot hog. "And furthermore—"

The magnified sound of ice dropping into hot water came as the dome overhead cracked in a million directions, the noise making the four of them stare in abject horror. Vague shapes on points of flame moved for the center of the spiderweb pattern but detonated prematurely as the shimmering lasers of the bubblecity fanned the water like a searchlight destroying everything they touched.

"That was very close to a full breach," said Emile, tying his long hair back behind his head. "All of this may be for nothing if the pirates win."

"Don't think about that," said Delphia, wiping his sunglasses. "Concentrate on the job, nothing else."

"Besides," Silver panted. "The pirates are to our advantage. Once we get inside her office, it's cake. The coldframe is kinda busy now, and won't be able to spend too many bytes trying to get rid of me."

"As you say," relented Emile, withdrawing Grand from inside his jacket and placing the creature on the ground. The ferret raced around his shoes for a bit, then sat up on his hind legs and yipped.

Studying the front door, Delphia gestured and drew his pistol. Emile recoiled from the act, his eyes bulging. His mouth opened to speak, but he only chewed air for a tick, before relaxing.

"One thing," said Delphia, screwing on a silencer to his weapon. "I'm not going to ace medics just to finish this run. If anybody in there gets brave and refuses to play, I'll try for a wound, but I'm not killing any healer."

"No prob," grinned Thumbs, brandishing a gnarled hand. He curled it into a fist and audibly cracked his giant knuckles. "I'll just reason wid 'em."

"I also specialize in defensive conjures," said Emile, caressing his wand. "Although my own humble sleep spells may not be as impressive as Sir Thumbs here."

"Tanks."

Emile studied the building across the street for a moment, then he gestured with hand and staff. The two guards at the front door yawned widely and slumped to the ground.

"Excellent," said Delphia, holstering his Manhunter. "Let's go." Abandoning the bikes to the shadows, they started for the complex.

"We can't go directly to her office," said Thumbs, holding his Mossberg behind his back.

Emile asked, "Why?"

"We need to hit the medical examiner to get some props for the show," he said. "Nothing opens doors faster than having a brain in pan."

"What a disgusting, but clever, notion," acknowledged Emile, nodding at the troll. "There must be some elf blood in your lineage."

"Still?" asked Thumbs brushing at his pants. "Damn, thought that would have washed out by now."

"Ha! I laugh."

"Too bad Moonfeather got flatlined," sighed Silver, as they walked up the front steps and past the snoring guards. "With two mages, we'd be going home by now."

"True," agreed Delphia, placing an ear to the door and pausing. "She was a bella ginzo, indeed. However, if wishes were drek . . ."

"Yes, yes, I know. Then sewers would be heaven. Ready?"

On a cue from Delphia, they kicked open the door with guns drawn, Emile gesturing at everybody in sight. The nurse slumped at the duty desk, an intern slid off his chair, two more guards dropped in their tracks. In seconds the lobby was clear and a wall alarm started beeping. Silver slashed at the exposed wiring with her fingertips, razors glinting under her nails. The wires separated and the alarm went still. Instantly, another took up its strident cry somewhere else deeper within the building.

"Elevators?" asked Emile, pointing.

"Stairs," snapped Silver, rattling the exit door handle. "Ghost, it's locked!"

Delphia's Manhunter boomed and the lock was blown off the frame. Then Thumbs slammed a fist forward and the door crashed open, falling to the floor on the other side.

"Arctic. Let's go!"

In the Old Dome Command Control, every screen was full of blips moving toward and away from the bubblecity. Half the view screens were dark, others so badly scrambled they resembled a pay-per-view trideo channel before you coughed up the nuyen. In various stages of dress, the staff members were racing in through the doors and jumping into the first empty seat they found. In the middle of the organized chaos stood Shawn Wilson. He was scowling and chewing an unlit deepweed cigar.

"Atlantic Security has scrambled a flight of Eagles armed with long-range underwater missiles. ETA ten minutes!" called out a norm holding a com to her head. "Missiles will be transferred to our control at a depth of one thousand!"

"A thousand what?" barked Wilson, reading a pocket computer while a City Guard belted a pistol around his waist. He then adjusted the belt to a more comfortable position.

"Meters, sir!" the fem hastily corrected. "Surface battleships with depth charges two hours after that!"

"We don't have two fragging hours!" stormed Wilson, lighting the cigar. Addiction be damned, he wanted a smoke! "Motherfragger, without a roof we're a sitting crab! Repair crew, what's the status of one and two?"

"Laser number one is still down, sir! Two is back at half power, nine has been zapped by a limpet mine," reported a tech. "Completely destroyed. The others are ready and still waiting."

"Sir, permission to use the rest of the lasers immediately!" called out a lieutenant, standing and saluting.

Crossing his arms, Shawn Wilson snorted at the newbie.

"Not yet. We get only one shot before those damn pirates hit back. We save 'em until . . ." The data screen and cigar dropped to the floor as the west view screen showed a single submarine rising above the mountain range. It was twice, three times—more—the size of any other pirate craft and there were so many torpedo launch tubes its bow resembled a honeycomb.

"Mother of gods and demons," breathed a technician, "it's the *Emperor Yamato!*"

"But that sank decades ago."

"Looks like they found her!"

A norm corporal snarled at them. "Gleebs, that's way too small for the *Yamato!*"

"It's too *what?*"

"Fire all lasers!" shouted Shawn Wilson, drawing his pistol for no sane reason. "Launch all AP torpedoes! Have the gunner go to independent firing! Call in the reserve subs! Prepare to detonate the land mines in the fields! Send out the suicide Jym suits!"

Nobody bothered to answer his commands, they just did it.

"This is it. Gods, I hope we're in time!" The City Guard rushed along the corridor, the race of the heavily armed soldier indecipherable in the full combat armor. Looking grim and serious, the medteam said nothing, just urged him on faster.

"What happened? Was she shot? A heart attack?"

"Shrapnel through the window," said a tall, thin medico wearing a surgical cap.

"One of our windows?"

"Yes."

"Zow! Didn't think that was possible."

"Drek happens," stated a troll, carrying a refrigerated trunk. The guard had checked inside when it arrived unannounced, and it was full of body parts packed in ice: arms, legs, lungs. He'd almost yarfed on the spot, but managed to keep his lunch internal.

At the end of the upholstered hallway, the Guard put his face against a receptacle that scanned his responsive retinas. He spoke a few words into a mike, placed his palm on a sensor pad, then the door opened and he stepped briskly out of the way. But the norm medico with the moustache shoved him into the office ahead of the rest of his team.

"Hey, what are you doing?" the Guard demanded, staggering, when the troll dropped the trunk of parts and threw a punch at him, the fist looming larger than a hairy express train.

"He'll live," said Silver, checking the pulse of the sprawled norm. "He'll be eating soymush for a month, but he'll live."

Closing the office door behind them, Delphia played with the lock using his unknown device, while Thumbs slid a chair under the latch and Emile tapped the door with his wand. The border of the door glowed red for a tick.

"Yowsa, nobody's coming through that thing without a Panzer," gloated Thumbs, running a finger around the inside of his uniform collar.

"Agreed," said Emile, kneeling on the plush carpeting and opening the two halves of a small medical bag. Grand leapt out onto the floor and immediately started cleaning himself.

Opening the trunk, Thumbs tossed aside the body parts they'd taken from the freezer and reached into the ice for his own Mossberg, the Predator, and the rest of their larger weapons.

Silver saw what she was looking for over on a huge wooden desk near the window. She sat down at Harvin's computer and tried a few commands. Good, no resistance. Perhaps Barbara Harvin thought nobody would ever penetrate this far into her sanctum. With the Fuchi on her lap, she slotted the cable, boosted every defensive program she had, took a breath, and then plunged into the bubblecity's coldframe.

The silver falcon of her icon soared through a mirrored universe of perfection. Pausing on an electric blue hilltop, she perched and looked about. The endless reflection of mirrors in mirrors was gone, replaced by colors and textures she had not seen before. Maybe this was going to work! Above was a plain of green-tinted glass separating her from the thousands of glowing lines that stretched from overhead and off into the incalculable distance of pixel blur. Underneath was a checkerboard of circuits and switches, coldframe representations of the real machinery supporting the incredible artificial world.

In the background a deep and steady throbbing sounded constantly. It was something she had never heard before, and guessed it was some kind of Matrix feedback from the combat. Torpedo hits, laser fire, she didn't know, or really care. She was here for a datasteal and every nanosecond counted.

Spreading her wings, she flew to a slim ramp that extended over swirling gray clouds. Rising higher, she soared into the air and grabbed hold of an overhead dataline. Her beak sizzled from the illegal contact, but she ignored the pain and alighted on the enclosed byte-stream. Perched there, she activated a shield program that covered her with armor plating. The pain in her beak vanished.

Booting her best can opener program, Silver then ripped open a chunk of the cable and blinding light bathed her like fire. Ignoring it, she stepped into the raw data and was whisked away like a leaf in a river. The currents carried her far and away before sending her plunging over a VR waterfall. With powerful wings, she dodged the jagged rocks. To the right was a vista full of twinkling lights and nodules of every shape and size. A wonderland of data sitting ripe and ready for quick harvesting.

Ignoring the trap, she flew onto the left shore. This plain was barren and empty, devoid of details. But circling about she suddenly saw a curved arch appear out of thin air. Inside the arch was a flat sheet of solid static, crackling and hissing. IC, and some of the blackest she had ever seen.

Appearing from out of the nothingness behind her, as if stepping from a thick fog, came a dozen mastiffs, their powerful, rippling, muscled, bodies covered with plates like armadillos, their fanged muzzles dripping foam. As the dogs bounded toward her, Silver waved a miniature version of the bubblecity—Jim Harvin's passcode—before the door, and the main lock clicked open. Yes!

After checking that the doors were closed behind her and the dogs unable to follow, Silver proceeded on. Throwing a cloak program over her, she now became a bronze samurai, hoping nobody would notice she was the only one about. A second arch led to another room. Here the rumble of feedback was gone and there were no other deckers visible. This inner locale was a quiet cool room of pastel marble, the air full of floating cabinets, each jammed with swarms of tumbling numbers and letters, encrypted files. The data vault. Hot damn!

Scanning the directory only took a nano, and she easily

found the subdirectory needed. However, this one refused to accept Harvin's code, so she pulled out her best can opener program. But the crowbar bent on the translucent node and shattered into bits. Drek! Not getting in this way.

Hmm, a bit of chaos might help things along. Give the coldframe something else to work on and divert its attention. Going to a smaller, less protected node, Silver easily decoded it and deactivated every door lock in the building. Then she changed her mind and sent out an executive order to disengage every internal lock in both domes; jail cells, arsenal, elevators, food storage, exits, everything was now available to her chummers.

The room around her dimmed as power was shunted else-where—probably to responses and alarm calls—and at the speed of thought, she hastily opened the directory. The warmth in her empty hands told her the Fuchi was nearly overloaded running the deciphering program, but it seemed to be holding out long enough to translate most of the minor file headings into readable text. Scanning the text as it flashed by, Silver went cold inside and as a beep sounded telling her the info-dump was done, she jacked out immediately.

"Hoi," she said, exhaling deeply, raising her fingers from the keyboard and flexing them. "I'm back."

"Did you get it? IronHell's location?" asked Thumbs.

She shook her head. "No, the coldframe doesn't know. It's why they hired us—to find it for them."

"What?"

Wiping moisture off his chattergun, Delphia frowned. "We were hired by Gunderson?"

"Yes. And Moonfeather was working for them covertly."

"She was a mole?"

"And our executioner if we succeeded."

"So they wouldn't have to pay us?"

"So it seems."

"The traitorous slitch!" growled Thumbs through clenched teeth, hands bunched into fists. "I'll kill her for that!"

"Already dead," reminded Emile, stroking Grand.

"Yar, but I didn't get to do it," grumbled Thumbs menac-ingly. "And somebody's gonna pay for that, too!

"Once I get the frag out of this aquarium," he added softly to the room at large.

"Done is done," Delphia said, waving one hand dismissively. He turned back to Silver. "Did you get an entry code for a sub? Anything at all useful?"

She swallowed. "I . . . I found out everything. Harvin's old code from the ork librarian worked down here also."

"Very strange," said Delphia.

Thumbs, however, gave a drek-eating grin. "Arctic. And?"

"And?" With a bitter laugh, Silver slumped in the chair. "And we are seriously fragged. Totally and utterly. Might as well put a round into our own heads. 'Cause we're already dead meat."

34

Weapons fire and explosions rumbled in the distance as the door to Barbara Harvin's office slammed open. She stormed in, flanked by six Guards carrying Vindicators, plus a couple of suits with computers and briefcases. The office was empty, but the limp body of a guard was lying under a table.

"What the frag is going on here?" Barbara demanded loudly. Then she stopped as the guards and suits all tumbled to the floor as if suddenly boneless. The door slammed shut behind her, and she spun about to find herself facing a dirty gang of street toughs who were securing it closed.

"Security! Intruder alert, Level one!" Harvin yelled, backing away from them. "Stat!"

"Their arrival will prove a bit difficult with the spell we got on that door," said a norm in a rumpled suit of exquisite styling.

"Plus we got the lady here." The troll patted an obvious decker on the shoulder. "She's running guard duty for us."

"Hallway is clear," Silver reported, fingers moving steadily over the Fuchi keyboard. "I've terminated the safeties and sent all the elevators down to the sub-basement. They're frozen. I've also turned on the fire sprinklers in the stairwell, blown all the circuit breakers, turned on every alarm, and I'm locking and unlocking the doors every other nano."

Through the Armorlite windows, she saw harsh light flash on the dome, then cracks spreading out and slowly closing. When she turned back to the room, the decker had a long cable attached to her deck that snaked off in the direction of her own desk.

"It appears I am your prisoner," she said, moving casually toward the bar. "For the moment."

With a rat of some kind prancing about his shoes, an elf wordlessly raised a fearsome-looking rifle at her.

At the sight, Harvin slumped. "I am your prisoner." She curled a lip. "Or is it hostage?"

"And how do ya know we're not here to kill you?" asked the troll, thrusting out his lower jaw.

Thunder boomed from different directions overhead, rattling the unbreakable windows.

"Because she isn't dead already," said the moustache. He kicked out a chair for her. "Sit, madam, we have much to discuss and little time."

"Such as?" she retorted coldly.

"Such as, we know everything," said the decker.

Barbara Harvin took the chair. "How nice. Infinite knowledge must be most gratifying."

"You can arc-store the drek, breeder," said the troll. "We got the goods and unless you play along, we all go to drek."

"Pray, continue," she murmured softly, somewhat taken aback by his crudity.

A thumb jerk. "Are you aware that you're at war, not with the pirates, but with your own brother?" asked the suit bluntly.

Harvin felt her expression freeze. "Explain that," she whispered.

The norm ticked off the reasons. "It was your brother who hired Emile here, an elf mage, to come down and help with your pirate problems. Even though any mage was the last thing you wanted in this place. It was your brother who secretly wrote a book about the pirates, and then let the personal passcode he gave to his ghost writer stay active for over a decade.

"And it was your brother who contacted a fixer to hire us in the first place," he concluded. "Hired us! To search for the IronHell headquarters, even though he didn't give a damn about them."

"You already have a plan to deal with the pirates," scoffed the decker, over faint detonations and the horrible noise of ice crackling. "And it's happening right now."

"He wanted us to find this dometown, then spill the scan," said the troll.

"What scan?" she asked him directly.

"About the twelve dead mages," spat the elf.

"Mages?"

The norm gestured and a Manhunter was instantly in his

hand. Harvin stared at it, stunned as much by the move as by the weapon being trained on her.

"Keeping answering questions with another question and you lose a limb," he said. "Which won't kill you, but believe me, it is more painful than you can possibly imagine."

"I believe you," she said after a heartbeat.

The muzzle of the massive pistol did not waver a micron. "Good. I rarely joke about business."

"And patching your stump will waste valuable time none of us has," added the elf, taking a seat himself.

She jerked at the word stump. "No more games."

"Download this," said the suit. "IronHell found this place and blackmailed you for the secret of its location in exchange for shiploads of supplies, protection from Atlantic Security, and the salvaged submarines you've been selling them. They got more subs, less hassles, and generally left your surface ships alone. Indeed, the companies and corporations you most disliked were targeted for pirate attacks. Am I correct?"

"An interesting theory."

"Theory, drek. We got the chips."

"And why would I want to pay such an exorbitant price for a farm? Food that hasn't been toxed or drowned in radiation is certainly valuable, but not at the level of nuyen you are discussing."

"That's hard copy. However, your brother discovered that you could utilize the abyss right next door to forge pressure-alloy chips worth billions on the weapons market."

"We don't manufacture chips. We're just shippers—importers and distributors of weapons."

"Natch. 'Cause you didn't want to get into a war with Ares. The megacorp would kick your hoop into tomorrow. But you do sell them the chips, and they sell you the weapons at a massive discount."

"A staggering discount," corrected the decker.

"Only then the pirates upped their demands, as they always do. The more prosperous the city looks, the more they want. And suddenly you needed an edge. So you built the coldframe to maintain a larger bubble and increase food production to hide the real profit from the chips!"

"Only you made it four times as large as necessary—we've seen it—so it could run a combat program for automatic weapons systems to blow them to drek."

"Weapons built specially for you by Ares," added the decker.

Harvin said nothing, watching their angry faces. They were leading up to something they wanted from her. This was not as one-sided a negotiation as it had originally seemed.

A pounding came from the office door, and muffled cries.

"My guards are here," she said. "If necessary, enough of them to physically throw your dead bodies out the windows."

The suit waved that aside. "Trivia. One flaw. Your brother decided to make sure nobody ever found the coldframe and for that he hired some mages to set up permanent wards of protection.

"Then he aced them to keep the location secret."

Outside, the concussion of the torpedoes was coming louder, the flashes of light filling the dome like fireworks. The streets were madness, but quiet ticks went by in the office.

"The pirates may win," Barbara said smoothly.

"If they do, we all die, and this is a meaningless conversation." The suit walked over to the bar and poured himself a brandy. "But if you win, you need us more than ever."

"Why?" she asked, wondering if they had truly figured it out. "Tell me, why would my own brother want people to know company secrets?"

"You know perfectly well why," said the decker. "Redemption. He's dying. The medical records are there for anybody to find. He only lives today because of the stolen flesh of others. He's no more than a collection of other people's spare parts."

"I see," Harvin said.

"Only it isn't working any more, and now he wants to clear his conscience before he flatlines," stated the suit. "Maybe not consciously, but he keeps fragging up in small disastrous ways."

"Like hiring us."

"And leaving holes in your security nets for others to find and exploit."

"Supposing this is all true," Harvin said slowly, "why don't I just kill you?"

"Then your brother sends more and more shadowrunners until the story is blown and you're naked in the sunlight."

"And we've taken steps to make sure the whole story of the food . . . additives will be released to the general population down here if we're harmed." The decker grinned. "Which would probably cause a riot big enough to make the pirate attack seem like simsense sex with a bouncebaby."

"Plus," said the elf, "we'll broadcast the story of the elves over a .Gertrude for the whole sea to hear. Maybe nobody hears the broadcast." A rueful smile. "Or maybe they do."

"And if word of it gets to Tir Taingire or Tir na nOg . . ."

"Every elf mage in the world would get himself here and smash this hellhole to bits."

"And then you would be dead."

"Or worse. Out of biz and penniless on the streets."

"Easy prey," chuckled the troll.

"A bluff," Barbara shot back defiantly.

"Try us," smiled the norm pleasantly.

An explosion shook the office door, but did not achieve penetration. Precious minutes ticked by in silence. Then a laser beam punched through the door in the office. As the beam winked out, the troll rammed in the muzzle of his Mossberg and fired off a full clip. Screams came from the other side.

"Guarantees will have to be given," she murmured.

"Half of us will always be down here as security for the safety of the others."

A horrible noise shook the whole building, knocking pictures off the walls and smashing glasses and bottles at the bar. Looking outside, they all saw a pirate sub looming large and then ramming into the city dome, cracks spreading out of sight. The honeycombed prow punched straight through the althropic plas and stopped, a circular spray of water from around the crumpled metal bow knifing into the city. Wherever it struck, buildings and bridges were cut apart, the chunks tumbling to the ground.

Lasers from below and the sides diced the sub into pieces, large sections falling off. The spreading cracks slowed their advance, and began to close. Then the bow was nipped off, the prow tumbling down to land in the street, where it exploded in a staggering fireball of flame, smoke, bodies, and vehicles spreading out from the mushroom cloud.

"We have a deal," Harvin said with a sigh. "You are now my new personal security staff assigned to the city for quote general info protection end quote. Satisfactory?"

"Once it's on chip," said Delphia, holstering his weapon. "And notarized."

"Agreed," she accepted grudgingly. "Maybe you truly will be a valuable asset for this corporation. Done and done. You there . . . decker?"

"Silver."

"*Hai,* Silver. Please give me a link to the guards."

She gestured. "Go . . . sir."

As Barbara Harvin spoke at length to her security people, and then her legal staff, the noise from outside diminished more and more. The flashes of light soon stopped and cheering came from the streets below.

"Seems we won," said Emile, leaning on his wand, looking out the window at the damaged city. Smoke and wreckage were everywhere, but so were dancing crowds.

"If you call this winning," said Silver, unjacking from her Fuchi deck. "Now we're trapped into working for these gleebs forever!"

"Nyah," snorted Thumbs, rubbing his arm. "Just until they geek us."

"Thank you, Captain Chuckles."

"No prob."

"All right," said Harvin, standing and going to her desk. Silver moved out of the way, and the older woman took the chair. "First thing to do," the older woman said, folding her hands on the desk top, "is kill my insane brother."

"No," said Delphia. "You will have to handle that yourself."

"We're bodyguards," agreed Thumbs resolutely.

"Not assassins," added Silver. "If we were . . ." she left the thought unfinished.

"I'll kill him," said Emile, with Grand purring in his arms. "Gladly and for free." To the astonished looks of the others, he added. "It is a matter of personal honor. He killed a dozen elf mages and must be made to pay."

Harvin gave him a slight smile of satisfaction. "Excellent. You'll leave first thing in the morning after we repair the sub docking stations."

"Immediately after I receive the antidote for the food poisoning," hissed Emile and Grand together. They ignored the hand.

Her face did not show any expression of surprise or

disappointment as she reclaimed her hand. "Of course. That's what I meant to say."

"Suits," snorted Thumbs softly to himself.

"Gaijin," corrected Delphia, sipping his brandy.

"Welcome to the Gunderson Corporation," added Silver, unlocking the door.

ABOUT THE AUTHOR

Nicholas Pollotta has written and published more than
a dozen novels, including *Illegal Aliens* which he co-
wrote with Phil Foglio for TSR, Inc. *Shadowboxer* is
his first Shadowrun® novel. He has also been a stand-
up comic who performed regularly at New York's
clubs in the mid-70's. Under the name "Nick Smith,"
he has published cartoons in publications like *Starlog*
and *Dragon* magazine. In the 1980's, he was the cre-
ator, producer, director and star of "The Adventures
of Phil A. Delphia," a series of humorous, science fic-
tion radio plays that were broadcast over college radio
stations. Hating boredom worse than almost anything,
his many hobbies include gaming, martial arts,
movies, books and guns.

Here's an exciting preview from
Headhunters,
the next *Shadowrun* novel by Mel Odom

"Elvis has left the building."

Jack Skater hunkered down in the shadows atop a four-story warehouse adjacent to the team's target. The new moon barely cracked the darkness that swallowed Tacoma except for the occasional pockets of neon advertising running the length of several skyscrapers and the illumination necessary in the around-the-clock dock areas. Wet salt air rushed over him, propelled by the easterly winds coming in off Puget Sound less than a half-klick away. The smell of the sea was almost stringent enough to claw the scent of the new tar roof underfoot from his nostrils.

He accessed the Commlink IV hardwired into his skull and said, "Our package?" The Crypto Circuit HD scrambled the transmission, making it impossible for anyone else to pick up. He especially hoped that held true for the city's blue crews working to keep the streets safe from crime. At least, Skater believed, to keep the streets free of any crimes they didn't get a percentage of. But maybe he was just being cynical. A guy got cynical quick when he worked the shadows.

"In place," Quint Duran answered. The ork mercenary's voice sounded deep and relaxed.

"Was he seen?"

The ork laughed gently. "Nobody's chasing him, kid, and with Knight Errant on the security, if they'd have spotted him, somebody would have been on his slotting hoop wanting to know just what the frag he was doing on the building."

"His idee should hold," Skater said.

"Now that he's dumped that Fiber-Optic Observation Link, it might. He's got too much heavy bodware to pass more than a surface inspection."

Skater knew it. But Elvis had been the one to send. Alone, with backup a few hundred yards away and the team maybe on the line if the run suddenly went to hell, the big troll samurai carried enough Arnie-Awesome cyberware that he might be able to break free and get away even from Knight Errant's best sec-guards.

"I'm clear, chummers," Elvis said in his basso voice. "Have you got contact with the sec systems?"

"Powering up now," Wheeler Iron-Nerve responded over the Commlink. "Okay, it looks like a go. Up to Archangel now."

"I'm here," the elven decker said calmly. "I'll let you know what I find."

Skater took a deep breath and tried to shake the feeling of dread that had been with him ever since the team had taken the Mr. Johnson's cred four days ago and agreed to the run. Too many details had been left hanging, too much danger possible.

But the bottom line was that they all needed the score. Living off the books, in between the cracks of society without selling out to the Mafia or Yakuza or the corporations was expensive even if a man or woman or meta lived by themselves and were responsible only for themselves. Now, though, Skater had Emma to figure into his personal equation of survival too. It made things harder in some ways, and easier in others.

Noise from the dock area thundered through the empty streets of Tacoma's business districts, and the whirling spotlights of the dock crews warred with the running lights of freighters. For decades, Tacoma had been the poor stepsister to glittering and decadent Seattle. But it was 2058 now, and wealth had come calling, spilling into the city from the deep pockets of the megacorps as they developed the shipping trade. The Yakuza, Mafia, and Seoulpa Rings worked the alleys and black markets for the crumbs.

The team had made their pickup of the Fiber-Optic Observation Link and paid a fragging slotful of cred for it at Basil's Faulty Bar, where Abe Heep ran a decent drinking establishment and a drekking-well inventoried backdoor supply house for illegal techware that he scabbed from intelligence circles. While they were there, Skater had spotted flags from Seattle, the United Canadian and American States, the Salish-Shidhe Council lands, California Free State, and even the Tir. The elves, though, ran the tightest security of all.

If the run somehow got hosed up, Skater was counting on the abundance of security to drek over the Lone Star squads that would be summoned to the scene. The team could buzz turbo for the dock area—provided they didn't get slotted over at the funeral home—and lose themselves among the international sec drawing rank and number down on the docks. A hidey-hole waited, already arranged and paid for, if they needed it.

He shifted, keeping his shadow against the line of the building so it wouldn't be noticeable from below. Dark and slim and dressed in combat black, there was no way he could have passed unnoticed along the street. He carried an Ares Predator II in a shoulder rig, and a Mossberg CDMT combat shotgun hung from his shoulder on a Whipit sling. A Cougar fine blade rode in his right boot. His Salish blood showed in his dusky skin, high cheekbones, and close-cropped dark hair.

He took the Ares low-light binox from his chest pouch and scanned their target. The light-multiplier circuitry banished most of the night.

The building stood like an imposing stone finger, fourteen stories high. The maglev controls listed fifteen floors, but that was because the thirteenth had been left out. Its outer skin was blued chrome the color of gunmetal or the broken heart of a razorboy, interrupted by thick sheets of bulletproof black duraglass. As far as skyscrapers went, it was dwarfed in comparison to the Shiwase Corporation Complex and other megacorp holdings downtown.

Over the last three days, Skater and his crew had uncovered everything they could about the building. Somewhere in Archangel's databases regarding the present run were the names of every business located inside, most of the legitimate renters' and shopkeepers' identities and their staff, and a number of the apartment dwellers in the top four stories.

The lower floors held office and shop space, which was how they'd been able to set up the connect for the Fiber-Optic Observation Link. Cullen Trey, suave and debonair, who had a sweet tooth for things and a lifestyle aristocratic, had rented a small office in the name of a street mage he knew to be dead.

Trey knew the man was dead because he'd killed him. Quint Duran had assisted in the trackdown, bounty-hunting for a Salish art dealer who'd found out he was suddenly holding forgeries of *object d'art* that he'd laid out an intense line of cred for.

When Trey and Duran had run the man to ground, the mage

had already established another identity, complete with SIN. Duran had taken care of the thief's accomplices, and Trey had taken out the street mage. As a combat mage, Cullen Trey was deadly.

When the Fiber-Optic Observation link was later found, the cable snaking through the rented office space to the link box Elvis had installed only moments ago, the trail could only lead to a dead man.

The target Skater wanted was on the ninth floor. Shastakovich's Funeral Home had moved in with the money coming into Tacoma, a branch office of a substantial chain that catered to corp execs and those who could afford a somewhat expensive send-off. The security was provided by Ares Corp and included most physical systems, with a wage mage on retainer for more important clientele.

"I'm in," Archangel said over the Commlink IV.

Skater took a deep breath. "The whole system?"

"Yes. It took awhile to sort through the Prism Switches till I found the one we needed. There was some white barrier IC that took a bit of sleazing, but I had some sleaze utilities that it hasn't seen before. I made it through without having to crash it."

Crashing it wasn't an option. Skater had been depending on the elven decker's skills to manage the Fiber-Optic Observation Link without being noticed. "What about the target?"

"I've accessed the database, but there's no listing for Coleman January."

Skater checked his chron. It was 1:43 a.m. "Any mention of a delivery being made?"

"No. I looked through those, too. I've got the deliveries that were already made this evening, and the ones that'll be made first thing in the morning."

"Fraggit!" Skater said without cutting in the Commlink. He wiped perspiration from his face with a gloved hand. It was too drekking hot in October to be dressed as he was, and the humidity was impartial to man, woman, or meta. But he couldn't chance being identified. The hose-up with ReGEN last year had cost him an eye, an ex-girlfriend, and nearly every bit of cred he'd had stashed away.

He was scared. He knew that and he hated it, but he was smart enough to admit it to himself. Twenty-six years old, he'd already been running the shadows for years. He was slotting good at what he did. But he glanced at his shaking hand, seeing Emma's face in his mind, his little girl's smiles as he tickled her.

"Kid," Duran growled, "there's no way we got the wrong funeral home."

"I know," Skater said, forcing his mind to wrap around the problem facing the team. He glanced back at the building. "The Johnson said Coleman January would be here no later than two o'clock this morning. There's only one way he could have known that."

"Sure," the ork mercenary replied. "The man was planning on slotting ol' Coleman's stick himself. Then let us pick up the pieces. Of course, then you gotta ask yourself why."

"We don't have time to ask why," Cullen Trey said. "We've fifteen minutes, providing Mr. Johnson's schedule is precise, to decide whether we keep a green light on the run or deep-six it. I for one, would like to see the other end of the cred we were promised."

Skater knew Trey had a cred Jones. The combat mage liked the good life even though he hadn't been born to it. "How do you call it, Elvis?"

"Well, chummer, we're into the funeral home's sec systems. I'd say that gives us a leg up on the situation. And we *are* here."

"That could be according to the Johnson's plan," Wheeler stated. "Welcome to my parlor, said the spider to the fly. Frag, we've been slotted over on runs before. Me, I'm for taking the front-end cred and taking a walk on this one."

"Archangel," Skater prompted. He lifted the binox again and tried to stare through the black duraglass covering the ninth floor windows. He wished he could peel it away, get a good scan inside. And he wished the thick greasy ball that had suddenly appeared in his stomach wasn't there.

"I'm with Wheeler," the elven decker replied. "Discretion is the wisest move at this point. We've been paid for our time. If the Johnson gives us any flack about how we've handled things, he'll have to find a way to leverage the cred back out of us."

The problem was, Skater was aware, that Johnsons could sometimes do that. When a shadowrunner made a deal with a Mr. Johnson, there was usually no telling who was really inside those Armani suits. And going back on a deal was sometimes worse than failing. The victim of a run didn't always know who'd come after him. Mr. Johnson *knew* who he'd made a deal with.

"Quint," Skater said.

"I want the action," the ork mercenary replied. "That makes it three to two. You gonna tie it up or go with the majority?"

Before Skater could answer, a footstep scraped against the pebbled rooftop behind him. He whirled, losing himself behind a HVAC unit.

"Told you I spotted somebody up here, Fontaine."

Three thrillers dressed in the jet and red colors of the Milton Dark Angels stood in the center of the rooftop. One young elf held two long knives in naked, scarred fists, while the other two, a human and a troll, were armed with a stun baton that crackled blue static and a glowing monofilament whip.

"Guess you were right, Hector," the elf said. "I have to give you that. Watch him, Wynn. If the fragger tries to slot it outta here, cut his legs off with that whip."

Skater drew the Predator from the shoulder rig. Dancing with members of a thrill gang didn't fit into his agenda at all. The problem was, if he cut loose with the Predator, every blue crew in the area would be on him and the team.

"Kid," Duran called. "We ain't exactly got all night."

"Busy," Skater said. "I've got unexpected company. A welcome wagon of Dark Angel thrillers."

"Hold on."

"Stay put," Skater said. "I'll see my own way clear. By the time you could get up here, it'd be over. One way or the other."

Fontaine waved his companions into motion, spreading out around Skater's position.

Skater knew they hadn't seen the pistol, but he was properly fragged over if he used it.

"Jack," Archangel called over the headset, "I just pulled a message from the funeral house telecom. Coleman January is now enroute. He's DOA and coming by DocWagon."

As Skater's mind reeled with the information, wondering who'd aced January and how deep his team was into the action, the troll thriller with the monofilament whip lashed out at the HVAC.

Sparks leapt in all directions as the single molecule edge sliced through the heavy piece of machinery and came spitting light at Skater's face.